HER IRISH SAVAGE

HER IRISH SAVAGE

A DIAMOND RING DARK ROMANCE

THE BOSTON MOB TRILOGY
BOOK 1

ALIX KEY

DIAMOND
FREEPORT PRESS

Published by Diamond Freeport Press
P.O. Box 42133, Arlington, VA 22204

ISBN 978-1-95018-482-8

Discover other titles by Alix Key at www.alixkey.com

091825ak

ALSO BY ALIX KEY

Find a complete, up-to-date list of Alix's books at www.alixkey.com.

Sinful Mafia Salvation

WORD OF WARNING

Her Irish Savage **is a dark romance.**

It contains hard-to-read scenes, graphic language, and explicit sexual content.

A complete list of potential triggers can be found at:

https://alixkey.com/books/boston-mob-trilogy

Please don't read this book if you are sensitive to any of those triggers. But if you believe in the power of true love to bring joy and fulfillment to consenting adults, then this is the book for you.

Welcome to the Diamond Ring.

1

FIONA

Someone has to be the grown-up in this relationship.

I'm determined to make Madden Kelly do the right thing. He has to return the money we stole from his brother three days ago. If I play my cards right—and I always do—Madden will believe giving back the cash is his idea.

That's my secret power: getting men to do what I want them to do. They think I'm a helpless twenty-four-year-old girl. But I'm actually a woman who has grown up in the heart of Boston's Irish mob. I can hold my own against anyone. I'm Fiona Fucking Ingram.

Capping my Louboutin lipstick with a decisive click, I purse my lips at my reflection in the mirror. Satisfied with the scarlet shine, I twitch the waistline of my Tom Ford leather corset to lie flat against its short matching skirt. The boned bodice is tight enough to make me regret the burger and fries I wolfed down at dinner. I should have stuck with a salad.

Fuck it. The fries were the best part of the meal. Regret is for losers.

I slip into my four-inch stilettos and head out to the living room.

I expect Madden to be on the couch, thumbing the remote between his precious Philadelphia sports teams—hockey playoffs to basketball playoffs to spring baseball. Instead, he's studying something on his phone, a diagram that looks like a subway map for a very crowded city. He's pacing as he looks at it, muttering under his breath.

I consider picking up my own phone from the coffee table and sending him a text to get his attention. Instead, I clear my throat, twice. When he finally looks up, he crams his phone in his pocket like I've caught him watching porn.

"What do you think *you're* doing?" I demand. Just last night, we added Headmistress and Naughty Schoolboy to our bedroom repertoire. I never expected he'd go off that fast. He was mortified about the sticky mess he left in his briefs. I sure as hell intend to use *that* information, going forward.

"Jaysus!" His Irish accent goes thick when he's startled. Or embarrassed. Or angry. "Don't ya be sneakin' up on a man!"

I raise my eyebrows, making it clear I didn't sneak. But I keep my eyes on my true goal—getting him to return Braiden's money. Crossing the room, I sway my hips a lot more than necessary. I raise one fingernail to trace from the tip of his chin to the bottom of his Adam's apple. "Let's go out tonight," I murmur.

He flinches. "I'm busy."

"Just a couple of drinks?" I need him relaxed and happy. I push my shoulders back, testing my corset's zipper.

He ignores the show and reaches for his pocket instead. He wants his phone more than he wants my body. "There's plenty of booze in the kitchen," he mutters.

"Fine. I'll fix us both a drink." But my fingers find his before he can tap his screen to life. Melting against him, I pull his hand under my skirt.

He growls when he discovers I'm not wearing panties.

I've been getting sounds like that out of Madden Kelly since the night we met in Dublin, six months ago. We were both visiting the old country. Da thought a month or two in Ireland would get the wildness out of my system, and I'd finally settle down like a good girl. Let him marry me off to one of his carefully selected mob associates. Secure more of his criminal empire.

Blah, blah, blah. Da's plan was boring.

Not like the high stakes poker game where I met Madden.

I made sure to lose three quick hands before I pleaded an empty purse. A handjob across the console of Madden's cheap rental car made up for the grand I owed him. We closed down a pub after that, and the blowjob I gave him after hours earned me an invitation to visit Pennsylvania.

I knew it would drive my father crazy, so I took Madden up on his offer. And ever since, I've had front row seats to Philly's version of *The Godfather*. More specifically, I've watched Madden's power struggle with his brother Braiden, the captain of Philadelphia's Irish mob. Madden is only second-in-command.

Sucks to be Madden, I guess.

Three days ago, he took me on the milk run, collecting envelopes of cash from every business on the long list of his brother's protection racket. I thought Madden was joking at first, stealing the money. But the joke was on me, especially when Madden headed into a back room at one of the brothels, at Mimi's place.

He kept me waiting a full hour.

Great. Madden proved he has power over me. We never said we were exclusive. I'm not allowed to get upset about his fucking a couple of whores.

But I need him to return his brother's money now, before

Braiden makes both of us pay. It's all fun and games until someone takes a knife beneath the ribs.

Now that I've got Madden's hand between my thighs, I finally have his attention. He hooks two fingers into me and I sigh his name. Panting like he has me racing, I handle his zipper. "God," I moan as I reach inside his jeans and his briefs. "That's so good." My fingernails on his dick seal the deal; he's hard in seconds.

I let him force me over to the couch. He pins my wrists overhead, and I catch a fake scream at the back of my throat. I breathe faster and faster as he pumps between my thighs.

He finishes with a single vicious thrust, holding himself deep inside me as every muscle in his body turns to stone. His cheek is sweaty against mine when he collapses with a grunt.

I hook my heel around the back of his knee and hold him close. "Hey, big guy," I whisper.

He isn't big. He's barely average. But I'll tell a lie or two to spare us both from Braiden's fury.

I rock a little, trying to get his attention. "Hey," I say again, while his dick is still inside me. "What should we do with the milk run?"

He freezes like I jammed a cattle prod up his ass. "It's mine." He sounds like a stubborn two-year-old.

"It is," I agree. "So you can do whatever you want with it."

"That's right," he says.

"Can you imagine how surprised Braiden would be if you gave it back? He'd shit his pants."

Madden plants a hand on my shoulder, pushing off of me hard enough to hurt. "Whose side are you on?"

"I don't choose sides."

"Then what the f—"

"Braiden's your captain. The money—"

Belongs to him. I was going to say *the money belongs to him.*

But Madden's fist lands in my belly, forcing all the air from my lungs and making me forget how to use my words.

I haven't been struck like this in years.

Madden scrambles off the couch, jamming his limp dick into his briefs and tugging his jeans over his hips. By the time he's yanked up his zipper, I'm finally able to push myself into a sitting position.

Don't fuck over the captain. I learned that rule sitting at my father's table, before I was old enough to tie my shoes. I've seen it play out over and over as Da keeps Boston in line, as he watches over the entire Grand Irish Union. It's the simple truth of life in the Irish mob, and part of me can't believe Madden Kelly doesn't know it.

I fight for a breath, for another, and then I say, "Braiden—"

Will come after you. After us. He'll make sure no one ever dreams of stealing from him ever again.

But Madden doesn't give me a chance to say another word. Because the instant his brother's name crosses my lips, Madden closes his hand around my throat. He drags me to my feet, ignoring my shrieked protest.

I'll do anything with a man. Dress however he wants. Play whatever role he needs. But no one—absolutely no one—gets to choke me.

Crimson fury mixes with blind panic as I try to force out the warning Madden needs to hear. "Your brother—"

But Madden Kelly has been replaced by a swearing, snarling demon. This time, when he punches me, he goes for my face. My lips splits over my teeth, and blood sprays onto the coffee table, darker than Louboutin red.

I raise my hands to defend myself, but I'm slow to move and everything hurts so much. He lands half a dozen blows—short, sharp jabs to my face, to my chest, to my stomach.

"Please," I gasp, and I hate myself, because I haven't begged a man since I was sixteen. "Stop," I plead, sharp and desperate, exactly the way I sounded eight years ago.

He waits until my knees buckle, until my spine melts, and I

collapse to the floor beside the couch. I can barely track his movements as he storms into the kitchen.

"You fucking bitch," he hollers, shoving a stack of envelopes in my face "*This* is what I'm doing with the milk run. I'm taking every goddamn dollar. And you're the one who made me do it! You goddamn fucking bitch." He lands a kick beneath my ribs before he stalks to the door.

Maybe I pass out. Maybe I just lie there, feeling a million tiny knives carving me apart from the inside. Maybe I'm pretending I'm dead, praying Madden won't come back to finish the job.

But eventually I have to find out how badly I'm hurt.

It takes all my concentration to stretch a hand toward the coffee table. I fumble blindly until I find my phone. My left eye isn't working right, but I manage to squint, to locate the little square icon for my camera.

My lip is split. My nose is bleeding, and I'm pretty sure it's broken. There's blood on my teeth, and a crimson line of drool paints my chin. My left eye is swelling shut, and a nasty bruise make me wonder if my cheekbone is broken too.

I snap a photo. My finger hovers over the tiny image. If I send it to my father, he might have Madden killed. Da's chief enforcer, Keenan Rivers, could do the job. He would make sure it takes a long, long time for Madden Kelly to die.

But Da has let me down before. He might ignore what Madden's done. Say it's my own fault, for staying with a bogger.

Or worse—Da could call me home. He'll say he never should have let me stay in Philly on my own. And as soon as my bruises fade, he'll make sure some man's ring is on my finger.

I won't do it. I'm worth more than my family name and a fucking marriage license. I know I am.

But there's someone else who can get revenge against Madden.

Holding my breath as I tap the screen, I call Braiden Kelly.

Earlier this spring, I lived in his house, spying at my father's command. When I wasn't flirting, I sponged up everything I could about how Braiden Kelly runs Philadelphia, how he keeps his Fishtown Boys loyal.

And I watched him tame his wife. I saw him exercise the power of a true alpha, a man who would never hurt a woman in any way she didn't crave.

He lets his phone ring three times before he answers. When he does pick up, his voice carries less emotion than the timer that tells me when my morning coffee has brewed. "Fiona."

"Your brother's a fucking bastard." I sound like I'm drunk, fighting to fit my swollen lips around the words.

"Tell me something I don't know."

"He took it all," I say.

"Took what?"

"The milk run."

"The money you two stole from me?"

I wince, and lightning explodes up every nerve in my face. "He beat me up." I actually mean to say I'm sorry, but the other words break out of me like a hiccup.

Braiden's voice is cold. "I'm not your knight in shining armor."

Braiden's no knight. And he's never been mine, no matter how I tried to tempt him with my stiletto heels and leather. But I remind him: "If you don't kick his ass, my father will. And you'll end up caught in the middle. Is your piece-of-shit brother worth burning every bridge to the Union?"

He doesn't say a word.

"Braiden…" I say, suddenly terrified he'll hang up on me.

I have to do something. I have to make him understand. I pull my phone away from my face and send him the fucking photo.

"Christ, Fiona," he finally says.

"Make him pay." I'm horrified to realize I'm crying. I never cry. "Please… Come get me, Braiden."

He keeps me waiting for long enough that I'm not surprised

by his answer. "I can't leave Thornfield." But then he offers: "But I'll send my Warlord, Patrick Moran."

I've barely seen Patrick, hanging around with the Fishtown Boys. I don't want a stranger to see me like this. "Please…" I say. And I don't even care that I'm begging for the second time in an hour. "Come get me yourself."

"Text me your address. Patrick's on his way."

I've heard that tone often enough over the past two months, since I started playing with fire here in Philly. Braiden Kelly won't change his mind. So I force myself to whisper, "Tell him to hurry."

Braiden ends the call before I do.

I should make my way down the hall to the bathroom. Pee and wipe away the mess Madden left between my legs. Wash my face. Brush my hair. Pull on a pair of panties, so my corset and skirt feel like armor, instead of a prison uniform.

But the instant I try to stand, the room begins to spin. I realize I'm only wearing one stiletto, and for some reason that strikes me as hilarious—until my cracked and broken laugh dissolves into more tears. I settle for kicking off the other shoe and bracing my back against the couch. I'll get to my feet… soon.

I must fall asleep, or maybe I pass out again. Because the next thing I know, someone has his hands jammed into my armpits. He's lifting me like I'm a splay-legged Barbie doll, or maybe a newborn foal. I try to protest, try to fight, but he only eases me back until I feel the edge of the couch behind my knees.

"Sit," he orders, which really isn't necessary, because I've already fallen onto the overstuffed cushions.

It hurts to look up at him. "Moran?" I ask.

He scowls. "Lucky for you," he says.

Patrick Moran is a wolf of a man. His hair looks like he battled a tornado getting here; shots of silver tangle with black. As he glares down at me, his eyes look black as well. His long-sleeve T makes it clear he never misses arm day at the gym. I don't know what color the shirt was when he bought it, but it's a weathered gray now, faded from countless washings. His jeans look even older.

He cuts off my gaping when he snarls, "Anyone could've walked in that open door."

I groan as I look over my shoulder. The door's closed now. "I didn't..." But it takes too much energy to explain that Madden left the door open. Madden took the milk run. Madden needs his ass kicked. Madden could be anywhere right now.

I'm shivering, my entire body shaking like I'm trapped beneath an iceberg. Each hammer-tap of my chattering teeth echoes through my head, and when I try to take a stifling breath, my side throbs so sharply I can't fill my lungs.

It was a mistake, calling Braiden. I need my own family after all. I need my da.

I point to my phone on the floor, an impossible continent away. "G— gimme..." My lips are too swollen to bend around the words.

But Moran must understand, because he picks up my cell. It looks like a toy beneath his scarred knuckles. "Who do you think you're calling?"

I force myself to look him in the eye. I'm Fiona Fucking Ingram, Crown Princess of the Boston clan. I swallow hard, so I don't stammer. "My da."

His sigh is like a wind blown all the way from the North Pole. "No, you're not."

I grit my teeth so hard, I see stars. Forcing myself to stand, I plant my hands on my hips. "I'm calling Kieran Ingram."

"Then you'll need a better phone." He tosses mine onto the couch, beyond my reach.

"What the fuck does that mean?"

His eyes spark bright with an animal fury. "It means your da is dead."

2

PATRICK

J esus Christ. That's not the way I meant to tell her.

But the Bell rang inside my head when Ingram's girl reached for her phone. Loud and clear, like the start of a boxing round, the clang broke all my resolve. I lashed out like I always do, giving in to impulse when I most need control.

Fuck.

My captain sent me here because he trusts me. Because somewhere in my forty-six years on this planet, I supposedly learned how to behave like a civilized human being. Because I know how to shove my temper onto an ice floe and do what needs to be done.

And probably because I lived in Boston half a lifetime ago. My boss thought I'd have something in common with Ingram's girl. That I'd find some way to break the news, soft and gentle as the springtime rain.

But Madden Kelly has pushed me to the feckin' brink. His handiwork here makes me want to rip off his bollocks and shove them down his throat. If I can't do that, then I want to beat his face to a bloody pulp and use his ribs like a fucking punching bag.

Because the dry shite sure worked over Fiona Ingram. And the whole time he was doing it, he thought her da was still breathing. Still able to take revenge against my boss.

I shouldn't fucking be here. I should be at my captain's side. Working for the Fishtown Boys. Keeping my adopted clan safe.

I fight the urge to put my fist through the nearest wall. Instead, I take a deep breath, inhaling on a count of four. Holding for four. Exhaling, slow and steady and even, counting four again.

Fiona Ingram played games with a sick fecker who has the morals of a great white shark, and she got served up for dinner. That's not my fault. I just have to manage the clean-up.

Which would be a hell of a lot easier if I hadn't just delivered another blow.

It means your da is dead.

Really, Moran? That's the best you could do?

Christ, I'm an eejit.

I take another boxed breath—in for four, hold for four, out for four, hold for four—and I'm focused again. Braced to handle the girl's grief. Ready to manage her tears. Prepared to do the job my boss sent me here to do.

Something shifts inside her, as if her bones are settling under the weight of what I said. I expect her to start shivering again. To wail. To sob.

Instead, she blinks hard, like she's a downed robot coming back online. "How'd he go?" she finally asks.

The old man died reading the Riot Act to my boss. He choked on seventy years of bile, on thinking he was always the smartest man in the room. He coughed up whatever tattered excuse for lungs he still had after smoking three packs a day for sixty years.

"I don't know," I lie.

She looks at her phone, out of reach where I tossed it on the couch. "No one's called me."

Of course they haven't. Her father's men are plotting war against my boss. They're gathered somewhere in Boston—in the old Ingram house in Southie, if I had to take a guess. They're figuring out how to get back at Braiden Kelly, how to turn disaster into triumph.

I've been at my share of tables like that. I watched Braiden settle the Boys after his father died, taking charge and putting dogs like Madden in their place. I watched Braiden's father before him, red-eyed and mourning the Old Man, but making sure every last soldier in the clan knew he was in charge.

No one's called Fiona because she doesn't matter. The men are pulling all the wagons 'round without her. They're fighting for the reins, bulling after the crown. She's been left behind. Forgotten.

"That's not right," she says, as if I lectured her out loud. And then, "I need to get home."

She's all elbows and knees as she tries to stand, but her legs don't cooperate. Something about slumping back to the couch hurts her side, and she closes her grass-green eyes, her apple cheeks stretching in a wince. She thinks I don't see her arm tuck close to her ribs, but I do. I see everything.

"You're not going anywhere," I say.

She starts to bite her lip but changes her mind when her teeth graze the nasty split that's still oozing blood down her chin. Gingerly, she touches the back of her hand to her mouth and hisses when it comes away red.

It takes her a moment, but then she fetches her phone without my help.

"Who the fuck are you calling?" I'm annoyed by her persistence. And touched with a bit of admiration too.

"My father's pilot."

Fucking princess. "He won't—"

She shakes her head to cut me off. I'm pretty sure she

doesn't realize she's smearing blood on her cell. And somehow, that only feeds my anger.

She has the volume set high enough that I hear each ring, crystal clear, and then the pilot's recorded message, telling her how important her call is and asking her to leave a voicemail. The gobshite's probably staring at his own feckin' screen, pissing his pants and wondering who will win the war of bloody succession.

"Fucker," Fiona mutters, ending the call without leaving a message. And then, as if I've challenged her out loud: "I'll go commercial."

Christ. She won't let it rest.

She wipes the screen clear on a sofa cushion, leaving a stain Madden Kelly deserves. Then her fingers flash over the glass, paging through information faster than I can follow. Her scarlet-tipped fingernails don't stop her from making plans, but my taking the phone out of her hands leaves her stranded. I toss it halfway across the room, onto a leather recliner with cupholders built into the feckin' arms.

"They'll never let you board, looking like that," I say.

"They don't care—"

"Commercial airlines don't want customers dropping dead in the middle of a flight."

"I won't—"

"You've got a broken nose and a busted lip. You'll be lucky if you can see out of that eye in a week, and I'll bet you a thousand dollars you've got at least one broken rib."

"But none of that—"

"You're a bad risk. You look like shite. Forget it."

Little Miss Know-It-All looks directly in my eyes. "Then take me to the emergency room. They'll patch me up, and I can still be in Boston by morning."

"You won't be through talking to the cops by morning."

That surprises her. "Cops?"

"Doctors are mandatory reporters. You look like the text-book example of domestic abuse."

This time she's thrown for all of thirty seconds. "Then take me to Thornfield."

Jesus, she won't back down. And there's no way in hell I'm taking Ingram's girl to Braiden Kelly's mansion right now. The place is crawling with Fishtown Boys, every one of them doing his best to keep her father's army from destroying us.

"No," I tell her.

"I know Braiden keeps a doctor on call."

"Braiden is busy."

"What the hell is he—" But she's smart enough to figure it out on her own. And when she does, her voice gets very small. "Oh."

With the fight gone out of her, she looks exactly like what she is: A frightened, bloodied kid. As she sinks back onto the couch, her face turns very, very white.

"I don't feel so good," she whispers.

"That's the blood you've swallowed. Lean forward. Don't let it run down your throat."

I wait until she's followed orders before I stalk to the kitchen. Every room in this place looks like it was cut out of a goddamn catalog. I'm willing to bet a year's salary that Madden bought the model condo unit, then paid extra for them to leave it staged.

Glasses are in the third cupboard I try. I fill one with tap water and snag both cotton towels hanging from the oven door.

Fiona's whimpering by the time I get back. Her hand shakes so hard when I pass her the glass that I leave my fingers on it, keeping it steady while she sips.

"Make it stop," she moans.

"It will, once your nose is set."

"Then set it."

"It'll hurt," I warn her.

Her laugh sounds like a shattered window. "Do it."

The couch is too low, so I settle my palm beneath her elbow and walk her over to the dining room table. I can feel her trembling through my fingertips.

"Sit on the edge of the table," I tell her. Her legs dangle, like she's a doll at a tea party.

"Hold on," I say, curling her fingers around the edge of the table. "Tight." And again, trying to warn her: "This'll hurt."

"Hurry up," she says.

"Blow," I tell her, holding the dish towel up to her nose. "As hard as you can." There's more blood and snot than any Kleenex could manage. "Again," I say, like she's a toddler with a head cold. "One more time." I try to ignore how that must feel.

When I put the towel on the table, I take care to fold over the cloth so she can't see what came out of her. Flexing my fingers, I remind myself I've done this for plenty of my soldiers. I know exactly what I'm doing.

Her left eye is swollen closed. But the right one stares at me —bloodshot and watering from who knows which pain, but a steady, unblinking green.

I resist the sudden urge to smooth her straight black hair off her face. I want to cup her cheek in my palm. I want to tell her she didn't deserve this, any of it.

Instead, I make a triangle with both my hands, setting my matched index fingers in the center of her forehead. Without giving her a chance to flinch, I slide my fingers down either side of her nose, pressing hard enough to realign the bones beneath.

A scream vibrates against the back of her throat, but she doesn't let a sound escape her lips. She holds onto the table for a full count of ten after I finish.

For the first time since I walked into this hellhole, I remember the rumors about Fiona Ingram: She's a killer. She's executed four men on her da's command. Taken out another three on her own accord, if the stories are right. Watching this slip of a girl manage her pain, I believe it.

"N— Now," she says, and it takes her a moment to stop her teeth from chattering. "Drive me up to Boston."

"I'm not—"

"Braiden sent you here for a reason. It wasn't just to tell me Da is dead. He could have done that over the phone."

"He wouldn't—"

"Drive me up to Boston, the way Braiden Kelly thinks you should."

"He doesn't—"

"Moran."

I don't remember the last time I let a woman cut me off while I was speaking—much less three times in a minute.

Then again, I interrupted her, earlier.

She's strong. And she's brave. But no matter how many men she's put in the ground, she doesn't have a clue how men will fight for the type of power her father took for granted.

I keep things simple. "No."

"Don't make me—"

My turn to interrupt again. "Fine," I say. "Walk across this room and pick up your phone."

She glares at me out of her one good eye. I watch her brace her arm against her side, cushioning her ribs as she slides off the table. She raises her chin, still streaked with dried blood from her lip.

She takes five steps before her knees buckle. That's four more than I thought she'd manage.

I catch her before she falls. She smells like sweat and blood and something sharp that might be despair. But I catch a whiff of something else, something clean. It's mint, maybe, or the chamomile tea my mother used to make when I had a dodgy stomach.

Holding her close, I collect her phone from the recliner. It's in one of those wallet cases—a Massachusetts driver's license pokes out between two credit cards. I jam it into my back pocket and drag her toward the door. "Let's go."

She's out of adrenaline. But she manages to slur, "Boston?"

"No. My place."

"F— fuck you."

I laugh, which almost gives her the strength to stand on her own. "Not everyone wants to get in your pants, sweetheart."

Since walking into this hellhole, I've been doing my best to ignore the fact that she's not wearing pants beneath that black leather skirt. The one that's small enough to double as a napkin. For a doll.

Her wordless snarl almost makes me laugh again. But I say, "You're in no shape to wait for Madden on your own. And if I'm here when he gets back, I'll have to kill him. My boss hasn't said I can do that yet. So do us both a favor, and let's get out of this feckin' dump."

She finally sees logic and nods. We move like we're fighting for last place in a three-legged race, but I get her out the door.

She manages to stay upright in the elevator, but the cold marble floor in the lobby makes her hobble. Enough. It's too late to go back for shoes now. I sweep her off her feet like she's a dress on a hanger.

"Fuck you," she tries again, but she curls against my chest.

She's too light. Too fragile. And I try to ignore that she's biting back sobs as I wrestle her into my Land Rover.

3

FIONA

The first time I wake, Moran is carrying me up a flight of stairs. There's noise behind us, music and people talking, and I hide my face against his chest, trying to escape the dull glow of a bare bulb hanging on the wall. Moran swears as he reaches a landing, Irish words Da uses when he thinks I'm not listening.

Words Da *used* when he *thought* I *wasn't* listening.

Da won't be swearing anymore.

Moran juggles me, a key, and the door, and then the noise of the crowd is locked safely outside. He brings me over to a couch and lowers me to a cushion. My muscles are overcooked spaghetti, and I slump to one side, which is fine because all I want to do is sleep.

"Not yet," Moran orders. "Sit up. It'll help the swelling."

It's easier to sit straight than to argue. I'm too tired to open my one good eye as I hear him cross the room. He must be in the kitchen, because a cabinet opens and closes. He runs water in a sink.

When he comes back, he presses something into my palm. I crack my eye open and stare, blinking hard enough to make out two round pills.

"They'll cut the pain," Moran says.

"Wh—What are they?"

"Oxy."

"Oxy's for b— bad shit." I'm slurring, but I need to make my point. "Gimme Advil."

He laughs. "Any worse shit, and you'll be in the feckin' hospital, mandatory reporting or not. Take them."

He could force me to swallow the pills. I put them on my tongue. He holds the glass for me, tilting it just enough for me to fill my mouth. I swallow.

"Good girl," he says.

Before I can remind him that I'm not a girl at all, that I'm twenty-four years old and I've killed men for the Old Colony Crew, he goes back to the kitchen. This time, I hear the rattle of a freezer drawer sliding open, and the clatter of ice cubes in a tray.

I'm dozing off when he eases a cloth-covered lump against my side. "Hold it close," he says. "No." He adjusts my arm. "Like this."

I suck in my breath as the cold pack bites my ribs.

"Here's another," he says. "Keep it on your nose. Your eye, too." He guides my free hand into place.

My fingers feel like they're rolling over tiny marbles. "What—"

"Frozen peas," he says. "They'll mold to your face better than cubes. Take it from an expert."

For just a moment, I wonder where he gained his expertise. Then I remember he's Braiden Kelly's Warlord. He manages his clan's soldiers for a living. He's seen every possible way a human body can be bruised and broken.

"Wait here," he says.

The frozen peas must be helping, or maybe the oxy's already in my blood, because I'm suddenly tempted to laugh. I don't know where Moran thinks I'm going. He could leave me here for hours, days even, and I wouldn't be able to follow him.

I don't know how long he's gone. I think it's only a couple of minutes, but my mind is playing tricks. It seems like I've been sitting on this couch for a lifetime.

I hear a scrape of plastic on plastic, the familiar sound of a lid twisting free from a jar. I recognize a scent as well—sage laced with rosemary. It's arnica cream, like the stuff I keep in my travel kit, next to my birth control pills.

That reminds me—my travel kit is back at Madden's apartment. And *that* reminds me of the last time I rubbed arnica into my wrists, when Madden fastened a pair of handcuffs tight enough to cut off circulation to my fingers, and he wouldn't listen when I told him to cut me loose but just kept pumping away between my legs.

"Hush," Moran says, and I realize I'm crying again.

I don't cry. But I've shed more tears tonight than I have in the past eight years. That's only because my body hurts so much.

I haven't cried for Da, and I won't, because he was King of the Old Colony Crew. Now I'll be the Queen. That's the way I'll mourn him. That's the way I'll honor his life.

Moran's thumb is gentle as he wipes tears from my cheeks. He's not at all like a warrior who spends day and night enforcing his mob boss's commands. His fingers are soft as he smooths on the arnica. He's still saying *hush*, so I know I'm still leaking tears, and he comes back with the soothing motion again and again.

I want to fight. I want to tell him I'm not a helpless child. He needs to know I'm Fiona Fucking Ingram.

Instead, I fall asleep.

≈

The second time I wake, I'm wedged into the corner of the sofa. Someone has piled cushions beside me so I stay upright. That same someone must have replaced my cold packs, because they're icy enough to make me shiver.

And someone has changed my clothes.

I'm free of my boned corset and my tight leather skirt. Instead, I'm swimming in a black hooded sweatshirt, with matching fleece pants rolled up to bare my ankles. My feet are lost in thick terry socks.

It's an ocean of softness, a universe of warmth. I'm floating on the memory of a stuffie called Bunbun—a once-pink rabbit with long floppy ears, bought by my mother the day she found out she was pregnant.

But my mother died giving birth to me. She's been dead two dozen years. And I threw out Bunbun when I was sixteen. I didn't need him anymore. Didn't want him after...

Forget about fucking Bunbun.

If someone dressed me in these warm clothes, then someone —Moran, I know it's Moran—has *undressed* me. He knows I wasn't wearing panties. He knows what Madden did before he beat me.

Groaning, I force myself to sit up straighter. I still feel pain —my face, my ribs, my tongue, where I must have bitten it. But everything is quiet now. Subdued. Like my injuries have been packed in cotton and layered in a shipping crate, and stored far, far away.

Moran was right. I needed the oxy.

I lower the ice pack from my face to my lap. I force my eyes —both of them—to open. My head feels like it's swaying in a breeze, like I'm one of those inflatable waving-arm tube men outside some store's grand opening.

"Go back to sleep," Moran says. He's sitting in the shadows across the room, knees spread wide, wrists anchored on the arms of a massive leather chair.

"I can't—"

"You can," he says.

"But you—"

"You're safe," he says.

"But I—"

"Sleep." It's an order, one I can't resist.

I do.

4

PATRICK

She's a pain in the arse, but I don't want her hurting any more than necessary. That's why I sit up, changing her ice packs every hour. I wrap the fresh ones in kitchen towels so she doesn't end up with frostbite, on top of everything Madden did. I make sure her breathing doesn't get too shallow.

I don't regret dosing her. Injuries like hers are the reason I keep a stash of oxy on hand. A slip of a girl like her, though… I probably should have started with one pill, instead of two.

But I wanted her out cold before I cleaned her up. Before I changed her clothes.

For the twentieth time, I tell myself not to think about the feckin' leather scraps I shoved into the bin beneath my kitchen sink. Even if she could get the blood out, she won't wear them again. She won't want the memories.

Sitting, listening to her breathe, my thumb fiddles with the ring I wear on the middle finger of my right hand. The titanium band has three sections so the middle part spins. I maxed out my meds hours ago. This fidget ring is my best chance to shut down the rabid squirrels inside my brain.

That, or rubbing one out while I sit here.

Christ. I can't be thinking about Fiona Ingram that way. I'm willing to bet she hasn't noticed me once in the past two months. All the flaunting she's done has been for the benefit of my boss. The rest of us Fishtown Boys are just props for her feckin' show.

I stare at the other ring I wear, the gold signet with a Celtic knot worked deep into the surface. The four-part circle says I'm a Fishtown Boy for life. My loyalty to my clan has no beginning and no end. I'll live and die by the family I've chosen.

Even if all of my brothers have been drooling over Fiona Ingram since she showed up at the start of Lent. Those tits... Those hips... That smart little mouth...

And now I know exactly what she looks like beneath the leather she wears like a uniform. I know how a steel zipper leaves a ridged, pink invitation down the middle of her chest. I know that buckles on her hips make grooves a man could measure with his tongue.

I know she waxes her pussy bare.

Jesus.

Fiona Ingram won't be wanting any man's touch for a long time. Maybe never for a man like me.

I shift in my chair, spreading my knees a little wider.

That moves my phone in my pocket, and I feel it buzz against my hip. Fishing it out, I find I've missed a whole string of messages, flowing through the group text for my soldiers. The first posts came in twenty minutes after I left Thornfield.

None of it makes sense. They're talking about a bomb. A fire. The garage went up in some sort of fierce explosion. The building's a total loss, along with all my boss's cars. It's a miracle no one was hurt.

I thumb through the posts faster now, until I find the real news: Madden Kelly set the bomb.

Fucking Madden Kelly.

I should have tracked him down before he shat all over Thornfield. Hunted him like the feral pig he is. Given him ten blows for every one he landed on Fiona tonight. Left him broken, blind, bleeding out in a dumpster.

I'm the Warlord. That's my job.

But now I'm stuck here, playing nursemaid because of what that dry shite did. Fiona needs someone to change her ice packs. And from the texts still flying fast and furious, the entire clan is after feckin' Madden. He'll get his soon enough.

Fiona moans, waking up. She waves a hand at me like she's trying to get a bad waiter's attention in a worse restaurant. "C'mon," she slurs. "Let's go."

She tries to get to her feet and fails. I wince for her as she sits down hard enough to clack her jaws together.

"You're not going anywhere but back to sleep," I say.

"Says who?"

She's a belligerent patient. But I'm bigger than she is. And stronger. And a hell of a lot more sober. "Sit back, *Scáthach*," I say.

"'M Fiona," she mumbles.

"My mistake," I say gravely, like I really give a damn. "Sit, Fiona. You need to sleep."

She shakes her head, and pain chisels lines into her forehead. "Need t' go."

This is worse than arguing with a drunk. I fetch another pill and bring her a glass of water.

"Wha's this?" She looks at me suspiciously.

"Take it," I say. "And then we'll go to Boston."

She grimaces as she swallows.

"Let it settle," I say.

"'N then we leave?"

"And then we leave," I lie.

She's out before she can make another demand. She barely stirs as I swap her ice packs again. She doesn't move when I smooth more arnica over the worst of her bruises.

I settle back in my chair and return to my phone. The men are reporting in, one by one. They've searched every inch of Thornfield, and Madden's nowhere to be found.

The arsehole's slipped away. But when I find him, he'll pay for all he's done.

~

Sometime before dawn, the texts start flying again—fire, bodies, danger. At first, I'm confused because the bombed garage was put out hours ago. But then I realize this is a second blaze, a bigger one, worse.

Within an hour, Thornfield's gone—an entire mansion, burned to the feckin' ground. Reports stay sketchy until my second-in-command weighs in. Rory O'Hare is doing his job, calming the enforcers.

Our boss went into that hellscape, trying to rescue two women in his care. Kelly came out alive. The women didn't.

It doesn't take much reading between the lines to know it was a close call. At Kelly's command, O'Hare is moving operations to a downtown hotel. He's called for the Fishtown Boys' tame doctor. He's set guards at the perimeter.

I should be there.

But despite it all—two fires, Madden missing, and the clan relocating to the feckin' Rittenhouse—I'm stuck following orders. It cuts me to the quick, but my boss doesn't actually need me by his side. O'Hare has everything under control.

The Bell rings, knocking out the brain squirrels. There *is* one thing I can do. Something no one else can.

Kieran Ingram's men threatened my boss's life earlier tonight, before Madden worked his shite. Now I've got Fiona Ingram, battered and bruised and clearly in my debt. If I stick with the girl, see her up to Boston, I can assess the threat up there. I can protect my captain that way.

But I've sworn never to set foot in Boston again.

Penance. I'm still paying penance for all the mistakes I made when I was younger than the girl on my couch. When I followed the ringing Bell and damned myself forever.

Fuck.

Fuck, fuck, fuck, fuck, fuck.

I pound my head with the heel of my hand, trying to knock some sense past the bone. I want to break something. Tear something. Holler until my throat bleeds.

But I'm not a feckin' animal. So I work out a plan. Test it in my mind. Find the weak points and lean in hard, correcting them. Test the fecker again.

When a few hours have passed and I know I have the best approach—at least until the ground shifts again beneath my feet—I take my phone into the bedroom, so I won't wake Fiona.

It takes four rings before Braiden Kelly answers.

"Condolences, Boss," I say. I figure that covers just about everything—the garage, the house, the bodies that didn't make it out.

He sighs. "We'll knock it down and start over." He sounds exhausted. I'm not the only one who's missed a night of sleep. "For now we're at the Rittenhouse," he says. "Presidential Suite. Liam'll get you a key."

My thumb crosses my palm to fidget with my ring. I should have eaten something before starting this call. Taken my meds. "About that, Boss." I lower my voice, because there are some things Fiona doesn't need to know. "Herself is… Madden did a lot of damage."

There's a longer silence than I expect. When Braiden finally speaks, his voice is frozen lava. "How bad is it?"

"She shouldn't be alone right now," I answer truthfully. And then I dig my own grave: "Not with her da gone and things gone arseways up in Boston."

"You're taking her up to Boston, then?"

Jesus, I don't want to go. I left that place for a damn good reason twenty-five years ago, for the best two reasons a man could ever have. I've vowed never to get within a hundred miles of the feckin' Old Colony Crew. I don't keep in touch with a single soul who knew me then.

But my boss needs to know what's stirring up there, how seriously he should take the threat on his life. And the girl on my couch needs to mourn her da. Needs to meet her new captain, too, to realize her silly dreams of taking charge will never happen.

I don't want to be the one to shatter her. But for the life of me, I can't think of anyone better.

Sighing, I say, "If you'll let me, Boss."

It takes a minute, but Braiden finally says. "Go ahead. But don't let me be surprised by anything you find up there."

"You won't be, Boss," I promise.

Spinning my ring, it occurs to me that the texts I've been reading have left a pretty massive hole. Madden Kelly made it onto Thornfield land to plant his bomb in the garage. An entire crew of Fishtown Boys—my enforcers included—scoured the estate for any sign of the gobshite, only to come up empty.

But Braiden hasn't called anyone to task. He hasn't questioned the search. He hasn't ordered new men to watch the gate.

My boss knows more than he's letting on in public. I can't ask him outright. Even with our phones secured, there are some questions no man should ever say out loud.

But I can work around that.

I clear my throat and say, "Speaking of surprises… I'll be taking Fiona round to collect her things before we leave. Any idea if Madden'll be there to give us trouble?"

He pauses for long enough that I have my answer. I don't know how and I don't know when, but Braiden Kelly has guaranteed his brother won't be wreaking any more havoc on the Fishtown Boys. On Fiona Ingram, either.

Nevertheless, Braiden *says*: "He was at the house last night. Blew the garage to smithereens, but no one caught him on the grounds. The boys couldn't find him."

My eyes narrow as I nod, my suspicions confirmed by the non-answer. I pitch my voice carefully, striving for just the right note of concern. "I'll let you know if we see him then."

"You do that." Braiden says.

Someone who didn't know my boss as well as I do might believe there's an honest chance Madden might walk through the door any second. But I'm armed with the truth.

Now that I know I'm heading north, I'm itching to get on the road. So I say, "If you need help while I'm gone, you could do worse than asking Rory O'Hare."

"Thanks," Braiden says. "Safe travels." It's gratifying that he sounds a touch reluctant to send me on my way.

I end the call and look around my bedroom. It's spartan. Bare. Some might say I live like a feckin' monk.

I do best when I'm surrounded by few distractions.

Pulling a duffel from under the bed, I start tossing in the things I need. A spare pair of jeans. Some T-shirts. Boxer briefs and socks. A tight-knit sweater, because I know how cold a Boston spring can be.

Two spare handguns, a throwing knife, and a pair of brass knuckles.

Glancing down the hall, I see Fiona hasn't moved on the couch. That gives me time to shower. Eat whatever passes for food in a kitchen nearly as empty as my bedroom. Take my meds.

And then I'll wake the hellcat so we can head to Boston.

5

FIONA

The third time I wake, bright light pries past the window shades. I've lost hours; it must be after noon. I look across the room, and the leather chair is empty. My ice packs are fresh, though. And from the rosemary-sage scent of arnica, Moran applied fresh cream to my bruises.

My brain is dull, like scissor blades used to cut through plastic. I'm thirsty, and my belly feels empty, but I'm queasy too. I'm not sure I can keep down food—which might be a first for me.

My phone sits on the low glass table in front of the couch. When I lean forward to pick it up, my body is out of sync. My head feels like it's tied to a string, floating up toward the ceiling. It takes a few breaths for my brain to catch up to my grasping fingers.

Sinking back into my nest of pillows, I hold the screen at arm's length, waiting for it to identify my face and unlock. The room is too dark, though, or the angle is wrong, or maybe my face is too swollen. I have to type in my code to access my information.

No messages from Madden. There's not a chance in hell I'm letting that asshole get anywhere near me, but I miss the chance to tell him so, in no uncertain terms.

There's nothing from my clan either. No one extending condolences about my father. No one calling his lieutenants together.

That makes sense. They're waiting for me to act.

Da started treating me like his Clan Chief—his second-in-command—a couple of months ago, when Uncle Aran was locked up in prison. With Da's sworn Clan Chief out of commission, he sent *me* to Philly. *I* was tasked to rein in Braiden Kelly.

My father had no idea I'd already made inroads with Madden.

Now, Uncle Aran's sprung from the pen; he went home just last week. Supposedly, the district attorney got worried about flimsy evidence, about losing such a high-profile case in an election year. I think she must have pocketed Uncle Aran's cash—enough to buy a summer home on the Cape. Or maybe she decided not to test the Old Colony Crew's reputation for burning out our enemies.

I haven't spoken to my uncle since he was released. That's a mistake. As my father's heir, I should have made a point of welcoming his Clan Chief home. We celebrate every loyal soldier who slips the noose.

Well, I'll make up for it once I'm back in Boston. I'll make a big deal out of announcing that Uncle Aran is still *my* Clan Chief, that I appreciate his serving as second-in-command, the way my father always did. Da has a stash of Jameson Bow Street in the basement. I'll give my uncle a bottle in front of all my men.

"You're awake, then."

I startle at the words, even as I recognize Moran's voice. "I am."

"Shower and get dressed. The clothes on the bed are clean. You can eat, and we'll pick up your things from Madden's place. We can be on the road by noon."

"On the road?"

"I'm taking you up to Boston. Get moving."

My head is doing that floating thing again, bobbing somewhere above the couch. I try to take a deep breath, but my bruised ribs think that's a crappy idea. I cover by giving Moran a slow blink and dropping my voice an octave. "You're pretty good at giving orders, aren't you?"

"You have no feckin' idea."

Even when he's agreeing with me, he sounds like he's making a threat. I probably should thank him for taking care of me all night long. But gratitude sounds an awful lot like weakness.

I settle for reaching toward the table, stretching like a cat as I put down my phone. That's the first time I remember I'm wearing sweatpants cut big enough for King Kong. A sweatshirt, too. How could I forget Moran stripped me while I was out cold?

Angrier than I have any right to be, I demand, "Did you like the show?"

"Somno's not my thing, *Scáthach*."

He called me that last night. I don't know what it means. I barely speak any Irish, just a word or two I've picked up from Da and the Crew. But I'll be damned if I'll ask Moran for the definition. I can look it up on my phone later.

He doesn't make a sound. His lips don't even curl. But somehow, I know he's laughing at me.

I pull the sleeves of his monster-size sweatshirt over my fingertips. There must be something witty I can say, something to put him in his place, to make him shift his weight as I charm his cock like a cobra. But for the life of me, I can't think of what it is.

I don't know if it's the oxy Moran shoved down my throat or the aftermath of Madden's fists or the looming realization that my father's been dead for well over twelve hours and I'm late showing up for the Crew. But my usual quick words slip away like fish over a coral reef.

"Do you need help in the shower?" Moran finally asks, and I hate that his voice is kind. He's not teasing me at all.

"I'm fine," I say. I bang my hip against the couch as I lurch toward the hall.

"The towels by the sink are clean."

"I'm fine," I say again, which doesn't make sense, but I'm concentrating too hard on keeping my balance to figure out why those words are wrong.

"Leave the door open," he calls as I sway down the hallway.

I pretend that I choose to lean against the doorjamb to the bedroom, that I'm not about to collapse. I cock a hip and throw my shoulders back. Maybe I look sexy, but I'm really just trying to keep my balance. "So you can get another free show?" I ask, my tone a few notes shy of the purr I want.

"So I can hear if you fall."

"Fuck you," I say, because if I let myself think I'm weak enough to slip in the shower, I'll cry again. And I cried enough yesterday to last the rest of my life.

I wait for him to make some scalding retort, to tell me exactly how he'll fuck me, precisely what he'll make me do. Instead, he says, "Go on, then. Coffee will be ready when you're done."

I don't fall in the shower. And I only have to turn up the cuffs on the clean sweatpants four times. Three on the sweatshirt sleeves.

The coffee is hot and sweet, charged with enough sugar that I can pretend it's a meal.

But I have a few things I need to take care of, before we can hit the road.

6

PATRICK

Fiona Ingram is a girl who is used to getting her way.

She wants to pile all of Madden's clothes in his bath-tub, douse them with cooking oil, and set them alight with a match.

I tell her no.

She wants to call the local cops, report a man who looks like Madden lurking by an elementary school, say he's jerking off near the kids.

I tell her no.

She wants to take her red Mini Cooper and drive all the way to Boston, with me riding shotgun in that tin can.

I tell her no feckin' way.

But I agree to call Rory O'Hare and have him park the Mini out at his place. And she agrees to pack. She's quick and efficient, filling just a pair of suitcases and a backpack. She eats both slices of toast I make for her. She sees the logic in wearing my clothes for the long drive north, not forcing her bruised body into her usual dominatrix gear. Once we're back in my car, she only tries to change the radio once, before I tell her we're listening to classic jazz.

She harrumphs, which makes me crank the music. That turns out to be a good thing, because Fiona Ingram isn't much of a talker.

What do I know? Maybe she usually has a lot to say. Just not when her father's dropped dead in the middle of the night. Or when her eejit of a boyfriend beat her bloody. Or when she's feeling kidnapped by a mob enforcer she'd never spoken to twenty-four hours ago.

I keep an eye on her while I drive, using the passenger-side mirror so she doesn't feel like an animal in a zoo. The ice and the arnica worked wonders. Her eyes are still puffy, like she's coming off a twenty-four-hour crying jag, and her lip is scabbed over where it split on Madden's fist. She's got a constellation of black and purple and deep dark green around both bloodshot eyes. But she looks a hell of a lot better than I thought possible when I found her on the floor last night.

Half an hour outside of Boston, we pass bright blue signs for a rest area. "Pull over here," Fiona says, like I'm a feckin' cab driver.

But she shouldn't have to beg for a chance to piss. And I wouldn't mind stretching my own legs before we get to Southie. So I negotiate the lane changes and guide us through a crowded parking lot. The car falls silent, my ears still ringing with Miles' trumpet asking *So What?*

Fiona climbs out and swings her backpack over both shoulders. "I'll be a few minutes."

I nod and open my own door. My spine pops as I unfold from the driver's seat. My knees register a protest when I straighten my legs. My arse has fallen asleep, and I get a stitch in my side when I stretch.

There was a time when an uninterrupted five-hour drive was just a warm-up. I could make a midnight run to North Carolina, fill a truck with cigarettes, and get home before noon. I'd sleep a few hours in the truck, then spend a night drinking and whoring at Mimi's place, getting back to my apartment just in time to watch the sunrise.

Getting old's a bitch.

There's a reason Warlords are supposed to sit in offices and manage naive young enforcers who'll do just about anything to become made men.

A minivan pulls into the space next to mine. Before the harried guy behind the wheel can cut the engine, both side doors glide open. Half a dozen ankle-biters spill out, dressed in identical green-and-white uniforms. Three boys start kicking around a football—*soccer*, I know they'd call it. The other three pound toward a water fountain like zebras at a watering hole. They're shouting loud enough to wake the dead, their voices sharp and clear like wrens.

I tell myself I'm grateful I don't have to wrangle the pack. But I don't believe a word of it.

Athawn would be just a few years younger than the man driving the team. If Athawn had survived being cut out of my dying wife. If I'd had only one body to bury, not two. Three, if I count my own mam, all in the space of one week.

Boston's plucking at my brainstem like a kid stripping wings off a butterfly. For all I know, if my son had lived, he might refuse to coach kids sport. He might be setting his roots as a doctor or a lawyer, too busy to launch a family. He might be—

Christ.

He's gone, and his mother, and my mother too, and there's no use dreaming otherwise. No use thinking things would be different if I'd kept away from the Crew in the first place, if Da'd never done the things he did, if I'd grabbed Jenn's keys before she could drive off in a fit of rage and disappointment.

Fuck Boston.

Fuck the Crew.

And fuck my da for turning everything to shite.

A muscle starts to twitch deep inside my jaw. That's the first sign my meds are wearing off. But If I dose now, I'll never sleep tonight—even after sitting up all last night to watch Fiona.

Instead, I focus on my breathing. In on a four-count. Hold for a—

"Jesus, Mary, and Joseph!" I swear under my breath as Fiona emerges from the red brick building.

I'm not the only one who notices her. The six little footballers stop dead in their tracks, every last one covering his crotch like he's defending a free kick. An elderly couple clutch each other, and I wonder how long it will take 911 to get here if they both stroke out. Three dude-bros wearing backward baseball caps and saggy jeans literally start to drool.

Fiona has poured herself into a sleeveless scarlet catsuit. The vinyl one-piece has a deep V at the front that isn't working very hard at covering her generous tits. The thing must zip up the back, because there isn't a hint of a seam from her sternum to her crotch. The shiny vinyl grips all the way to her ankles, showing off her five-inch-high black stilettos. Her arms are cased in tight black gloves.

None of that, though, is the reason I'm staring like a sex-starved teen-age boy. Over forty-six years, I've seen more than my share of tits and hips, of flat bellies and smoothed-over cunts.

But I've never seen what Fiona has managed with her face. Her face and her neck and the generous spread of flesh between those magnificent tits…

I sponged her clean last night. I rubbed arnica into her skin. I held ice packs against her body, beside her nose, under her eyes. She's battered and she's bruised and no single night of care could ever heal what Madden Kelly did to her.

But apparently makeup can.

"What the actual fuck?" I ask as she strikes a pose in front of me.

The young father in the minivan hollers for his charges. The octogenarians stagger back to their car. All three horn-dog bros gape at me like I'm a feckin' god.

"How the hell…"

Fiona dips her chin, using the motion to look at me through eyelashes coated in a gallon of black goop. "I keep a few tricks up my sleeves." Her rippling shrug is designed to deprive every straight man in a hundred-mile radius of all blood-flow north of his belt.

"Get in the car."

Her lips are the exact same shade as the catsuit, and somehow twice as shiny. My cock knocks against my zipper as she pouts. "I didn't have change for a soda. Will you buy one for me?"

"Get. In. The. Car."

"I'll pay you back." Her sultry tone leaves no doubt about how she'll make good on her debt.

"Fiona…" I glance around like I'm transporting moonshine over state lines. One of the drooling bros has his phone out, catching video. The thought of her headlining his spank bank tightens my fingers into fists. "Get in the car," I choke out a third time. "And I'll get you a soda."

She smiles like I've just offered her the sun, the moon, and the stars. "Mountain Dew," she says. "Diet."

I wait until she closes the Land Rover's door before I stalk to the vending machine. I make a point of bumping into the delinquent with the phone. We both hear the screen shatter when he drops it, but he's not suicidal enough to say a word.

Mountain Dew. Diet. I flash a credit card at the machine and a bottle drops with a sound like a soul arriving in hell. Storming back to the car, I get in on the driver's side. I shove the drink at her, hard, like I'm not afraid of any feckin' vinyl.

She makes a sound like a kitten sighing. "No straw?" she asks.

"It's a goddamn vending machine," I growl. "Of course there's no straw."

She sniffs and puts the drink in a cup holder. I jam the Land Rover into reverse and flee the parking lot like I'm driving the getaway car on a million-dollar bank heist.

We're ten miles from Boston before my breath stops feeling like barbed wire in my throat. By the time I pull off the interstate, I'm angry with myself for playing her game. When we cross into Southie, into Old Colony Crew territory, I force myself to sound bored.

"What's your plan here? Beyond painting your face and pouring yourself into that thing?"

She fiddles with the cap on the unopened bottle of soda. "We'll go straight to the *dún*."

The *dún*. The fortress. The house her father claimed in the heart of Southie, decades ago. I know it better than I'm willing to admit. I've seen a lot of blood flow there.

"And what?" I ask. "You'll just waltz up to the door and knock?"

She gives me a look like I'm a poor eejit child. "I won't *knock*. I'll walk right in."

"Just like that."

"I'm Queen now. The *dún* belongs to me." She lets me go another three blocks before she says, "Take a right at the next street."

"I know how to get there."

Surprise flashes across her face, but it only takes a heartbeat for her to tamp it down to boredom.

Fiona wasn't even born when I left Boston. When Da… When Mam… When Jenn… When Athawn… When the Moran name turned to shite.

I take a left turn, and then a right.

The *dún* looks exactly as it did on the day I left. It's a dark gray clapboard building. Three stories above ground, and one below. It fills a city block. That's bulletproof glass in the windows. Walls reinforced with steel. Doors three inches thick.

No cars park on this block, on either side of the street.

Cameras are mounted on telephone poles. They used to dump a grainy feed onto computer screens in the basement, but the equipment must have been upgraded by now.

Two kids stand on the closest corner, hunched in denim jackets against the late April chill. Their twins are at the far end of the block. Relaxed. Casual. At least until I stop the Land Rover in the middle of the road.

Two grown men flank the door. I don't know them. I suspect I don't know most of the Crew these days. But Fiona's sharp little inhale says she recognizes the pair.

"What's wrong?" I ask, not taking my eyes off them. They're making no secret of the handguns they carry. They're right-handed, both of them. Their shoulder holsters hold something heavy.

I'd put backup in the house across the street. Long guns on the second floor.

When I leave the engine running, the guy on the left taps an earpiece. His eyes don't shift, but I catch a flicker of curtain across the way. Like I said, extra manpower across the street.

Maybe a sniper on the roof. You can't be too careful these days. Southie's a lot rougher than the Philadelphia suburb my boss calls home. And every criminal in Boston must be dreaming of an unexpected payday, now that the Old Colony captain's dead.

Fiona has gone perfectly still.

"What's wrong?" I ask again.

"They're not Da's men."

I didn't think they would be. Fiona's told herself a fable. She believes in fairy godmothers and magic castles and unicorns farting rainbows across the sky. But she's about to wake up to the real world.

"You know who they work for?"

She nods, a single tight jerk of her head. "Uncle Aran."

Aran Dowd. Old Ingram's Clan Chief, his second-in-command. A man I know far too well. A man I hate.

Her fingers scramble for the latch on her door.

"Hold on," I say. My voice is sharp enough that she obeys. "You need a plan. You aren't just walking in there."

She shakes her head. "That's exactly what I need to do. I'm not afraid of those two. I'm not afraid of anyone." I wait for her to tell me she's a killer, like that's news. She misses the opportunity, which gives me a hint of just how thrown she is.

"You should be," I say.

"He's my uncle. He's waiting to welcome me home. He knows this is what my father wanted."

If her father wanted to make her captain in his stead, he'd have kept her close to Boston, not sent her down to Philadelphia. Not tried to marry her off like a broodmare, to a thoroughly uninterested Braiden Kelly. Not ignored her, when she stayed on with feckin' Madden Kelly.

Her breath is coming fast now. She's closer than ever to spilling out of that suit.

"Let's think this through," I say. "We can come back tomorrow. You can sit down with your uncle like equals."

"We aren't equals," she says. "I'm his captain." She's like a child, announcing the Easter Bunny will deliver baskets after midnight. The Tooth Fairy will take her front tooth and leave her a silver dollar. Good old Santy will fill her Christmas stocking.

"Fiona—"

But I don't get to say the rest. Because she pulls back firmly on the latch. She climbs out of the Land Rover, steady on her towering heels. She throws back her shoulders, and the light from the streetlamp cascades over her catsuit. She heads toward the *dún* like she's Queen of all the Celts.

"Stop!" the guard on the right shouts.

Fiona doesn't stop.

"You are not welcome here," says the guard on the left, like he's memorized one line for a school play.

Fiona keeps on walking.

"This house is the property of the Old Colony Crew," the first man announces.""

Fiona pauses then, one foot on the curb. She cocks a hip. Twists her lips into a knowing smile. And she says very loudly, very clearly, carving out each syllable like a perfect diamond, "Then this house belongs to me. I'm Fiona Ingram. Queen of the Old Colony Crew."

Gunshots echo down the street like the voice of an angry god.

7

FIONA

My ears are ringing, but I can still make out the sound of an engine racing behind me. An engine, and Moran shouting: "Fiona! Move yer feckin' arse!"

I stumble toward the car. One of my shoes catches on a manhole cover, and my ankle turns. That sends me tumbling forward, but the Land Rover's there, the door open. I'm still fighting for balance when Moran grabs my wrist. He yanks so hard I think my arm's coming loose from its socket. My already bruised ribs crash hard against the center console.

Tires squeal, and Moran peels away. My legs are half-in, half-out of the vehicle. Moran grips my biceps like a vise, anchoring my throbbing ribs against the gearshift.

He takes a corner wide. Slams down a block like he's on the straightaway of a Nascar track. Turns left, then left again, hurtling down an alley.

He only releases my arm after he's thrown the car into Park and punched the emergency brake.

"Close your door," he says, voice surprisingly mild, like he's talking about the weather.

"They fired at me!"

"Close your fucking door." His tone is still perfectly even. I wonder if he's some sort of sociopath.

I scramble clumsily, half-kneeling on the seat before I get my legs inside. Once I'm sitting, my stilettos force my knees to an awkward angle, too close to my chin. I realize I'm leaning forward, trying to draw a full breath against the constriction of my catsuit.

I close my door.

The instant it latches, Moran shoves the car into gear and flies down the alley.

"They tried to kill me," I say, as he returns to a city street.

"Bullshit." He ignores a stop sign.

"Didn't you hear those shots? They wanted—"

"To scare the shite out of you." He soars through a red light too. "You were three feet away. If they wanted to kill you, you'd be dead by now."

Southie sails by—sagging houses and tired cars and dimly lit packies with beer signs hanging in their barred windows. "I didn't think they'd—"

"You didn't think." He cuts me off. "Period." He finds one of the streets that crosses beneath the interstate. Shabby tents line the underpass.

"My father made me his—"

"Your father did shite."

"He—"

"Shut it."

"I'm—"

"Yer a girl," Moran sneers, his accent thicker than it's been all day. "Yer nothin' but a feckin' girl."

I smooth my catsuit. The action's automatic, but I take some comfort in the feel of the smooth vinyl beneath my palms.

When I catch Moran looking at me, I arch my spine. I can't

help it. I almost laugh when I hear his hard swallow. I say, "I'm taking over the Crew."

"Sure you are." He's humoring me.

"It'll just take a little longer than I planned."

"Uh-huh."

"The captains will vote on a new general for the Grand Irish Union in one hundred days." That's the post my father held, the way he ruled over all the captains in the States. Tradition says all of us mourn, counting off the days, and then we act, choosing our new leader.

"And you think you'll be that general."

I shake my head. "Some of the captains have never even met me. It's unrealistic to think enough will vote for me in just three months."

"Unrealistic, eh?"

The Irish at the end of his question—a combination of good humor and raw doubt—makes me angry, but it locks in my determination. "Every man in the Old Colony Crew will swear his loyalty to me as Queen by the Grand Irish Union vote."

I've watched a bunch of podcasts about achieving your dreams. They all recommend setting SMART goals. S—make it specific. M—measurable. R—relevant. T—time-bound. I've just done all that.

Yeah, there's an A in there too. The goal's supposed to be attainable. Moran's going to tell me I'm being utterly unrealistic. I might as well say I'm going to win an Olympic gold medal in the decathlon.

But Moran doesn't say anything at all. Which only makes me want to work harder to prove him wrong.

He's slowed the car to a normal speed. We're in a busier part of town; restaurants and bars line the streets. We're getting close to the Commons, where tourists throng.

He nods toward the backpack by my feet. "You still have my clothes in there?"

My chin juts defiantly. "Yeah."

"Get dressed."

I snort as I look out the window. "Here?"

"Just do it."

Knowing it'll drive him mad, I moan as I reach for the hidden zipper along my spine.

"Jesus Christ," he mutters. "Just cover yourself. Put those on over your…whatever."

"It's vinyl," I say.

"So help me God…"

I peel off my long black gloves, plucking the fingers one by one. I have to undo my seatbelt to pull his sweatshirt over my head, and an alarm shrills like the vehicle is about to self-destruct. I slip off my stilettos so I can negotiate the sweatpants. Moran mumbles something in Irish as I raise my hips, definitely making me wish I'd learned more Gaelic.

He takes a sharp right turn into a well-lit driveway.

"Where are we?" I ask, peering through the windows.

"A hotel."

"Which one?"

"A Hilton. A Hyatt. What the fuck do you care? It's somewhere not connected with you in any way. Your uncle won't have any reason to look for us here."

A uniformed attendant hovers by my door. I shove my shoes into my backpack and try not to argue with Moran. I'm barely successful, especially when he looks like he wants to de-nut the man who helps me out of the car.

Moran wrestles both of my suitcases out of the back and slings his own duffel over one shoulder. I see what it costs him when the valet asks for his car key. Moran doesn't like giving control to anyone.

Once we're in the lobby, he orders me to stay close to his side. There's no one waiting to check in. The one clerk at reception is carrying on an animated conversation with a bellhop.

"And then——" says the clerk. His name tag reads *Nelson*. I don't know if that's a first name or a last.

"Excuse me," Moran interrupts.

"And *then*," Nelson tries again. The bellhop has the grace to look uncomfortable.

Moran taps the corner of his credit card against the counter. It's an American Express platinum.

Da carried a black card. I wonder if I can access his account. How long will it be before I get my own black card?

The clerk doesn't take the hint. Instead, he angles his shoulders, as if he's sharing a secret with his uneasy coworker. "I *told* her——"

"Cut the crap," Moran warns, his voice dangerously low.

Nelson isn't quite as stupid as he looks. He raises his eyebrows in fake surprise. "I'm sorry, sir," he says in a voice that is anything but. "I didn't realize you were waiting."

Negotiations for a room go about as well as I expect. There's nothing on the highest floor. All the suites are taken. They don't have anything with two queen beds. If we have special requirements like that, we should have made a reservation.

Moran finally settles on a fourth-floor room with a single king-size bed. Nelson eyes his computer screen with a spark of malevolence. "Are you eligible for any of our discounts?" he asks, flicking a dismissive glance at Moran's disheveled gray-shot hair. "Senior citizen?"

Moran is Braiden's chief enforcer. The Glock in his shoulder holster can't be the only weapon he's carrying. But he takes the insult, only gritting through set teeth: "No discounts."

The clerk nods and types and blinks like he's innocent as a newborn lamb. "And will your daughter need a key too?"

My laugh comes out as a sharp bark. Moran glares like he's trying to incinerate the entire front desk. "We both need keys."

"Very well, sir," Nelson says. He puts two plastic cards in a paper sleeve. "Have a wonderful evening. Don't hesitate to let me know if I can do anything to make your stay more pleasant."

Moran growls as he snatches up the keys. I need to jog to keep up on our way to the elevator.

The room door closes noisily behind us. The bed fills almost every inch of the stained beige carpet. A quick glance out the window confirms we're facing an air shaft.

Moran throws his duffel into the only free corner. "Where do you want your bags?" he asks.

I snort. "The bathroom? Or maybe we should use them as pillows."

This time, he swears in English.

Before I can tweak him again, he edges past my suitcases and stomps into the bathroom. I'm pretty sure he's practicing deep breathing and maybe counting to ten. The door is thin enough I'd hear anything else.

I take advantage of his absence to wiggle out of his sweats. The only problem with this catsuit is that the zipper catches if I take too deep a breath. And I've done plenty of deep breathing since I left the rest-area bathroom.

Twisting my arm, I try to grip the zipper's tiny tab. It moves less than an inch before it snags in the middle of my back. "*Motherfucker!*" I say, because that's the way *I* learned to swear.

Moran throws open the bathroom door as if I'm being attacked. Feeling a little foolish, I look at him from under my arm. "Hey, Daddy," I say, channeling the asshole clerk who put us here. "A little help?"

His eyes go flat, like a rattlesnake eyeing a mouse for supper. "What did you just call me?"

I hear the warning in his voice, sharper and far more deadly than the alarm that rang when I shimmied out of my seatbelt. I catch my breath against the unexpected belly-swoop that jacks my heartbeat into overdrive.

Maybe it's the aftermath of being shot at, the leftover adrenaline from fleeing the *dún* like a pair of action-adventure heroes. Maybe it's rage at the Crew for not letting me in, or it's how Moran was taken down by the desk clerk, or it's because I want new memories to replace the shitty ones of Madden Kelly's fists.

But I want more of this breathless feeling—of this sudden raw desire. I purposely soften my tone before I look up at Moran through my lashes. "Daddy?" I coo. "Won't you help your little girl?"

He closes the distance between us like he's been shot out of a cannon.

His hand moves with precision, fingers seizing the zipper tab like tweezers. His pull is steady and strong. The front of the suit compresses my chest, then my ribs, then the small of my back before he peels the vinyl down to my ankles.

I barely have a chance to snatch a full breath before he shoves me onto the bed. My feet are trapped as I balance on all fours. Moran orders: "Stay."

I'm tempted to woof like a dog. Instead, I look over my naked shoulder and say, "Yes, Daddy."

I watch something snap inside him. He toes off his shoes like they're doused in acid; he strips off his socks too. He pulls off his long-sleeve T, tossing his head like a bull once he's free. He doesn't bother pulling his belt all the way clear, just undoes the buckle, then his button and zipper. He pulls his boxer briefs down with his jeans.

He's naked, except for a scattering of scars and the tattoos that cover his right arm. A lighthouse stretches from his shoulder to his elbow, wreathed in black clouds and thready lightning that boils over his biceps. The design is executed in exquisite detail; I can make out windows on the tower and every bar of the iron cage at the top. Storm-whipped ocean waves cover his forearm. The tattooed zigzag of a heart monitor races across his wrist, cut short with an unflinching straight line.

I reach for the design because it's beautiful and it's terrible and I can't imagine how many hours he sat in some artist's chair, getting the ink pumped under his skin.

He bats my hand away. I'm not allowed to touch.

For a single gobsmacked moment, I think he's retreating to the bathroom again. But then I realize he's tearing into his duffel in the corner. He's digging into a leather kit, shoving aside a comb, a razor, and an amber bottle of pills. He comes up with a chain of foil squares, victory glinting in his eyes.

I twist to help him as he tears open a packet. I want to roll the condom over his cock. I want to run my fingers down the rubber, feel the length of him, hard and ready. "Please," I say. "I'm Daddy's little helper."

He slaps my hand again and turns me around, his chest to my back. When I arch against him, I feel his dick between us, pressing hard against me.

His fingers close around the nape of my neck, and he pushes me forward, his grip steady and commanding. I balance on hands and knees again, but he wants more. He *demands* more. He lowers my face toward the mattress until I sink onto my forearms. My bare ass is full exposed.

"Is this what you want, Daddy? Is this how you want your little girl?"

I've never played this game before. I only say the words now because they're sparking something deep beneath Moran's surface, something fierce, something animal.

I need that savagery. I need to forget what Madden did, forget that Da died, forget the surprise of gunfire at the *dún*. I need Moran to fuck the last twenty-four hours out of my mind.

He digs his fingers into my hips, tugging me back until I feel the tip of his cock between my legs. I gasp—not because he's hot and not because he's hard and not because he's bigger than any man I've ever had before. I hiss because his fingers find my bruises. They burrow into dark places where Madden shoved his fists.

Moran growls something, Irish again, ending with that word he calls me: *Scáthach*. He shifts his grip and folds an arm around my belly. He's holding me tighter than he was before, but now it doesn't hurt. He's not pressing into my old wounds. He's found a new way to pull me close.

"Thank you, Daddy," I say, pushing back against him.

He reaches between my thighs and slides his thumb inside. I'm wet. Soaked. He must like how I feel, because he groans deep inside his throat.

He drives home like he's staking a claim in a gold mine. I gasp at the pressure, at his weight, at his strength. He fills me, going deeper than any man has ever gone before. A flutter immediately starts inside me, a ripple, a swirl.

He eases back, slow and steady, almost pulling free. I need him, though. I don't want to let him go. I whine, a silly, desperate sound, and then I whisper the same order he gave me: "*Stay.*"

He stays. He tightens his arm beneath me. He shifts his weight and he fills me again.

It's easy to find our rhythm. We move without shame, without awkwardness, without any of the little slips and stumbles new lovers make.

Sex with Moran is hard and fast and dirty.

He says my cunt is amazing. He tells me I'm strong. He says I'm brave, and no one has ever said that before, and I don't believe him, I can't believe him, even though I'm opening up beneath him, and I'm spinning…hanging…waiting…

I come.

I come with a man's cock deep inside me.

An actual orgasm around an actual dick. No fake gasping and thrashing and calling on God. No toy, vibrating in a monotone until my nerves short-circuit. No fingers of my own, rubbing and pushing and pulling by rote.

I come with a man for the first time in my life.

And just as the seizing, grasping, pulsing begins to slow inside me, Moran comes too. He groans my name like it's a magic spell or maybe like it's a prayer. He finds some way to slide a little bit deeper. He spreads his hand wide across my back, claiming me, owning me.

When he's done, when he's empty and I'm full, he says that I'm the most beautiful girl he's ever seen. I don't know how it happens, I don't know where my body finds the strength, but suddenly I'm coming again—and multiple orgasms are another thing I've never done with an actual man.

Every sensation is deeper this time and stronger and I stretch beneath him and take his weight on my back and I never want to leave this place, not ever, not for the rest of my everlasting life.

8

PATRICK

Fiona whimpers when I finally pull out of her. This close, I can see the makeup she painted on, the way she covered up her bruises. I can count her ribs.

I push off the bed and reach down for her dangling feet. She twitches when I go for gentle, so I take hold of each ankle firmly. I have to work at getting the catsuit over her toes.

When I finally drop the vinyl on the floor, it looks like it couldn't cover a doll. I kick it toward the door, then fold the snow-white duvet over Fiona's still body so she doesn't get cold. I find my skivvies, tangled in my jeans, and I stalk to the jacks.

Once I'm behind the closed door, I take care of the johnny and pull on my boxer briefs. I run water in the sink until it starts to steam, and then I splash my face. Hands planted on the counter, water dripping from my chin, I stare at the eejit in the mirror.

We were high on the adrenaline of being shot at. I let that gobshite at the front desk get under my skin—did I need a feckin' pensioner's discount? Fiona's never met a man she wasn't ready to tease. She's a charmer, that one. And I couldn't wait to dip my own oar.

The Bell rang, and I fucking answered.

Jesus Christ, this was a mistake. She's a kid. And I don't need anything tying me to this godforsaken city one second longer than necessary.

I trace the heartbeat inked on my wrist—up, down, up, down, up, down, flat—the way I have a million times before. The tattoo isn't changing. There's no going back.

But, fuck me, the drumbeat inside my brain is taking a breather. The twitch in my jaw is gone.

I know the science behind my brain's jumbled chemicals. Mam read every one of the reports I carried home from school. She gave them to me and explained all the words I couldn't understand, even though she couldn't change the diagnosis.

The doctors call it a neurodevelopmental disorder—severe attention deficit hyperactivity disorder, combined-type. I know every last one of the scientific terms—endorphins and neurotransmitters, norepinephrine and serotonin, frontal cortex and basal ganglia and locus coeruleus. My highly genetic brain-based syndrome results in a failure to regulate my executive functioning skills.

Bottom line: My brain always craves something new. New activities. New sensations. New problems. I've got squirrels inside my skull, and a Bell that shatters any thought of impulse control.

I could write a book on all the ways I've learned to manage. I live and die by the apps on my phone—calendars, alarms, timers, reminders. I use my fidget ring to bleed off excess energy. I try not to get too hungry, too thirsty, too tired. I take my feckin' meds.

And one of the best tricks of all: Exercise.

Sex is the best type of exercise a man can have. My life as a

Dom tames the worst of my brain's misfires. Controlling women in my bed forces me to focus.

Jenn understood that. She was my first sub; we learned the life together. She had a masochistic streak as wide as the Grand Canyon, and our endless experiments locked away the brain squirrels for hours at a time.

When Jenn died, I knew I'd never find another sane woman who would tolerate the things I demand. Not in a so-called loving and mutually beneficial *relationship*. So I visit Mimi's girls to get what I need. I pay well and I tip better. I always get consent.

But I never—not once—dreamed I'd be the sort of sick fuck who gets off on playing Daddy.

Daddy. Won't you help your little girl?

Closing my eyes, I can still see Fiona's cherry-red lips. I hear the taunting in her voice. She knew exactly what she was doing.

And Christ, was she good at it.

I grab a towel from the rack and start to dry my face. Before I can finish, a phone rings in the other room—a light and airy tone that sounds like the theme for a puppet show.

Fiona's stirring when I come back from the jacks. "My backpack," she mutters, and I find it by the foot of the bed. She digs out her phone but then she stares at the screen like she's forgotten how to answer. When she finally looks at me, her face is stricken. "It's my uncle."

"Put it on speaker."

She obeys, which pulls something tight in my throat.

"Uncle Aran." Her voice is flat.

"Fiona."

I haven't heard him in twenty-five years. Dowd's a Clan Chief now, his captain's right-hand man. He's spent his entire life in the Irish mob, and he's made it somewhere north of sixty without being taken down by the feds, a competing mob, or fights within his own clan.

I thought about killing him myself a quarter of a century ago. He deserved it, for what he did.

But Aran Dowd is a man who gets his way. He's got that in common with his niece. Instead of killing Dowd, I left Boston.

Fiona pulls the duvet closer, as if a feckin' quilt can keep her safe from the shitehawk. But she's smart enough to hold her tongue. Dowd's the one who placed the call. He's the one who wants something.

And sure enough, he finally says, "I understand there was a misunderstanding tonight, at the *dún*."

"At my home," she says. Good girl. She's not afraid to stake her claim.

"At your father's home," Dowd clarifies. "May he rest in peace."

Fiona doesn't bother with religious sentiment. "Your men tried to kill me."

"Like I said," Dowd replies smoothly. "A misunderstanding. They weren't expecting you to show up like that. Tonight."

"To my *home*," she insists.

He ignores her point. "Tonight," he repeats. "Your father's wake isn't until tomorrow."

"You have no *right* scheduling my father's wake." Fiona's voice shifts up a couple of notes. I take a step forward, lowering my chin, trying to remind her she's a feckin' force.

"So many locals want to show their respect," Dowd explains. "We're holding his funeral till Saturday. Leaving time for the Dublin family to fly in."

"I get to decide that! I'm his d—" she catches herself, just before she says *daughter*. "Only child," she says, like that will get her the prize she wants. "I should choose the date."

"Wait too long and people start plotting. They need to see a King on his throne." Dowd sounds like he's teaching catechism to a slow student. But it's no coincidence he uses *king* and *his*. Fiona hears it too.

"No one's ever pushed out a rightful Old Colony captain," she warns.

"And they won't now," Dowd says smoothly. "Seven o'clock for the wake. Tomorrow night. At the *dún*."

"And you can promise we won't have any more *misunderstandings*?" Fiona pushes, clearly trying to salvage some hint of authority.

"Good night, *neacht*."

It's not an answer. Some might say his calling her *neacht*—niece—is a good sign. Family doesn't murder family. But I'm inclined to say he's putting her in her place. Patting her on the head and sending her to bed. Telling her the grown-ups will take care of the Crew.

From the look on Fiona's face, she agrees with my interpretation. "Asshole," she breathes, tossing her phone onto the mattress.

The motion pulls the duvet away from her chest. I do my best to ignore the view, focusing instead on the point of her chin. "And what do you intend to do about it?"

"What *can* I do? Show up for my father's wake. Once I'm there, I'll let everyone know in charge."

She's fierce. I'll give her that. "The first thing we can do is get there early. Seven o'clock is arrival time for the public. We'll be there by five."

She eyes me steadily. "We?"

"We. You need someone watching your back."

Plus, once I'm inside the *dún*, I'll have a front-row seat to the Old Colony Crew's infighting. I'll find out if Dowd has already completed his coup. If he's pulled his men into line, they can move against the Fishtown Boys.

After all, that's why my boss gave me leave to make this trip north—to monitor the risk to my adopted clan. Not to fuck a girl young enough to be my daughter.

Fiona raises her eyebrows. "Watching my back. Is that what old men like you call it?"

There's a moment when I know I can have her again. All I have to do is tug away the duvet that's barely covering her lap. I can grab another johnny and pull her ankles to my shoulders and give her another ride she won't soon forget.

But she didn't call me *Daddy* just now. And I'll take that as a sign that she's as tired as I am. Worse, likely, because Madden beat the shite out of her just twenty-four hours ago. Ice and arnica and makeup disguise a lot, but sleep is the only thing that will truly heal damage like hers.

I edge sideways around the bed and fight to loosen the blanket and sheet from the mattress. "Play your cards right, *Scáthach*, and I'll buy you breakfast in the morning."

"What does that mean? Ska-ha?"

She pronounces it like an American girl. I climb into bed and make a show of fluffing up my pillow. "Come to bed."

She huffs in exasperation, but she gets in on her side of the mattress. "Seriously," she says. "Why are you calling me that?"

"Go to sleep," I say, because I like being the one in control.

She clicks her tongue as if she's ten years younger than she is. Rolling over, she does her best to steal both the sheet and the blanket.

I put a quick stop to that. I throw my arm around her and spread my fingers wide across her belly, pulling her spine to my chest. I purposely aim low, avoiding the mottled bruises Madden left across her ribs.

"*Oíche mhaith*," I say, trusting she has enough Irish to know *goodnight*.

She shifts her weight, and I catch her wrist before she can land an elbow in my side. I pull her even closer, anchoring my position by arcing my leg over hers.

"Goodnight," I murmur for good measure, setting my lips against her ear.

She holds herself stiff for a full minute. I think I'll have to relent because pinning her here does neither of us any good.

But then she exhales, long and low and steady. Her spine

transforms from an iron chain to a length of heavy rope. Her hips rock, and she finds a better angle, and she sighs again inside the cage of my body.

I won't sleep like this. I never do more than doze at night anyway—a hard-won hour here, getting up to check the door and windows, another stolen hour there.

But things are different with Fiona. I lie still so I don't disturb her. I relax my grip around her belly. I let her take the full weight of my leg. I match my breath to hers.

And I sleep.

9

FIONA

Moran wakes before dawn, if the gray light leaking in from the air shaft is any guide. I feel the pressure of his morning wood against my ass, and I wait for him to nudge me awake for some relief.

But he only brushes a kiss against the sensitive skin beneath my ear before he pulls away. Once he's out of bed, he shifts the sheet and duvet up to my chin.

I must fall asleep while he's taking a shower, because the next thing I know, he's setting a paper bag on the shelf that passes for a nightstand. He waits for me to sit up, and then he gives me a cup.

I take it with both hands, breathing in the steam. Sadly, while it smells like coffee, the brew is so weak it tastes like water. Sugar water—I'll give Moran that—but water all the same.

"There's an apple," he says, nodding to the bag. "And an everything bagel."

That's barely a start. I'm ravenous. But I ask, "What are you eating?"

"I'll get something while I'm out."

"Where are you going?"

"I need a suit for the wake tonight."

He's talking like this is all perfectly normal. Like he didn't turn me inside out last night. Like he didn't keep the nightmares away, giving me five, six, seven straight hours of sleep.

He's also ignoring the fact that I'm stark naked beneath the bedclothes. He hasn't tried to cop a feel once this morning. He doesn't even let his eyes linger.

Daddy.

That's the magic word. That will get him back in bed. I know it in my bones.

Before I can say it, though, before I can decide if I *want* to say it, he heads into the bathroom. He leaves the door open, so I can hear him rummaging around; he must have filled the room's plastic ice bucket while he was out on his morning rounds.

"Here," he says, coming back to the side of the bed. He shoves a scratchy white hand towel toward me. "Keep this on until it melts."

The makeshift ice pack isn't as nice as a bag of frozen peas. But it feels good against my cheek and the bridge of my nose.

"Do you need anything?" he asks, halfway to the door.

You.

I could say it. I could throw back the covers. I could give him a glimpse of everything he's walking away from.

But I don't really understand why he's leaving. Why he didn't take care of his morning hard-on by using my body. Why he's being so kind and why he's ignoring everything we did last night.

So I shake my head no.

He comes back to the bed, and for just a moment I think he's changed his mind. Or maybe—is it crazy to think this?— he's going to give me a sweet kiss goodbye.

But he picks up my phone from the shelf. He holds it in front of my face, and when that doesn't open the screen, he gestures for me to put in my code. Once it's unlocked, he types in his number. I hear his own phone, buzzing in his pocket.

"There," he says. "Call me if you need anything. Get room service if you're hungry. I put out the Do Not Disturb sign. I'll be back by three."

Don't go.

It's not too late. I can say it. I can ask him to stay. I can beg.

I'm Fiona Fucking Ingram. I'm going to be Captain of the Old Colony Crew. I don't beg.

The door clicks closed.

I eat my bagel. I drink the rest of my lousy coffee. I sit with my ice pack covering my face. And I try not to think about how Patrick Moran shredded my life last night.

Moran comes out of the bathroom dressed like the mobster he is—black suit, black shirt, black tie. His hair is combed back, the gray more prominent in the hotel room's dim light. He's freshly shaved.

I can't glimpse the ink on his arm—the lighthouse, the storm, the severed heartbeat. He doesn't bother with his shoulder holster. No guard will let him into the *dún* with an obvious gun.

I wonder what other weapons he's carrying.

And I wonder why that thought tickles something between my legs. I'm sore from Madden's beating, but all that ice at Moran's apartment worked wonders toward easing my pain. I could easily go for a round or two in bed.

Maybe the wires are crossed in my brain, and I'm mistaking annoyance for horniness. Moran said he'd be back at three, and he didn't show up until five minutes after four. I spent the extra hour wondering if something terrible had happened, if the

Crew had tracked him down, if he was paying for driving me to the *dún* last night.

I told him as much when he finally came back to the hotel room, carrying a new suit and a half-drunk energy drink. He shrugged and glanced at his phone, like the screen should have told him he was running late. He hit the shower while I was still mid-tirade.

I'm starving. It's been hours since I ordered lunch—a large Caesar salad with extra anchovies and a grilled cheese sandwich with fries and a chocolate chip cookie the size of my head. After eating every last bite, I took a steaming shower. I applied a perfect mask of makeup to cover my bruises.

I'm wearing my favorite corset, the one made out of black leather, with scarlet lacing up the sides. Staring straight at Moran so he can't misunderstand my meaning, I raise my chin. Shifting my weight, I let my hips issue a familiar invitation.

But Moran doesn't take the bait.

"Go on," he says. "Change into something decent, and we can be on our way."

"I'm decent." I push my shoulders back to better make my point.

"You're not going to your da's wake with your tits hanging out for every man in the Old Colony Crew to ogle."

"Who made you the fashion police?" The corset doesn't show my tits. It just helps men with no imagination.

"I'm not police," he says. "I'm just the Fishtown eejit walking into the *dún* like I have a right to be there. And if you think you're going to convince any member of the Crew that you're their rightful boss, you'd best dress for the feckin' job. Show some respect for the dead."

It's *my* da's wake. I get to choose how I dress.

But it's not worth fighting with Moran. Maybe there *is* some member of the Crew who'll think less of me for looking like the woman I am.

I put on my cobalt-blue jacket, the one that buttons from my chin to my thighs. But I'm still wearing my leather pants. I have a reputation to maintain.

"Satisfied?" I ask, once I'm covered up.

"Hardly," he says.

I grip the handle on my closest suitcase and sling my backpack over one shoulder. "Let's go, then."

"Where are you going with that?"

I fight the urge to roll my eyes. "You want to spend another night here? We'll sleep at the *dún* tonight. After the wake."

After I've taken charge of the Crew. After I've stepped into my role as my father's true heir.

With a good night's sleep and hours to think, I've realized I don't actually have to wait for the Grand Irish Union vote. If I sweep in today, bold and determined, the Crew can be mine by nightfall.

That's the trick: Making those men understand I won't give up. They'll accept my leadership now, or they'll accept it later. And I'll be a far kinder Queen if they recognize my status now.

Moran says, "We missed checkout hours ago. Leave the bags."

But that's ridiculous. There's no reason for Moran to drive back to fetch them after I'm settled in the *dún*.

Men need to get used to my leading. Might as well start now.

It's awkward for me to get both bags out the door of the hotel room, but I manage. I'm pressing the button to call the elevator before Moran catches up. He's swearing in Irish, not quite under his breath.

As we cross the lobby, I see that Nelson is back on duty at reception. His face twists as we move toward the door, like he's caught a whiff of rancid beef. I consider waltzing over to the desk and thanking him for his biting comments last night. Tell him I got lucky. That I'm grateful.

Moran herds me out the door, and the moment passes.

He's got the Land Rover waiting just outside. Good tips to valets will do that. He throws my suitcases and backpack into the rear compartment and adds his duffel. He doesn't say a word as he navigates the city streets to Southie.

That silence is unfortunate. It gives me a chance to think about what I'm about to do: Claim the Crew as my own.

This is it. The moment I've waited for since I turned sixteen. Since I realized the only way for a woman to control the world around her is to take a stand against the men who want to destroy her. Since I learned to be twice as calculating as any man and ten times as ruthless.

My stomach twists beneath my cobalt armor. I start to bite my lip, but I remember not to get makeup on my teeth. Instead, I drum my fingers against the armrest, a staccato tapping that does nothing to slow my racing heart.

I can do this. It's the only thing I've ever truly wanted. It's what I deserve.

The street in front of the *dún* is clear, of course. It always is. Moran parks directly across from the door, like he has every right to be there.

"Ready, *Scáthach?*" he asks.

"What does that—" But he doesn't wait for me to finish my question before he comes around to open my door.

It's time.

Well past time, based on Moran's original plan for us to arrive by five. It's nearly 6:30. Other guests will be here soon. That's fine. It won't take me long to establish that I'm in control.

As if they've already accepted me as their captain, the guards don't lay a finger on me, though they give Moran a thorough patting down. He submits, jaw locked, eyes riveted to the front door. I don't know who breathes easier once we're allowed inside—him, me, or the soldiers who don't have to fight him.

The fireplace is cold in the parlor, framing a massive casket on a draped stand. The coffin is made out of mahogany, so polished that it reflects the room. The top half is propped open to reveal its white silk lining. A velvet-lined kneeler waits for my prayers.

From here, I can just glimpse my father's body. His eyes are closed. His hands are crossed on his chest, his fingers twisted around a rosary I never saw him hold in life. Someone has worked over his face with makeup, adding pink to his sallow flesh. His hair is combed with a perfection he would have hated.

They say the dead look like they're sleeping. They're wrong.

My father is gone. There's nothing but a shell inside that casket. Nothing but a symbol, waiting for someone—for *me*—to acknowledge, so we can all move into the future.

"Fiona! Darlin'! We weren't expectin' ya till seven!"

Uncle Aran enters from the door that leads to the hallway, to Crew offices and the stairs that head to the second floor. I know the *dún* like I know the lines on my own hand. I'm surprised by how good it feels to be home.

I assume Uncle Aran is playing up his Irish brogue to impress the handful of Old Colony soldiers who follow him into the room. He usually saves the County Mayo shit for when he's seriously drunk.

Give him credit, though. He's dressed for the occasion—a fine black suit, complete with a well-cut waistcoat. He's wearing his Old Colony tie, deep emerald green with gold emblems of the Liberty Tree scattered among matching shamrocks. His full beard is so white it looks powdered, which makes his red-veined nose seem even larger than it actually is.

He glances at Moran, who is standing behind me, silent as a stone wall. Something tightens in my uncle's face, or maybe it's his throat, or the hand he raises to draw me forward. He recovers, though, before I can be sure of what he's thinking. "Come raise a glass," Uncle Aran says. "T' yer dear, departed da!"

Someone's moved the furniture out of this front room, the matching armchairs that were decades old before I was born and the sagging couch with its tired floral print preserved beneath crinkling plastic. Instead, a table's been set up against the far wall. It's draped in black cloth and covered with crystal glasses, Da's best Waterford tumblers. Whiskey bottles stand sentry at the back.

Uncle Aran is generous, pouring my father's twelve-year-old Jameson. I wonder if that's what the Crew are drinking, the men hovering by the hallway door. No one pours for Moran. I'm about to correct the oversight when Uncle Aran cries out: "To Kieran!"

He touches his glass to mine. The toast is echoed by the Crew. All of us drink.

And before I can bring Moran into the circle, a ghost steps out of the crowd. "Fiona," he says.

Of course it's not really a ghost. It's Keenan Rivers. My father's Warlord, chief of all his enforcers.

Rivers clears six feet easy, maybe six foot three. He's thin as a whip—narrow shoulders, narrow waist—but he has all the coiled strength of a snake. His eyes are the sharp blue of a winter sky, and I can't remember a time his stick-straight hair wasn't ice white. He wears it long, pulled into a club at the nape of his neck.

He terrifies me. He always has. But I'm going to be his captain now, so I pretend my blood hasn't frozen in my veins.

"Keenan," I say.

He looks past me and sniffs, like I've tracked in dogshit on my shoe. "Cujo," he says to Moran, raising his glass in greeting. "Come to check if anyone's bleeding out in the basement?"

I have no idea what Rivers is talking about. But before Moran can finish bristling and shoot off some smart reply, Rivers says to me, "Send your dog to the kitchen."

Now's a perfect time to take a stand, to let the Old Colony Crew know there's a new boss in the *dún*. I pull myself to my full height, grateful for the extra four inches of stiletto that bring me closer to Rivers' eye level. "His name is Patrick Moran," I say, pitching my voice to be heard all the way to the second floor. "And I'm not sending him anywhere."

"No Moran is welcome in this house." Rivers says it like I've forgotten how to multiply, or maybe how to write in cursive.

Before I can answer, Moran steps up. He's as tall as Rivers and broader across the shoulders, across the waist too. His dark eyes meet Rivers' blue ones, obsidian chipping the sky. "I'm Warlord for the Fishtown Boys now," Moran says. "My captain sends condolences on your loss."

"Your *captain*," Rivers spits out the word like a piece of gristle. "Is the reason we're gathered here today."

"With all due respect," Moran says, which means with none at all. "We're here because your man smoked three packs a day."

"*With all due respect*," Rivers counters with the bite of a sudden cold snap. "You'll give my King his proper title in his own *dún*. You used to know that, Cujo. Have you forgot how men behave?"

"Go to feckin' hell." Moran says it casually, like he's commenting on the weather.

Rivers shoves me out of the way to get to him. Half a dozen of my father's best enforcers join the fray.

"Gentlemen!" I say, because that's what a captain does. She manages her men when they go too far, even when they think they're acting in her best interest. "A toast! To Kieran Ingram!"

My diversion works—at least to the extent that Moran and Rivers back off to glare at each other. Before I can force them both to drink to Da, Uncle Aran raises his own glass.

"So the prodigal daughter returns," Uncle Aran crows. "Your poor da's last great wish was to see you married by Easter. Alas, you failed at that. But if he could know his little girl came back to pay her respects…"

He wipes a finger beneath his eye, and I'm close enough to see it come away dry.

"To little Fee," my uncle shouts.

And every one of the fuckers but Moran repeats the toast: "To little Fee."

Just like that, my uncle has locked me in a box. I'm the naughty child. I'm the bad girl who didn't follow her father's orders. I'm the brat—little Fee—who barely made it home to spit on her father's grave.

I've never gone by a nickname, not once in my entire life. And I'm not about to accept this one now.

But Uncle Aran turns his fucking back on me. He raises a bottle of my da's whiskey, and he tops off the glass of every loyal man in the Crew. He clamps a hand on Rivers' shoulder, leaning close to mutter something I can't catch.

The soldiers savor their drinks. More than one of them eyes me, taking the measure of the bad girl come home.

Suddenly, I'm sweating inside my tailored jacket. My leather pants are clammy. Swallowing an unexpected wave of panic, I wonder if my makeup is holding up, if the shame of my bruises is on display for every member of the Crew to see.

Uncle Aran turns back, as if he's only just remembered I'm still here. "You must be tired, Fee, after coming such a long way," he says. "Why don't you go to the kitchen? Ask Oona for some biscuits."

Oona Maguire was my nanny, the woman who dressed me and bathed me and made me feel safe in this nest of vipers. Da plucked her from the kitchen to take care of me and on my tenth birthday he sent her back downstairs, without a word of warning.

So Uncle Aran's landed another blow. It's not enough to load me down with a new nickname. Now I'm impossibly weak, exhausted after a five-hour drive from Philly. I'm only fit for visiting with a woman in the kitchen, for snacking on cookies while the grown-ups mourn.

If I go to the kitchen, I'm a child. He wins.

If I stay in the room, I'm a defiant brat. He wins.

If I look to Moran for support, if I explain that Da sent me to Philadelphia, if I shout that my uncle's men shot at me last night, if I demand my rightful place as heir to my father and captain of the Old Colony Crew—anyway I play this: He. Fucking. Wins.

So I choose the least dangerous of all my terrible options. I stalk to the coffin by the fireplace. I drop to my knees, and I bow my head. Crossing myself, I move my lips in the barely remembered words of the rosary.

My uncle can't stop me from praying over my father's body.

I can't afford to look up. I can't gauge his reaction. But from the corner of my eye, I see him turn toward the front door, toward some newly arrived guest, come to honor my father. I don't take a full breath until I hear Uncle Aran's hearty laugh across the room.

This has all gone horribly wrong. I *am* my father's heir. This wake is supposed to be *my* first act as captain of the Old Colony Crew.

But Braiden Kelly warned me, weeks ago, in Philadelphia. How did he phrase it?

You're holding no cards. No one even gave you a seat at the table.

It's seven o'clock. The room is filling rapidly now. I hear lively exclamations as men greet men. Bottles clink against glasses.

The door opens for long enough that a chilly breeze snakes across the floor. The Crew's tone changes; their voices get softer. Laughter dies away.

I'm not surprised when I hear Father Bertram's bass rumble, scratchy as he greets mourners. He accepts a drink, comforting whoever pours for him: "God bless you, my son."

My fingers knit tighter. *I'm* the reason Father Bertram ministers to the Old Colony now. *I'm* the one who got rid of Father Colin.

I dare to look over my white-knuckled hands. Uncle Aran is holding court beside the bar. I have to blink twice, because the man he's talking to doesn't belong inside the *dún*.

It's Nero Sacco, Boston's mafia don.

Sacco is paying his respects. Sacco is honoring my father.

Sacco is making a very public statement that he accepts Aran Dowd as the next King of the Old Colony Crew.

The mafioso is taller than he looks in newspaper articles. Fatter, too. He's still got a full head of gray hair, even though he's older than my da was. His eyes are dark as they study the room, but his skin has an unhealthy yellow cast. Maybe he drinks too much. Or maybe he's just uneasy on enemy ground.

Keenan Rivers sidles up to the don. The Old Colony Warlord's lips twist into something that's supposed to be a grin as he offers his hand. The men shake, which is something that might have killed my father, if he wasn't already dead.

And what do I do? I remain kneeling by the coffin, hands clasped, neck bent, trying to figure out how I can possibly leave this room with any dignity intact.

10

PATRICK

How the fuck will I get Fiona out of here now?

Half the room is watching that guinea Sacco kiss up to Dowd, and to Rivers too. The other half is staring at Fiona as she goes through the motions of praying over her da. They're wondering how long the show will go on, and when she'll be tossed out on her pretty little leather-clad arse.

Well, in for a penny, in for a feckin' pound.

I cross the room and kneel beside her. I haven't been to church in twenty-five years, but lessons from my childhood don't die easily. My hand moves with automatic precision, making the sign of the cross as I bow my head.

Things couldn't have gone more arseways for Fiona. Wake or no wake, I never should have let her come back to the *dún*. Sure, I admire her fierce determination. It's almost sweet, the certainty she has that she'll win out in the end.

But if Dowd stops patronizing her for long enough to label her a threat, the Crew will follow his lead. At the very least, they'll lock her in one of the upstairs bedrooms. At the worst, they'll drag us both down to the basement.

I wonder if the cellar still stinks of heating oil. If the grout's still stained a rusty brown by the drain. If anyone's bothered to sharpen the bone saws and the cleavers, or whether the dull blades are still considered part of the game.

My shoulder blades twitch, sparking alarms to every one of my brain squirrels. I shouldn't have my back to the room. I shouldn't take my eyes off the Crew for a single goddamn second. But no one will know I'm not whispering a Hail Mary as I mutter to Fiona, "Ready to leave, *Scáthach?*"

"Don't call me that," she says automatically.

Despite the danger, my lips twitch. This girl has spirit. And that may be enough to get us out of here alive.

"Head high," I murmur. "Eyes straight ahead."

I cross myself again, and then I lumber to my feet, ignoring the shouted message from my knees that I should leave kneeling to younger men. For a moment, I think Fiona will ignore me, but then she seems to conclude I'm her best chance for something approaching a graceful exit.

She stands. She reaches out to touch her father's stiff claws. I haven't seen the fecker in more than a quarter century, but I have to question the morticians' skill. I wonder if the clan still uses the Callahan Funeral Home.

Maybe Ingram really did look like a vulture at the end. My boss certainly thought he acted like one.

Fiona shifts her fingertips to rest on the center of her father's chest, where his heart would be if he'd had one. Old Colony King. General of the Grand Irish Union.

All that power, and the gobshite's still dead.

"Sleep well, Da," Fiona says, in her normal voice. The sound carries to every corner of the frozen room. "I'll make you proud at the Corman Gala. The Crew will give ten million dollars in your name. You'll sponsor this year's event. I promise you that."

She brushes a kiss against her fingertips, then brings them to rest against her father's lips. Every boyo in the room watches—and now it's not just her leather gear that has them so excited.

Fiona just issued a challenge. She made a promise. And every man here expects her to fail.

You can't grow up in Boston without knowing about the Caterina Marcus Corman Museum Gala. It's held on June 30 every year, an old-school formal affair, complete with a feckin' red carpet. Boston's richest families gather in the museum's courtyard, competing to show off their generosity. If your ancestors didn't show up on the Mayflower, good luck getting a ticket.

Except the mayor's allowed in. The City Council, too. The Chief of Police attends and the Fire Commissioner and the lucky eejit in charge of building inspections for the entire city.

But an Irish mob boss from Southie? Kieran Ingram wouldn't be allowed to sweep the sidewalk in front of the museum. Which is why the Crew captain famously angled for an invitation—year after year after year.

Fiona might as well have just promised to build the Kieran Feckin' Ingram colony on Mars. Or engineer a cure for hunger. Guarantee us all world peace.

I'm not certain Fiona has a credit card to her name. If she had a cool ten mill to drop on an art museum, we wouldn't have spent last night in a closet.

A closet with a feckin' king-size bed. But a closet, all the same.

What the hell is she thinking, making promises like that in front of a pack of yokes who'd gladly see her dead and buried? Or married off to make peace among the clans? Or forgotten altogether, because she's just a girl, and not one of the men present thinks she can ever be a real threat?

I can't make her take back the words. And standing here won't get her any closer to finding ten million dollars.

For a moment, I think about offering her my arm. But the last thing she needs is for the Crew to see her leaning on a Fishtown man, especially when rumors still run sharp that my boss killed her da.

So I settle for shouldering a path through the room, slow enough that she can follow.

Head high. Eyes straight ahead.

She listens to me. She even folds her fingers into fists, like she'll beat down any man who hints this is her last time inside the *dún*.

The road in front of the gray clapboard building is lined with vehicles now, the usual rule about clear streets set aside for the wake. A pair of Boston's finest makes their way down the sidewalk, snapping photos of license plates.

They spend extra time at the gate to the *dún's* side yard, getting the number for a black Cadillac Escalade. One of them starts to test the driver's door, but his buddy calls him back, reminds him they don't have a warrant. They turn back to the street.

They don't bother with the car on the corner, on the opposite side of the street. From here, I can make out two people sitting inside the dirty gray sedan—a man and a woman, both wearing dark suits with shirts so white they shine like flashlights.

They could be mobbed-up guests, finishing a conversation before they honor the dead man inside the *dún*. They could be real estate agents, making a late-night survey of Southie properties for prospective clients. They could be tourists, straying way off the beaten track for Boston nightlife.

But in my bones, I know they're feds.

I saw a car like that parked outside my da's house, long before I knew what he'd done. Suits like that. Agents like that. Not afraid to be seen. Not afraid to let the mob know someone's under investigation.

The FBI got my da killed in the basement of the building behind us.

Who the fuck am I kidding? Da got himself killed. No one forced him to turn traitor.

But the car on the corner says there's another turncoat in the *dún*. It could be anyone in the Crew. It could be Nero Sacco, the prick that's run the Boston mafia since long before I left. Hell, maybe the feds have a hard-on for the priest that showed up while Fiona was on her knees by the coffin.

There's no way to know for sure. And tonight, I don't care— because I got Fiona out of there alive.

The damage has been done, though. She made a promise she'll never be able to keep. She boasted. She bragged. And the Crew will make her pay.

11

FIONA

W hat the fuck have I done?

I could have left the wake without saying a word. Moran said it in the hotel: he had my back. He proved it, kneeling beside me in front of Da's casket.

But I had to make a scene. I had to promise ten million dollars to the fucking Corman Museum. Ten million dollars my father will never know about. Ten mill he'll never respect me for.

I wait for Moran to tell me I'm a fucking idiot. But he only starts the Land Rover's engine and says, "Got your phone? Pick out a hotel for us."

"Us?"

"I'll stay through the funeral," he says.

"Why the fuck would you do that?"

His shrug doesn't shift his grip on the wheel. "Because it'll piss off Aran Dowd. Because Rivers called me Cujo. Because you need someone keeping an eye on you, before you spend a billion dollars getting Fenway Park renamed for your da."

My father would have sold me into slavery to own the Boston Red Sox. But I don't want to talk about Da. Or about how easy it was for Uncle Aran to manipulate me back there. So I settle on asking, "Cujo?"

Moran's lips part on a puff of disgust. "It was a book. Horror. Came out about twenty years before you were born. It was about a—"

"Rabid dog. I know." If he's surprised that I've read Stephen King, he doesn't show it. So I push: "Why did Rivers call you Cujo?"

"The whole clan did. When I was a soldier."

I can just make out the white scars on his knuckles beneath the passing streetlights. "You were an enforcer for the Old Colony Crew?"

He grunts, in a way that confirms my question even as it shuts down conversation. Still not taking his eyes from the road, he gestures toward me with his elbow. "Phone?" he asks. "Hotel?"

I ignore him. "What happens after the funeral?"

"We need a place to stay tonight."

"After the funeral?" I push.

"*You* figure out some scheme to raise ten million dollars. *I* go back to Philadelphia. I'm Warlord for the Fishtown Boys. My captain needs me."

I need you too.

The words are right there, heating up my lips. My fingers are already moving toward the buttons on my jacket. My right knee bends, bringing my foot to rest on the seat.

I know how to do this, how to make a man give me what I want. God knows I've had plenty of practice in the last eight years.

I need Patrick Moran to put his arm around me at night. I

need him to give me blinding orgasms. I need him to hold me tight enough that the nightmares stay away.

But I'll clean the dark-tinted windshield of this Land Rover with my tongue before I'll say any of that out loud.

So I take out my phone. I pretend to look for a hotel. I tap an address, because Uncle Aran made up my mind for me the second he called me "little Fee."

I know where I'm living while I get back the Crew.

My phone's mechanical voice tells Moran to proceed to the route. I wait until he's made the first turn before I say, "You can go back to Philadelphia now. I don't need you babysitting me until the funeral."

"I want to make sure your father's in his grave. Tough old fecker like him… He might change his mind about this dying shite."

I snort. Da changed his mind about plenty of things. But even he can't cheat death.

We're well after rush hour, but the streets are still crowded. Fortunately, we don't have far to go. We pass a couple of public alleys. Turn left on Beacon Street. My phone announces: "Arrived."

Moran taps the brakes and sighs in disgust. "Forget about GPS. Just tell me the hotel, and I'll get us there."

"There's no hotel." I gesture toward the red brick building with its gleaming black door. "We're staying here."

"I'm in no mood for games."

I point down the street, where an SUV is pulling out of a space. "You can park there."

He clearly wants to argue with me. But instead, he negotiates the parking space flawlessly, even though there's less than a foot of extra space. When he takes my suitcases out of the back, I grab his duffel.

A metal mailbox is mounted on the brick wall to the left of the door. I enter the four-digit code for Unit 4. The box is stuffed with mail, which I hand off to a mystified-looking Moran.

A magnetized box clings to the top of the mail compartment. I pry it loose and enter another code, six digits this time. Two shiny brass keys wait inside.

I use one to open the building's front door, which swings back on silent hinges. "Ready?" I say to Moran. "It's a walk-up."

He grunts a non-answer. I reach for the larger suitcase, because I don't want to be responsible for his heart attack, but he bats my hand away. Shrugging, I take the smaller one and lead the way.

I'm more out of breath at the top than he is. That must be because he's wearing more sensible shoes.

The second key opens the condo door. I let him enter first. I see the way he automatically twitches his jacket out of the way so he'll have easy access to his gun. But he doesn't have his pistol in its holster. He packed it, because he was going to the *dún*.

Inside the apartment, everything is just the way I left it. The air smells like dust, but with a hint of cinnamon, a touch of lavender and leather. The kitchen and living room are to the right. The bedroom is to the left, with its en suite bathroom.

I lead us toward the living room. One wall is exposed brick, backing a flat, black TV screen. Another is floor-to-ceiling bookshelves, filled with everything from novels to essays on economics. The huge windows have a southern exposure.

I pull the shades before I flip on the lights and set Moran's duffel bag by my feet.

"What the hell is this place?" Moran asks.

"My home away from home."

"What's that supposed to mean?"

"I stay here when I want to get away from the *dún*."

He looks toward the bedroom with an edgy frown. I can tell he wants to make sure no one's lurking with a machete.

"Relax," I say. "No one in the Crew knows about this place."

"And you know that how?"

I point toward a framed photo on the counter that divides the kitchen from the living room. It's Aunt Siobhan and me. She's wearing Tory Burch couture, a ruffled white top so sheer it's immediately obvious she isn't wearing a bra. I'm in my first-ever leather bustier, the one with the straps that barely cover my nipples. I was sixteen when she bought it for me. I could still smell gunpowder on my hands when I smoothed the leather over my breasts.

Moran squints at the photo. "Who's that?"

"Aunt S."

"That means something to me?"

"Siobhan Dowd. My father's sister. Uncle Aran's wife."

Now he looks at the photo more closely. I can practically see him scrubbing off Aunt S's smoky eye and contouring makeup. He pulls her hair back into a respectable messy bun. He puts her in jeans and a long-sleeve T. Maybe a frumpy dress.

And then he looks around the apartment more closely. "So this is, what? A hideout?"

"Aunt S got tired of my uncle's *cailíns*, of cleaning other women's lipstick off his underwear. So she bought this place. Sort of an escape pod. Her lawyers hired lawyers who hired lawyers. She sold some jewelry and paid in cash."

His chin juts toward that Tory Burch declaration of independence. "And now she comes here to turn tricks?"

"Fuck you," I say. I'm surprised by the sudden heat of my anger.

His eyebrows barely twitch. "I'm just saying... It looks like she knows her way around a bedroom."

He doesn't say anything about me. He doesn't have to. But I drip acid over a single word: "Knew."

"What?"

"Aunt Siobhan *knew* what she wanted. And that was a place where her husband didn't micro-manage her every move."

He gives the apartment one more look, suspicion narrowing his eyes once again. "Until Dowd found out."

"Uncle Aran never knew! Aunt S just got sick." It's harder for me to say the words than I expect it to be. "But when she was here, she dressed the way she wanted."

I don't tell him about the trench coat she kept in the closet, the one that still hangs in front of the wall safe. She covered up, even for a walk around the block. She never, ever got to live the life she deserved. Not before the cancer. And definitely not after.

But she taught me how to be the woman I am. Never afraid. Or ashamed. If not for Aunt S, I might have listened to the nightmares. I might have carried a sharp razor into a hot bath...

Moran's looking toward the bedroom again. "And we spent last night in the smallest hotel room in Boston because?"

Despite his judgmental, patriarchal comments about Aunt S, he deserves an answer. "Until ten minutes ago, I was the only person on earth who knows about this place."

"Except the tax assessor. The real estate clerk. The utility companies and all your neighbors."

"Everything's hidden, six layers down. Aunt S took care of it before she died. My name is a million miles away from any of this."

"And you live here." His voice twists with disbelief.

I correct him. "I visit. When I can't stand being in the *dún* for one more minute." When there are too many men. Too much testosterone. When I can't stand my father's lies and his rules and his double-crossing—

Da's gone. It's time for me to claim what's mine.

Moran still looks skeptical.

"You have to trust me," I say.

"I don't trust anyone."

"I'm good at what I do." It's important that he understands that. "Very, very good."

He looks at the photo again. "I can see that," he says. My nipples get hard at the tone of his voice, and I'm glad he can't see beneath my blue jacket.

"Now you really can fuck off."

"The mouth on you," he says evenly.

For about ten seconds, my response echoes inside my head: *Want to fuck it, Daddy?*

But I wait too long.

He takes my large suitcase and rolls it down the hall to the bedroom. I hear him open the closet door. Shuffle through the hangers, presumably making sure no Crew enforcer is hiding among my shoes. He goes into the bathroom and checks the linen closet there.

He comes out with one of my extra pillows and a blanket. Kicking aside his duffel bag, he deposits his makeshift bedroll on the couch. "Are you washing up first, or am I?"

I don't trust any of the things I want to say.

Don't sleep out here.

Let's take a shower together.

How the hell did you do that to my body, make me come while you were inside me, and why haven't you done it again?

"You go ahead," I say.

I pretend not to see him shrug out of his black jacket. I don't watch as he takes his well-worn Dopp kit out of his duffel. I tell myself not to think about the chain of foil-wrapped condoms I know are inside.

He heads back down the hall and closes himself into the bathroom. I ignore the running water, forcing myself to sort the mail I took out of the box downstairs.

It's junk, all of it. Bills are paid through the complicated system Aunt S set up, and no one knows to reach me here.

But I read all the ads for pizza delivery like they're the world's finest literature—which only makes me starving for an extra-large pie with pepperoni, sausage, and mushrooms. I study the flyers from real estate agents like every one is a museum masterpiece. I stack everything neatly, then sort recyclable paper from shiny cardstock.

Finally, centuries later, Moran's back. I catch a whiff of mint as he crosses to the couch; he's brushed his teeth. The light flashes on the gray in his hair as he picks up his pillow in both hands. "Goodnight," he says, staring at me levelly.

"Hey," I answer. "Thank you for what you did back at the *dún*." I brave his gaze. "It didn't go exactly the way I thought it would."

No shit.

He'd be justified in saying that. But instead, he just nods.

So I say, "*Oíche mhaith.*" Goodnight. Just like he said last night.

Behind the bedroom door, it takes me longer than it should to unpack my suitcases. It already seems like my stay in Philadelphia was a long time ago. A lifetime ago.

I go to the safe in the closet and work the combination. I'm pretty sure I left it empty—spending the last few hundred-dollar-bills on a leather bodysuit, one with steel-framed cutouts for my nipples and snaps across the crotch.

I'm right. The cupboard's bare.

I take out my phone and pull up a translator app. I'm not sure how to spell that word he calls me—*ska-ha*—but I try typing it in phonetically. Nothing comes up.

I switch to an English-Irish dictionary, but it's no more help. I try pulling up an Irish dictionary, one that leaves the words in Gaelic, but I can't make heads or tails out of that.

Frustrated, I throw my phone on the bed. I get undressed, and I hang up the clothes I wore to the wake. I put on one of my favorite sleep sets—a plum-colored cropped cami and matching high-waist shorts. I wash away my careful makeup, obliterating my smoky eye and exposing my bruises. I smooth on fresh arnica, and I brush my teeth.

Moran's out there.

I can't stop myself from thinking it. But I don't allow myself to do anything.

Instead, I climb into bed and stare at the ceiling. I should be exhausted. My body's still healing from the beating Madden gave me. I honestly never imagined the day I'd see my father lying in his casket. I still can't say what drove me to make my ruthless promise to the Crew.

Ten million dollars.

I barely have ten thousand in my savings account. Most of that was birthday gifts from family. I haven't worked a day in my life, aside from the job I just lost: Being Kieran Ingram's daughter.

Moran's out there.

With a good real estate agent, a better lawyer, and a lot of luck, I could sell this apartment by the end of the month. But— as high as Back Bay real estate is—I wouldn't clear enough to meet my goal.

I could go back to Philadelphia with Moran and beg Braiden Kelly to lend me the money. But the thought of groveling in front of him, of admitting that I need help, that I can't do this on my own… And I can't be sure he'd even let me borrow the cash. Not after I stood by and watched his brother steal his own protection money…

Moran's out there.

The bedroom is too hot. I toss off all my covers.

My pillow is too flat. I double it over. Crane my neck because now it's too high.

I slip my hand between my legs, edging my fingers past the lace at the top of my shorts. But even before I start to rub, I know my body won't cooperate. Touching my clit is as exciting as rubbing the tip of my nose.

Moran's out—

When he comes into the bedroom, he doesn't try to be quiet. He turns the doorknob hard and shoves the door all the way back to the wall. He comes to the foot of the bed, a shadow in the night. Two rings glint on the hand that grips his pillowcase.

"Are you asleep?" he asks, in a voice loud enough to wake me if I was.

I shake my head, then realize he can't see me. "No."

"This doesn't mean anything," he says.

"Of course it doesn't."

"I just need to sleep," he says.

"Me too."

He circles around the bed and places his pillow beside mine. His eyes must have adjusted to the dark, because he pulls back my tangled bedclothes without hesitation.

Only then does he climb onto the mattress. It's higher than the one at the hotel, but my bed is only a queen. He slips beneath the sheet and the blanket and the duvet.

His chest is bare, but he's wearing boxer briefs. His arm is heavy as he pulls me close to his body. His chub presses against the lace of my shorts until he shifts his leg, caging mine.

This shouldn't work. I should feel too closed-in. I should be choked by the memory of incense and altar candles, by the starch that Oona ironed into my uniform top.

Instead, I smell amber and oak, the warmth of fresh-turned earth baking in the sun. I feel the velvet-covered steel of muscles at rest, even though they've been trained to kill. I hear the rough whisper, so soft it's more a vibration than actual sound, "Stop worrying, *Scáthach*. Go to sleep."

I want to know what he's calling me, but not enough to risk his backing away. He has me. I'm safe. The nightmares won't come while he's here.

So I move my lips but make absolute sure not a whisper of sound slips free. "Yes, Daddy."

12

PATRICK

I'm not a total feckin' coward. I wait until Fiona's out of the shower before I leave the apartment. I look her in the eye and tell her I'll be back by mid-afternoon. I ask if she needs me to pick up anything while I'm out.

I can be a civilized human being.

But the keychain she gives me burns like a bar of uranium in my pocket. The brain squirrels want it to mean something. They want to chew on it. Bury it so they can enjoy it later.

Lying on that couch last night, replaying that disaster of a wake, I couldn't stop thinking of the girl behind the bedroom door. I wanted to soothe her. To protect her.

The Bell was clanging, calling me into the boxing ring, telling me to start a round. Don't think. Just act.

Just go be her Daddy.

But how fucked up is that, when the reason she needs comfort is because her real father's dead? How can I think about calling her my little girl when she's in the middle of mourning?

I swear to God, I think she said it. So soft, I *felt* it, instead of heard it.

Daddy.

But that's not enough. That's not right. The scrambled signals in my brain aren't an excuse to take advantage of her.

So we spent last night sleeping in that bed, instead of fucking. And this morning, instead of figuring out a dozen ways to make her scream the one word my twisted brain wants to hear, I'm out of the apartment.

I should go for a run. A long one. Get ten miles in, enough to tire out my body and get the brain squirrels back in their cage.

But I've never been good at doing what I ought. I'm back behind the wheel of the Land Rover before common sense—and my morning meds—can kick in.

I take the long way around Southie, staying close to the water. Emotions are sure to be high at the *dún*, with folks hung over from the wake and the Crew gearing up to put Kieran Ingram in the ground. No reason for a chance encounter to turn sour.

A smart man would skip going to Yankee Roast altogether.

I'm not a smart man. Or maybe I'm just stewing in nostalgia. Twenty-five years is a long time to be away from the streets where I was born, where I joined the mob, where I thought I'd live forever.

I end up parking three blocks over from the bakery. This part of town is busier than the last time I was here. I hurry past a handful of little bistros, a yarn store, and a shop selling chocolates that cost nearly as much as my Glock.

Yankee Roast looks like it's enjoyed the high tide. The outside has a coat of fresh paint; the door is a brighter blue than I remember. There are tables on the sidewalk now, and decals on the door announce delivery through three different services.

A bell rings as I walk in. I'm slapped in the face with the

smell of cinnamon and coffee, with fresh-baked bread and melted chocolate.

Kimi Mulroney is working behind the counter. An apron covers her faded plaid shirt, and her sleeves are rolled up as she wipes down a counter with a clean white rag. She's thinner than I remember; her face is drawn in a way that's more than tired. Her head is wrapped in a brightly colored scarf, and I'm willing to bet she's lost her hair.

"Motherfucker," she says, in a tone that's equal parts greeting and a warning to get the hell out.

"Kimi," I reply.

"It's Kimberly now."

I nod, but I don't repeat her name. "Looks like business has picked up."

"After twenty-five years? Yeah. Things have turned around."

Of course she knows how long it's been. I wouldn't be surprised if she gave me the number of weeks. The specific number of days.

I look at the cases of baked goods. Athawn's Apple Fritters still hold place of pride on a top shelf. Jenn's Jam Tarts gleam with their cherry and apricot fillings. Patrick's Peanut Butter Cookies are notably missing. I'll go out on a limb and assume it's not for fear of allergies.

"Can I get a cup of coffee?" I ask. "Pour one for yourself too."

She wrinkles her nose, and it's the exact same expression I saw twenty-eight years ago, when her sister brought me home to meet their parents. She waves a hand toward her scarf. "Everything tastes like I'm chewing on tin foil."

"I'm sorry to hear that," I say. I mean it.

She selects an over-size mug from the shelf above the sink and turns her back to me as she pours. "Another six weeks of chemo," she says. "The doctors are *cautiously optimistic.*"

"Joe's helping out around here?"

"Joe left fourteen years ago. Thought he'd be happier

fucking double-D implants and collagen lips that could suck a baseball through a straw."

Before I can figure out another way to say I'm sorry, she hands me my coffee. I salute her with the mug and take a good slug.

It takes every ounce of my willpower not to spit all over her counter. "What the fuck?" I say, after I manage to swallow. "Did you dump in a cup of salt?"

"Whoops," she deadpans. "Meant to add sugar."

I put the mug on the counter.

Kimi—*Kimberly*—stares at me flatly. "What's your plan, Patrick? I'd ask what brings you to town, but I've already heard you're fucking Ingram's daughter."

I've always been impressed with the Southie grapevine. Gossip moves from one end of the enclave to the other faster than birds can fly. And now that everyone and her sister has a cellphone permanently attached at the fingertips, information travels that much faster.

I start to deny that I'm fucking Fiona. Whatever happened in that hotel room was just between the two of us, and it won't be repeated, because I'm leaving town after the funeral.

But even if I clear my record with Kimi, she's not likely to defend me to the rest of South Boston.

So I settle for saying, "I head back to Philadelphia on Sunday."

She snorts in disgust. "Running away as usual."

"I didn't run, Kimi. I left. Because there was nothing to keep me here."

"You had friends, asshole. Family."

"Jenn had friends. Jenn had family."

"We loved you!"

She sounds like she means it, which is news to me. So I remind her: "You loved Jenn."

"Until you killed her." There we go. That's the Kimi I know so well. Hits the target in less than one feckin' minute.

"Jenn died, Kimi. No one killed her. She drove too fast and she hit a patch of black ice and the Escort flipped three times."

Jenn worried about crashing the Ford. She'd read articles about seatbelts harming unborn babies. She left hers off so she didn't hurt Athawn. That's why they both died—my wife, and our son who was never born.

Kimi's face twists with an expression of pure hate. "Why was she driving too fast, Patrick?"

I don't know. No one does. But a fair guess would be she was terrified of me, after she found out what I did.

When I got home that day, I told her my father had ratted out the Crew, turning witness for the feds instead of facing up to a heroin beef. The clan found out, and its Warlord—Keenan Rivers—punished Tommy Moran on the killing floor in the *dún's* basement.

That's all I thought Jenn needed to know.

But Aran Dowd had already told her the rest.

He called before I ever got back to the apartment. Maybe he was getting revenge for all the shite Da did. Maybe he was testing me. Maybe he did it just for laughs.

Jenn asked if the rest was true, if I'd really done all the things Dowd said. I told the truth then, all of it. And Jenn just shook her head. She took her keys. She walked out the door of our crappy apartment, and she drove the Escort into a fucking tree.

Kimi repeats her question: "Why was she driving too fast, Patrick?"

After twenty-five years, I thought I could be here. I thought I could remember my wife with the sister who'd loved her. I could mourn my unborn son with the woman who would have been his aunt.

I shove back from the counter. "This was a mistake."

"You're damn right, it's a mistake. You're the same fucking savage you ever were."

The bell jangles on the door behind me. Kimi looks past me,

and a smile splits her face, like the sun breaking through a bank of thunderheads. "Hannah!" Kimi says. "I didn't think you were coming in today!"

"I've got an hour before rehearsal, so I thought I'd stop by and grab some lunch." My niece moves behind the counter with the ease of someone very familiar with the space. "Go on," she says to her mother. "Sit down. Take a glass of water. You know you aren't drinking enough."

Impossibly, Kimi obeys the force of nature she brought into this world. She fills a glass with tap water and takes a stool at the counter.

Hannah turns to me with a bright smile. "And what can I get you today?"

She doesn't recognize me. I left before her first birthday.

Kimi watches me warily.

"Thanks," I say to Hannah. "I was just leaving."

As I walk back to the Land Rover, I try to figure out how I could have left them both some money. It wouldn't be enough. Nothing would. But I'd feel a little better.

And there's my answer. The women in that bakery don't need my money. The only thing they need is for me to stay out of their lives forever.

This time, I cut through the heart of Southie, because I don't give two shites who sees me. I pass the old after-hours joints. I drive by Ingram's tame bookie. There's the strip club, and the whorehouse.

I'm a dinosaur, crashing through the jungle, oblivious to the meteor hurtling through the stars. I can't tell if any of the old businesses are left. Probably not, in this age of online betting, of Internet porn.

I'm out of Southie, nearly back to the tourist-friendly parts of the city, when I realize I never got my cup of coffee. The second I start thinking about it, the wiring frays inside my skull. Deprived of caffeine, the brain squirrels gnaw away.

There's a Dunkin' in the next block. Who am I kidding?

This is Boston. There's a Dunkin' on every block. I can get mine back at the apartment, before I climb four flights of stairs.

That promise doesn't still the squirrels. In fact, they shift into hyperdrive when we drive past the next orange-and-pink store. This one has a parking space open at the curb—two in front of a huge black Escalade.

An Escalade with a familiar license plate. One I watched being tracked by cops, just last night. I'm good that way, remembering strings of letters and numbers. Playing with the symbols usually makes the squirrels back off a while.

That Cadillac was at the *dún's* side yard last night, but it's out of Southie now. Which is as good a reason as any for me to stop for coffee now.

Waiting in line, I monitor the crowd. The habit is as deeply ingrained as spinning my fidget ring. I'm a Warlord. I keep tabs on everyone around me.

It's the usual mix of students and tourists and—this close to Back Bay—folks taking a break from crouching over their home computers.

Two men sit in the far-left booth, barely visible in profile. They're dressed in casual clothes. Middle-aged. Nothing remarkable. I wouldn't notice them at all if the Escalade wasn't parked out front. And if the man with his back to me didn't have a full white beard.

What the hell is Aran Dowd doing in a Dunkin' outside his Southie territory? And why the fuck does the guy sitting across from him look so goddamn familiar?

From the expression on Dowd's face, he hasn't clocked me yet. He's leaning forward, pointing his finger at Other Guy. Dowd's cheeks are flushed, and he's dangerously close to knocking over his cup of coffee.

The Bell rings inside my head. I should walk back to the booth. Let Dowd know I haven't left town. Find out who he's lecturing.

But I grit my teeth to tamp down the impulse. Dowd's presence here is fucking bizarre. I don't want him to know I've seen him.

I slip out of line. I head back to the door, moving slow and steady, like I've already got my coffee and a donut. It's not until I'm back in the Land Rover that I hear Kimi's voice, echoing loud in the brain squirrels' scrambled nest: *What's your plan?*

I don't have one.

I want to find out what Dowd is doing in a donut shop.

I want to remember who the guy is, sitting across from him.

I want to get back to Philadelphia, to my captain, to the clan that adopted me a quarter of a century ago.

But most of all, I want to drive back to the Beacon Street apartment, order Fiona to call me Daddy, and fuck her until neither of us can move.

She's younger than my niece. Younger than my son would be, if I'd ever had a son.

She's vital and she's smart and she's strong—the opposite of me in every way. Is that why I itch for her? Am I too old, too tired to keep doing the job I've done since before she was born?

What's your plan?

It's time to feckin' get one.

13

FIONA

I'm balancing a shrimp on my chopsticks when my phone rings, so I don't bother to answer. The only person in the world I want to talk to is Aunt S, and she's never using a cell phone again.

I ordered all her favorites from the Chinese restaurant around the corner. Pan-fried crab dumplings. Mu shu pork with extra pancakes. Hunan broccoli with brown rice. Eight treasures lo mein.

I don't care that it's enough food for a small army. Aunt S would do the same in my memory, if I'd been the one to kick off first.

Plus, I thought Moran might be hungry when he got back from his errands.

He said he'd be back by the middle of the afternoon. He lied.

It's five minutes after seven now. I waited half an hour after dinner was delivered to put the food on the coffee table. I took out two bowls. Four lacquered chopsticks. I only started eating ten minutes ago.

I did *not* spend the extra time skimming through local news stories on my phone, looking for news of gangland warfare erupting in Southie. I just wanted to see if anyone was talking about Da, if his death is being discussed by people outside the Crew.

And I didn't check the traffic report to see if a Land Rover was involved in a major crash that was snarling all the roadways. I only wondered if the roads are clear from Logan, so anyone flying in for Saturday's funeral has an easy time getting in from the airport.

And I definitely didn't search for reports of a desk clerk being assaulted at a downtown Hyatt, or Hilton, or whatever-the-hell type of hotel. I'm merely curious about how hard it is to find lodging, in case funeral visitors need some help.

My phone rings again. It's on silent mode, so it rattles against the granite counter in the kitchen, jittering close to the edge like it's trying to commit suicide. Ignoring it, I catch some broccoli with my chopsticks.

The ringing stops but immediately starts again. Annoyed, I drop my chopsticks onto my plate. Whoever's calling has won themselves a lifetime block.

The call is from *Patrick*.

For two full rings, I don't recognize the name. Then, the connection finally clicks. It's Moran. He entered his first name when he added his information to my phone. I don't know why that tugs at something in my chest, but it does.

I consider letting the call go to voicemail again. It's what he deserves, when I expected him hours ago. But I don't want him to know I was worried.

I answer on speaker. "You're late."

"Throw down a key."

"What?"

I cross back to the three tall windows at the front of the

apartment. Sure enough, the Land Rover is parked across the street, in front of a fire hydrant.

"You'll get a ticket, parked there," I say.

"Fuck it," Patrick says. And then he repeats: "Throw down a key."

"Where's the one I gave you?"

"I don't know. I thought I had it when I left this morning. Maybe I lost it. Maybe it's in my suit pocket, up there. Throw down the feckin' key, Fiona."

Patrick Moran. Warlord of the Fishtown Boys. Cujo to the Old Colony Crew. Can't keep track of a house key.

I end the call and pluck my key from the bowl on the counter.

The window shrieks a protest as I open it. I brace my hands on the sill, displaying the boned bodice of my corset. It was a pain in the ass to lace up the back on my own, but now I know it was worth my time to get the ties even.

"How do I know you won't lose this one?" I call down.

I can tell this isn't the first time he's run his fingers through his hair because it's standing on end. "Give it a rest," he says, just loud enough for me to hear.

"What if you don't catch it?"

"Enough, Fiona."

"If it falls in the storm drain, we're in all sorts of trouble."

"I'll show you trouble," he grumbles, and something catches deep beneath my belly.

I dangle the key like I'm teasing a kitten. "I'm not sure I like your tone," I say. My own tone is surprisingly breathy. I must have laced my corset too tight.

"What the fuck do you want from me?"

My brain is suddenly flooded with an image of exactly what I want: Patrick Moran standing at the edge of the bed. One hand tangles in my hair as I'm splayed before him on hands and knees. The other hand grips my hip as he pounds home with enough force to make me scream.

And I know exactly what it would take to get it. There's only one word I have to say: *Daddy.*

Ask nicely, Daddy.

Here's the key, Daddy.

What will you give me if I'm your good girl, Daddy?

But I'm not going to call any of that from the fourth-floor window of a Back Bay townhouse. I'm not going to say any of that ever. Anywhere. To anyone.

"Catch," I say, and I toss the key before I make a mistake I'll regret forever.

I've closed and locked the window by the time he's climbed all four flights of stairs. I'm standing in the middle of the living room. The lace pants that match my boned corset have a scalloped hem. I cock my leg to one side, knowing that angle will accentuate my silky black boy shorts.

Patrick closes the door. Locks it. Crosses to the kitchen counter and puts my key in the bowl.

Only then does he look at me. He swallows hard enough for me to hear him, and his hand finds his hair again. "Let it go, Fiona."

"Let what go?" I add just the right amount of pout to the words.

I know he wants me. I can see it in the tight lines of his throat. I refuse to let my eyes drift south of his belt, but I'm certain if I did, his jeans would prove I'm right.

But he only shakes his head and goes down the hall to the bedroom.

I could follow him. But I'm Fiona Fucking Ingram. I'm not chasing after any man. It's his loss, if he doesn't follow up on what I've offered.

I hear him move things around in there. I'm pretty sure that's the sound of his duffel bag being tossed on the bed. Yes, those are the zippers being pulled, each of them, slowly, then all of them, more rapidly.

He goes into the closet. I hear him sliding the hangers—his dress shirt, his suit jacket, his pants.

I'm not sure why he bothers, but he slams into the bathroom. He rummages in his Dopp kit, and for just a moment, I picture gold foil squares raining from his fingers. But he's not looking for rubbers, because he stomps back to the front of the apartment and heads straight to the kitchen.

He empties the bowl on the counter. Pulls open the silverware drawer. He checks the cupboard that holds the mugs, and the one with plates and bowls. He looks in the refrigerator, and then the freezer.

And when he's done, he braces both hands on the counter. He stands there—legs spread, head down. And I wait for him to explode.

14

PATRICK

F iona played me with the key, and I fucking know it. She's looking for power, for a way to make me pay for being gone all day. But she wants to be in control, and I don't allow that for any woman of mine.

Besides, she's less than a week out from the beating Madden gave her. Youth heals quickly, I'll give her that. But I know there are still bruises beneath her expertly applied makeup. And I know a woman who's survived what that dry shite did will be hard-pressed to accept what *I* need in bed.

All the same, I almost fuck her.

I could bend her over this kitchen counter. Rip that feckin' lace to shreds. Plant one hand between the wings of her shoulder blades and use the other to shove my cock into her hot, wet cunt. I could ride her until I forget all the things the brain squirrels are throwing at me.

I'm a feckin' idiot, unable to hold onto a key.

Primary school boys are better at tracking their belongings than I am.

Why the hell would any right-thinking captain have me in his clan, when I fuck up everything I touch?

I want to touch Fiona right now. I want to push her to her knees. I want to bark out short, sharp orders, let her know who's in charge here, who runs the show. She'll suck my cock. She'll dig her fingernails into my thighs and take me deep enough to gag. And when I let her rock back on her heels, I'll wipe the tears from her cheeks and tell her she's my *Scáthach*, and I won't have to think about how fragile the walls are around my world.

Back home, I have systems. My keychain has a shamrock medallion. I can feel it in my pocket, know exactly where it is, know if I've set it down and forgotten it by mistake.

Back home, I have obligations too. My captain expects me to enforce his rules. On Mondays, I do the milk run, collecting the protection money my boss is owed. On Tuesdays, I check in with my men, see that the Fishtown machine is working as it should. Wednesdays, Thursdays, Fridays—every day has its tasks, its goals. Not like here, in feckin' Boston.

And safe back home, I have my apartment to myself. It's quiet, and the walls are bare. The furniture is plain. The wall-to-wall carpet is smooth beneath my feet. I'm not distracted by framed paintings that look like a close-up of some blushing woman's clit. I'm not left wondering if I should lean against throw pillows or toss them on the floor. I don't have to stare at the patterns in three antique rugs, stacked one on top of the other, like they're on loan from a museum.

God, I want to shove Fiona down on those rugs. Jam a few of those throw pillows under her arse. Tie her hands together with my belt when she gets too antsy. Take that scrap of silk she thinks are knickers and shove it into her mouth, let her moan and groan without ever saying a word. Then I can fuck her as slow as I want, as hard as I want, tease her pretty clit until it's as hard and pink as whatever the fuck is in that painting.

I stare at the fidget ring on my third finger, fighting the urge to spin it. I eye my Fishtown ring, the one that means I belong in Philly. I box my breathing.

It takes me three rounds, but the squirrels die down. I push back from the counter and walk down the hall like a man this time, instead of like a rabid animal. I find the amber bottle in the bathroom, and I dry-swallow a small orange pill. I shake my head at the eejit in the mirror, and then I head out to the living room to pay my dues.

Fiona's on the couch now. She's sitting in the precise center of the three cushions. One foot is folded beneath her, stretching that black lace over the sleek muscle of her thigh. The other foot rests on the floor, the scarlet polish on her toenails shining like a beacon. Or maybe a stop light.

Cartons of Chinese food fill the table. I pick up the empty plate and use clean chopsticks to shovel out generous portions from each of the containers.

I ate a protein bar this morning. Downed one slug of salted coffee at Yankee Roast. Stood in line at Dunkin' but left before I got anything to eat or drink.

And then I spent the day driving around the city like I was on a personal "greatest hits" tour—the alley Jenn and I parked in the first time she let me get in her pants. The Common, where we brought a picnic lunch the day she told me she was pregnant. The run-down Southie apartment we were renting the night she died.

I went by all of it after I left Kimi and Hannah, after I found Dowd where he shouldn't have been. I stared at my past for hours, like some sort of homesick kid. I forgot about eating, forgot about drinking. No wonder I lost the feckin' key.

Now, Fiona watches me chew. She eyes my throat when I swallow. Her face is set hard; she's fighting what she wants too.

So I set down my chopsticks. I take the time to meet her stony gaze. I nod once, because I recognize when I've been wrong. "I'm sorry," I say. "I should have let you know I'd be late."

Something eases in her jaw. I wonder if she's ever heard a man apologize before.

I wonder why I did, just now. It's not my way. Not with any other woman. Maybe it's the meds taking hold. Maybe it's the food filling my belly. Maybe it's the fact that I still want to rip those lace pants off her so I can take all she's advertising and more.

I won't. Not when I can still hear her teasing voice, from back at the hotel. Not when I know she's called me Daddy once, and she knows how to do it again, if she wants, if she isn't disgusted by what I need.

But when she does, if she does... God help her. God help both of us.

I spear a scallop out of the lo mein. I chew it well and swallow hard. And then I say, "I'll have a new key made tomorrow."

15

FIONA

I'm standing in the walk-in closet, surrounded by Aunt S's clothes. I couldn't bear to throw anything away after she died.

All of it is couture and most of it would give Patrick a heart attack if I staged a private little runway show. Aunt S loved her peekaboo tops and cutaway trousers. She honestly believed the human body was a work of art. That's why she hung the original Georgia O'Keeffe in the living room.

There's one outfit at the very back of the closet. Aunt S kept it here in case she had an unexpected command performance at the *dún.*

Her black A-line skirt hits me mid-calf. A matching silk shell looks like something an English princess would wear to tea at the Ritz. There's a double-breasted jacket with cloth-covered buttons and a wide-brim hat with a somber black ribbon.

"Holy hell," Patrick says, when I enter the living room.

I genuflect, like I learned to do for my first communion.

"You look amazing," he says.

My face ignites.

I'm not a girl who blushes. I spend my time figuring out ways to make *other* people flush. But Patrick's praise hooks something deep inside me, and for just a moment, I'm back in our crappy hotel room, balancing on my knees and forearms as he fucks me blind, telling me I'm beautiful, I'm strong, I'm brave.

His lips turn up as he registers my reaction, just the corners, and something inside me trembles as I wait to see if he'll really smile.

"Good girl," he says, crossing the room to tuck a strand of hair behind my ear. The tiny hairs on the backs of his fingers brush my cheek, and I catch my breath like I'm about to come.

No. Not *like* I'm about to come. He's taken me from zero to sixty in less than ten seconds. My clit throbs, and I squeeze my thighs together to keep from straddling him on the couch.

He laughs, as if he can see straight through Aunt S's proper skirt. "Give me a minute," he says. "And we can be on our way."

On our way? Right. We're going to the funeral. We're burying my father. That's why I'm wearing this outrageous costume.

He closes the bedroom door behind him, and I cross to the living room windows, fanning myself with one hand to get some air. I lean my head against the glass, wondering what the hell he's done to me.

I'm Fiona Fucking Ingram. I've been fooling men with my fake orgasms since I turned sixteen. I don't cream at a few nice words. I've got a hell of a lot more control than that.

Patrick takes more than a minute. He takes five. But he comes out of the bedroom dressed in the plain black suit he wore to Da's wake. This time, he's wearing a white shirt, so bright it takes away all the breath I've managed to gather. His tie today is the dark green of grass under starlight, with a sprinkling of Celtic knots that match his golden ring.

He squirms under my inspection. "It's a Fishtown tie," he says defensively.

I don't care if the silk was woven by the devil himself. I just think about how it would feel, lashed around my wrists. I gulp air like I've just downed a ghost pepper smoothie.

"I need to stop at a drug store," I make myself say. "I need sunglasses."

"So no one sees you weeping over your da's grave?"

"So no one sees my bruises," I snap. I won't be crying. Not today. Although the thought of how little sorrow I feel makes me wonder if I'm some sort of monster.

My makeup skills are excellent, but I don't trust the results in broad daylight. Not when I'm going to be under intense scrutiny as the grieving daughter. Or the girl making an upstart bid for Queen.

Moran's phone starts to serenade him from his pocket. He takes it out with an automatic motion and thumbs an icon to stop the song. "Alarm," he says to my unasked question. "Don't want to be late."

Another alarm goes off fifteen minutes later, as we're leaving the CVS. This sound is louder and faster paced. I blink behind my cat's-eye sunglasses. As he turns off the music, he says, "Sorry."

Fifteen minutes later, we're caught at a traffic light and a third alarm goes off—the steady beeping of a smoke detector. He grimaces and kills the sound. It's not until he opens my door at St. Augustine's, handing me down from the Land Rover, that I realize I didn't tell him our destination.

This is the oldest Catholic cemetery in Boston. The tombstones cluster around the chapel like giant sea urchin spikes. A place has been reserved for my father since he was a child; he'll spend eternity between his own parents.

My mother is buried an hour south of here. I've never visited her grave.

Father Bertram conducts the service in the chapel. I sit in

the front row, with Patrick by my side. Uncle Aran is in the pew across the aisle.

The chapel fills behind us, most of the Old Colony Crew sitting behind my uncle. Keenan Rivers is on the aisle, directly behind Uncle Aran. Sacco, the mafia don, sits a few rows back. The pews fill in with the people who paid my father protection money for decades—the ones who've run his brothels and gambling dens, along with legitimate business owners who only want to guarantee smooth operations. Everyone lines up behind Uncle Aran.

A handful of people sit behind me. There's Oona, my former nanny, back to her job as a cook at the *dún*. There's a reporter, scribbling on a pocket notebook. I'd love to throw him out the door, but it isn't worth making a scene.

There are a couple of young women who join us, so similar in appearance they could be twins—wide-set eyes in heart-shaped faces, plump lips, and breasts so huge there's no way they're real. One has dyed black hair; the other is a platinum blonde, but my father clearly had a type for his girlfriends, his *cailíns*.

A few men at the very back look like they've been sleeping rough. The chapel is warm and dry, and they can nod off without anyone taking great offense.

Just before the service starts, a few Irish relatives slip into the pews behind me. There's an aunt and three uncles I last saw on my trip to Dublin, each of them with red eyes and drawn faces, exhausted from travel, if not from sorrow. None of my cousins have made the trip.

But when my family realize how the crowd has lined up, they shift over to Uncle Aran's side. I want to stand up, to demand they come back to me. Uncle Aran isn't flesh and blood. He married into the family, married Aunt Siobhan. But the Irish Ingrams understand power when they see it.

I set my shoulders, refusing to look at them again.

Even the latecomers stand at the back, instead of sitting with me. They'll pay, all of them. They're all betting on the wrong horse.

Father Bertram starts the service half an hour after the announced time, to give everyone a chance to settle. He looks lost in front of the altar, like he's floating on a sea of flowers. Every captain in the Grand Irish Union has sent a display to honor his general. There are blankets and wreaths and horse-shoes, and one huge round of white carnations trimmed with red roses, made up to look like a baseball. I wonder if there are any flowers left in Boston, maybe in all of New England.

Father Bertram wears purple vestments, a sign of penance.

My father never repented a single thing he did, not in his entire life. He lived hard. He died hard. And he truly believed that a single hint of regret might kill him. His men would refuse to be led by a man who showed even a shadow of doubt.

Maybe that's why he never announced who would take over when he died. He was like an expectant parent, keeping the name of his baby secret until the birth, so he didn't have to listen to every last friend and relative who thought he was making a mistake.

But goddamn it, he *owed* me. I did everything my father ever asked of me. Almost everything. I tried.

Water under the fucking bridge. He didn't name me his heir. And now, I'm fighting for my life with the Crew. Fighting a battle no sane man would say I can win.

It doesn't take long for Father Bertram to finish saying mass. Uncle Aran takes communion. All the senior officers do.

I don't go up to the altar rail. I haven't gone to confession in eight years.

Outside, by the open grave, the wind has picked up. Father Bertram's fleshy lips look like liver in the daylight. I wonder how much he knows about his predecessor, whether he has night-mares about Father Colin's untimely death. I do.

I hear the echo of that shot eight years ago, and I flinch. Patrick feels it. He puts his hand beneath my elbow to steady me. If anyone's watching, they'll think I'm overcome with emotion as Father Bertram leads us all in the Lord's Prayer.

The service ends and the crowd breaks into clusters of two or three. Before I can tell Patrick I'm ready to go, Oona Maguire bustles to my side. When she was my nanny, she marked my height on the frame of my bedroom door every year, on my birthday. When I turned nine, I stretched on tiptoe, and I was taller than she was. In the intervening years, she's shrunk even more. Her face looks like it's carved out of a dried apple.

"*Coinín beag*," she says, hugging my waist, calling me her little rabbit. I don't know where to put my hands, so I wave them in the air, helpless.

Oona looks up at me. Her eyes are red. Her lips are chapped. Tears stain her cheeks, and I realize she may be the only person in the entire cemetery who honestly mourns my father.

"*Coinín beag*," she says again. "I brought something for you." She slips a battered tote bag from her shoulder and begins fumbling inside.

I imagine she has something that belonged to my father. One of his cigarette lighters. Maybe a pen from his desk. Even though there's nothing I want, my throat tightens at the kindness.

But I'm wrong. I very much want the thing she pulls out of her bag.

It's a cigar box, cedar, decorated in gaudy green and red. The metal clasp is tarnished. One of the hinges slips when the lid opens too far.

I know that last bit, because I kept the box tucked under my mattress for years. I filled it with my treasures. My secrets. My past.

"Oh my God," I whisper, clutching it close to my chest.

"Your uncle is changing things," Oona says, pursing her lips.

"And not for the better. He'll be turning your bedroom into an office, he says."

Of all the petty, manipulative…

She says, "I couldn't have him taking all your things."

I hold the box closer, catching a whiff of its clean-smelling wood. "Thank you," I say. "Thank you so much."

She stretches a hand up to cup my jaw. "You be a good girl, now."

"I will," I lie.

Turning to Patrick, she cocks her head to one side, like a bird on a ledge. "You take care of our girl, Paddy Moran."

I'm amazed that she calls him by a nickname. I'm even more astonished by his grave tone as he says, "I will, Miz Maguire."

She harrumphs. "It was *Oona* when ya lived in the *dún*. It can be *Oona* now."

"Oona," he says meekly.

"Go on now," she says. "Carry that box for Herself."

I'm shocked when he takes the cigar box from my hands. He looks like he's a schoolboy in some black-and-white movie, carrying home an innocent girl's books.

"Now get her out of here before her uncle decides to work some mischief." Oona makes a shooing motion, as if she's frightening off a mouse with her non-existent apron.

"Do you need a ride back to the *dún*?" Patrick asks courteously.

"Don't worry about me," she says. "Go on. Be a good boy, Paddy."

Obediently, he takes my arm. We're halfway to the parking lot before I manage to splutter, "*Be a good boy, Paddy?*"

A smile ghosts his lips.

I can't let it rest. "When did you live at the *dún*?"

"Before you were born," he says. I'm astonished to hear his voice grow wistful as he clarifies his words. "Before I was married."

"When the hell were you going to tell—"

Patrick cuts me off, shouldering in front of me before I reach the car.

"I need to talk to Fiona." The voice beyond Patrick's broad shoulders is high and nasal, like someone fighting nasty spring allergies.

"Call and make an appointment." Patrick's snarl sounds like he's three seconds shy of ignition. There's a violence in his words, a savagery like a pickax to the base of my skull.

"I—I don't have t— time—"

I've finally placed the voice. And Patrick's bodyguard act is amusing, but I can't imagine being threatened by anyone who's reduced to absolute stammering by a few gruff words.

"Down, boy," I say to my self-appointed protector. I put a hand on Patrick's arm before I step around the wall of his body.

He scowls, but I'm too busy smothering a laugh to put him in his place.

The man waiting to talk to me is half Patrick's size. His rumpled brown suit looks like he's been wearing it for weeks, and a button is missing from his yellowed shirt. Dandruff dusts his shoulders. His smudged eyeglasses slip down the bridge of his nose, causing him to blink like a startled frog. The finger he uses to push them back in place is stained with ink.

It's something of a miracle that Quentin O'Roark has made it to my father's funeral. Q is—*was*—Da's Quartermaster. He knows where every dollar of the Old Colony's Crew wealth came from and where every penny is stored. His office is in one of the townhouses across from the *dún*. I was only there once, on a summer afternoon, when the room easily topped one hundred degrees from the heat of all Q's computers. I'm pretty sure he hasn't left the house for years.

"Quentin," I say, like we stand around chatting on a regular basis. A flash of surprise widens his eyes. I wonder how many other people in the cemetery remember his full name.

"Fiona." His gaze stays glued to mine. He sounds like he's

reading lines from a play as he loudly announces: "I'm sorry for your loss."

"Thank you," I say.

And then, before I can think of something civil to continue the conversation—ask about his family (does he even have one?), or maybe about his health—he leans in close. Talking fast, like he's reciting all of the Generally Accepted Accounting Principles in less than a minute, he says, "The ten million dollars you promised for the museum. You need to pull it from sources no one else knows about. Dowd will do everything he can to stop you. Call Rónnad."

"Who?" I ask, feeling like I've been caught in the spray of a machine gun.

"Call her," he says urgently. "Today."

"I don't—"

He reaches out and shakes my hand. His palm is sweaty, but he's holding a scrap of paper. He grips my fingers until he's certain I've accepted the transfer.

"Who is she?" I ask. "Why are you helping me?"

But Q answers in that too-loud, too-fake voice. "Great to see you, Fiona. Wish it was under other circumstances."

He leaves before I can force out any more questions, darting across the parking lot like a pack of wolves is nipping at his heels.

Patrick shakes his head, but he opens my door and sees me settled in my seat. He hands me my cigar box after I've fastened my safety belt.

I'm already studying the paper by the time he locks his own door. "What's that?" he asks.

I show him the scrap. It's blank, except for ten inked numbers divided into three neat groups—a phone number. But there's no sign at all of who this Rónnad is, or why Q believes so strongly that I can trust her to get me the money I need.

16

PATRICK

F uck.

I'm not driving back to Philadelphia today.

I remember Quentin O'Roark. The last time I saw him, he was a low-level runner, but he's clearly found a way to succeed with the Crew. That makes sense. The man was born with a computer attached to his fingers.

But I stepped in front of Fiona because he *could* have had a gun. He could have pulled a knife on her. Broken her neck with a twist of his hands.

Okay. Maybe not *his* hands.

But Fiona isn't safe—not with Aran Dowd prowling for the King's throne. And even though Keenan Rivers has kept to the shadows, I don't trust him either.

The simplest thing for me to do is to pay attention to the Fishtown ring on my finger. That Celtic knot stands for something. It tells me who my true family is, where I've been for the past twenty-five years, where I belong.

But a feckin' ring doesn't say anything about a girl trying to do what's right. Fiona dressed like a Queen today. She stood by her father's grave as if he deserved her respect. She held her tongue when that dry shite of a priest rushed through his prayers like he was shoving a pauper in a pit.

And she nearly came apart at the seams back in the apartment, when I spared her one kind word.

I've been counting kinks for longer than she's been alive. I know some people get off on praise. Plenty of subs get more from a few kind words than they do from whips or cuffs or butt plugs.

But I've never seen anyone turn on so fast, so bright. Fiona lit up like a feckin' lightbulb, and my fingers are itching to pull her chain again.

When we return to the Back Bay, I linger on the little patio at the back of the house. I have phone calls to make, and Fiona needs time to gather her thoughts. I saw the way she clutched that cigar box like it was a lifeline. I'm curious about what's in it, but I had no business asking at the churchyard when she'd just buried her da.

I check in with Rory O'Hare first. He's been my second-in-command for a few years now; I trust him keeping an eye on our boss. It's Saturday afternoon, but he answers on the first ring, ready with a full report. He fills me in on Kelly's whereabouts, on his state of mind, on the day-to-day challenges of running a criminal empire from a five-star luxury hotel.

That gives me what I need to check in with Himself. But Kelly doesn't pick up, even though I'm calling his personal phone.

On the one hand, I should be pleased O'Hare's serving well enough that I'm not needed. On the other, I feel a bit bruised for being set aside so soon. I leave a message, saying Dowd and Rivers are chasing their own tails; I don't think they'll bother Fishtown anytime soon.

But I also say I need a little more time to investigate. A little more time to be sure.

I don't mention Fiona.

I knock on the apartment door when I get up to the fourth floor. Somehow, I forgot to get a replacement key made yesterday. I meant to do it; the plan just slipped my mind with everything else going on.

Fiona's changed out of her demure outfit. She's wearing yoga pants now, ones that sit low on her hips so I get a clear view of her skinny crimson thong. She's pulled on a top that's more lace than cloth.

She plants one hand on her hip. "So you're staying?"

"Yeah," I say, even though I'm half-convinced it's a mistake. "For now."

"Thank you," she says. "For now."

She doesn't have to tilt her head to that angle. She has no cause to lick her lips. There isn't a reason on earth she needs to pause with her tongue just barely visible in the soft, dark cave of her mouth.

My hands need something to do, so I strip off my tie. I'm still thinking about what I could manage with that knot-marked silk when I turn to the note she's left on the counter—a 617 phone number.

"Are you going to call?" I ask. My question's a test. I want to know how she thinks.

"Q was right," she says. "I need to act fast. The Gala's at the end of next month."

"But why reach out to a stranger? If O'Roark really wants to help, why not just hand over your father's accounts?"

"If Da made a will, I haven't heard about it. It'll take days to pull together his records. More days—maybe even weeks—to jump through hoops with bankers, investment guys. I don't have that time, especially with Uncle Aran fighting me every step of the way."

"But you trust O'Roark with this?" I jut my chin toward the number.

"He's old-school, belts-and-suspenders. It was dangerous, what he did today. He wouldn't take that risk if it wasn't safe for me to follow up."

"What if Dowd put him up to it? Or Rivers?"

She shakes her head. "Q was terrified they'd see him talking to me. His hands were so sweaty... That stammer... I know a thing or two about nervous men."

Her words are matter-of-fact, but her tone tightens the crotch of my trousers.

"Trust me," she goes on. "Quentin O'Roark doesn't have the balls to play both ends against the middle."

"So you trust whatever random woman he tells you to call?" I eye the slip of paper.

"Of course not." She sounds indignant. "I know nothing about her."

"Good girl."

She smiles as her cheeks turn pink, and it's like someone turned on an entire bank of stadium lights to flood a football pitch. "But I will call her." She sounds a little breathless, like she's just run up all four flights of stairs to this apartment. "I'll meet with her. I'll see what she has to say. And if it makes sense, if her terms are good, I'll get the money I need."

That's a good answer, so I pull a clean burner from my pocket. I always keep one on hand. "Go on, then."

Fiona swallows as she takes the phone. She smooths the piece of paper on the countertop. She glances out the window at the brownstone across the street, at the sky, at the Land Rover parked in front of the fire hydrant.

But her hand is steady when she finally puts the phone on speaker and punches in the number.

It rings three times before someone answers: "Speak."

The voice is female.

Fiona looks at me as she responds. "I was told you can help me. I need to raise some funds."

"Who gave you this number?" The accent is Boston, born and bred, and the woman is old.

Fiona asks a question with her eyebrows. I shake my head. "Someone who trusts both of us," she says.

"I don't talk to strangers on the phone. Can we meet in person?"

"Yes," Fiona says.

"Monday morning," the woman says.

"Tomorrow," Fiona says. She clearly doesn't want to wait.

"Tomorrow is Sunday. I go to church. Spend time with family. We can meet on Monday."

"Fine," Fiona says, resigned, but not happy about losing the round.

"Caffe Isabella," the woman says. "On the waterfront. Ten o'clock."

I shake my head. On principal, I won't take the first place offered.

Fiona says, "Monday at ten. But let's meet at The Black Sheep."

I wince. The pub is in the heart of Crew territory. There's no telling how many eyes and ears will report back to the *dún* before we've settled in a booth.

But the old woman seems to have her own rules. She makes a spitting sound, then says, "Not three blocks from the gray house."

She knows about the *dún*.

Fiona holds up empty hands, asking for suggestions. I haven't been in Boston for more than two decades. I don't know the best place for black-market shenanigans.

But I know a place that's easy to get to. That's far enough from the *dún* that none of Dowd's men is likely to happen by. That's got tables outside, where it'll be a hell of a lot harder for this woman or any of her associates to plant a camera or a bug.

The Bell clangs. I know better than to act on impulse. But sometimes impulse is the only thing I have to go on. I grab one of the menus from the bowl, along with a pen, and I print in big letters on a patch of white paper.

"Yankee Roast," Fiona says. She reads off the address as I add it.

"Yankee Roast," our mystery woman says. "At ten. On Monday." And she ends the call without another word.

Fiona shakes her head as she hands back my phone. "You think this will work?" she asks.

"As long as I'm not the one ordering," I say.

But somehow I suspect that salt in the coffee will be the least of our problems.

17

FIONA

Patrick sends me into the bakery, telling me to get him a cup of coffee. As I wait in line to place my order, I watch him edge the end table further away from the others. I set my sunglasses on top of my head to better watch him working.

Two women stand behind the counter. From the structure of their cheekbones and the curve of their lips, I'm guessing they're a mother/daughter team. But Mother isn't exactly welcoming when I get to the front of the line.

Glaring out the window, she asks, "You're with him?"

I shrug, like I'd rather be anywhere else in the world. "He's just moving the table so he can sit in the sun," I say. "Old bones."

She's building up a head of steam, and I wonder why Patrick chose this place for my summit with Rónnad. But the younger woman steps forward with a smile as soothing as foam on a latte. "It's time for your break, Ma," she says. And when her mother hesitates, "Go on. Take your tea. Put your feet up in the office and close your eyes for a bit."

The older woman grumbles, but she drops a bag of chamomile into a glazed mug. She stares out at Moran as she siphons off hot water, her lips moving like she's muttering a spell.

"Don't let those chairs block the sidewalk," she warns me.

"They won't," I promise.

Still grumbling, she disappears through a door in the back.

"Sorry about that," the younger woman says. "She's having a bad morning."

I spotted the headscarf and the yellow cast to her face the moment I walked in—not to mention wrists as thin as broomsticks. But I say, "Happens to the best of us." I order a caramel latte for me and two drip coffees, figuring Rónnad can doctor one with cream and sugar, if that's her preference. When they're served up, I find a trio of little cherry pastries on the tray as well —Jenn's Jam Tarts, according to the label inside the bakery case.

"On the house," the woman says. "Come back in for free refills on the coffees."

I thank her and carry out the tray. Patrick takes his mug, but he glares at the miniature pies as if they're poisoned. Tired of old people being pissed off with me, I polish off one in three bites.

Jittery, Patrick is twisting his fidget ring. I think about telling him to take a walk around the block. Or maybe he should stop mainlining coffee.

The skin looks tight around his eyes, but I know he slept well last night. We both did—sliding beneath the duvet and curling against each other, my back to his front. His arm felt like an iron shield clamped around me, banishing even a hint of nightmare.

I know it's strange that we haven't talked about it. Neither one of us has mentioned that we're sleeping in the same bed, touching, closer than close, but apparently we're never having sex again.

I'm Fiona Fucking Ingram. There is literally nothing I won't say out loud. Nothing I won't try in bed. Nothing I won't tease a man about, if I think it'll help me get my way.

But every time I start to say something—*I haven't slept this well in eight years*—I know exactly what he'll do. He'll run stiff fingers through his hair. He'll look at a point exactly three inches above the bridge of my nose. He'll let his thumb drift toward the titanium ring on his middle finger, the one that spins.

And I somehow know that if he thinks he's being soft, that he's slacking off on what he owes Braiden Kelly or the Fishtown Boys or some perfect version of himself packed deep inside his memory, then he'll stop. He'll deny himself a night of sleep, just to prove he can. And I'll lose out too.

Fuck.

I rub my arms and consider stealing another one of the cherry tarts. Before I can reach for the pastry, though, a bundle of rags rolls around the corner of the building.

Patrick stands. It takes me longer to realize there's a person inside all that cloth. She's wearing three different skirts, one hem bunching at her ankles, another at her calves, the last around her knees. Her waist looks like someone cinched a frayed rope around a broken-down mattress. One of her sweaters has horizontal rainbow stripes; the other is covered in filthy white polka dots on black. Both are torn at the elbows, revealing a yellow and black plaid shirt underneath. Her hair is woven into four braids that flop around like snakes.

She looks like a cross between a crazy woman, a witch, and some sort of Roma fortune teller.

She waddles over and sits in the middle seat, the one Patrick was in. Without saying a word, one hand crams a cherry tart into her mouth. The other grabs my latte. Her fingers are gnarled like ancient pine trees, swollen knuckles stretching paper-thin skin.

Her face is as wrinkled as her hands, the skin so shiny she might buff it. Her red-rimmed eyes are the tired brown of sun-baked grass, and that braided hair is the colorless gray of a field mouse. She wheezes, spraying flakes of pastry over the table as she says, "Rónnad."

"Fiona," I say, wondering if Q has played an elaborate joke on me.

Patrick doesn't say anything. He just scowls.

Rónnad downs half my coffee in three noisy swallows. She wipes her mouth with the back of one hand and says, "How much do you need?"

I can't believe I actually answer her. "Ten million."

She puffs air out of her mouth, like she can't be bothered for so small a sum.

"By no later than June 15," I add.

That's only six weeks. But Q said she could do it. And no matter how odd this witch-like woman is, no matter how strange our conversation, Q never led my father astray, not once in twenty years. The same instinct that tells me Uncle Aran will destroy me, the one that says Keenan Rivers is looking for a way to tear me apart too, that's the inner thought that says Q is on my side. So Rónnad must be too.

"Ten million," she says, finishing off my latte. "Another," she says, shoving her mug into Patrick's ribs.

His face darkens, and I imagine all the ways he can put this woman in her place, but I give him a single shake of my head. It's a risk. I've never given him a direct order before.

But he takes the cup and goes inside.

"Ten million dollars," Rónnad says. "I can do that."

"How?"

"You don't trust me?" She laughs without any humor.

"I don't *know* you. How the fuck am I supposed to trust you?"

She clicks her tongue, but I'm not sure if she's protesting my swearing, my lack of faith, or Patrick's failure to return instantaneously with her sweet, milky coffee. "Give me a bank account," she says. "I'll deposit one hundred thousand dollars by tomorrow night. One million by next Monday. The rest by June 15."

I shake my head in disbelief. "Just like that?"

She smacks her lips. "Just like that."

Patrick finally returns. Rónnad accepts the fresh latte like she's doing him a favor.

"And what do you want in exchange?"

She drains off all the coffee at once, as if her mouth is made of asbestos. When she sets the empty mug on the table, she cocks her head like a curious pigeon. Her braids bounce. "Those sunglasses."

My fingers go to the frames of the glasses I picked up at the drugstore before the funeral. "You'll deposit one hundred thousand dollars into my bank account by tomorrow night. And all you want is a pair of *sunglasses?*"

She shrugs. "They're nice sunglasses."

"They're rip-off designer shades I bought at CVS."

She nods and repeats: "They're nice sunglasses."

She's fucking nuts. I don't know what sort of joke Q is playing. I don't know if this woman is wearing a wire, or if she plans on hacking the banking system, or if this is all an elaborate scam to get two lattes and a cherry tart.

But I made my crazy vow in front of the entire Old Colony Crew. I need ten million dollars by the end of June. So unless I can figure out some way to spin it from thin air, I need Rónnad.

"How do I send you the account information?" I ask.

She digs in the pocket of one of her skirts. Patrick tenses, but he holds off from putting her in a wrist lock for long enough that she can produce a smartphone.

It's an Apple. Top of the line. More camera lenses than my own phone, which is only a year old.

She holds the device to her face, unlocking the screen. Peering closely at the glass, she searches for an icon. Her knotted finger lands heavily on the green-and-white image for texts.

"Here," she says, passing the phone to me. "You send yourself a text."

I stare at the phone like it's a live tarantula. There's no way in hell I'm giving her my personal information.

Patrick grunts like a silverback gorilla. He takes his burner out of his pocket and I pass him Rónnad's phone. He types in a number, hits send, and nods when the message arrives.

Rónnad returns her phone to her pocket, then points at me with an index finger so twisted it points in three directions at once. For a moment, I think she still wants me to hand over my own device. Then, I think she's asking for a third latte. But she raises her chin, gesturing toward my glasses.

I take them off slowly and pass them across the table. Rónnad picks them up using both hands, reverently, as if they're some sort of holy relic. When she puts them on, they cover half her face.

"Tomorrow," she says.

And then she's gone.

18

PATRICK

E very nerve in my body is screaming at me to go after that bitch. Shove my Glock in her face. Find out what game she's really playing.

But one game she *might* be playing is drawing Fiona out in the open. We're on the edge of Southie. On the border of the Crew's territory. And Aran Dowd is ruthless enough to know his life would be a hell of a lot simpler with Kieran Ingram's daughter in a grave.

So I'm not leaving Fiona to chase that woman.

Instead, I spin my fidget ring and gulp the last of my coffee. It's surprisingly good, without an ocean of salt dumped in.

Fiona makes a show of being fascinated by the mugs. There's one of those jam tarts left on the plate, and she pushes it around with her index finger. She's too busy avoiding my gaze to put it in her mouth.

In fact, avoiding me leads to her collecting the dishes and bringing them inside, like she's been paid to do the work. She takes her time, maybe talking to Hannah or Kimi; with the sun's reflection on the window, I can't see what's happening in there.

But when Fiona comes out the door, she walks directly to the Land Rover. She's all legs and tits and shiny black hair. She's opted for a strapless lace bustier, and she's wearing tight black trousers that look like they'd feel slick under my palms. They cut off mid-calf, allowing her to show off her shoes—five-inch stilettos with cuffs around both ankles that make me think of every wicked thing I've ever made a woman do.

I follow her to the car like a dog on a feckin' leash.

We're halfway to the townhouse, and she still hasn't said a word. So I go ahead and start the fight.

"Sunglasses aren't the last thing she'll want from you," I say, staring at a red light like it's the most important thing in my life.

"No shit." Fiona seems fascinated by her manicure. Her fingernails look like they've been freshly dipped in blood, and she's studying them like they're engraved with all the secrets of the universe.

"No one hands out hundred-grand gifts without expecting something in return."

"Contrary to what you seem to believe, I'm neither a child nor an idiot."

"She's not your fairy godmother."

"Jesus Christ," she shouts. "Give it a rest."

I hold my tongue for five full minutes. That takes us into the heart of Back Bay. The space in front of the fire hydrant is open, so I take it.

She gets out before I put the car in Park. Barely looking both ways, she crosses the street, and she's got her key in the door as I come up behind her. She turns the stairs into a track meet, and I'm honestly impressed at her speed in those heels.

I wait until she's slammed and locked the door before I say, "There are worse things than going back on your promise at the wake."

"Are there?"

I've seen Fiona scheming. I've seen her egging on a room of grown men, making every single one of them believe they've got a chance to fuck her. I've seen her recovering from a beating she never deserved.

But I've never seen Fiona furious—until now.

"I made that promise to my *father*," she says, spitting out the word like it's acid on her lips. "That means something. Not like —" She cuts herself off.

"Not like what?" I press.

She storms into the kitchen and assaults the cupboard, taking out a bag of coffee.

"Not like what?" I ask again.

She slams a filter into the coffee maker. Throws coffee into a grinder. Pounds the button until the entire apartment is filled with the racket of beans being reduced to dust.

When I can finally be heard, I repeat my question a third time. "Not like—"

"*Him!*" she shouts. "Not like my father. Not like Saint Kieran, holy captain of the Old Colony Crew."

She grabs a mug like she's thinking of using it to brain me.

"He made me sit at his table, family dinner every fucking night, and I was never allowed to say a word. But I did it. He ordered me to attend the mayor's Patriots Day fundraiser, year after year after year, even though every single person in the room sneered like I smelled like fish. But I did it. I visited family in Dublin, I brokered a peace in Philadelphia, I knocked down Braiden Kelly in favor of a mafia piece of shit, because that's what my father told me to do. Everything. I fucking did it."

"Fiona—"

"I shot four men on his orders, after he said I wouldn't have the guts to follow through. I proved I was a good soldier. I showed him."

"You—"

"I killed three more on my own. One word from Da, and those assholes could have been buried at sea. But he didn't care.

He didn't punish them. I did, though. I promised I'd get revenge, and I keep my fucking promises!"

She slams the mug onto the counter so hard it collapses into a pile of knife-sharp shards. I don't think she realizes how much she's told me, how much of her past I know now. She howls—in pain or fury or frustration—and she starts to grind her hand into the mess.

"Stop!" I shout, one syllable that she can't cut off, that she can't deny.

I've known girls who cut. Women who hurt themselves because pain is the only sensation that registers. Hell, I've been a Dom for plenty of subs who need to ache before they can come.

But I won't stand here and watch Fiona do that to herself.

She's startled enough by my shout that she freezes. She's breathing hard. She bites her lip. Then, with perfect calculation, she flexes her wrist and slowly leans into the shattered mug again.

"I said stop," I tell her. And I close the distance between us, grabbing her wrist to keep her from harming herself.

I feel the small bones beneath my fingers. This close, I can see her eyes are dilated; they flicker with every rapid breath she draws. Her lips are parted, just enough that I can see her sharp, white teeth.

"What will you do if I don't?" she asks. And then she shifts her weight onto one of those cuffed stilettos, jutting out a hip and raising her chin. "Daddy."

I pull her arm to her side, stepping even closer. "Don't call me that unless you mean it."

She looks at me steadily. "Whatever you say, *Daddy*."

She's perfectly, devastatingly calm, so I force my voice to stay even. "This isn't a game."

She pouts. "But what if I like to play?"

"I have rules."

Her smile is radiant. "Then it *is* a game!"

"Number one," I say, ignoring her brattiness. "No little girl of mine hurts herself."

She looks at the ruins of the mug on the counter. Her fingers curl, protecting the red marks on her palm where she hasn't yet broken the skin. Rubbing her hand against her hip, she does that devastating thing again, looking straight at me. "Yes, Daddy."

"My little girl doesn't throw tantrums."

I see the precise second she realizes I'm serious. I watch her start to argue. She wasn't throwing a tantrum. She was justified. We're standing in her home; she gets to make the rules.

One by one, she throws away her protests. Eyeing me steadily, she says, "Yes, Daddy."

Only a hint of breathlessness gives her away. That, and the heat rising off her, carrying the scent of lemon and clove. I've smelled that soap in her shower. I'm suddenly throttled by the desire to lather up my hands, to run them over every feckin' inch of her.

I'm still holding one wrist as she moves her free hand to the scalloped edge of her top. Catching the tip of her tongue between her teeth, she traces the lace design with her fingertips. This close, I can make out the twin darts of her nipples, straining at their black silk cups. I brush against one with the back of my fingers.

"Oh, fuck, yes," she says, closing her eyes and throwing back her head.

I want to suck on the pulse point just beneath her jaw. I want to scrape her throat with my teeth. I want to bury my face between her magnificent tits.

But more than that, I want to make more rules for my little girl.

Because this is different for me, even though I've spent thirty years learning every way it's possible to fuck a woman.

As a kid, I paid attention in Health class. It didn't take long to realize the importance of all those line drawings, the location of a woman's clit, what it's actually good for.

As a man, I learned how to listen to a woman's body. Every one is different, each one can tell me what she needs, what feels good, when she's about to come.

As a Dom, I explored being in control, setting limits for my subs, pushing each beyond her expectations for herself. I know the line where pleasure turns to agony, where anticipation collapses into mindless terror. I've mastered power, every single way I can wield it.

Sex cages the brain squirrels. Sex silences the Bell. Sex heals all the broken bits inside my brain—rough sex, hard sex, sex that leaves my women bruised and aching. That's why I haven't fucked a woman without laying down cold, hard cash since Jenn wrapped our Ford Escort around that goddamn tree.

So whatever the fuck this is between Fiona and me, it's new. It's different. It washes my brain in a soothing bath of menthol, slowing everything down, making everything slip into place.

Her neck is still arched like she's waiting for a vampire to suck her dry. She moans again before she whispers, "Fuck me, Daddy."

I know exactly what I need to say. What I need to do. I catch her chin between my fingers and force her head up. I shake her once, hard, until she looks me in the eye. I say, very slowly, very clearly, so there can be no misunderstanding, "My little girl doesn't swear. Because if she does, *when* she does, my little girl is punished."

I don't give a fuck about swearing. But I very much care about obedience. I want my rules to be a challenge. To be difficult for my sub to follow.

I think Fiona will test me, then and there. But I can see she isn't certain. She barely knows me; we've only been together for a week. She's just a little afraid of what will happen, now that she's awakened the animal inside me.

"Yes, Daddy," she says, visibly swallowing every foul word she knows. She's proving she can be wise.

"What was your favorite stuffed animal when you were a kid?" I ask, still holding her chin.

"Bunbun," she says, clearly confused. "A rabbit."

"Bunbun," I repeat. "That's your safeword. That's what you'll say when you need me to stop."

"I won't—" She's already twisting, already shifting her hips toward me, shoving her tits against my chest.

I step away, dropping my grip. "You have it if you need it."

"I'll never use it."

I stare down her defiance. "You'll be safe."

She wants to protest further, but she's already learned better. "Yes, Daddy," she says, so soft it's almost a whisper.

"Good girl."

The rush of blood to her cheeks is like a wildfire. Her eyes go wide and she rocks back on her heels, just enough to let me know she didn't expect her own reaction. And if that's enough to surprise her, then she doesn't know what's about to hit her.

"On your knees," I order, snapping my finger to enforce the command.

She drops like I've shot her with my Glock. When she gulps for breath, that black lace stretches across her tits. She doesn't hesitate to go for my belt, sliding it from its loops and draping it around her neck like a towel after a workout. But she hasn't begun the exercises I have in mind. She looks up at me and says, "Thank you, Daddy."

I think about sliding the belt through its buckle, about wrapping the leather around my fist and cinching it tight enough for the edges to crease her throat. We'll get to breath play eventually. But for now, I just need to remind her I'm the one in control.

"Suck my cock."

I realize *control* is a lie, the instant she takes me in her mouth.

Sure, I have her calling me Daddy. I've got her on her knees. I'm dreaming about holding her feckin' leash.

But when her lips close around my dick, the menthol bath in

my brain starts to boil. She whines a little as she accepts the size of me. I feel the back of her throat. Her fingers dig into my thighs as she fights her gag reflex. She loosens her jaw and stretches her neck and then she does it—she takes my full length.

She's good with her tongue. Her lips, too. Her mouth is hot and wet and she knows just how hard to suck.

I've been hard since she called me Daddy, but now my bollocks actually ache. I bury one hand in her hair. I slow her down because I mean to last.

"My God, *Scáthach*," I groan. "You have no idea how good that feels."

This time, when she blushes, she whimpers, and the little sound vibrates all the way to the base of my spine. As I catch a stuttering breath, I get a whiff of hot, excited girl.

"You're amazing, little girl," I tell her. "You're doing such a good job."

Her grip tightens on my thighs. Her tongue swirls down to lick my balls. I see stars, sprayed across the wooden cabinets in the kitchen.

"Stop," I gasp. And when she doesn't listen, I tug on her hair, sharp enough that she has to pay attention. "Stop, little girl."

She shifts back to sit on her heels, easing my cock from her lips. "Why'd you do that?" she asks, looking up at me. "You were so fucking close."

Fucking close.

I told her not to swear. And now, staring down at her past my raging hard-on, my fingers still wrapped in her hair, I realize just how much I hoped she'd break one of my rules.

Now, my little girl has to pay.

19

FIONA

"That's it," Patrick says. "On your feet."

I'm so stunned, I don't know how to respond. My lips tingle, like I've been eating shishito peppers. My eyes are tearing because he's just so huge, and I wipe the back of my hand under my nose.

"Come on, Daddy," I purr, looking up at him. I don't want to follow his order. I want to finish him off. I want to feel him lose control.

But when I raise my hand to stroke his obviously eager cock, he tightens his grip on my hair. A lightning bolt sizzles from my chin to my thighs. He angles his wrist so I have no choice but to rise from the floor.

"No," he says. "*You* come on."

The pressure releases for a moment, just long enough for him to tug his boxer briefs from around his knees, to savagely tuck himself into his pants. Then, he's pulling me around the kitchen counter, through the living room, and down the hall to the bedroom.

I finally realize what I said. But he *was* fucking close. And if he thinks I'm going to change my entire vocabulary just to keep him satisfied, just to make him think he's the boss of me…

"Strip," he says once we're standing in front of the bed.

"No fucking way," I say, because I want to know what he'll do.

I don't expect him to dust his palms together, like he's finished some dirty task. "No more games," he says, stepping back. I must make some sound of protest, because he shakes his head. "I gave you three simple rules. And you couldn't follow them for an hour. This was a bad idea. You're not ready to be my little girl."

A month ago, in Madden's apartment, if you'd asked me if I got off on role-play, I would have laughed. Mind games like that are for weak, spineless men.

A week ago, in that joke of a hotel room, if you'd asked me if I liked calling Moran Daddy, I would have shrugged. It got him hot and bothered, and after everything we'd been through, we both needed to get laid.

But right now, at this very minute, in the bedroom of Aunt S's apartment—where I first laced up a corset and figured out the pull I could have on men—I'm devastated.

I don't know how this happened. I don't know who I am. But at this moment, in this place, more than anything else in the world, I want to be Patrick's little girl.

"Please," I say. "Give me another chance."

I'm wearing more clothes than usual. My lace bustier has opaque cups. My silk pants cover every inch from my waist to my ankles. My satin panties hide my bare pussy far more than the thongs I usually choose.

But Patrick's eyes are as dark as charcoal, as hard and sharp as obsidian knives. And I flinch in front of him, because I've never felt more naked.

"I'm sorry," I say, "Let me make you feel good. Let me help you finish."

I don't say *Daddy*. I'm not allowed to say *Daddy*. Not until I've made this up to him. Not until I've proven I can follow his rules.

I don't realize I'm holding my breath until my lungs start to burn. I'm stretched like a rubber band, almost at my breaking point. I'm waiting, waiting, waiting.

And finally, he turns to the bed. He grabs the duvet, the blanket, and the sheet, tugging hard enough to strip them all from the mattress at once. He snaps his fingers, the same way he did in the kitchen, kindling a tiny flicker of hope inside my belly.

"Strip," he says again.

This time, I don't weigh whether I should be sexy or sweet. I don't debate wriggling my hips or fingering my nipples as I free them from their lace. I simply follow his command, shoes first, corset next, pants and panties last of all.

"On your back," he says. "Middle of the bed."

I do it.

He straddles me then. His jeans are rough against the sides of my breasts. He's still erect, and he gets harder as he pulls my arms above my head, as he lashes my wrists together and ties me to the iron headboard with his belt.

I raise my head, craning my neck as he steps into the closet. I hear the thud of his shoes hitting the floor, and the rasp of his zipper. I think I'm prepared when he comes back to the room naked, but then I realize he's holding two neckties.

The black one, the one he wore to Da's wake, loops around my right ankle, securing me to the footboard. The Fishtown one, from the funeral, anchors my left leg. He's ruthless as he ties his knots, brutally efficient.

Muscles ripple beneath his lighthouse tattoo as he clenches his fist after a job well done. The scars stand out on his body, evidence of all the years he's lived in the mob. His cock stands proud as he studies me from the foot of the bed.

I'm used to men staring at my body. I do everything I *can* to make men notice me.

But Patrick's gaze is different from all those other men. He's looking at something more than my exposed pussy. He's staring into my soul.

So I'm more than a little surprised when he climbs onto the bed and kneels between my thighs. "Tell me what you did wrong," he says.

Back in the hotel, I would have laughed. I would have said I don't have to play by his rules. I don't have to do anything he demands.

But now I say, "I broke one of your rules."

"Which rule?" He strokes the insides of my thighs with his fingertips, striping me with velvet fire.

Go to hell, I could tell him. But instead I say, "I'm not supposed to swear."

His fingers find my folds. I'm so slick. So ready. "Why aren't you supposed to swear?" he asks.

Don't ask me—you made the fucking rule. That's the first thing I think. But I say, "Because I'm your little girl."

He sinks a finger into me, and I shudder from my toes to the roots of my hair. "Who makes the rules, little girl?"

Anyone who isn't tied to the goddamn bed! But I say, "You do." And I swallow before I add, "Daddy."

He gives me another finger. My hips flex, straining to take him deeper. I think he'll ask me another question, make me pay with another truth, but I must be doing something to satisfy him, because he slips in a third finger, hooking me, stretching me.

He fucks me with his hand, and I've never felt anything like it before. He is absolutely, completely fixated on filling me with his fingers. My own hands and feet are tied; I can't do anything to reciprocate, anything to escape.

No other man has done this to me before. Sure, I've been

tied up. But that was only so someone could shove his dick down my throat. Pound my cunt. Come inside my ass.

This is the first time in my life a man has concentrated on what *I* want. What I need.

When I lift my head, I can see a bead of precum gleaming in the light. He's primed. He's ready. But he isn't using me.

Instead, he curls his fingers. He finds that patch of nerves deep inside me, the place I can never reach myself.

He strokes me, pressing hard. My toes point. The arches of my feet scream on the edge of cramps. And then he whispers, "You're *my* good girl."

And I come. I come screaming. I come gasping. I come straining my hips against his hand, wanting his fourth finger, wanting his thumb, wanting him to fist me, but instead he says, "That's it, beautiful. That's right, gorgeous. You're so tight, *Scáthach.* So strong."

His words fill me more than his hand ever could. They wrap inside me, curling up my spine. They knit into my bones.

"Give it to me, little girl. Give me all you've got. My good, good girl," he murmurs, and I crash into a second orgasm.

I don't know why I need this. I don't know what makes his words spin inside me. I don't know how he understands exactly what to say, what to do, but he completes me in a way I can't explain.

I think he'll untie me, once I've collapsed back to the mattress. But Patrick is a man who doesn't believe in part measures.

He cages me with his body. Squeezing my hips between his knees, he strokes my throat, from my chin to the hollow between my collarbones. He pets me like I'm an animal. I can smell myself on his fingers, as he paints with my arousal.

My lips purse. I want to be back in the kitchen. I want to feel my mouth stretched by his cock. I want to fight to swallow him.

Instead, he gives me his fingers to suck.

They're salty and sweet. I roll my tongue over them, around them. I pull hard, trying to fill all the empty places inside me.

And he lowers his head to my right breast, sucking my nipple past his teeth. His mouth threads a wire straight to my clit, and just like that, I'm on the edge of coming for the third time.

"Oh my God," I moan around the fingers in my mouth. He starts to trace my lips, making them hum again, the way they did in the kitchen. Before I can beg, though, he uses his wet fingers to pinch my nipple—hard, harder, hardest, almost more than I can bear.

At the same time, he slides down my body and buries his face between my thighs.

Patrick Moran knows how to eat pussy. He draws my folds into his mouth, pulling with a steady pressure that makes me strain for more. He fucks me with his tongue. He sucks on my clit.

I've never been with a man who wanted to go down on me. Sure, a couple of guys have licked me like I'm an ice cream cone. One worked down there for long enough that I produced my usual fake orgasm—shouting his name, pulling his hair, the whole nine yards. But five minutes later, I realized he only did it so he'd get his own pipes cleaned.

Patrick isn't checking off items on a spreadsheet. He's paying attention to what I want. What I need. When his thumb stretches my taint, my clit starts to pulse, echoing the heartbeat that's hammering through my head. He spears my pussy with his tongue until I beg. "Please," I tell him. "Just do it," I plead. "Let me finish. Please."

He raises his head, those coal-black eyes peering at me over the curve of my waxed mound, over the plane of my belly that rises and falls as I pant for release. His thumb is heavy, pulling me, stretching me.

"You've got the prettiest pussy I've ever seen," he says.

And I'm coming before he sucks my clit into this mouth.

My feet fight against the silk neckties that bind them. My arms strain against the leather belt. My entire body is electrified, on fire; every nerve is shattered.

I can't tell where his lips are, what his tongue is doing as he works miracles between my thighs. All I know is I'm cresting again, before I ever imagined my body could respond.

I scream without words as every cell in my body explodes. I never imagined sex could be this way, could be this good, could empty my soul and fill it back to overflowing.

Somehow I realize that Patrick has left the bed, but before I can complain, he's back. I slit my eyes open, barely able to make sense of shapes, of shadows.

He's worked a condom out of its foil and rolled the rubber over his cock. He's pressed himself against me, against my clit, against my pussy that still flutters with electric aftershocks.

There's no way I can come again. I might never have another orgasm in my life.

When he fills me, my entire body stretches. My lips open, eager, wanting, and I didn't know I needed to kiss him until his mouth covers mine. He moves inside me as our tongues meet, slowly, effortlessly, opening new paths to bliss.

I'm bound. I can't clutch him. I can't rake my fingernails down his back. I can't dig my fingers into the muscles of his ass, speed him up, slow him down, do anything to make this right.

I'm helpless.

But the ocean waves rise from somewhere deep inside me. They're a slow roll, a deep flex, something calmer and more profound than anything I've ever felt in my life.

Patrick breaks our kiss, but his lips stay close enough to mine that I feel him form the words: "You're incredible, *Scáthach.*"

I fold around him.

This isn't an orgasm like any I've had before. This is perfect balance, perfect ease. I'm not falling, because he's already caught me. I'm not soaring, because he's already gathered me close.

And this time when I come, he does too. His body tightens. His mouth melts against mine. He pulses inside my body, binding us, merging us in the darkness.

He calls me *Scáthach* again, and then he speaks in Irish, soft words, sweet words, words my soul already knows. And even before he comes back to English, I know I'll do anything to be his little girl forever.

20

PATRICK

After I ease out of Fiona, I unfasten my belt from the headboard. I help her to lower her arms, making sure she doesn't move too fast, doesn't set off waves of cramps in her toned, stretched arms. The knots around her ankles take more time; she's pulled them tight by straining against the bed.

She's still dazed, but she's free and curled onto her side. It's safe for me to go into the jacks, to take care of the johnny. Back in the bedroom, I pull my last pair of boxer briefs from my duffel. That's enough clothes for me to head into the kitchen.

After I fill a glass of water at the sink, I open the refrigerator. I want to layer slices of sharp cheddar onto crisp, sweet apples. I want to peel clementines and section out tiny half moons that I can slip between her lips. I want to unwrap chocolate, sweet with milk, like something inside a Christmas stocking.

She doesn't have any of that. The only thing in the fridge is leftover Chinese food. We'll get to that, but water will have to do for now.

I climb onto the bed and pull Fiona onto my lap. I help her with the water, giving her a sip at a time, making sure she doesn't get too greedy, taking care not to spill.

I hold her as she settles back into her body. I rub arnica into her wrists, and I smooth the cream into the creases etched around her ankles. I tell her she's my little girl.

After I set aside the plastic jar, she runs her finger over the knuckles of my right hand. "You have a lot of scars," she says.

"They come with the job."

She sets her palm against the wrinkled flesh on my left shoulder. "What happened here?"

"I was shot." She doesn't need to know about the Fishtown Boys' bratva enemies.

She traces the long ridge above my liver. "And here?"

"Knife." No reason to tell her I was foolish enough to open my front door to some mafia goons who thought I was carrying the clan's cash.

"And here?" She traces the long gouge across my right thigh.

"Shot again." That's one I took for Kelly, when the two of us went after the Colombians, before he ever stepped up to captain.

She kisses the raised skin on my shoulder. "Don't get hurt again, okay?"

I don't bother lying, telling her I won't.

Her fingers spread across my biceps, closing around the dark lantern of my lighthouse tattoo. "What are you covering up here?"

"Not covering up," I say. "I got it after my wife died."

Even half-asleep, she's not stupid. She sees that the lighthouse is dark. That the storm clouds threaten. I watch her start to ask questions, stop, start again, give up. Instead, she runs a nail down the inked side of the lighthouse. She ends up touching Athawn's broken lifeline.

"And when did you get this?" Fiona asks.

"The same time. My son died too."

She swallows the rest of her questions. She grew up in Southie. She knows how easy it is to track down stories about the past.

So instead of pushing for more, she nuzzles closer to my side. I offer her the glass and make her sip until it's empty.

After that, she dozes for a while. I sit up, leaning against the headboard while she stretches out beside me. My hand lingers over her hip, my fingers spread wide.

Sleeping, she looks so young. All of her fierceness is drained out of her. All of her fight.

What the fuck am I doing? Living in a Back Bay brownstone —a far cry from the rough Southie streets where I grew up. Playing with a sub who has a wild praise kink—because I've never been with a woman as quick to come as Fiona when I tell her she's amazing.

I've never been a pleasure Dom. Sure, I've left my women satisfied. I've given them what they want. What they need.

But I've never had a woman who *needs* pure pleasure. Fiona's not ready for anything really rough. Sure, she dresses like she wants to be fucked hard against a brick wall in a back alley. And she's willing to take a little correction. But after what Madden Kelly did to her, she needs to take it slow.

I've never played Daddy before. The thought of any shite-hawk going after an actual child disgusts me. I'd gut him, prick to chin, without a second thought. But protecting Fiona? Keeping her safe from herself and the rest of the world? Making her see that she doesn't always have to be the one fighting, the one in ball-busting charge?

That's satisfying in a way I can't begin to describe—except it suits my brain squirrels just fine. My mind feels…settled.

Calmed.

Fiona wakes sometime after sunset. She stretches at first. Burrows in closer. Then, all at once, she comes awake. Her eyes look wild against her smeared makeup.

"Go on, *Scáthach*," I tell her. "Take a shower. And then we'll eat some dinner."

Scáthach is better than *little girl* right now. The Irish word doesn't make her worry about what we've done. What we're doing.

I get dressed while the water's running. She takes longer than she needs to, and I consider going in to complain about the delay. But my little girl deserves some time to herself. A chance to think. Some space to adjust, just as I've had for myself.

She finally comes out of the bedroom, her hair toweled dry, her face scrubbed free of makeup. She's wearing a pair of black yoga pants and some sort of knit top that looks like it belongs underneath legitimate clothes. I think they call those little bits of string *spaghetti straps*. All I know for sure is I could snap them with one quick tug.

Her bruises are healing well—better than I ever would have predicted back in Philadelphia. She's young. She's healthy.

And she's ravenous.

Reluctantly, I turn away to open up the fridge. "There's enough Chinese food—"

"I want pizza," she says.

"All right. Pizza."

She digs in the bowl on the counter and comes up with a menu. The restaurant answers on the first ring. Caesar salad, she orders, and garlic bread and mozzarella sticks. An extra-large pizza with pepperoni and sausage and olives.

"Anchovies?" she asks me, and I feel like it's a test.

"Whatever you want," I say.

"Extra anchovies," she tells the person taking her order. "Two liters of Coke. And some of those cheesecake bites."

After she's given her credit card number and hung up, I look around the living room. "Do you have half a dozen friends, coming to join us?"

"Don't tell me you aren't starving too."

She's right. And I'm tempted to start eating now, before

dinner arrives. I pull her close, easing my hands under that flimsy little top. She leans back, letting me hold most of her weight, sighing as my lips find the pulse point in her throat.

"They work really fast," she says. "The food will be here in twenty minutes."

"I work fast too," I growl.

"Liar," she says. But she laughs, low and throaty. The only reason I don't strip her out of her clothes then and there is that she was right, earlier. I *am* starving.

It takes twenty-three minutes for the food to arrive. We're both still dressed by the time the buzzer sounds from the front door, but we're breathing like we've raced to the top of Bunker Hill.

"I'll be right down," Fiona says into the intercom. And then to me, when I reach around her to open the door: "I'll be back in a sec."

"You're not going down there alone."

Annoyance darkens her face. "What? You think the pizza-delivery guy will kidnap me?"

"I think it's impossible to be too cautious."

"Let me guess. You're going to carry your big long gun downstairs and scare the crap out of some poor schmuck who's earning minimum wage on his bike."

"Not a bad idea. Wait here."

As I shoulder past her to the bedroom, I can see she wants to protest. But she wants to eat more. So she lets me retrieve my Glock and shove it into my waistband, at the small of my back. She lets me follow her down the stairs. I watch her open the door to the street and collect a pizza box and two grocery bags from a kid who looks like he's five seconds away from leaving it all on the doorstep.

Upstairs, Fiona eats like she hasn't seen food in a year. She downs two pieces of garlic bread and a mozzarella stick before I have plates on the counter. She pours extra dressing onto her salad, then cleans her bowl with crust from her first piece of pizza. Two monster slices later, she's finally starting to slow down, but that doesn't keep her from making satisfied little mews of contentment as cheesecake melts across her tongue.

Two pieces of pizza are more than enough for me.

To fill the time, I ask her stupid things. Who sings her favorite songs. What's her favorite movie.

She names three singers I've never heard of. When she pulls up their music on her phone, they all sound the same— anguished girls with high, thready voices, spitting out the word *fuck* in the middle of complicated rhymes about boys who screwed them over.

Fiona has never seen *The Shawshank Redemption*. So after we put the leftovers in the fridge, we settle on the couch and watch my favorite film on her phone. She curls up against me like a kitten. We both ignore my full-blown hard-on, because Morgan Freeman deserves that much respect.

Fiona doesn't love the movie.

"It's just a bunch of men," she says. "It can't be one of the best movies of all time if there aren't roles for women."

"There's Andy's wife," I remind her. I know that's not enough to win the argument, but I want to wind her up. I'm thinking Fiona and I can go a round or two, that I'm ready to see if I can make her scream *Daddy* as she comes.

But before she can deliver a scathing reply, she yawns—and not some dainty, catch-it-at-the-back-of-her-throat little ladylike yawn. Her mouth opens like a cobra's, and her tongue curls up as a sound like half a scream scrapes her throat.

Obviously embarrassed, she winces like she's nursing a physical blow. She catches her lip between her teeth and glances at the front door, like she expects me to pack up and leave.

"Okay," I say. "Let's go, *Scáthach*."

"What does that mean?" she says, like she hasn't asked before.

I play dumb. "What does what mean?"

"Ska-ha?"

"That's something only Daddies know." I say it because I want to get a rise out of her. I want her to stop thinking about how she just yawned like a banshee.

"That's absolute bullsh—" She swallows mid-word.

I know she won't stop swearing forever. I don't even want to apply my rule outside this game we're playing. She can say whatever she wants when we aren't actually fucking.

But I love the way she's suddenly thinking, suddenly *aware* of everything she says.

"What's that, little girl?"

"Nothing," she mutters.

"I'll tell you what," I say, because playing games with her is fun. "I'll tell you what *Scáthach* means if you show me what's inside the cigar box Oona gave you."

She looks scandalized. "Never! No one's looked inside that box."

"Well, then." I don't push. I can wait until she wants to share.

But I see the way fatigue is shaping her face. Her eyes are heavy. Her lips are soft. "Come on," I say. And then I repeat: "Let's go."

"Go where?" She's suddenly wary, like a cat ready to hide beneath a table.

"To bed. Before I have to carry you there."

She's so transparent, my little girl. She juts her chin. She gives a sidewise glance to the crotch of my jeans where, mercifully, my cock has decided to behave. She licks her lips, ready to say *something* designed to get a literal rise out of me.

I shake my head. "Be good."

And she must truly be exhausted, because she obeys.

But at three in the morning, I'm the one who wants to go another round. I pad into the jacks to piss, and I come back with another johnny. I'm hard enough to roll it on before I climb back into the warm space beside Fiona.

I spread my hand across her belly, and she wriggles close. I lean down and whisper in her ear, "You're gorgeous when you sleep."

She's barely half-awake, but her body reacts like a cat hearing a can-opener. I can't see her blush in the darkened room, but heat rises off her back in waves. I slip my hand under the waistband of the skimpy little shorts she's wearing as pajamas. "You feel so good, little girl."

Her eyes stay closed but she moans a little, and her hand reaches between her legs. Her fingers thread with mine, and we find her clit together.

"I'm so proud of you, for what you took this afternoon."

We circle around her clit, catching it between our fingers. We dip into her sweet pussy and spread honey across her throbbing pearl, again and again and again. And when she breaks, we cup her smooth mound, holding her steady, pulling her close.

I slip into her from behind, which is easy because she's soaked. She trembles when I sink home, and I don't know if she's coming a second time, or if it's still the first, drawn out long and slow.

All I know is she feels like silk beneath me. She smells like cloves and lemons. She sounds like she's laughing, soft and low, like we're sharing the best joke in the world.

And when I come, pulsing hard inside her, I know it will be a while before I get back to Philadelphia.

21

FIONA

Father Colin holds the chalice, waiting for me to sip the wine, but when I raise the silver rim to my lips, the liquid inside is blood. Frantic, I look at the priest, but his face is a mangled mass—eyes burst, nose shattered, jaw hanging from a thread.

My knees ache as I stand, and my ears are filled with the howling of wild dogs. They're snarling around me, cutting me off, driving me into a dark stone corner.

I'm bowled over by the stink of incense and the sulfur smell of snuffed out candles. Blood fills the chapel, soaking my plaid uniform skirt, rising until it covers my chin, until it covers my lips, until I'm drowning…

I wake up screaming.

For one solid week, I slept without nightmares. Seven precious nights of feeling safe and protected, of knowing no one could harm me.

Now, everything's back to the horror of *normal*. My throat

aches. My eyes are gritty. My head pounds like I'm coming off a one-week drunk.

Patrick is gone.

His pillow is cool to the touch. I don't hear him in the bathroom, or in the kitchen, or in the living room.

I hate the feeling of panic that surges through me. I shouldn't have called him Daddy. I shouldn't have dropped to my knees in the kitchen. I shouldn't have let him tie me to the bed.

"Patrick?" I call out, my voice shakier than I'll ever admit.

Silence.

"Patrick!" I try again, louder this time.

Nothing. Goddammit. He's gone.

Bunbun. That's all I had to say. He gave me a fucking safeword. If I'd used it, I wouldn't be trying to swallow this beach ball of shame.

Furious with myself, I rub my hand from my forehead to my chin, trying to scrub away memories of last night. I nearly retch when I smell my fingers. He held my hand while he fingerfucked me in the middle of the night. He whispered lies to me in the darkness, and I believed him, because my body isn't smart enough to understand facts my mind knows all too well.

He's a grown man dealing with his own ration of shit. I don't know why the Crew call him Cujo. I don't know why he left Boston. I don't know what the fuck he thought he was doing, bringing me back from Philadelphia, but I never should have let myself lean on him.

I'm so fucked up. I called him *Daddy.* I never wanted to fuck my father. That's disgusting. I just wanted a man to keep me safe. Someone to take care of me, after Madden fucked me over.

Jesus Christ. I shouldn't have let any man distract me, not for a minute. Not when it will take every ounce of concentration I have to get control over the Old Colony Crew.

Rónnad. She's supposed to deliver a hundred grand today, but she doesn't have the number for my bank account yet.

Goddammit! I should have just given her my own phone number. The only way she has to reach me is through Patrick's burner.

Fuck, fuck, fuck. I am so fucking stupid.

I throw back the covers. Going into the bathroom, I run water in the sink, letting it get so hot steam curls from the faucet. I wash my hands with five pumps of soap, dripping lather onto the counter. I'm brutal as I rub my fingers dry on a towel.

At least I don't smell like middle-of-the-night fucking anymore.

I don't realize how sore I am until I head to the kitchen. My shoulders ache like some giant tried to pull them from their sockets. My thighs protest every step I take down the hallway. The soles of my feet ache, like I spent all of yesterday wearing my highest heels.

He has a lot to answer for, Patrick Motherfucking Mor—

There's a note on the counter, pinned under a corner of the coffee maker.

Gone to get coffee.
Don't forget to send your account info.
P

His burner sits next to the empty bag of dark roast beans.

Patrick isn't gone.

My fingers shake as I dig in the bowl on the counter, shoving aside the menus, digging beneath the pens and notepads. At the very bottom is a fake leather wallet. I can't remember the last time I wrote a check, but the account numbers are printed there, like some ancient computer spit them out at the dawn of time.

Patrick isn't gone.

The burner phone doesn't have a password, so I go straight to the text screen. I find the message from Rónnad's phone.

Carefully, double-checking before I hit Send, I type in the numbers for my account.

Patrick isn't gone.

My knees are doing something tricky. I'm not sure I can stay on my feet. I need to sit down before I fall down.

Patrick isn't gone.

I hear footsteps on the stairs. A key in the lock. I look up, and he's framed in the doorway, his silvering hair scrambled like it's windy outside. He's carrying a grocery bag in one hand and a box of donuts in the other.

"You're awake," he says.

I nod.

"I picked up a few things," he says.

I nod again.

"Did you send the account number?"

I nod one more time and finally make myself speak: "No word back from her yet." My voice sounds like I've just inhaled an entire box of saltines.

My phone is in the bedroom, charging on the nightstand, which gives me a convenient excuse to escape Patrick's curious gaze. I take longer than I need to, retrieving my cell, and when I come back to the kitchen Patrick is almost through loading groceries into the fridge. There's cheddar cheese, the white kind that's so sharp my mouth waters when I look at the package. Perfectly round apples, their red peels speckled with gold. A bag of bright orange clementines, pushing against their red netting. He leaves a bag of Ghirardelli chocolate squares on the counter.

Blushing for no good reason, I sign into my bank account and tap the screen to check my balance. There's no change— just the couple of hundred dollars I expect to see.

I refresh the screen. Again. Again.

The balance changes.

"Holy shit," I say.

Patrick looks up from the ground coffee he's loading into the machine. "What?"

"She did it." I blink several times, as if that might make the numbers disappear. "She actually fucking did it."

One hundred thousand dollars. A pending deposit from an anonymous string of letters and numbers.

Patrick holds out his hand. Once I give him my phone, he drags his fingers across the glass, zooming out to make the numbers bigger. He shakes his head, like he doesn't really believe what he's seeing.

And then he reaches for his burner. He puts it on speaker and punches the screen to call Rónnad's number.

She answers on the first ring. "You got my gift?" Her Boston accent sounds fake, like she's an actor in some black-and-white movie, probably something Patrick would like.

"What the fuck're ya doin'?" he demands, his accent gone thick. "Where're ya gettin' th' dosh?"

She clicks her tongue, like a mother schooling a child. "I'm not working for you."

"Ya may not've put yer dirty money into my account, but yer answerin' t' me all the same."

"I made my promise to the girl."

"'N' I made *my* promises t' that same girl."

That's news to me. Sure, Patrick brought me to Boston. And he stayed by my side as I buried my da. But a promise?

I look at the box of donuts on the counter, next to the golden bag of chocolates. I think about the groceries he just put away—apples and cheese and clementines, like he lives here. Like he *belongs* here.

They say something, the food he's brought home. Just like the words he directs to his phone, his brogue thicker than ever. "Speak, ol' woman. Or I'll hunt ya down. I'll find ya in th' middle o' th' night. I'll drag ya t' my car, 'n' I'll take ya to a place where no one'll hear ya scream, 'n' I'll cut th' words outta ya, right b'fore I break yer fuckin' neck."

He delivers his threats in a low voice, with a deadly certainty that turns my veins to ice—a million times more terrifying than if he shouted. He won't act in passion. He won't be fast. He won't offer a shred of mercy.

He'll be an enforcer, striking a blow for his clan.

No. Not for his clan.

For me.

He's a savage, taking aim at a crazy old lady, and I can barely swallow because I'm so fucking turned on.

When Rónnad finally answers, her words flow fast. "I've got my boys stealing cars. I have customers overseas, in Dubai and Doha and Riyadh. Every month, they send me a shopping list, the cars they want. High end, some of them, Mercedes and Lexus and such. But other cars too, Toyotas and Hondas and Hyundais. My boys find the make. They find the color. They take the cars off the streets, most of them. Encourage the owners with a little...direct pressure, when necessary. I have contacts at the Boston port. And New York too. Philadelphia. Baltimore. There's almost no risk, after the containers are sealed."

"'N' what're ya takin' out o' th' middle?" Patrick asks.

"Five percent! That's all! Just five percent off the top. I pass on all the rest."

"Five percent." I can tell from his tone that he doesn't believe her.

He makes her go over all the details again. How many cars are on her *shopping list*. How many men are on her team. The ports, the containers, the bribes she's paid up and down the Eastern seaboard.

Whenever she balks, he reminds her of his threats. He never raises his voice. He merely makes promises with the crystal clarity of a man who never needs to lie.

I could duplicate her system if I had my own team. But I'm not in charge of the Old Colony Crew—yet. If I took this game to my father's men now, they might not do the work for me.

In fact, it makes no sense—Rónnad doing this for only five

percent. The number of cars she'll have to boost… The number of containers she'll have to commandeer…

Patrick sees that too, of course. "Why?" he finally demands. "Why take th' risk fer Fiona?"

"The sunglasses!" Rónnad says. "She gave me her sunglasses!"

He rattles something under his breath, words that end with *motherfucking sunglasses.*

But no matter how hard he presses, she won't give him any other explanation. The money is mine. No strings attached. It's a gift, from one woman to another. Like the sunglasses were, from me to her.

Patrick finally gives up and ends the call.

Rónnad is certain she can steal the cars. And I'm certain I need the funds. So I decide to continue working with her.

And just like that, a week goes by. Rónnad keeps her end of the bargain. Seven days after her first pay-out, I receive one million dollars.

I can't just let the money sit there forever. I withdraw fifty thousand dollars in crisp hundred-dollar bills, half-expecting the transaction to draw unwelcome attention from the feds. But no one at the bank blinks an eye. I stash the money in my safe in the closet, feeling like I'm paying Aunt S back for something.

The second million comes in even faster, only three days later. The third arrives two days after that.

And then Uncle Aran calls, demanding that I meet him at the *dún.*

22

PATRICK

F iona won't listen to feckin' reason.

I tell her not to meet with Dowd, that she has nothing to gain from answering his summons. She says she's not afraid of him, that she has to put him in his place before she becomes his Queen, and now's as good a time as any.

I tell her not to go to the *dún*, that she shouldn't meet on his territory. She says her father's name is on the city records, the *dún* has been Ingram property for more than one hundred years, and she'll be conceding something vital if she treats it like Dowd owns it now.

I tell her she still doesn't know that witch's game, that no one takes all the risk and pays out ninety-five percent of the take without having some ulterior motive. She says she's not an idiot, and that she appreciates my looking out for her, but there isn't an angle to this that she hasn't already considered.

And then she calls me Daddy.

I take her to bed, just as she intends me to do.

She's a good little girl. She comes when I praise her, three separate times, because I think that might be enough to change her feckin' mind about the trip to Dowd.

But then I'm pulling on clean clothes, a new shirt and trousers I bought to hang in her closet. My shoulder holster feels like a bridle. I pocket an extra magazine for my Glock.

And I drive her over to the feckin' *dún* because I'm not *actually* her da, and I'm not her boss, and there's nothing I can do if she's determined to risk her goddamn, gorgeous neck.

Dowd sees us in his office, which is another bullshit power play. As Clan Chief, he's had a private room in the *dún* for decades; it's the same one I stood in after Da died. It's the same huge desk, sized for a man who uses paper and pen in his daily work. It's the same executive chair, framing him like he's the villain in a movie made from a comic book. It's the same row of gilded plates on the wall, awards from the South Boston Eire Association, honoring him for his fine work over the years.

"Thank you for bringing Herself," Dowd says, with a civil tone that almost makes me forget he's a feckin' animal.

I nod, because the alternative is speaking to him, and I don't trust what I might say.

"You can wait in the kitchen," Dowd says, not bothering to look me in the eye.

That requires an answer. "I'm happy to stay here."

"I wasn't asking, Cujo."

There's a knife behind his words that only a fool would ignore. But the past three weeks have turned me into an eejit, because I turn to Fiona and say, "I'll stay."

Her eyes are bigger than the fancy gold plates behind her feckin' uncle. She swallows before she remembers to throw back her shoulders, before she raises her chin. She looks at a point somewhere north of my forehead when she says, "That's okay, Patrick. I'll swing by the kitchen when I'm through."

It hurts more than I expect. I've known from the moment I wrapped one of my kitchen towels around a bag of frozen peas that Fiona Ingram had her own agenda—first with Madden Kelly, then up here in Boston. She's determined to take over her father's empire. She knows that'll cost her, and she's prepared to pay.

Nevertheless it feels like pure shite, being part and parcel of the currency she's handing over.

I could call her bluff. Refuse to go. Keep her safe, at least until I'm cut down by the men Dowd surely has in earshot. The Crew knows I fight like a savage. Dowd must have taken that into account when he planned this goddamn summit.

Summit. Not exactly. A summit is a meeting of equals. And Fiona Ingram isn't an equal to her uncle. Not in this room. Not inside the *dún*. Not in the city she's called home for all her twenty-four years.

And if I disobey her now, I'll make her worth even less.

So, God help me, I leave her in that feckin' snake pit. I make my way to the kitchen, clearing my throat outside the door, so I don't take anyone by surprise.

And sure enough, Oona Maguire is sitting at the head of the scrubbed wooden table when I enter the room. She's in the middle of fixing Sunday roast; that's a leg of lamb in the roasting pan and a mountain of potatoes she's peeling for roasties.

"Have a seat, Paddy," she says, nodding to the chair next to her. "I've just put on the kettle. I thought you might want a cuppa."

It stings that she knew I'd be coming. Dowd must have put her on alert. Or she figured I'd be sent here, tail between my legs, the instant word spread that Fiona and I were inside the *dún*.

But I thank her, because the woman's never done a thing to hurt me in the past. She might be the only true ally Fiona has inside this house. "You'll have one too?"

Her smile is genuine as she heaves herself to her feet. I suspect there aren't a lot of men who talk to Oona here. She's invisible to the Crew, making meals happen, keeping the fridge well-stocked. But no one sees a woman working behind the scenes.

She brushes a gnarled hand against my shoulder on her way over to a cupboard. After fetching a second mug, she reaches for a brightly colored tin. It takes some effort for her to work the lid loose, but then she reveals a cache of homemade shortbread. She sets a dozen squares on a plate.

I fiddle with the sugar bowl in the center of the table. I shift the creamer. My fingers find the ring on my third finger, and I spin the titanium band, trying to beat back the brain squirrels.

I shouldn't have let Dowd call me Cujo without fighting back.

I shouldn't have left Fiona behind.

I shouldn't be sitting at this table like a feckin' child.

The electric kettle comes to a boil, its eerie blue light switching off. Oona takes the lid from a stoneware teapot. She pours in a bit of hot water and swirls it around to warm the pot. Tosses in a handful of dark leaves from a battered green tin. Fills the pot with water. Sets a strainer over the first mug and waits.

And it occurs to me, as I watch Oona Maguire's perfect efficiency, that she might have some useful information to share.

I wait a few minutes, until she's poured for both of us. The tea is black as tar, and I don't blame her for cutting hers with a dollop of heavy cream. I salute her with my mug, and when I take a sip, it tastes like close calls and late nights and the first time I ever bled for the Crew. I chase it with a bite of shortbread that crumbles over my tongue like crystallized butter.

"You still have a way with the baking, Oona."

"The only sweets Aran Dowd will eat," she says with pride, going back to peeling her potatoes. She doesn't have any way of knowing she's opened a door wide.

I march through before she can get suspicious. "Except for Dunkin'," I say.

"Aran won't touch those lumps of lard!" She sounds indignant.

I push a little harder. "I'm certain I saw him there, just the other day. On Beacon Street, near Back Bay."

Oona laughs. "Listen to you, pulling my leg. You know as well as I that if Aran got a sudden mad itch for store-bought shite, he wouldn't cross out of Southie to scratch it."

I laugh too, because I don't want her remembering we had this conversation. But when I raise my mug to my lips, I try to recall the face of the man who sat across from Dowd. The face that was familiar that day. The face that still lingers in my memory, just beyond my grasp.

I change the subject before Oona can think too much about Dowd straying. "Father Bertram's words were lovely at the funeral."

She makes a face. "Father Bertram's learned to recite a few good prayers."

"That cigar box you gave to Fiona. She was certainly pleased to get it."

For the first time since I've entered the kitchen, Oona looks at me with suspicion. "Herself's told you that, has she?"

"I could see, just from the expression on her face. And later, when she was going through her treasures…"

Oona shakes her head, her lips turned up in the faintest hint of a smile. "You'll not get me telling my Fiona's secrets that easily. If you want to know what's in the box, you'll have to ask her. Honestly, Paddy. Do you think I was born yesterday?"

She ruffles my hair before she carries my mug to the counter. Shortbread, strong tea, and now an old woman treating me like a kid. I'm surprised by the wash of warmth I feel.

As Oona tops off my mug with hot tea from the pot, she offers her own overly casual observation. "Fiona's not yet twenty-five years old."

I don't say anything, because every direction from here is dangerous.

"How long has it been since you left Boston?" Oona asks. She sets my mug on the table with enough force that a little tea splashes over the side. Rather than clean it up, she stares at me with watery blue eyes that don't blink.

That's a kinder question than she could have asked. She doesn't say, "How long has it been since your wife died?" Or, "How old would your son be if he'd been born alive?"

I'm willing to bet every cent I've earned in the last ten years that Oona knows the answer. My life shattered twenty-five years ago, and yes, Fiona Ingram is young enough to be my daughter, and no, I don't know what the fuck I'm going to do about that.

But I have to say something, so I start with, "If you're asking if my intentions are good—"

Before I can figure out how the hell to end that sentence, there's a clatter of shoes on the hardwood floor outside the kitchen. Oona looks up with a start. I've got my Glock out of its holster before I'm on both feet.

And Fiona crashes through the door like she's being chased by all the hounds in hell.

23

FIONA
Fifteen Minutes Earlier

I almost call out as Patrick closes the door to Uncle Aran's office. I want him to stay, to hear whatever my uncle has to tell me, but I know that relying on him will only make me look weak.

Weaker.

Because my uncle is gazing down at me with the sort of tolerant smile grownups use when they watch toddlers play. I feel like I'm pedaling a tricycle or standing over a wooden stove, serving up plastic fruits and vegetables.

"Fee," Uncle Aran says. "I'm so glad you could join me today."

"You didn't give me a choice. You said the future of the Crew depends on it." Disapproval flickers across his face. I'm only supposed to agree with him. But as long as I have his attention, I say, "And my name is Fiona."

I want him to respect me, but he only tilts his head and

presses his lips together, like he's biting back a tolerant smile. Goddamn it. I should have ignored the fucking nickname.

I try to wrestle back command. "What's going on? Why do you need me?"

He doesn't answer my question. Instead, he says, "We missed you at mass this morning."

I don't know who *we* is, but I remind him, "I haven't gone to mass since I was sixteen."

Aunt S and I used to skip church, staying here at the *dún* to help Oona with the Sunday roast. After my aunt died, I let my father believe I was with one boyfriend or another. And some Sundays I actually *was* fucking someone he wouldn't approve of, over at the Back Bay apartment.

"You'd be surprised by how much business a captain can get done at church," Uncle Aran says.

I bristle. *He* would be surprised by how much business a captain can get done in the ladies' room of a club. In the men's room, too, if she plays her cards right. And wears a skirt for easy access.

My voice is brittle. "I don't need lessons from you on how to run my clan."

"Apparently you do," he says, hotter than I expect. "Because *your clan* became quite the topic of conversation this morning, after mass. Chief Flanagan has all sorts of concerns about *your clan*."

Boston Chief of Police Daniel Flanagan keeps his distance from the Crew. He never let himself be seen with Da in public. He rarely sets foot in Southie at all, unless he's preening at a photo op to reassure *The Globe* that he has crime under control.

So Flanagan attending mass at St. Brigid's *is* a big deal—which Uncle Aran makes sure I understand: "Chief Flanagan is quite concerned about the increase in car thefts over the past couple of weeks. Twice the norm, he says. And moving higher."

"How unfortunate." I stifle a fake yawn.

"You think I haven't heard the same rumors? I keep men on

the street, girl. Eyes at the dock. And half of Boston heard you at your sainted father's wake. Ten million dollars to the Corman by June. You aren't fooling anyone, Fee."

"I've never stolen a car in my life!" I'm used to lying about my innocence. But I have to call Rónnad, as soon as I can get to Patrick's burner. She'll have to be more careful, slow down her thefts. There should still be plenty of time to hit my goal if—

"Cut the goddamn crap!" Uncle Aran shouts, slamming one fist on his desk.

Heart pounding, I study my fingernails. Gel polish really is an amazing thing. I got this manicure eight days ago, and there isn't a single chip.

"You're putting the Old Colony Crew at risk, girl," Uncle Aran says.

I meet his gaze, eyes blazing. "I'm doing all I can to save us."

"I covered your tracks this morning, paying off Flanagan. But the car thefts have to stop. Now."

I smooth the seam of my corset over my hip, taking care to emphasize the garment's boned lining. "That's not going to happen," I say, back to faking boredom. "Maybe in July. After the Corman Gala."

"I'm not asking, girlie. I'm telling." He steps out from behind his desk, like a school principal laying down the law.

I can't count the number of principals I've talked back to in my life, the number of times I was expelled for my smart mouth. So I feel like I'm belting out the refrain from an old familiar song when I say, "What have I *ever* said or done that could possibly make you think I care?"

His fingers curl into fists. "You will not win this game, Fee."

I'm fucking *over* that nickname. But I simply freeze my tone. "I'm not aware of any *game*."

He takes a step closer, using his height to make me look up. "The Old Colony Crew will never follow a girl."

"Woman." I settle my hands on my hips to emphasize my point.

Uncle Aran's face flushes dark. "This is a man's world."

"Go on telling yourself that. But when I present a ten million dollar check to the Corman Museum, everyone who is anyone in Boston will know my name. They'll recognize my power. They'll understand who gets things done in this town."

"They'll know a spoiled little brat is throwing one last temper tantrum, trying to get the attention of her father, who's dead and buried. By next year's Gala, the Ingram name will be completely forgotten in Boston."

My throat grows tight when he says *dead and buried*. But looking up at his overgrown white beard and his red-veined nose, I say, "The Ingram name will live forever."

His fingers clamp down on my arm, hard enough that I know he's leaving bruises. "Not after you become a Dowd."

"What?" I'm so shocked by his words that I can't keep the question from huffing past my lips. I immediately hate that I've given him that much. I despise that he's starting to smile.

He repeats himself, slowly and carefully, setting down each word like I've only learned the language this morning. "Not. After. You. Become. A. Dowd." And then, in case there's been any misunderstanding: "I'm putting a ring on your finger by the day the Grand Irish Union meets to name a general."

"You're my uncle!" I gasp, as if that's the most objectionable thing about his insane plan.

"By marriage." He harrumphs.

"Aunt Siobhan—"

"Would be grateful we've found such an elegant solution. A Dowd marries Ingram's brat, and the clan will be stronger than ever."

"You are out of your fucking mind!"

"Language," he says.

Patrick gets to tell me to watch my language—and only when we're in bed. There's not another man on earth who's earned that right. So I enunciate very carefully when I say, "Sure thing, motherfucker."

"Get it out of your system now. Because once you wear my wedding band, you'll stop talking like a sailor. Stop dressing like a slut, too. You'll be a good girl, a good wife, and once I get a baby into you, you'll be a good mother too."

Good girl.

My stomach twists so violently over those two words that I almost miss the rest of his threat. *Good girl* is another thing only Patrick is allowed.

My uncle's proposal is revolting. He's family. He destroyed my Aunt Siobhan. I know all about his affairs, about the diseases he brought home from his *cailíns*.

"You're a smart girl, Fee. This is how the Crew keeps its power."

"Over my dead body."

"Don't turn me into some villain out of a Bond movie. Don't make me say I can arrange that."

"You're disgusting!"

He's still holding my arm. And now, he uses his other hand to grasp my jaw. Squeezing hard, using his certainty and his weight, he forces me back against his desk.

I'm stunned, like a fish yanked out of water. My brain has stuttered to a stop. But I feel him force my head back. I know he's raising my face to his. His lips grind on mine, his teeth backing up his demand. As he settles his body against me, the dead weight of his erection pushes into my belly.

With a wordless cry, I bring my knee up, as hard as I can. I feel the breath whoosh out of him, and I shove him off my body.

My fingers scrabble on the door. The knob catches, and I think he's locked me in, but then it finally turns, and I gulp a breath of fresh air. I run blindly down the hall.

Tumbling into the kitchen, I fight off waves of nausea. I want to spit out the disgusting taste of my uncle. I want to rip off my clothes, everything he touched, everything he ruined.

"Fiona!" Patrick says, and it takes me a moment to realize he's holstering his gun.

I throw myself at him, desperate for his touch to scrub away Uncle Aran's. I try to disappear inside him, grabbing at his shoulders, at his back, at the hard, tight muscles of his ass.

"Hush," Patrick says. "I've got you." There's more, in Irish. He calls me *cailín beag*; I know that's *little girl*, and that's all right, that's what I want, what I need.

"Uncle Aran," I choke out. "He wants... He says... He..."

Patrick's palm brushes over the red marks my uncle left on my arm. I don't have to tell him. He understands exactly what my uncle wants. He looks toward the office, and his hand drifts back to the holster nestled under his arm.

Oona says, "You're in the *dún*, Paddy. Don't be a fool."

He looks like he wants to argue. Instead, he pulls me a little closer before he says to Oona, "I'm taking her out the back."

She twists her hands, but she nods.

"Come on," Patrick says to me. "Daddy's got you now."

Disapproval blooms on Oona's face, the same as eight years ago, when I told her what I did to Father Colin and the others. But she crosses to the steel door that leads outside, shooting all five bolts with fingers strong from kneading bread. Poking her head out, she looks left, then right like she's expecting company.

"Go on, then," she finally says, directing her words to Patrick. "Get her out of here."

His arm is heavy around my waist. I lean into his strength, letting him half-carry me down the three concrete steps. He hurries us down the brick walk to the street.

Before we duck out of sight, Oona calls out from the top step. "We haven't finished our conversation, Paddy Moran."

He waves a hand over his head, a signal that's equal parts acceptance and refusal.

"I'm sorry," I say, after he's helped me into the Land Rover and taken his own place behind the wheel.

He's checking the mirrors, calm, methodical, like another

man might tie his shoelaces. But I see the look he throws at the glove box. I wonder what weapons he has stashed in there.

"Hold on," he says, his attention snagged by something outside the car.

By reflex, I follow his gaze—just in time to see the two guards at the *dún's* front door assume tactical stances in the middle of the road, raising their guns with stiffened arms.

24

PATRICK

My fingers spread wide across the back of Fiona's head as I shove her to the floor of the car. "Stay down," I growl as she protests. Flooring the accelerator, I fight the gut-wrench of desperation as the engine shrieks before the wheels grip the road. The Bell clangs, loud and clear inside my head, urging me to wheel around and send those shitehawks running. Driving away from Southie gunmen is starting to feel far too familiar.

This time, no shots are fired.

I don't know if that's because Dowd calls them off, shouting orders through their high-end earpieces, or because they think better of starting a shooting war in the middle of Boston, or maybe it's the unmarked car I hurtle past at the end of the street.

The brain squirrels start justifying the space they take up inside my skull. I'm handling half a dozen things, and I'm ready to manage twenty more.

One hand hovers over Fiona, as if that will keep her safe

from danger. I'm steering clear of the curbs, grateful the Crew's ban on parking still applies to this street, glad I don't have to lose time sideswiping vehicles. I'm watching the eejits in my rear-view mirror, making sure they lower their arms, waiting for them to holster their weapons. I'm thinking of where I'll take Fiona, where she'll be safe, where we can be certain no one is following us, because the last thing I want is to draw Dowd's men to the Back Bay apartment. I'm watching a group of boys beside the streetlight, still dressed in their Sunday best, and if they're anything like I was at that age, they're lying about touching some girl's tit or getting a hand beneath her pants, but all I care about now is that they don't decide to dart across the street, don't decide now's the time to head home for Sunday roast. I'm watching Michelangelo Barbieri stare at me from behind the wheel of his Chevy Tahoe, a paper cup of coffee halfway to his mouth.

Mike Barbieri.

Fuck.

The brain squirrels pelt me with a shitload of memories, all of them bad. Twenty-five years ago, Barbieri was a kid fresh out of the FBI Academy. If there was a rulebook, he had it memorized. If there was a risk, he'd jump in arse-first.

He was the agent who turned my father. I first saw Barbieri at the back of a bar, buying Da rounds of Guinness that no man with cirrhosis should ever have touched, Irishman or no. I saw Barbieri in the power tools aisle at Lucky's Hardware, pretending to buy a nail gun as my father coughed up facts about Kieran Ingram. I saw him under an umbrella outside St. Brigid's after a priest told lies about Da's saved soul.

Barbieri must be forty pounds heavier than he was back then; his neck swells over his collar. He's lost most of the thick black hair he used to wear slicked back like a Wall Street banker. He's drinking Starbucks coffee, instead of Dunkin' like a proper Boston boy.

Courtesy of the brain squirrels, I clock all of that as the

Land Rover shoots across the intersection. It takes me another block to realize I've already seen him on this trip to Boston. He was Other Guy, sitting across from Dowd in the Back Bay Dunkin'.

The feds are surveilling the *dún*—not just Ingram's wake, but daily operations. They had enough leverage on Dowd to force him to a meeting outside of Southie. They're running him, same as they ran my da.

Fiona's swearing from the floor. I gather she's broken a motherfucking nail, and Dowd's a cocksucker if he thinks she'll give him the Crew just because he says he'll put a ring on her goddamn finger, and if he tries, she'll shove it up his jizz-stained arse.

She's creative, that one. Colorful, too. And I figure I better let her off the floor after my third stop at a traffic light, or she'll turn some of her rage on me.

The Bell's a constant jingle as Fiona settles back in her seat. I manage to sound neutral as I ask, "Dowd thinks he'll marry you?"

She lets loose with another stream of profanity, all adding up to the fact that Dowd says he'll drag her to the altar. As Fiona goes through a show of yanking her corset and twitching her trousers, I realize the steering wheel is cutting into my palms.

Aran Dowd has finally gone too far.

He's talking to the feds, the very thing that put my da in the *dún's* basement twenty-five years ago. Dowd didn't make my father turn traitor; I've always known that. I never tried to get revenge against the man—not for Da, not for Jenn or Athawn, and not for my poor mam.

But now? The gobshite's singing to the FBI. The clan must have its due. And I'll get my revenge too, because that fat fuck was stupid enough to go after my little girl.

All I have to do is prove Dowd's sold out to Barbieri.

For now, though, I need to figure out where to take Fiona—

someplace Dowd will never think to look. Somewhere she can relax and forget the shitehawk mauled her.

I don't know if Mary's Place is still standing. Jenn's been gone for two and a half decades, and she was always one of their best customers. But I'm already heading north and west of downtown, and if it's not still there, I'll find something else.

The neighborhood is a lot more built up. Entire blocks of old frame houses have been replaced by modern mansions. But just as I'm thinking I'll have to come up with Plan B, there's a change to the buildings. Houses give way to a run of small stores —baby clothes covered with dinosaurs, a bakery for dogs, another for humans with a sign in the window that says they have four dozen flavors of cupcakes.

And there, at the end of the next block, is Mary's Place. The little parking lot still stretches on the side, ten angled spaces. The front room is filled with the "curiosities" Jenn loved—antique coffee tins and silver serving spoons and mugs shaped like animals. The back room is an old-fashioned soda fountain— black-and-white tile, a counter lined with red-leather stools, and five matching booths.

At the counter, a harried mother asks for extra jimmies on her kid's double scoop of chocolate. Two teen-age boys are sampling every one of the thirteen flavors in the ice cream case. Everyone gapes as Fiona enters in front of me, staring at the leather laces barely keeping her corset from bursting open, at the trousers so tight I know she had to lie on the bed to zip them.

I lead Fiona to the last booth. She sits with her back to the door. I keep an eye on things, just in case.

"What is this place?" she asks.

I pluck the menu from the side of the display that shows all the songs on the jukebox. At first glance, it's the same list as the one Jenn ordered from twenty-five years ago. Ice cream, shakes, and malts on the front. Boozy versions of the same on the back.

But things have changed. The prices are ten times what they used to be. And the jukebox takes credit cards, one dollar a play.

"Figure out what you want," I tell her. "I'll order at the counter."

She doesn't want to give in that easy. "You've been here before?"

I give her a look. There's no way in hell I just happened to drive to this old-fashioned little storefront by accident, on this quiet street, in this particular suburb. "What do you want?" I ask, pushing the menu toward her again.

She barely glances at the laminated page. "A Millionaire Malt," she says.

My girl has good taste. It's twice the price of anything else on the menu, made with eighteen-year-old Glenfiddich.

I wait until the counter's clear before I place our order. One Millionaire for Fiona. A bowl of vanilla ice cream for me.

Back at the table, I make a show of choosing music. The options are old— even for me—big band and barbershop and crooners my gran used to love. I punch in codes for a Rat Pack serenade—Dean Martin's "The Lady is a Tramp," Frank singing "You're Nobody till Somebody Loves You," Sammy Davis Jr. going after "I've Got You Under My Skin."

The old man who brings us our ice cream looks like he's been here for fifty years. His face is a perfect mask as he serves Fiona's malt. He leaves her the metal mixing cup and a long spoon, along with a whipped-cream-capped glass.

Fiona laughs at my bowl of ice cream. "Vanilla?" she asks.

"It's a flavor," I say defensively.

"Not one I ever thought *you'd* be interested in." *Daddy.* She starts to say it. I see her tongue curl behind her upper teeth. But something makes her think better of yanking my chain in public.

Maybe she's remembering the look on Oona's face. Maybe she's thinking about Dowd.

Her fingers go to the red marks on her arm, the ones already turning to bruises.

She's definitely thinking about Dowd.

My own fingers curl into fists by my thighs.

But she takes a sip of her malt, drawing on a straw that's as big as my little finger. The hollows of her cheeks tug something inside me, something that turns to melted beeswax as she registers the taste. "This is amazing," she says.

I nod, because I knew she'd like it.

She takes another long draw. And then, casually, like she's commenting on the music: "I'm going to kill him."

Not if I get there first. But I humor her. "That'll cost you, in the long run."

Defiance turns her jaw to stone. "I've done it before. Four times."

I keep my gaze steady. "More like seven, from what I've heard."

She sucks on the straw, like she doesn't care. But sometime in the past three weeks, I've learned to read the expressions on her face. She's embarrassed. Angry. Determined as fuck.

"Who were they?" I ask, when she's swallowed enough whiskey and cream to soften the blow.

"It doesn't matter."

"It does," I argue. "Because killing your own uncle will haunt you like those three you don't want to count. The ones you forget to mention when you tell men how tough you are. The ones you want to erase."

She pours from the silver cup into her glass, concentrating like it's brain surgery. She applies the same careful attention to her lipstick-stained straw, placing it in the bottom of the glass like it's a fuse on a nuclear bomb before she matches the print of her lips.

When she's finished, not getting close to answering my question, she sits back on her side of the booth. "I'd like another one of those," she says.

I think about telling her to slow down, but she's the one who got pawed back at the *dún*. And she's the one fighting, body and soul, to keep from telling me about her past. If she's not afraid of an ice cream headache, then she can do as she wants.

I play my role all over again, going to the counter and ordering her drink. I choose more music—"You Make Me Feel So Young," "Bewitched, Bothered and Bewildered," and "The Things We Did Last Summer."

She's halfway through her second Millionaire before she starts to talk. She looks at the glass instead of at me. She traces a pool of condensation on the table, running her fingertip in circles.

"Some men need to die."

I nod, because that's obviously true.

"But da said *a good King chooses his battles*."

I wait, because that's another truth. And finally she goes on: "There were two of them. But Da said it must have been my fault. I picked a fight. Went irregular with my uniform. Whatever—I started it, Da said, and he'd have nothing to do with ending it."

I still don't know what *it* is, but I'm pretty sure I can take a guess.

"I made things look like a robbery," she says. "And I gave the money to St. Vincent-de-Paul's."

"Good thinking, that."

"I wasn't keeping blood money."

She's half-drunk by now. Her words are slippery in a way that might mean her mouth is cold from the ice cream. But I'm willing to bet it's the four shots of Glenfiddich that have softened her lips, especially after her adrenaline-fueled flight from Dowd's office. She stares at me defiantly, like she thinks I'll say she was wrong to give to charity.

Instead, I say, "I'm sorry."

She focuses on transferring the last of her second malted from the silver cup to her glass.

"Your father should have protected you," I say.

Her straw makes a slurping sound as she polishes off the dregs.

"Your da should've been the one to get revenge."

She shrugs, like she doesn't care. But she pushes her glass toward me. "One more?"

I don't know where she'll put it, but I know she can eat me under the table with pizza, so I shouldn't be surprised. Once I'm up at the counter, I think about ordering some food, French fries or a burger, something to soak up some of the booze.

But Fiona doesn't want food. She wants another malted. That's what she *needs*, and the only reason I'm in Boston is to help her, to protect her, so another Millionaire Malt it is.

This time, she's drinking to get drunk. She doesn't bother with a straw. That's a shame, because the shape of her lips closing around that bit of plastic is a feckin' work of art.

Then again, when she drinks from her glass, she ends up with a healthy dose of cream on her upper lip. I think about wiping it off with a napkin. I want to taste it with the tip of my tongue. But I settle for watching her swallow.

"Mmm. Like mother's milk." She fakes an Irish accent. Or maybe that's supposed to be Scottish. I can't tell.

"Your mam fed you Scotch by the glassful?"

"My mother died the day I was born."

Somewhere in the back of my brain, beneath the leaf litter left by all the squirrels, I knew Kieran Ingram's wife died giving birth to his only child. "I'm sorry," I say, which is part a condolence on her loss and part an apology for forgetting it.

She shrugs. "Can't miss what I never had." She peers at me over the rim of her glass. I'm not sure what she sees, but it makes her want to talk. "What about you?" she says.

"What *about* me?"

"Were you close to your mother?"

I don't know how to answer the question. My mother moved to

Boston when she was twenty-five years old, after a fire burned down her house in Providence, Rhode Island. She caught Da's eye her first morning, walking down a street in Southie. Tommy Moran marched her to the altar, she had me, and she never looked back.

Mam knew all my favorite foods, and she made them on my birthday. She spent hours poring over doctor's reports and fighting with my schools to get me even a fraction of the help I needed. She did her best to hide my father's violent world until it became clear I was walking in his footsteps, as close as I could follow.

After Da died, and Jenn and Athawn too, Mam took a header off the Longfellow Bridge, the night before her forty-sixth birthday.

Christ. I'm older than Mam ever was.

Fiona's not too drunk to see she's touched a nerve. She makes a show of finishing off the drink that's in her glass then, with the careful precision of a driver at a sobriety checkpoint, works the metal-cup transfer one last time. She gives a sly glance to my long-empty bowl of vanilla ice cream and makes a show of licking her lips. "Want a taste, Daddy?"

I *want* to pull her onto the table between us. I *want* to shove a hand down that corset. I *want* to squeeze a hand into those trousers, to see if she's as wet as I think she is.

I think about telling her she's a marvel. She's smart and she's strong and she's gorgeous, and I'm lucky to be the man she's taunting.

But as intriguing as the game would be—can I get her off without actually laying a finger on her?—I won't take advantage of her when she's drunk.

So I shake my head. I load up one last round of songs on the jukebox—"Hit the Road to Dreamland," and "Let Me Go Lover," and "Fools Rush In." I tell her to drink up.

By the time I get her to the Back Bay apartment, she's unsteady on her feet, like Bambi on an ice-covered pond. Four flights of stairs are a lot longer when I'm half-carrying a girl who's trying to get her hand past my zipper.

Once I work the lock on the squeaky front door, she's a lot more docile. Back in the bedroom, she stares at my fingers as I strip the laces on her corset. She raises her arms when I ask, and she lets me slip off the boned leather. She sits on the edge of the bed and gives me one foot and then the other, watching as I toss her shoes into the closet. The trousers are a bit more of a struggle, but I finally get her under the sheet, and under the blanket too, resting her head on her pillow.

"Go to sleep, little girl."

"I'm not tired," she says, slurring like a professional drunk. But before she can argue further, she yawns. "Keep me company?" she asks.

I want to. I want to peel off my clothes and climb under the covers and rail her till we're both blind, until Dowd's threat seems like an idiotic joke and not a legitimate bid to steal the Crew out from under her.

But more than that, I want to protect Fiona. I want to keep her safe. I want to be closer to her than I've ever been before. So I lean over and brush a kiss on her forehead. "You need your rest. We'll have a full day tomorrow."

"What's tomorrow?" Her held tilts. I'm pretty sure she's shooting for *rebellious*, but she miscalculates badly and lands on *sweet*.

"We're going to the doctor."

"I don't like doctors."

"No one likes doctors."

"Why do we have to go? I'm not sick."

I stroke her hair off her forehead. "That's exactly what we'll check for. Make sure neither of us can pass anything to the other. Because I won't be satisfied with johnnies for much longer."

"You don't need to wear one. I'll be fine."

I head to the jacks, but I'm not going after a string of foil squares. Instead, I shake some Advil out of a bottle. I fill a glass of water. By the time I bring her both, she's fallen asleep, lying on her back, arms and legs spread like she's trying to fill as much of the bed as possible.

I leave the tablets on the nightstand, and then I head out to the living room with my phone. First, I need to see if Jenn's doctor is still in practice. I remember the woman's name, and I can picture the medical building we visited for sonograms.

After, I'll find out what Mike Barbieri's been up to for the last twenty-five years.

And then I'll try to figure out what leverage the feds have on Aran Dowd.

25

FIONA

Fuck Madden Kelly. And fuck the fucking chlamydia he gave me as a fucking going-away gift.

It had to be him. I've never let anyone else go bareback.

Doctor Prescott is matter-of-fact. Three million people a year get infected. It's easily cured with a week of antibiotics. I should keep taking my birth control pills. Contact all my partners from the last six months. Test again in three months. Have my partner wear a condom for the next week.

There's no partner for the next week.

At first, I tell Patrick I'm hung-over after he fed me all those milkshakes. I go to bed, and he goes out for a run. He's started doing that every afternoon, leaving the apartment for a couple of hours. When he gets home, he watches something in the living room, keeping the TV so low I can barely hear it.

Next, I say the meds make me sick to my stomach. He makes me plain rice, which would be wonderful if I really felt like I was going to puke, but instead it just makes me feel more sorry for myself. The next day, when I tell him I'm still sick, he goes out to the store and buys fresh bread for toast, along with applesauce and bananas. I eat everything he fixes for me, but I'm starving by bedtime. I don't dare tell him I'm lying.

Then, I pretend to have a migraine. He leaves me in the cool bedroom with the shades pulled, and he brings me fresh water and painkillers every four hours. Sometimes I swallow the pills. Sometimes I palm them and flush them down the toilet.

Patrick's taking antibiotics too, even though he wore a rubber. The doctor said it was a good precaution. If he's feeling any ill effects from his own meds, he doesn't say a word.

Each night, he sleeps with me in the big bed, but that's all we do—sleep. I'm grateful for his arm around me. It weighs me down, anchoring me to the mattress, keeping me from floating off into my usual nightmares.

I feel so stupid for getting this disease. I feel dirty, no matter how many times I take a shower. I feel ashamed, especially because I might have made Patrick sick too.

We finish our packs of baby-blue capsules at the same time. Patrick goes out on a run and comes back with a bouquet of white daisies. I put them in water and head back to the bedroom for a nap.

When I wake, I take yet another shower. I go to my closet, but the leather and lace make me want to puke. I tug open my dresser drawers, but the options there aren't any better.

Instead, I sneak open the drawer Patrick is using. I find one of his T-shirts and a pair of his boxer-briefs. I remember that I still have his hoodie and his sweatpants hanging in the closet, the ones I wore when we left Philadelphia.

I wear them for three days straight, only taking them off to shower, every morning and every night.

When I come out of the bathroom on Wednesday morning, my body is wrapped in a towel. My hair, too. His clothes, the ones I've been wearing, aren't on the bed where I left them.

Patrick leans against the closed bedroom door, his arms

crossed over his chest. He's wearing jeans and a black T-shirt that's a twin to the one I've had on. His feet are bare on the hardwood floor.

My heart starts to jackrabbit, but I tell myself I'll be fine. I'll just get a different T-shirt. I cross to the dresser and open the drawer where he keeps his clothes.

"Don't touch my feckin' things." His voice is mild, like he's commenting on the weather. *They say it might rain today. It's hot for this time of year.*

"I'll wash them with my laundry," I say. The cool khaki of a T-shirt and the clean white cotton of his shorts vibrate against my fingertips.

"Put those down, or there'll be consequences."

I snort a little, because the type of game he's talking about seems ridiculous now. Turning my back to him, I pull the boxer briefs on under my towel. Once my ass is covered, I feel more comfortable baring my back so I can pull on his T-shirt.

I've dropped my towel, and I'm about to pull his shirt over my head when his arms close around me from behind. His fingers circle my wrists. "You're not very good at following rules, little girl," he growls by my ear.

I don't fight him. I don't want him thinking this is a game. "I'm not your little girl," I say.

He kicks my towel out of the way. When he pulls me closer against his body, his abs flex against my back. His forearms tighten around my ribs, pulling my hands up to my chest. The storm clouds that surround his lighthouse tattoo look like they're leaking from the side of my breast.

"Let me go," I say.

He lowers his lips to my neck, to the pulse point beneath my jaw. I squirm to escape his kiss, twisting around to face him. The clean T-shirt I'm trying to put on is crumpled in my fist.

"Stop it," I say, but he only pulls me closer. "Dammit, Patrick! Leave me alone!"

I push at his shoulders, and he lets me go. I take two steps back, until the mattress hits behind my knees. I try to cover my chest with his shirt.

He asks, "What's going on, little girl?"

"What's going on?" I laugh a little as I repeat his question. He's not going to leave until he makes me say it out loud, so I might as well choke out the words and get him to leave me alone. "I'm gross. That's what's going on."

I don't like the look on his face, the softness, the kindness. It scrapes something slimy that pools beneath my lungs. I've made a mistake these past few days, hiding inside soft clothes. Right now, I'd give anything to be laced into my sexiest corset, to be poured into one of my vinyl dresses. I need the armor. I need the defense.

It's too late to build a wall with clothing, so I try for the next best thing: words. "The pussy you said was the prettiest you've ever seen? It's disgusting. *I'm* disgusting."

"That's enough," he says, and I didn't realize I was shouting until I hear how quiet he is.

I try to retreat when he closes the distance between us, but there's no place left to go. I flinch when his palm cups my face, when his fingers frame my cheekbone. I try to turn my head away, but he won't let me.

"You got sick," he says. "And you did the responsible thing. You went to the doctor, and now you're cured. You're not disgusting. You just had sex with someone who'd had sex with someone else."

"Fucking Madden Kelly," I say, filling the words with ten days of venom.

"Language, little girl," Patrick says.

It's a warning. He's told me he doesn't want me swearing in bed. It's a test, too, because we're not in bed yet, and he wants to know if I'll take the gift he's giving me. And it's a promise, because if I accept, he's going to fuck me. And this time, there won't be any sleeve of latex between us.

I lick my lips. I close my eyes. I feel him waiting, waiting, waiting. And finally, I force myself to say, "I'm sorry, Daddy."

He shifts his hand to the towel that covers my hair and gently, gently, he works the terrycloth loose. Wrapping his fingers in my damp hair, he pulls me close for a kiss.

This time, I go. I let his mouth heat against mine. I let him tilt my head to a better angle. I let his tongue force open my lips.

My knees start to buckle, and he follows me down to the bed. He lets me pull his T-shirt over his head, lets me toss it onto the floor. But when I go for the zipper on his jeans, he pushes my hands away.

His denim-clad leg presses between mine, and my knees drop to either side. He tightens one hand on my hair and slips the other inside the fly of the boxer briefs I wear.

I stiffen as he strokes my folds. "Don't do that, little girl," he says, and he slips one finger inside me. "Don't do that to me." He pushes deeper inside me. "Don't do that to yourself." He curls his finger and does something devastating.

In just a few ragged breaths, I'm stretching and I'm melting and I'm balanced on the edge of a cliff. Even if I wanted to shut him out, I couldn't. Not when he makes me feel like this.

"More, Daddy," I whisper. "Please give me more."

He adds a second finger. At the same time, he tightens his grip on my hair. Now when he strokes me, my clit begins to sing.

My brain believes what he's told me, that it's not my fault, that I got sick and I got clean, and everything's all right. But my body doesn't have the message yet. It needs punishment. It needs to be redeemed.

"Harder, Daddy," I gasp.

My damp hair squeaks beneath his fist. Inside the boxer briefs, his hand moves faster. His strokes are longer. I shift my hips to catch the heel of his hand against my clit.

I bite my lip. I point my toes. I'm close, so close, almost, almost there.

"Please, Daddy," I moan. "Please, please, please…"

He releases my hair, and I cry out because that's not what I want. That's not what I need. I thought he knew me better than I knew myself, and I'm devastated to learn that I'm wrong.

But then he asks, "Is this what you want, little girl?"

His left hand, the one that was pulling my hair, closes around my throat. His thumb digs in beneath one ear. His fingers tighten on the other side, and the heel of his hand lowers against my voice box. Slowly and steadily, he starts to squeeze.

My knees slam closed. My heart somersaults against my sternum. My lungs burn like acid, even though it's too soon for them to starve, too soon for me to suffocate.

Every cell in my body is dipped in gasoline, and I can't run, can't fight. All I can do is freeze.

But no. That's wrong. There's one more thing I can do, one last way to save myself. Patrick told me, the first time we fucked on this bed.

"Bunbun!" I gasp, praying to all the saints I don't believe in that what he said was true.

26

PATRICK

I jerk back as if Fiona's landed a Taser lead on my bollocks.

The squirrels inside my head start clamoring like wild-fire's broken out in the forest. My cock presses against my zipper with a fury that's already shifting into ache. The hand I used to choke her curls into a fist like it wants to disappear up my arm, and the one that was inside her hovers over her body, wanting to touch, wanting to soothe, wanting to make it all better, even though I don't have a fucking clue how I'm going to do that.

I shift my weight so I'm no longer straddling her body. I say her name, so she knows I'm not going anywhere. "You're fine, Fiona," I tell her, even though I don't know if it's true. "You're a good girl. You're my good girl. You're fine."

It takes her a minute or more to come back from wherever she went. When she does, her face flushes crimson. She throws an arm over her eyes and says, "I'm sorry."

"You don't need to be sorry."

She lowers her arm to her side, but she doesn't open her eyes. "I feel so stupid."

"For stopping me? For keeping yourself safe? For doing exactly what I told you to do when things get out of control?"

She looks at me, her expression flat. "I'm so fucked up."

The savage inside me wants to remind her she's not allowed to swear in my bed. The human says, "You're not." And when she just shakes her head, I ask, "Do you want to tell me about it?"

Defiance sets her chin. "No."

That's not the answer I want, but it's the choice I gave her. I sit back, taking care to keep my hands in full view. "That's your right."

She glares at me, as if I've told her she'll be my prisoner until she dumps her bleeding heart at my feet. I shrug, because I can't give what she doesn't want to take.

Well, fuck. At least she isn't flogging herself over the doctor's visit any longer.

Most of the time when I'm with Fiona, I forget she's barely half my age. She's smarter and more driven and she's seen more of the world than most other women I've met.

But her embarrassment about the clam makes me remember how young she is. How vulnerable. There are things she's never faced before, things she's never done—like accepting the fact that her body isn't perfect. It can fail her. She can get hurt. She can get sick.

I hate the fact that it was easier for her to accept Madden Kelly beating her bloody than it's been for her to face the rest of what he did. But I know how fast she heals.

All I have to do is give her time.

I push myself to the far side of the bed and come to my feet. "Put on some clothes," I say. I want to order her to raid her own feckin' closet, to leave my things alone. But I figure it'll take another few days to get us past this setback. "I'll make us breakfast."

I'm almost out the door before she says anything, and when she speaks, it's nearly too soft for me to hear. "Don't go."

I freeze, my hands braced on the doorjamb. When I catch my breath, I can smell her on my fingers.

"Please," she says. "Can we try again?"

I turn slowly.

She's sitting on the edge of the bed, one knee up so she can face me. Her hair is still damp, standing out like she's rubbed it against a balloon. My shorts were already too big on her, and now they're twisted, the fly stretching open to show her hip. Her tits are bare.

"Is that really what you want?" I force myself to ask.

She nods. "Yes, please." And she cements it: "Daddy."

She stands as I cross back to the bed. This time, when she goes for the button on my jeans, I let her. Her fingers shake, just a little, but she gets the zipper down without much fuss.

Holding my gaze like we're having a silent conversation, she reaches inside my fly. I expect her fingers to be cool when she closes them around my cock, but I'm wrong. Her hand is hot. Ready. She finds the slick of precum left over from before, and she works it around my head with her thumb.

I groan as a shudder rises from my bollocks to the base of my skull. She smiles at that, the corners of her mouth turning up in a wicked little grin. "Does that feel good, Daddy?"

"It feels amazing, little girl."

I let her pull my jeans over my hips, along with my boxer briefs. Her eyes flash wide as she remembers the size of me.

"You're wearing too many clothes, little girl," I say. She stands in front of me obediently, letting me slip my hands beneath the elastic around her waist. She shivers as I palm her arse.

I kneel as I slide the boxer briefs down her legs. With my shoulders, I force her back to sitting on the edge of the bed. I slip one hand under her leg, easing her knees apart. She shivers and her hands curl into fists by her sides.

I know this is hard for her. I know she's embarrassed, that she somehow thinks the gorgeous flower of her pussy is permanently stained. I can't think of any way to prove how wrong she is, other than drinking as deep as I can.

"Patrick!" she gasps as I bury my face. I pause then, because my body has already memorized our code. My name isn't the same as a safeword. It's not an absolute command.

But it's not *Daddy*, either. I need to give her time to remember I'm not like the others. I'm the one man in the world she never needs to fear. When she's with me, she can be the woman's she's always meant to be.

After forever, she moves. She flexes her knees. She tilts her hips so her cunt opens beneath my lips.

"Good girl," I whisper, just before I fuck her with my tongue.

She comes on my mouth, chanting to God and finally calling me Daddy again. She's still pulsing when I slip my thumb into her. I pump my fist against her slowly, steadily, all the while telling her she's beautiful, she's precious, she's mine.

She whines as she breaks the second time, and her hands scramble to find my hair. She tugs, just a little, whimpering, "Please, Daddy." And when I don't rise from my knees: "Haven't I been a good girl?"

I can't resist her. I don't think I'll ever be able to resist her again. I pull her with me as I climb onto the bed. I want this first time, bare flesh to bare flesh, to last for hours. As I rest the tip of my naked cock against her soaked, trembling folds, I set my thumb against her mouth.

She hesitates. She still doesn't believe me. She can't accept she's clean.

"Go on, little girl," I urge her. "Have a taste."

I won't look away. I won't let her escape that easily.

And I see the moment she decides to trust me. Her lips open. She sucks my thumb inside.

"Good girl," I tell her, as she tastes her own honey. She

closes her eyes, but she pulls hard with her lips. She circles my thumb with her tongue.

I forget whatever stupid ideas I had about taking it slow, about staying controlled, about making this first time last. She's too slick, and I'm too hard. She shifts her arse, letting me sink even deeper into the heat between her thighs.

"You're the best girl," I tell her. "You're everything I've ever wanted. Sweet Jesus, little girl..."

She's a miracle, because she's already coming again. And feeling her break around me, knowing she was afraid but I'm the one who gave her courage, that I'm the one who made her feel safe, who gave her the strength to trust me again...

There aren't words for how it feels to come inside her, without a johnny between us. All I can say with that first miraculous pulse is, "You're mine, little girl." And then, each time I seize inside her: "Mine. Mine. Mine."

And when she whispers, "Thank you, Daddy," my heart is as full as my body is empty.

We sprawl across the bed, sweaty and sticky and naked. My breathing slows before hers does. I keep one possessive hand on her hip.

Which is why I feel her body move before I hear it—the echoing gurgle of an empty belly. She tenses for just a moment, and then she laughs. "Oh my God," she says. "I'm starving!"

I want to keep her locked in the bedroom for a while longer. See how many times I can make her come in a single hour. Shower with her and watch soap sleek over the waxed V between her thighs. Lace her into one of those leather things until her tits push up like a buffet.

But she's my little girl. I'm her Daddy. I'm responsible for her.

So I haul my arse out of bed and make her the sort of breakfast she deserves.

27

FIONA

There's a problem with having a rogue witch send you ten million dollars over the course of six weeks: You need to manage ten million dollars.

The first account number I gave Rónnad was for a checking account. I realized my mistake after the first day. I set up an offshore savings account, something invisible to the US authorities. Tax sheltered. Secure.

But getting money from that account into a form I can give to the Corman museum turns out to be a lot trickier.

The Irish mob used to be expert at laundering money. We had cash-based businesses, everything from laundromats to casinos. Legitimate customers handed over their money. We inflated the numbers with our dirty wealth, depositing fresh, clean funds into lawful accounts. Everyone went home happy at the end of the day.

But the world runs on credit cards now. And even gambling

—traditionally the Old Colony Crew's greatest cash cow—now thrives on the Internet.

I spend days trying to come up with a solution. I have some decent ideas for cash-based businesses. Nail salons. Strip clubs. Food trucks, farmers markets, and good old-fashioned barber shops.

But none of them makes ten million bucks in a couple of months.

I finally give up and do what I should have done in the first place. I call Quentin O'Roark.

I have his number in my contacts, same as I have Uncle Aran and Keenan Rivers, all the men who ran my father's empire. I use a burner, so I know he won't pick up, but I trust he'll recognize my voice when I leave a message: "Q. Meet me at three, tomorrow afternoon. Main Reading Room of the Boston Public Library."

I figure Uncle Aran will be allergic to the place; there is absolutely no chance he'll show up to force his claim on me. But the next day, as I'm getting ready to leave the apartment, Patrick insists on coming along.

"No one will try anything in a place that public," I say.

"You aren't stopping me," he says. "So why don't we just skip over the arguing stage?"

I roll my eyes. But I'm secretly glad to know I'll have him by my side. "Fine," I say. "Be an overprotective old man."

"Spoken like the brat you are."

I stick out my tongue. Patrick says, "Don't write checks you aren't willing to cash."

"What does that even mean? I guess if I was old, like you, I'd know about writing checks. Want some help setting up payment options on your phone?"

"Careful, little girl."

"Or what? You'll send me to bed without any supper?"

"I'll do *something* with you in bed."

Before I can think of another smart-ass comment, he scoops

me up, folding me over his shoulder. Pounding on his back, I try to kick my way free, but he tosses me on the bed like I'm a rag doll.

An hour later, I remember how to speak. "What the fuck was that?" I ask, resting my cheek on his shoulder.

His laugh rumbles through my body. "Just a little trick from the Old Man's Manual."

"Jesus," I gasp, almost catching my breath. "You could be a menace."

He steals a quick kiss. "Let's get to the library, *Scáthach*."

"Are you ever going to tell me what that means?"

"Are you ever going to show me what's in the cigar box?"

Ignoring him, I cross to the closet, surprised and grateful that I'm steady on my feet. I don't want anyone paying attention to the conversation Q and I will have so for once, I dress like a nun. If a nun wore blue jeans. And a Boston Red Sox T-shirt. And beat-up old Nikes that look like they've been through a washing machine a hundred times.

Patrick and I get to the library half an hour early. He sits next to me in the reading room, both of us on the same side of one long wooden table, facing a green-shaded lamp. He fiddles with the titanium ring on his middle finger. I watch the door, fighting the urge to stand every time a new person walks into the room.

Libraries aren't the sort of silent temples they used to be ages ago, when Patrick was a kid. One librarian is talking to a patron two tables over, using a normal speaking voice. Two women are looking at some sort of catalog, debating whether or not to make a purchase. A man speaks into his cell phone, checking on the status of a court filing.

I'm confident Q and I can meet safely here. We just have to watch what we say.

Three o'clock comes and goes. 3:15, and I take out my phone, in case I missed Q's call. 3:30, and I fight the urge to phone him.

At 3:42, Q finally rushes into the room. He collapses into a seat across from us, slipping two fingers into the collar of his dress shirt and pulling like he can't get enough air. His hair is damp and sweat beads on his upper lip. I catch an acrid whiff rising off him, the gritty stench of a rained-out campfire.

"You were supposed to be here at three," I say. Once I'm his captain, he'll obey my commands to the letter.

"I thought I was being followed." Q half-turns to the door. Patrick leans across the table, as if he's prepared to use Quentin O'Roark as a human shield. When Q turns back to me, he gives a visible start.

"I need your help," I say, once Q gets over his surprise. "I need a washing machine that works. The ones I'm looking at don't have enough power."

Q's quick nod proves he understands we're talking about money laundering. But then he asks, "Why aren't you watering the tree?"

I glance at Patrick, but he only shrugs. So I ask Q, "What the fuck does that mean?"

"The Christmas tree."

I take a closer look at him. He's nervous. And he's out of breath. But he doesn't *look* like anyone hit him on the head.

"You don't know," Q finally realizes. He takes a small spiral notebook out of his breast pocket, the kind that's bound across the top with a battered wire. He produces a pen, too, and slips off its well-chewed cap. Flipping past several pages covered in tiny, precise writing, Q finally draws a circle on a blank sheet. Inside, he writes the letters *KI*.

He looks at me, and I nod. That symbol represents my father.

Below that circle, he draws three more. One gets labeled FI—that must be me. Another gets labeled KI, LLC—a corporation owned by my father. The third is "my" corporation, FI, LLC.

When I nod again, Q goes to town, with more drawing and

labeling. These get combination names: KI and FI; KI and KI, LLC; KI and FI, LLC. The corporations share circles. The combined entities share circles.

By the time Q gets to the bottom of the page, there are two dozen labeled blobs, arranged in tiers, like a Christmas tree. He looks up at me and says, "And so on."

I nod one more time.

"Tend any branch, and water overflows to the rest of the tree. Siphon off however much you need."

Tend—make small enough deposits that I fly under the radar. Siphon—collect payments for something important, like donating to the Corman Gala.

I ask, "Where can I get details on the branches?"

Q frowns. "Aran has all that."

My uncle's name curdles something in my stomach. I press: "But you do too, right?"

He doesn't want to admit it. But Patrick's getting restless, putting his hands on the table again, so Q finally says, "Yes."

I tap the drawing. "My name is on those documents?"

He delays even longer this time, looking across the reading room as if the rows of tables and their green, glowing lamps are the most fascinating things he's ever seen in his life.

"Quentin?" I ask, testing a tone of command I heard my father use more times than I can remember.

He squirms visibly, shifting on his chair as if the wooden seat has kindled beneath him. "Yes," he finally says. "Your name is on the documents."

"I want the details now."

"I'll get them to you."

"No. Now." I'm getting the hang of this tone. All I have to do is think of every man who ever thought he could tell me what to do because I was shorter than he was, because because I weighed less, because I didn't have a cock between my thighs. "You aren't leaving this library until I get them."

Q puffs out a tiny gasp of despair. "I don't have them *memorized*. I need a computer."

I glance at the sign by the reading room door. "Like the public access ones? On the second floor?"

Q's face twists with intense disgust, as if I've suggested pegging him on the table between us. I don't know what sickens him more—handing over the account information to me or doing it in a public place.

Patrick stands. "Ready to stretch your legs?" he asks, as if we've been sitting too long at lunch.

"I'm not..." Q's answer fades away. "I can't... If the Crew finds out..."

I stand too. I'm not afraid to invade Q's personal space, but I lower my voice because some threats have to be kept quiet. "By *Crew*, you seem to mean my uncle. But he's not in charge of the Crew. *I* am. And if I don't get those account numbers in the next five minutes, the *Crew* will no longer be needing your services."

Patrick rounds out our cozy little circle. He's trying to be subtle, reaching beneath his jacket like he's about to pull a business card from his inside pocket. No one else in the reading room even notices. No one else even suspects there's a holster hidden there. But Q swallows so hard, I'm afraid he'll faint.

Patrick gets a hand under his elbow, keeping him on his feet. All three of us move toward the door, up the wide marble steps, and down the hall to the library's public access computer terminals.

Q's hands shake like he's in the throes of heroin withdrawal. Sweat trickles down his temple, tracing his jaw to get lost in his collar. The ashy stink of a burned-out campfire gets even stronger.

But he logs in to the terminal. He navigates to a new-to-me website, something with a Liberty Tree surrounded by a Celtic knot. He enters a username and one of the longest passwords I've ever seen.

The screen reveals dozens of blue file folders. Q clicks on one, and the screen refreshes to show ten more. He moves fast, working on muscle memory. It takes him less than a minute to reach his destination.

One click, and it's all there in a single file. Bank names and locations. Accounts set up as long strings of numbers and letters.

"Send it to me," I order. Q has worked for my family long enough that he doesn't have to ask an address. I take out my phone and watch the screen until a red badge tells me the file has arrived.

He licks his lips. "Okay? I can log out now?"

I'm about to set him free, but Patrick steps forward. "Go back two screens."

Q only hesitates a moment before he hits the right buttons.

"One more," Patrick says. Then: "There. What's that?"

Q looks like he wants to melt into the floor. "A list of assets."

Patrick flicks a quick glance at me, and I pick up the ball without any hesitation. "Assets?" I ask.

"Physical holdings," Q says, cringing like a beaten dog. "Belonging to your father."

"What sort of *physical holdings*?"

Q licks his lips. He looks past Patrick and me, to the door, and then he glances at Patrick's hidden holster. Correctly concluding that escape is not an option, he says, "Artwork." Before I can turn his statement into another question, he taps an address at the top of the screen. "In this warehouse."

"This one? There are others?"

He shrinks three sizes, trying to disappear into his chair. But Patrick isn't giving him any extra space, and I start to crowd the screen too. Finally, Q says, "Another storage unit has maps dating back to the Revolutionary War. And there's one with rare books, Irish authors. Some jewelry too." He clears his throat. "A lot of jewelry."

I should have expected to find something like this. My father was captain of the Old Colony Crew for decades. General of the Grand Irish Union, too. He's accumulated a lifetime of wealth, far more than the cash value of the *dún*.

"Send me the list," I tell Q. "Along with where it's all held."

Q hesitates until Patrick leans into his chair. "Send it," Patrick says.

Q finally complies. After I confirm receipt on my phone, he starts to log out again. But Patrick says, "Wait." He points to a file named *Philadelphia*. Of course it caught his attention. He's lived in Philly for decades. "What's that?"

Q's face pales to the color of the keyboard beneath his hands. Instead of answering Patrick, he looks at me. "That's not for your father."

The evasive answer just makes Patrick loom larger. "What is it?" he asks, in a voice designed to make Q dissolve into a dusty puddle.

"Nothing important. Just a side project. For Aran."

Now *I* want to know what Q is hiding, because I'll take any ammunition I can use against my asshole uncle. "What sort of project?"

The look of pure desperation on Q's face tells me I can't afford to back off now. He finally says, "It's nothing. Just a little asset diversification."

"Asset—"

"An international investment."

"Open it," Patrick says.

A whine escapes Q's lips. His eyes plead with me. But I only repeat what Patrick said: "Open it."

Q's finger falls on a single key, like a head dropping from a guillotine. The computer screen flashes.

It takes me a moment to parse what I see. It's a spreadsheet —words and numbers scrolling across the screen in columns.

Euros going to Germany.

Shipments arriving in Philadelphia.

The name *Herzog* is repeated on the document. And *Crash*. Transactions began six years ago, and they picked up significantly over the past twenty-four months—until they stopped dead, back in April.

"Send that one too," Patrick says.

All the fight has gone out of Q. He sends the file without arguing.

The information means nothing to me. But it's obviously important to Patrick. Maybe it's a way to make my uncle pay for what he did to me in his office at the *dún*. I nod once my phone says the file has arrived.

"Okay," Patrick says, pushing his knee into Q's chair. "You can go."

Q scarcely takes time to log out of whatever dark system he's been in. The instant the library's logo displays on the computer screen, he sprints for the door. He doesn't look back, even when a librarian calls out, "Excuse me, sir! No running in the library!"

Patrick waits until everyone else in the room has returned to their own captivating computers. Then he says, "Should we grab dinner on the way home? It'll be a long night, going through all this."

There's a lot I love about those words. *A long night*, with Patrick by my side. *Home*, the apartment we're sharing. And *dinner*. I worked up an appetite before we ever got to the library.

"A burger?" I ask. "With extra fries?"

Patrick laughs, exactly the way I knew he would. As we reach the stairs, he says, "We should make that lobster. With caviar. And a damn good bottle of wine."

I think about the files we'll be going through. Artwork. Maps. Rare books. Jewelry. And that's before we get to any of the German stuff.

I'm rich.

Very, very rich.

So rich that I'll never need Rónnad's money again.

28

PATRICK

F iona is sitting at the small desk in the bedroom, working through the accounts she got from Q. On the drive back from dinner, she told me her plan to automate a lot of the book-keeping. I understood about every third word she said.

She'll work it out. She's a hell of a lot better with computers than I am.

And I'm a hell of a lot better at being a mob enforcer than she'll ever dream of being. Right now, I'm doing my best to smother the Bell, to keep it from sending me after Aran Dowd. The dry shite has to pay for daring to touch my little girl. For talking to the feds, too—but I need proof of that before I can take real action.

And the *Philadelphia* file Q handed over just might be that proof.

Pacing the living room, I realize I can use my time for some-thing productive. I take out my phone and call my actual captain, because I've been in Boston for more than a month, and I owe him a little direct communication.

"Boss," I say when Braiden Kelly picks up.

"When the hell are you coming home?" I know that tone. He's tired and he's wary and he's feeling the burden of running a full-time criminal empire.

The first thing I need to do is prove my loyalty. "If O'Hare's slacking off, I'll be the first to show him the door."

I can picture Kelly pinching his lower lip, the way he shows frustration. "O'Hare's doing his job," he finally says. "*Your* job."

"My job is keeping you safe," I remind him.

"Let me guess." He's in a foul mood, his voice sticky with sarcasm. "Fiona Ingram's plotting to take me down. The only way you can stop her is to stay by her side."

I glance toward the bedroom. "It's not like that, Boss."

"Then she's got your bollocks in her pocket, and you've forgotten Philadelphia's your home."

Tapping my Fishtown ring with my thumb, I take a chance. "We both know her trousers are too tight for pockets."

He laughs. It's more a sharp bark than anything expressing actual humor, but it's the crack I hoped to find in his sour mood.

I try to make things better by promising, "I've forgotten nothing, Boss."

"But you still aren't coming home."

"Are you giving me an order?"

He could do it. He knows how to keep all the Fishtown Boys in line. And if he does, I'll be up against a wall, facing a decision I hope to put off for quite a while longer.

But Kelly's a good man, the best captain a soldier could ask for. So he doesn't force me to make the choice. Instead, he sighs and says, "Tell Fiona I asked after her."

I exhale a breath I didn't realize I was holding. "I'll do that." And then, before he goes back to whatever business I interrupted, I say, "One more thing, Boss."

"Didn't anyone ever teach you to quit while you're ahead?"

His voice has shifted back to acid, but I bull ahead like I don't have a care in the world. Fiona doesn't know it yet, but she needs some information Kelly has. "That place you go to, down in Delaware…"

"Diamond Freeport?"

I nod, even though he can't see me. "It's what? A tax haven?"

"It's a port. I send assets there for safekeeping. If I sell those assets to someone else who keeps them there, the transfer isn't taxed."

"It's secure then?"

"Secure enough for a dozen billionaires to trust it." And then, with a cool tone: "So Fiona's paying you enough you need to play some tax games?"

"I'm asking for Herself."

"Where the hell is Fiona—" He cuts himself off. "So she got her hands on her father's estate." He doesn't make it a question.

"And she'll get the Crew too."

Fiona is determined. I'm willing to bet she's already taken over every account Q gave her today. She'll use it all to take down Dowd.

Which brings me to the last thing Kelly needs to know. "Boss," I say. "Fiona got some information today. A report that mentions Philly."

Kelly's voice sharpens with interest. "What sort of report?"

"A balance sheet. With names. And notes."

"Go on." That's his captain voice, the one that makes every one of us men jump to comply. Fiona exercised hers with Q earlier today, but she's far from being a master.

Challenged by Kelly, I find myself reciting like a first-year runner. "Aran Dowd started wiring money to Germany six years back. Payments for shipping into Philadelphia. There's a steady increase in dollar amount, doubling quarter over quarter. But two months ago, everything stopped."

Kelly scoffs. "That could be anything. Electronics. High-end automobiles. Raw chemicals for labs."

"The early payments went to Klaus Herzog."

Silence.

A few years back, a video went viral—a group of Diamond Freeport billionaires sitting around a table, feasting on seafood and hundred-dollar-a-shot booze. One of those billionaires— Klaus Herzog—died in a spectacularly bloody way. And Kelly was caught on camera, watching the entire thing.

"And the later ones?" my boss finally asks.

"To his brothers. The records I saw didn't even try to hide their names. Didn't hide the nature of the goods either. It's Crash."

I take a little credit for Kelly's fluent Irish curses. He learned our mother tongue in a classroom. I taught him how real men speak.

Crash is a drug created in a German lab. It's designed to target kids' developing brains, and a single dose is addictive.

With Kieran Ingram as head of the Grand Irish Union, there've been few things the mob won't touch. Whores? No problem. Running guns? We've got that covered. Extortion, blackmail, an occasional political hit? Bring it on.

But Ingram put out the word on Crash. Sell it, and kiss the mob goodbye. You're out. You're dead.

A few years back, Kelly fell into a sweetheart deal—kilos of the stuff, taken from the Herzogs in a warehouse raid and worth millions on the street. He ordered me to charter a boat and dump the shite at sea.

But it looks like Aran Dowd didn't get the same memo.

"How much is he selling?" Kelly asks.

"Three months ago, he was bringing in millions."

"Three months ago, he was in prison."

Dowd's stint in jail was the reason Fiona came to Phil-adelphia in the first place. She took her uncle's place, running a meeting for her da. But Kelly and I both know how easy it is to keep an import/export business running from inside the joint.

I say, "The sales cut out ten weeks ago. Like someone came at them with a cleaver."

"When did Dowd get out?"

"Ten weeks ago."

"Because the district attorney didn't want to chance losing a major case," Kelly says slowly, like he's solving a jigsaw puzzle.

"That's the story I heard."

I've seen a lot of criminal enterprises. Some make good money. Others are write-offs. The only thing I've seen cause a complete drop-off like Dowd's line on Crash is death.

Or the closest thing to dying: Being turned by the feds.

All the facts are in front of me. Q's records make things clear as crystal. This isn't about bruises on Fiona's arm, about Dowd trying to shove his tongue down my little girl's throat.

This is about betraying a clan. About selling out the Irish mob to avoid years of prison for distributing a drug more deadly than heroin.

I weigh my words carefully, because I know exactly what they'll cost. I measured out the payment for my own dead da, twenty-five years back. But I finally tell Kelly, "I saw Dowd a month ago, in a place he had no business being. With a man he had no reason to meet. A federal agent."

Kelly's whistle is long and low. When he speaks, he doesn't mince words. "Your Dowd's a fucking rat. He ran his shite through Philadelphia. Make him fucking pay."

29

FIONA

"We can absolutely conduct auctions," Alix Key says. "Art, maps, books, jewelry… We can deliver top dollar on all of them."

I've read up on Diamond Freeport. It serves people with a hell of a lot more in assets than I'm taking from my father. Alix herself is calm and sophisticated; she looks like she was born in that designer suit. She took this meeting on short notice, and she's treated me with nothing but respect.

But I don't know how willing she is to skirt the law.

"Let's talk about the artwork for a moment," I say, glancing at Patrick to see if he thinks I should tip my hand. He offers the slightest nod, which loosens my tongue enough to say, "What if it wasn't all acquired through strictly legal channels?"

I've had a chance to review the long lists of assets Q handed over. I'm starting with art because everyone's heard of Picasso.

In fact, everyone's heard of my father's Picasso—*Screaming Woman in Mirror.*

It was stolen from the Caterina Marcus Corman Museum in the most famous art museum heist of all time. Thieves managed to walk off with the precious canvas in the middle of the June Gala, thirty-five years ago.

I'm certain Da didn't arrange the theft. That sort of thing requires expertise far beyond what the Old Colony Crew can handle.

But I'm also certain my father was willing to pay a shitload of money to acquire the painting after it was stolen. Even if he could never show it in public—maybe *because* he could never show it—he did whatever he had to do to get the Picasso. It's a perfect *fuck you* to the museum that never let him sponsor the Gala.

A frown ghosts across Alix's face, but it's quickly replaced by serene competence. "In general, buyers expect a rock-solid provenance, proof of a painting's prior ownership. Museums require it. But certain private parties are willing to be more... flexible."

Yeah, she's saying. *I can sell your hot Picasso.*

"Of course, the reappearance of...missing work can generate a lot of attention from law enforcement. There have been several recent incidents where people were required to return artwork stolen by Nazis to the families of original owners."

But, she's saying. *If word gets out, you might lose everything.*

Sitting back in my chair, I remind myself that I'm Fiona Fucking Ingram. The painting is mine, no matter what I decide to do with it. Just like the Crew will be mine.

My deep sigh shifts my black silk corset, the one that's embroidered with cream-colored roses. It's strapless, with a sweetheart neckline. I loved the way Patrick's eyes flared when he saw it this morning—or maybe he was reacting to my thigh-high black boots, the ones with stiletto heels. It might have been the flash of bare flesh between the top of the boots and the bottom of my tight leather skirt that got him going.

But sitting across from Alix, I feel less like a woman taking on the entire universe and more like a little girl playing dress-up. I wish I'd taken a cue from how Patrick dressed for this meeting. He's in his black suit, wearing a blinding white shirt and his Fishtown tie.

Fuck.

Right now, his raised eyebrows are an invitation for me to ask more questions, but I'm not sure what else I need to know. I flick my hand, telling him to say whatever's on his mind. He asks Alix, "Does it make sense to move the artwork here if we aren't ready to sell it?"

She gives him a professional smile. "Of course, I have a vested interest in answering that question." She immediately returns her attention to me. She recognizes that I'll be her client, not the man sitting beside me. For that reason alone, I want to do business with her. "Our galleries are designed to withstand fire and flood," she says. "The entire building is hurricane-proof, tornado-proof, and built to withstand a direct hit from a one-thousand-kilogram bunker-buster bomb."

I haven't seen the storage facility where my father put his stolen goods, but Da was famous for pinching every penny until it screamed. I'm fairly certain he's kept the Picasso in a heat- and humidity-controlled environment. But the rest of it? I suspect he never considered bomb-proofing his collection.

Alix continues: "We shelter some of the world's great art treasures here at the freeport. We've auctioned Monets, Van Goghs, and Matisses. One of our premier clients, Braiden Kelly, is selling an illuminated manuscript in two weeks. It's a medieval Irish book that has never before been offered on the open market."

I don't know why Braiden's name makes me uncomfortable. I have nothing to hide about the time I spent in his mansion. Nothing happened between us—no matter how many offers I put on the table.

But Patrick is the one who fills the awkward silence by telling

Alix, "Kelly and I are…business associates. He's the one who gave us your contact information."

Alix doesn't blink, although she surely knows exactly what *business* Patrick and Braiden have in common. She says, "Of course. And I'll be certain to thank Braiden for sending you our way."

Wracking my brain for an appropriate question, I ask, "What sort of security measures do you have for individual galleries?"

Alix flicks her fingers over her laptop keyboard, sending an image to the screen at the front of the room. "As you can see, we have state-of-the-art biometric controls—both fingerprint and retina scans." She brings up another picture, which looks like an office in any high-end building in the world. "Of course, you can furnish your gallery any way that works for you. Some of our clients maintain business offices down there, along with whatever storage they need."

She goes on with various facts and figures, details about computer access, Internet connections, some sort of direct link to banking systems in the Caymans and in Switzerland…

Alix passes a thick binder across the table. "This document summarizes everything we've talked about so far. I'm sorry our General Counsel couldn't be here today, but if you have any legal questions, Samantha will be happy to answer them."

"Samantha?" I ask, even though I'm pretty sure I know who she's referring to.

"Samantha Mott. She's served as our chief legal officer since the freeport opened. She—"

"I know Samantha."

I spent the better part of the last six months jockeying with Samantha for power in Braiden Kelly's Philadelphia household. I did my best to make her think we were competing for Braiden's attention.

I never had a fucking chance.

Now I stand, because I can't think of anything else I could

possibly need to know about Diamond Freeport. Alix shakes my hand first, before she turns to Patrick. Her fingers are cool on mine.

We exchange pleasantries, and I promise to keep in touch. Alix escorts us to the building lobby, where a limousine waits to take us back to the nearby private airfield and our chartered jet.

I chose not to use Da's private plane this morning. I didn't want any chance that Uncle Aran would find out where Patrick and I went. I don't want to give my uncle any hint that I know about Da's hidden property.

"That went well, *Scáthach*," Patrick says once we're aboard, sitting in massive leather chairs beside a polished teak table.

My frown at the Irish word is erased by the flight attendant coming in with a tray. She's remembered that Patrick doesn't take ice in his orange juice, and she found the perfect balance of sugar for my cup of coffee. She leaves us with a plate of fresh fruit, promising lunch once we're in the air.

"We learned a lot," I say. "Thank you for setting up the meeting."

He brushes aside my thanks as the jet taxis down the runway. I stare out the window until the freeport fades to a tiny dot in the distance. When I look up, I'm surprised by the indulgent smile on his face. I say, "I can't believe this is my life now."

"Welcome to the big time, little girl."

The endearment snags my breath. From Patrick's wicked smile, I know that's exactly the reaction he planned. But I shake my head and set my shoulders. I know he'll disagree with what I'm about to say. "Even if I move everything to the freeport tomorrow, I still need to get the last million dollars from Rónnad."

Predictably, his face darkens. "You can't trust that—"

"I have to. She's kept her end of the bargain so far."

"Bargain? You gave her a feckin' pair of sunglasses. You have no idea what angle she's really working."

I shake my head. "Her deposits have shown up like clock-work. Just one more, and we'll be done."

"Sell the feckin' Picasso."

"You heard Alix. I can't sell it without getting the law involved."

"You can't sell it *publicly*."

"The Gala's in three weeks, and I need my ten mill before that."

He scowls, but he can't contradict me. Even Diamond Freeport has its limitations.

I try to change the topic. "What do you think it's worth? The Picasso, and those maps? The books and jewelry and everything else Da hid away?"

He makes a sound between a sniff and a snort. He knows exactly what I'm doing, distracting him from Rónnad. But he agrees to be led away from the raw topic. "Depending on what Q meant by *a lot of jewelry*?" he asks. "You might be looking at a billion dollars."

I count the zeroes in my mind, but they make no sense. They're a magic spell. A fairy tale. I wave my hand over the fruit tray and my coffee. "So I can afford to get us both refills on coffee?"

Patrick sits back in his chair. "Do you have any idea how much a billion is?"

I shrug.

"Let's say you put a million pennies in a stack. They're almost a mile high. But if you stack a *billion* pennies, they'd go all the way from Boston to Chicago."

I laugh. "And you just happen to know that off the top of your head."

"I've thought a lot about it. That's what I get, working for a feckin' billionaire."

I don't think he says it to remind me Braiden Kelly is his boss. After all, we both know he's sworn to Philadelphia. The past six weeks have been temporary. This—whatever we have between us—will end when I take the Old Colony throne. Once I defeat Uncle Aran, Patrick has to head back to his real job.

Unless I can convince him to change his mind. Once I'm Queen, I'll need a Warlord, just like Braiden. Patrick can be part of my Council.

I just have to convince him he wants to stay. That he wants to work for me.

Sliding my ass forward on my chair, I stretch out my foot until the toe of my boot nestles between Patrick's legs. At the same time, I pluck a slice of pineapple from the fruit tray and bring it to my mouth, extending my tongue to catch a drop of golden juice.

"Mmm," I moan, just loud enough for him to hear over the plane's engines.

His fingers close around my ankle, tight enough for me to feel through the leather of my boots.

The flight attendant chooses that moment to return from the plane's tiny galley, carrying a tray with silverware and glasses and two huge snowy napkins. I pull my foot back quickly, balancing on the edge of my seat like a proper young lady. The attendant shakes out my napkin and places it on my lap.

Patrick snatches his own napkin from her fingers. Covering himself, he shifts in his seat, grimacing in obvious discomfort. I fight to smother a laugh as the attendant returns with a charcuterie board and a basket of bread.

I make a point of eating very slowly. I purse my lips a lot more than necessary. I use the tip of my tongue to test my food.

Patrick's eyes narrow with an unspoken promise.

There's nothing he can do to while we're six miles in the air —not with the flight attendant standing guard just inside the galley. But after we land in Boston, our driver meets us at the charter terminal. As soon as we're secure in our rented limo, behind a privacy screen and tinted windows, my Daddy makes me pay for taunting him.

Three times, he makes me pay, because he knows exactly

what to say, exactly how to make my body melt under his touch. I'm still recovering from his last lesson when his burner chimes with a message.

Swearing fluently in a mix of English and Irish, he tugs his phone from his pants pocket, which would be a lot easier to do if his zipper wasn't tented like a circus big top. When he glances at the screen, his face shifts to unreadable stone. "There," he says, before he finally shows the phone to me. "You won't have to deal with her, ever again."

The message is from Rónnad. She's delivered the last of her promised money.

I wait. We both do, for some final demand, for a threat to expose our business arrangement, for something that explains why she made it so easy to collect the money I needed.

Nothing.

No further texts. No claims. No commands.

I want to get back to the game interrupted by the burner's chime, but one look at Patrick's scowling face tells me the moment has passed. That's fine, though. It has to be.

There's plenty of work to be done after we climb the stairs to the Back Bay apartment. I need to find a photo of my father, one presentable outside the *dún*. I need to decide what to wear. I need to issue a press release, to put the media on high alert.

Because tomorrow morning, I walk into the executive offices of the Caterina Marcus Corman Museum and hand over ten million dollars—on condition that the Gala publicly recognizes Kieran Ingram's dying gift.

30

PATRICK

I give up on figuring out the physics of how Fiona's dress covers the mission-critical parts of her body. It wraps around her neck like she's wearing a collar. It falls from her hips to the floor. But in between, big triangles are cut out of the sides so anyone who cares can count her ribs. The back is completely bare. The blood-red fabric barely covers her tits.

A leather belt snakes around her hips, challenging every man in the Corman Museum's courtyard to keep his mind on cold showers, snowstorms, and icebergs floating in a frozen sea. I already made one unscheduled trip to the jacks before we left the Back Bay apartment, and I'm starting to feel the need for another.

"Fiona!"

The woman who sails down the steps is a mass of white hair and heavy makeup and a cloud of perfume that arrives twenty feet before she does. I don't know if anyone on earth can wear gold and black stripes without looking like a pregnant bumble-bee. This woman certainly can't.

"Marjorie," Fiona responds, dutifully accepting air kisses on each cheek. "My father would be so touched by the memorial."

"We were afraid you weren't coming," Marjorie chides.

I'm the reason we're late. I set three alarms, but somewhere between the studs for my tuxedo shirt and the clasp of my cummerbund, I got distracted. We ended up leaving the apartment five minutes after we were supposed to arrive at the museum.

Fiona doesn't flick a glance toward me. She just settles her hand on the older woman's arm and says, "You know I wouldn't miss this for the world."

Together, Marjorie and Fiona look toward the head table. Places are set for Fiona and me to sit dead center, like a bride and groom sandwiched between twenty of our closest friends.

A gigantic headshot of Kieran Ingram is suspended between the balconies that frame the museum's second floor, at least twenty feet tall. Fiona had the good sense to dig out a vintage photo of her da. The giant looming over us still has a full head of thick, dark hair. The only creases on his face are the laugh lines by his eyes. His cheeks have a healthy flush, nothing like the sallow tinge even the morticians couldn't hide at the end.

An even larger scroll wraps around the bottom edge of the photo's frame. *In Memoriam*, it says. *Kieran Phelan Ingram*.

Smaller images of the photo, frame, and banner are set into floral centerpieces on every table—overflowing Easter lilies and shamrocks. The Gala menu has taken on an Irish flair as well. Waiters walk around with trays of little lamb chops and caviar-topped potatoes. The entrées promise to be chicken in Jameson sauce and baked salmon. Someone managed to bring in the entire East Coast supply of Guinness for the bars on either side of the courtyard, and rumor has it there are vats of Bailey's for after-dinner drinks.

It's amazing what ten million dollars can buy, even on short notice.

Marjorie Hindman continues cooing over Fiona, bringing her into a circle of the museum's greatest supporters. There's the mayor and the chief of police. The chief fire inspector. The head of the city's tax division.

Every last one of them knows exactly who Fiona is. And every last one of them is forced to shake her hand. To gesture at the portrait of her father. To thank her for her generous donation to the museum they all support.

"Our girl's loving every feckin' minute of it."

I've let my guard down, watching Fiona bask in the glory of her donation. That's the only reason I didn't see Aran Dowd approach—and now he's close enough to rumble in my ear.

I resist the urge to reach for my Glock, which isn't even here. The shoulder holster doesn't fit under my tuxedo jacket. Besides, I knew we'd be forced through a metal detector before anyone would be allowed near His Honor, the mayor.

Clenching a fist against the Bell that starts echoing inside my skull, I manage to respond with a level tone. "So the Corman's open for all sorts now."

"They could hardly refuse a request from their Platinum Donor's brother-in-law, could they? Especially when he came armed with his own seven-figure check."

So Dowd was willing to cough up a million of his own dollars to get through the door. Giving in to one clang of the Bell, I ask, "Which table are you at?" I already know he's not sitting with us at the front of the room.

He scowls, and I think he'll tell me to fuck off. Instead he says, "Isn't it about time for you to leave town, Cujo? I think I hear your Philly master whistling."

What a feckin' tool. If Dowd *could* hear Kelly calling, that would mean he's a dog too. The Bell starts an in-skull symphony, but I can't exactly rip off his bollocks and shove them down his throat. Not here, amid Boston's wealthiest art-lovers. So I settle for raising my glass like I'm toasting his brilliant wit. "Shove it up your fucking hole," I say evenly, before I sip the Jameson.

His face turns the color of Fiona's dress, and I realize I've made a costly mistake. I should've challenged the gobshite to a game or two of poker before we had it out, if that's the best he can do at hiding his emotions.

Fiona's laugh rings out across the marble floor. A circle has gathered around her, mostly men, with a couple of curious women flashing their own feather-bright colors to get close to her. I've seen Fiona like this before, drunk on the attention of the crowd, flushed with the power she holds. She's gorgeous when she's *on*.

Dowd says, "She's meant for a finer man than you, Cujo."

"So she reminds me every morning," I answer. "After I bring her breakfast in bed."

Fiona's playing her admirers. "We Irish have a tradition," she cries. "Telling limericks to mark a grand event. Here's one my da would love."

Christ. I've heard Fiona's limericks before. She may be misjudging this crowd.

As if he's reading my mind, Dowd says, "She's young. She makes mistakes. But I'll bring her in line in no time."

Doing my best to ignore the feckin' Bell, I fight to sound like I'm talking about the weather. "Touch her like you did the other day, and I'll break every bone in your fucking hand."

Fiona holds her glass aloft. "There once was a lad from Nantucket," she begins.

Everyone around her laughs. Some think she's funny. Others are politely appalled.

Dowd says, "I'll touch her however I choose. That's what a man does to his wife."

"You haven't been paying attention," I say. "Fiona's not the marrying type."

As if to prove my point, Fiona says from the front of the

room, "Wait. That's not right. Let's try again. In Southie there lived a young buck—"

This time, the laughter is a little more nervous. Marjorie sails forward, like the Queen Mary coming in to dock. "Fiona, dear," she says. "Why don't you tell us a little more about your father's love of art?"

Fiona says, "There are so many stories I could tell!" She gestures toward the photo of her da and drops her voice, reeling in the crowd. From the shocked expression on Marjorie's face, whatever Fiona says isn't fit for polite company, but that's never stopped my girl a day in her life.

Dowd spits, "You're choosing the wrong side, Cujo. You'll pay for that, the instant she's back in the *dún*, where she belongs."

"So we agree on one thing," I say. "Fiona does belong in the *dún*. She's the next captain of the Old Colony Crew." I've never thought she has a chance at leading Boston's mob. But if the alternative is letting Aran Dowd get the upper hand, I'll throw in my lot with Fiona.

Dowd laughs, loud enough that a few art lovers look around. When he claps a heavy hand on my shoulder, the Bell tells me to twist him into an armlock, to break some feckin' bones. I resist until he sneers, "There's not a man in the Crew who'll follow that minge's lead."

That *does* require a clear response. I grab Dowd by the elbow as I shrug out from under his hand. My fingers tighten on his ulnar nerve, the one they call the funny bone. His lips turn gray as I squeeze. "Mind your fucking mouth," I tell him. "She's your dead captain's daughter. You'll give her the respect she deserves."

"I'll give her *something* she deserves," he says through gritted teeth. "My ring on her finger and my cock up her ass."

I think about *my* ring, the Fishtown one, connecting with the point of his beard-covered chin. He's spent too many years as Kieran Ingram's second-in-command. Too much time in meetings, figuring out *strategy*. He's soft, and I could knock him on his arse without half trying.

But the Bell hammers away, reminding me there's an even better way to take him down a peg. Still keeping a casual tone, I ask, "When's the last time you had Mike Barbieri's cock up *your* ass?"

He stiffens beneath my hand. For a moment, I think he'll take a swing, which would be grand, because then I could knock his teeth down his feckin' throat. But he just spits out, "Mind your tongue, Cujo. Lies like that get a man killed."

Maybe that's his way of telling me he's innocent, that my incorrect assumption could put his life at risk. But I'm pretty sure the gobshite's making a threat, and *my* life is the one on the line.

Before I can force him to take a stand—his life or mine—Fiona calls out: "To my father!" She offers her glass in a toast. At least a dozen men are eager to drink at her command. Something twinges beneath the pleats of my white shirt, and I fight the urge to tear through the crowd, tossing the eejits aside like paper dolls.

"Fiona!" Dowd calls, yanking his arm from my grasp to shoulder his way through the gala guests.

She turns a look on him that would wither an ordinary man's wedding tackle. But Dowd's a stupid cunt, and he wades in like he has a stand beside Fiona. The hand he lays on her arm looks like a farmer's, claiming a racehorse that's refused to enter the blocks. I bite off an oath and push my own way forward.

Before I can get there, Dowd delivers a kiss. He stops short of shoving his tongue down Fiona's throat, but his fingers move from her elbow to her hip. He uses his height to force her back a step, then slides an arm around her waist to keep her steady.

She stumbles, as if she's lost her balance on those needle-sharp heels. It's all an act, though. Fiona's as steady as they come, and Dowd can't keep from bellowing when she pins his foot with her stiletto. At the same time, she paints a look of pure shock across her face. "Please!" she exclaims. "Uncle Aran!"

Murmurs ripple through the crowd. From the cheap seats, the dry shite looks like the lech he is, trying to manhandle a sweet, vulnerable young thing.

All right.

Maybe not sweet.

Not vulnerable, either.

But young, and not happy with the attention of the old man grimacing and shifting from foot to foot in front of her.

Fiona's got a flock of new suitors ready to defend her honor, and they do it with more finesse than I would do. One invites Fiona over to a display case, showing off the museum's latest purchase, a bowl that looks like it was painted by kindergarteners set loose in a mud pit. Two more deliberately put their pickleball-honed bodies between Dowd and his prey, squaring their shoulders like they have the first idea how to throw a punch. The smartest of them looks across the room toward the head caterer, catching the guy's attention and sparking an order issued through an earpiece.

By the time I get to Fiona's side, she's regained her composure. She sends one fan running to fetch her a fresh drink. She squeezes the arm of another, clearly admiring his bravery. With the steely determination of a queen, she ignores the muted commotion as two security guards escort Dowd from the hall.

"There you are!" Fiona says to me, looping her arm through mine. "Patrick, dear. I want you to meet my new friends!"

Her voice is half an octave too high. Her eyes are dilated, like she somehow found the time to sneak a joint. She's trembling just a little; I probably couldn't feel it if I wasn't fighting my own impulse to crush her against my side and get her the hell out of this madhouse.

But I shake hands like I wasn't raised by feckin' wolves. And I admire the pottery bowl like it isn't painted to look like shite. And I escort Fiona to the head table when the waiters glide through the crowd, playing their little xylophones like they've only learned the first three notes of a song.

I shouldn't look at the phone in my pocket. It's the public one, the number I've held for decades. It buzzes with texts every hour of the day and night.

But when a dozen messages come through while I'm spooning up my cold potato soup, I excuse myself between courses. Fiona's eyebrows peak, a question if everything's all right. I brush a kiss against her cheek. "All's well, *Scáthach*."

She sticks her tongue out at me, like she isn't being watched by three hundred cultured eejits.

I head to the jacks, into a stall where I can check my phone in peace.

DOWD

> Down, Cujo.

> She's mine.

There's a video, a string of videos, close-ups of some cock railing a dripping pussy.

DOWD

> But you can watch me fuck her once I'm captain of the Crew.

31

FIONA

When Patrick comes back, his face looks like someone reached behind his eyes and switched off the thing that makes him human. Taking his seat with a belligerent air, he digs into his salmon with the determination of a marathon runner carbo-loading before a big race.

"Everything okay?" I ask.

"Just peachy."

I think about asking if *peachy* is a word old men use when they want out of a social commitment, but I suspect I won't like the answer. Plus, it's a hell of a lot more fun to tease him about being ancient when we're in the privacy of our own apartment.

I settle for putting my hand in his lap. I'm pretty sure the table has drapery in front of it, a modesty panel for everyone sitting up here on the stage. Fuck it, if it doesn't.

He doesn't react when my fingers slip beneath his napkin. He reaches for his water as I trace his inseam with one nail. But when I shift to the tab on his zipper, he says, "Stop."

He doesn't raise his voice, so I figure I still have a little room to play. I shift my wrist so the heel of my hand rides the line of his stirring cock.

"Fiona," he says. "Stop." And this time, he reaches beneath the table and returns my hand to my own lap.

I shift my attention to Marjorie Hindman, on my left, spending the rest of the meal learning about the Corman's building fund. That leaves Patrick to make small talk with the museum's oldest living board member, Mildred Fuhrman, who just celebrated her ninety-fifth birthday. She falls asleep as dessert is being served, slumping against Patrick. He manages to hand her off to a waiter before she can drool on his tux.

There are speeches after the meal. Three different liars get up and say how much they wish they'd met my father, how certain they are that he would have loved tonight's gala, how wonderful it is that I'm here to show my support.

A band starts to play at the far end of the courtyard, their cover of Donna Summer luring couples onto the dance floor. I tilt my head with an invitation for Patrick, but he says, "Not on your feckin' life."

One of the men who got between Uncle Aran and me asks for a dance. Patrick puts his hand on my wrist and says, "Not tonight." I'm tempted to take the man—Nigel? Edmund? Oliver?—up on his offer, dancing with whoever-he-is just to remind Patrick that he's not the boss of me. But good-old-what-shisname takes one quick look at my guard-dog's face and remembers he has to finish an urgent conversation on the far side of the room.

I turn to Patrick, fury knitting my shoulder blades together. "You have no right—"

"Say your goodbyes. It's time for us to leave."

"If you think I paid ten million dollars, just so I can duck out of here halfway through the night—"

"You have fifteen minutes. And then I carry you out."

The motherfucker will do it, too. So I make a quick tour of

the room, interrupting a conversation between the mayor and the police chief, then kissing the cheek of the fire inspector like we're old friends. I can't bring myself to lean in toward the tax inspector, but we give each other chilly goodbyes. That leaves Marjorie—one more gush about her gold-and-black gown—before Patrick ghosts up to my side.

I'm too furious to speak as he marches me out to the valet stand. The Land Rover has been kept in the loop of the driveway—one advantage of being the guest of honor. A boy with terrible acne helps me into my seat on the passenger side. When I catch him craning his neck for a glimpse of side-boob, I figure what the hell, and I pretend to have an itch at the back of my head. The kid practically groans as he gapes at the extra flesh my stretch displays. Patrick has to remind him to close my door.

I wait for Patrick to tell me why it was so urgent for us to leave, but he's busy managing the Land Rover like I'm administering a driver's license exam. He comes to a complete halt at a four-way stop sign, looking left, then right, then left again. He uses his turn indicators when he changes lanes. He doles out his concentration between the road in front of him, the rear-view mirror, and both side mirrors.

He ignores me when I lean forward to turn on the radio. I think his jaw tightens when I flip away from the cool jazz stylings of some guy who was older than my father. Patrick's back to the role of Perfect Driving Man by the time I find Metallica. I crank the volume.

When I kick off my shoes and hitch up my skirt so I can rest one heel on the edge of my seat, he does glance over at me. I see his eyes travel from my crotch to my ankle. A muscle twitches by his temple, and he clamps his hands around the steering wheel, his palms perfectly positioned at two and ten.

"You're supposed to put your hands at nine and three," I say.

He grunts.

"It's safer with, you know, modern cars. Ones with airbags."

The rear-view mirror captures his attention for longer than it should.

I say, "I guess they still taught the old way when *you* learned to drive."

"Fasten your seatbelt."

I ignore him.

"Fasten your goddamn seatbelt," he says, splitting his attention between the rear-view and the road.

I wish I had some bubble gum. I'd blow a huge bubble and pop it just before it got to my hair.

"Goddammit, Fiona. This isn't a fucking game. We're being followed."

I want to tell him to go to hell. But I fasten my seatbelt before I turn around. There are two lanes of traffic. There must be ten cars behind us. "How can you tell?"

"Hold on," he says, and he cranks the wheel to the right, hard, without any warning, without slowing down.

I'm thrown against the door as Patrick handles the wheel with the casual grace of a Formula 1 driver. Flooring the accelerator, he weaves between cars, narrowly skating through three yellow lights in a row. Whoever's behind us ignores the same lights, hurtling through cross-traffic as the June night fills with the sound of screeching tires and honking horns.

"Get down," Patrick says, reaching over to cup the back of my head with his hand.

"No one's shooting—"

"Goddammit!" he bellows, shoving my head between my knees.

I can't see where he's going, but I hear the crash. Something splinters in front of us, wood and metal ripping apart. I sit up in time to see we've shattered a gate.

"Where—" I start to ask, but Patrick's too busy steering across a recently painted parking lot.

There's a low building to our left, walls of windows dark for the night. The Land Rover's headlights pick up gently rolling hills in front of us. Green grass swoops to either side, trees carving out windbreaks.

It's a golf course. Patrick's driven us to the municipal golf course.

Correction.

Patrick's driving *on* the municipal golf course. And the car that's chasing us follows.

It's a Cadillac Escalade. Black. Classic. Big enough for a grown man to sleep on the back seat. Or for a couple of bodies to fit in the rear compartment.

Patrick slams on his brakes, turning the wheel with practiced precision. The Land Rover spins in a perfect half-circle, coming to rest facing the torn-up greens and somewhere—beyond our line of sight—the shattered gate. Patrick cuts the engine, along with the lights.

The Cadillac brakes too, but its driver doesn't spin the wheel. The Escalade barrels past us, hurtling toward a pitch-black shadow.

That's not a shadow. It's a water hazard.

The Cadillac stops with its front wheels on the edge of the drop-off. Its nose extends into mid-air. Its headlights beam into space.

Patrick reaches between my legs. I don't have time to be surprised before he yanks open the glove box, and his fingers settle over the grip of a gun.

Looking up, I can barely make out the shapes of two men using the Cadillac's back doors as shields. Someone calls from the driver's side: "Let's keep this simple, Cujo."

Patrick's jaw sets in concrete.

"Give us the girl," the driver shouts. "And you won't end up dogshite, like your da."

The passenger probably thinks he's being clever by howling like a mad dog. Patrick calls out, "Fuck you."

"Dowd gave us orders."

Of course he did. I *know* the car poised on the edge of the water hazard—it belongs to Uncle Aran. And the man driving it is one of his favorite runners.

"Fuck Aran Dowd," Patrick calls.

At the same time, I shout across the green. "You're making a huge mistake, Kevin Joyce!"

Patrick flicks his attention to me for a heartbeat. "That gobshite's still in the Crew?"

"Uncle Aran uses him for special jobs." Which means that one of us—Patrick or me—isn't expected to get out of this alive. Maybe both of us. But no... Joyce could have fired through the Land Rover's back window by now if Uncle Aran wanted both of us dead.

Joyce has finally figured out a response. "Your man's the one making a mistake. Now get out of the car, both of you. Slow and easy. And keep your hands where we can see them."

Patrick reaches for his door latch, but he doesn't open his door. Keeping his eyes on the Escalade, he says in a low voice, "Do you trust me?"

"Yes." It's one word. But it's two months of thought. Two months of living on top of each other in the Back Bay apartment. Two months of this game we've been playing, Daddy and little girl.

"Good girl," he says. "Get out of the car. Walk straight over to Joyce."

In a twisted way, that makes sense. Joyce will have to focus on me, on dragging me into his car, on getting the back door closed. Patrick can come after him as Joyce backs up from the edge of the water hazard.

If the other guy doesn't take out Patrick first.

Joyce is getting restless. He calls out, "I'm counting to three. One!"

Patrick nods toward the Cadillac. "Go on, then," he says. He holds the gun in his lap, the one he took from the glove compartment.

The other guy will definitely take Patrick out first. He'll have no reason not to open fire on the Land Rover, the instant I'm safely away.

I lick my lips. I don't want to leave the car. I don't want to leave Patrick.

"*Scáthach*," Patrick says.

I have to delay, until I can come up with a better plan. "Tell me what that—"

"Later."

There'll be no later.

I run my fingers under the halter of my evening gown, settling the seams in place. I try to think of another way to play this. Some way that doesn't end up with me a captive and Patrick gunned down by my uncle's soldiers. "Patrick—" I say.

"Go."

I climb out of the car. It's a June night. My brain knows that the air around me must be warm, hot even, and heavy with summer humidity. But the grass feels like miniature icicles under my bare feet. Goose pimples rise on my arms, and my back feels like it's pressed against an iceberg.

I can't see in the dark. The Land Rover's lights are turned off, and the front of the Cadillac faces the water hazard. I squint, trying to make out some refuge in the darkness—a line of trees, bleachers for spectators, *something* I can run to.

This is wrong. This is a mistake. Patrick doesn't understand. He's forgotten that the Old Colony Crew takes no prisoners.

Except for me.

I'll be their prisoner. I'll belong to Uncle Aran, and he'll use me any way he wants because Patrick will be dead.

I don't have any delusions about my uncle's plans. We'll marry in front of the entire clan so he can claim he's captain by right. He'll throw out my packets of birth control pills my first night at the *dún*. He'll have me knocked up by the end of July, but if it's a girl he won't let me keep it. I won't be allowed out of the house until he has his heir. Maybe not even then.

I can't do this.

Joyce calls out, "Two!"

I don't have a choice. I jam a rod of iron through the ice that lines my spine. I close my eyes and take my first step toward the Cadillac.

32

PATRICK

She said she trusts me.

But that can't prepare her for what I've planned.

I wait until she takes her first step toward the Caddy. I'm hoping those dry shites can't resist gawking at her tits. God knows, Kevin Joyce never met a woman he didn't want to fuck, no matter the cost. We all learned to cover for him the mornings after big payouts, when he spent every last cent in his pocket on whores.

Eejits like that don't change over time.

I reach up and turn off the dome light inside the Land Rover. I take a deep breath. I double-check my grip on the Magnum. The Desert Eagle lives in the glove box because it's too big to strap on under a jacket. I've got twelve rounds to make my point.

Fiona takes another step.

I barrel out of the Land Rover. I don't bother crouching,

don't try to hide. My goal is to move fast and get where they can't hit me.

Which means I'm pressed against Fiona's back before they have a chance to fire. I catch my arm around her chest, pulling her close to my body. I steady her head against my left shoulder as I raise my right arm. I fire past her—two quick shots through the car door on Joyce's side, then a pair at whatever jackass thought it would be a good idea to drag out Joyce's Cujo jibe.

The Magnum's big enough to take down a deer or a charging wild boar. It shreds the Escalade doors like it's tearing through paper, first on Joyce's side, then the other.

I march forward, driving Fiona in front of me, clamping her even closer as panic makes her fight. I must have scored direct hits on both of Dowd's trained monkeys; they aren't offering a hint of resistance.

But I'm not taking any chances. I wait until we're just three strides from the Cadillac, and then I push Fiona behind me, shoving her toward the ground.

"Stay down," I order, as I advance on the enemy.

I don't know what his name was. His own mother won't recognize him now. The thing that used to be his face is a mass of red-splashed bone. The stink of blood and shite rises from shiny bits that have spilled onto the cool green grass.

My first shot must have gutted him. My second caught his head as he collapsed.

That leaves Joyce.

I stalk to the other side of the car, arms stiff, Magnum ready. It's a dark night, only a sliver of moon. The Caddy's headlights are useless. Its interior light casts a wavering yellow circle, like someone's pissed on the shadows.

Swinging around the car door, I automatically adjust my aim.

Joyce has managed to pull himself halfway into the car. One of my shots pulverized his right arm; nothing but meat and gristle hangs from his shoulder. His legs sprawl on the ground. It looks like he tried to shift his revolver to his left hand, but he dropped the gun on the transfer.

I kick it away and point my Magnum at his face.

"Dowd'll eat yer bollocks fer breakfast," Joyce says.

"He'll have to catch me first. And if you're the type he's sending round, I'm feeling fairly safe."

Joyce shakes his head, his teeth gleaming red in the weak light. "He'll make ya watch him fuck that cunt."

I'm close enough that I barely need to twitch my wrist. The Magnum explodes, and a black pool spreads where Joyce's cock used to twitch.

The motherfucker howls, his eyes going wild. I think he's watching the demons who'll drag him down to hell until I hear Fiona's trembling voice. "Let me finish the job."

One quick glance shows she's picked up Joyce's revolver. The dim light makes her bare arms look like they're carved out of marble. Her ribs are heaving, her breath coming sharp and fast. Her hand shakes as she aims at Kevin Joyce, and her lower lip quivers like she's about to burst into tears.

Joyce starts to beg. He says he didn't mean it. He says he had no choice. He tries English, tries Irish, and then he stops arguing and just cries for his mam.

Fiona's killed before—the four she's proud of and the three that give her nightmares. She's followed orders, and she's made her own choices. She knows how this game works.

But the Bell rings inside my skull, crystal clear in the summer night. Fiona shouldn't have to bear the weight for this one. She doesn't need to remember this sack of shite, sobbing, desperate, snot running down his face as he pleads.

One more twitch of my wrist. One more pull on the trigger. One more blast from the Magnum, and the thing that used to be the head of Kevin Joyce explodes all over the interior of Aran Dowd's Cadillac.

I take a deep breath before I lower my weapon.

But before I can turn around and take my little girl in my

arms, tell her it's over, tell her she's safe, she throws herself at my back.

She pounds me with her fist. She does her best to bite me as she screams beside my ear. She throws her head back and howls louder than Joyce ever managed—no words, nothing human, just a flood of feral rage.

33

FIONA

R ed.
   I'm blinded by a curtain of red, darker than my dress under moonlight. I *told* him what I wanted. I *said* what I needed. I claimed that writhing sack of shit as mine.

But Patrick Moran is just like every other man I've ever met. He plays a good game. He says he isn't interested in the Old Colony Crew. He acts like he's willing to let me take the lead, to let me be his captain.

But the instant I didn't do exactly as he demanded, he made his own choice. He took charge. He stole what belonged to me.

"Put down the gun, Fiona."

I hear the words, but I don't care. I continue to beat him with my fist, pounding at his chest, because he's finally turned to face me.

"Put down the fucking gun."

That animal sound still tears across my throat. I hear it. I know I'm making it. But I can't stop. I don't *want* to stop. I want to scream at him forever.

"Goddammit, Fiona!"

His fingers close around my wrist, squeezing the pressure point above my thumb. My howl turns to a wail, and the revolver drops onto the grass.

"You fucking *asshole!*" I scream.

He folds his arms around me. He's trying to smother me against his chest. His hand spreads across the back of my head, and I hear the things he's whispering, soft, like I'm a wounded animal, like I'm a baby he can rock to sleep.

"You're safe, little girl. You're fine, little girl. No one's going to hurt you."

"I'm not your little girl!"

"I'm sorry I used you like a shield. I didn't have time to tell you my plan. I'm so, so sorry, little girl."

"I'll never be your little girl again!"

He sucks in a sharp breath like I've kneed him in the balls, but he doesn't let me go. Instead he tightens his arms around me and says, "Daddy has you."

I shove against his chest, pushing off like I'm trying to topple him into the water hazard below. He lets me go, but he doesn't back away.

"You're not my fucking Daddy," I growl, planting my fists on my hips.

"*Scáthach*—" he says.

"Don't call me that!" My scream is so loud, they must hear it at the top of Old North Church.

He could break my neck if I gave him half a chance. He could punch me hard enough to lacerate my liver. Hell, he still has that fucking Howitzer of a gun—he must have tucked it into his waistband, beneath his rumpled tuxedo jacket—and a shot from that thing at this close range would turn my body into mist.

But he takes a full step back, saying, "Let's get out of here."

"I don't want to get out of here!"

"The cops will—"

"Fuck the goddamn cops."

I watch him swallow down an argument. I see him shift gears. "I only wanted to help you, Fiona. To keep you safe."

"Fuck you. I can fight my own fucking bat—"

"You *can* fight. But you don't have to."

"Of course I have to fight! Every Queen has to fight!"

"Captains issue kill orders every day."

"*Not if they're a fucking woman!*"

My shout is loud enough to echo off the moon. It knocks away every patronizing argument Patrick Moran could ever make.

Now that I finally have his attention, I tell him *my* truth. "I don't get to captain the Crew like anyone who's gone before me. I have to be stronger than my father ever was."

"Your father's dead—"

I interrupt him. "You think I don't know that?"

"—and buried. But you're still giving him free rent inside your head. You're stuck trying to be his perfect daughter. You want him to pat you on the head and tell you he loves you. Well, I've got news for you. That is never going to happen."

"Go to hell."

"He would have been ashamed by that show you put on tonight, back at the museum. Sure—flaunt your tits at a few gobsmacked mobsters. But don't think you can go after civilians the exact same way. Limericks. Jameson. Toasts to the old country. No one wants that type of show."

"Careful, old man. Your jealousy's showing. You didn't like the way those poor, bored fucks paid attention to me."

"I don't give one shite about society yokes. But your uncle's another story."

"Fuck my uncle."

"That's what he wants, yeah. That's what you're scared of. *That's* why you wanted to kill this shitehawk—to prove you can pull the trigger when you face the man who sent him. But Dowd is smarter than this eejit. Richer and stronger too."

"He's Da's age. He's too fucking old to run the Crew."

"And you're too fucking young! You don't have the experience. You make too many bad choices. The sooner you accept that, the sooner you can figure out what you want to be when you grow up."

My voice freezes. "I'm going to be captain of the Old Colony Crew."

"The fuck you are."

"When the Grand Irish Union votes in six weeks—"

"Wake up!" He interrupts me, snapping in front of my nose. "Sure. You can wait till the Union votes to make your move. Wait till you sit on Santy's lap, begging for a Christmas gift. Wait till hell freezes over, because you are never, ever going to lead the Old Colony Crew."

It feels like he's slapped me. Like he's landed a punch in my ribs. All these weeks, I thought he understood. I thought he knew. I thought he believed in me.

I have to hit back. I have to land a blow as hard as the one he's just struck. Harder.

"I *will* lead the Crew," I tell him. "And you know why? Because I can concentrate on something for longer than thirty goddamn seconds. I can show up where I'm supposed to be on time, without setting a dozen alarms. I can keep track of a fucking key for an entire day. I can show a little goddamn impulse control and keep from blowing some motherfucker's head to smithereens!"

His throat works. He starts to explain. Stops. Starts to fucking apologize. Stops again.

And I take my one last shot, the one I should have put into Kevin Joyce's brain. "I can't trust you, because you can't trust yourself. You're not a man. You're an animal. You don't belong here, Cujo. You never did."

34

PATRICK

Cujo.

Kieran Ingram was the first man to call me that, and he used it as a sign of respect. I was a mad dog. I was *his* mad dog. He could point me toward an enemy, and I would tear the poor fecker apart, limb from goddamn limb.

But the meaning changed when Da died. Cujo meant I was sick. I was damaged. I was everything corrupt about the Crew I'd sworn to.

Fiona can't know all that. But she knows she wants to hurt me. She wants to pierce my heart.

Which is exactly what I tried to do to her. I knew what I was saying, telling her she was young, telling her she was naive. I placed a wedge, and I pounded it hard, knowing she'd never accept what I said.

There's one long moment when we can both say we're sorry. We can both take back our words.

But I'm a mad dog. A savage. I can't fix this.

And she doesn't want to.

The time-bomb is ticking, ticking, ticking. But it doesn't explode. Instead, it eats a gulf between us, chewing away at everything we ever had, leaving a gaping canyon neither one of us can cross.

I stare at the mayhem around us. The water beyond the Cadillac's nose is deep enough to swallow a frustrated golfer's clubs, but it's not a lake. It can't hide bodies or a car.

It's something of a miracle we haven't been found already. If the golf course wasn't on the edge of a busy college campus, someone would have already phoned in the noise. Any cop who drives past the splintered front gate will investigate the situation.

This is one of those times when my broken brain is an asset. It can replay every single frame of the movie we've just shot. I can watch every step Fiona and I took. I can see we never touched the Caddy. I know we've left no fingerprints behind.

We're too far from the clubhouse to worry about a security camera. There's probably one trained on the gate. They'll run the Land Rover's Pennsylvania plate. Maybe show up with a warrant at my place down in Philly. I need to swap plates *now*.

I stalk to the gun I forced Fiona to drop. It's a snub-nosed Ruger, with a textured grip. It could be useful down the road, especially since there's nothing to connect it to this slaughter-house. I drop it in the pocket of my trousers.

"Let's go," I say to Fiona.

"I'm not going anywhere with you." She sounds like she's twelve, instead of twenty-four.

She squawks when I swoop her into a fireman's carry. She tries to elbow my face, but she can't get any leverage. She kicks like a mule, but she can't make contact with her feet either.

I drop her onto the Land Rover's passenger seat, hard enough to clack her teeth together because I can't risk her getting any brilliant ideas about running away. I slam her door closed and don't waste any time circling around and getting behind the wheel. It's easy enough to flip the switch that child-locks the doors—great for families, I hear, but better for kidnappers.

Neither of us says a word as I drive across town. I follow the speed limit like I'm a priest taking communion to my elderly granny. I treat yellow lights like they're red. I count to five at stop signs.

When I get to Beacon Street, I stop in front of the apartment. I ignore my open space at the fire hydrant. I turn on my flashers so I don't cause an accident.

Flicking the button to release Fiona's door, I say, "Get out."

She stares straight ahead, as if she's been struck deaf.

"I swear to God," I tell her. "I will throw you over my shoulder and drop you in front of that goddamn door."

That makes her look at me. "Of course you will," she says, etching each word with acid. And then she nails my coffin shut: "*Daddy.*"

She's not trying to seduce me. She's not even playing bait and switch.

She's shoving an ice pick into the base of my brain and dripping in venom after.

As if there could be any doubt, she gets out of the car then, closing the door like she's cradling a basket of eggs. She walks up the steps like a queen on parade, like she's reviewing the troops of her own private army.

It takes every last fiber of my shredded self-control to keep from flooring the Land Rover as I turn off the flashers and pull away. Two miles down the road, I turn into a public parking garage. I navigate three levels of the ramp before easing into a space between a twenty-year-old Camry and a sleek BMW sedan.

The Camry owner takes care of his car. He's made it last, even in Massachusetts, where winter salt and sand eat everything on the road. So I'll fuck over the Beemer's owner instead.

Pennsylvania only requires plates on the back of a car, which leaves the BMW's front looking empty after I swap the plates.

Fuck it. The owner will notice. That means I need to make another stop.

I exit the garage and drive a few more well-regulated miles before I pull into another garage. This one's less crowded. I have to work fast, but I switch the Beemer's plates with the ones on a family minivan.

That's good enough for now. I only have to get far enough to sell the fucking car.

Who am I kidding? I'm leaving this one at a chop shop. And the shops I know best are all down in Philadelphia.

I'm nearly at Boston's city limits when I realize Fiona left her stiletto heels behind.

I toss one out the window as I merge onto the interstate. The other one goes when I cross into Connecticut. After that, it's a long, mind-numbing haul, sticking to the speed limit every mile of the road.

35

FIONA

The man lived here for two months, but there's little sign of him around the apartment. There are six hangers in the closet, holding dress shirts, pants, and his plain black suit. There's one drawer in the dresser, filled with socks and under-wear, with solid-color T-shirts folded into perfect dark rectan-gles. There's a shelf in the medicine cabinet—a razor, a can of shaving cream, and a toothbrush.

And an amber bottle of pills.

Fuck the pills. Fuck Patrick Moran. He's a fucking criminal mastermind. He can get more fucking pills whenever he needs them.

I shove all his crap into the duffel bag he carried when we drove up from Philadelphia. While I'm at it, I add my dress. I'll never be able to look at it again without thinking about this fiasco of a night.

I want to drench it all in lighter fluid and set it on fire in the backyard, but one of my neighbors would probably complain about the smoke. With my luck, they'd call the cops. And the *Globe* would be monitoring the police scanner. Along with every podcaster in the state. Every last one of them would show up on my doorstep, and my face would be spread across the Internet with enough information to let any idiot track me: *Beacon Street Bonfire Battle.*

Fuck my life.

I'll take it all to the dumpster down the street tomorrow. Toss it into the bin behind the Chinese restaurant. Let it get buried beneath cabbage leaves and moldy pork.

For now, I pull on my oldest pair of yoga pants. I find an ancient cami, a plain one without lace. I go into the bathroom and scrub my makeup from my face. And when I'm done, when I'm clean, when I'm nothing like the woman who faced down the Corman Gala and my uncle's trained kidnappers, I grab a bottle of vodka and climb into bed.

I down shots like medicine. Two off the bat, then one more every thirty minutes. In between, I scan my phone, looking for news about murders on the golf course.

I pass out before the story breaks.

36

PATRICK

I make it to Philly before sunrise. Part of me knows I should report to my boss, tell Kelly I'm ready and willing to take on whatever work he needs done. But more of me knows my second-in-command is doing an excellent job managing the Fishtown Boys' enforcers without me.

It wouldn't be fair to Rory O'Hare to show up without warning. To take over the reins like I've never been gone. To act like the last two months never happened.

So I convince myself it's a good idea to check into a hotel. And I know myself well enough that I don't go for some luxury high-rise downtown. I'm going to be here for a while.

I stay close to the freeway, far north of town. I choose the place at random—Embassy Garden or Holiday Suites, whatever —and check into a sterile, white room with a black-and-white photo of the L-O-V-E sculpture in downtown Philly. Luck finally breaks my way—they have a room. I don't have to wait for an afternoon check-in.

My eyelids are lined with sandpaper. My knees ache, and I'm second-guessing my decision to drive straight through without stopping. My stomach says it's going on strike if I don't get something to eat within the hour.

But the brain squirrels are on overdrive. At the hotel's complimentary breakfast bar, my first slice of toast pops up in ten seconds because I forget to set the heat level. The second one turns to charcoal when I get distracted by the coffee machine.

All I want is a caffeine IV, but I have to page through three computer screens, past lattes and cappuccinos and something called a feckin' Mocha Mist. Across the room, a kid is pounding his table with his fist, demanding that his father get him frosted flakes.

"Long night?" the beaten-down father asks, as he approaches the milk dispenser.

It takes me too long to realize he's nodding toward my tuxedo. No wonder the front desk clerk stared at me oddly. They'd both go ape-shit if they knew I still have Kevin Joyce's Ruger in my pocket. At least my Magnum's back in the glove box.

I press the button on the coffee machine, and a thick stream of something that looks like motor oil spurts straight into the drain. I forgot to put a cup beneath the spout.

"Fuck," I say, louder than I should, because Frosted Flakes Boy starts shouting, "Fuck! Fuck! Fuck!" between spoonfuls of poison. His father gives me a dirty look.

I pull a hand down my face in a desperate effort to focus. I finally get a cup of coffee, a packaged Danish, and a banana from a bowl.

Part of me knows I should reach out to Doc Kelleher, the sawbones kept on call by the Fishtown Boys. He can set me up with a new scrip, get me my meds.

But for now, I need my brain working overtime. I need to figure out what went wrong in Boston. I need to make sure no one's traced me down here to Philly. I need to get out of this goddamn tuxedo.

And I need to ditch the Land Rover.

Stopping at a Target on my way downtown, I throw things into the red plastic cart—jeans, a package of T-shirts, a bag of boxer briefs, runners, and socks. I grab a toothbrush and tooth-paste, a razor, and shaving cream. On the way to checkout, I toss in a box of protein bars, even though I know the brain squirrels will have a field day with the sugar. I make it past the beer and wine without clearing the shelves.

My life should fill more than two plastic bags.

I change clothes in the jacks at the store. I can't leave the Ruger tucked into the small of my back, grip showing above my belt, so I bury it in one of the bags, between my satin-striped pants and my pleated white shirt. I try to ignore the feeling that the guy collecting carts in the parking lot has X-ray vision.

There's a chop shop I know, down by the docks. It takes time to get there, threading my way through morning rush hour traf-fic. There's a crash near one of the exits that backs up traffic for three and a half miles. I spin my fidget ring until I finally get past the cops' flashing blue lights.

I feel like my red-and-white Massachusetts plates are set on strobe. I wonder if anyone's reported the switches I made back in Boston.

The brain squirrels want me to pull off the road. They chitter that I'll be better off on surface streets. I can put the Land Rover in a garage. Back into a space and take off the Massachusetts plate on the front. Leave the car there for days. Maybe weeks. A month?

It's a stupid plan, leaving too much to chance. The sort of grand scheme the brain squirrels feed me when they're acting the maggot, screwing around for the sheer joy of driving me mad.

I bite my tongue, hard enough to force me to focus. I wind my way through the warehouse district. I empty out the glove box—the Magnum, a pair of throwing knives, and a retractable baton—and I hand over the keys.

It takes a little negotiating, but I have Ramirez's guy drop me at a used car lot out by the airport. The place is the size of a postage stamp; it's mainly a front for selling drugs. But I'm carrying enough cash for a ten-year-old Chevy Trax, and that will keep me going for a while.

The sun is blinding as I drive back to the hotel. I should have grabbed sunglasses at Target. I can stop at a drugstore and pick some up.

Fiona bought sunglasses at a drugstore. Fiona gave away her glasses. Fiona—

Fuck. I have to stop thinking about Fiona.

She was a mistake.

Everything that happened in Boston was a mistake.

Squinting into the morning light, I weave my way back to my hotel.

37

FIONA

E very night, I twist beneath my sheets, dreaming I'm pinned against a chapel's stone floor, dreaming I'm shoving a gun in Father Colin's face, dreaming he's Kevin Joyce. At midnight or at one or at three in the morning, I give up and pour myself a juice glass full of booze.

I work my way through all the vodka in the apartment. Then the rum. Then the gin.

I pour the Jameson down the sink.

Each morning, I wake to a pounding headache. I stretch one hand toward my nightstand, because I'm smart when I drink. I leave myself a glass of water and a couple of Advil.

But after a week of my new routine, I forget. I don't set out my morning cure. And when I wake, my stomach feels like the inside of a lava lamp.

As I steel myself to stumble into the bathroom, a nasty little voice whispers at the back of my throbbing brain. *Patrick left you water and Advil when you got drunk on Scotch and ice cream.*

Patrick's gone. And he's never coming back. That's what I want. I only have room in my life for people who believe in me, for people who support my fight to take over the Crew.

That's Q.

And, um, Oona, if she even knows what I'm trying to do.

And… and Rónnad.

Fuck.

I get my own water. And I swallow my own Advil. And an hour later, when I think my stomach can handle it, I go into the kitchen and make some toast, telling myself that only rookies puke.

Over the last seven days, I've paced every square inch of the apartment. I've turned the photo of Aunt S to the counter, because I don't want her to see how I've let one idiot man take me down.

Goddammit, I'm not letting him win. I can't stay in this apartment forever. I have to get back to work, to taking over the Old Colony Crew. I need to start acting like a Queen, if I'm ever going to claim that job.

The Grand Irish Union meets in a little more than a month. By tradition, Boston hosts that meeting. When my father became general, the vote was held at the Four Seasons.

What was good enough for Da is good enough for me.

I spend an entire morning on the phone with the most professional conference coordinator I could ever imagine. I reserve a conference room for the vote, complete with coffee service and a guarantee that no hotel staff will set foot anywhere near while we're meeting. I rent suites for all the captains.

I'm so exhausted when I finish the job that I take a nap. I sleep all afternoon and into the evening.

And when I finally wake, I decide it's time to celebrate the work I accomplished. I'm keeping the GIU on track. That's the sort of responsible thing a captain does. I *will* end up in charge of the Old Colony Crew, even if it takes me a little longer than I originally planned.

Going to my closet, I choose a never-fail corset: Black leather, six buckles down the front, metal studs tracing my ribs like fingerprints. I pair it with a latex miniskirt cut so short I won't be able to sit down.

That's fine. The only sitting I plan to do will be on some man's face.

I eat an apple, and when that doesn't turn my stomach, I follow it with a glass of milk.

There. I'm ready to go out.

I tuck my phone into my cleavage, step into my highest needle-heel shoes, and head downstairs. One quick stop to leave my key in the mailbox, and I'm on my way to Wicked Sins.

Henry's behind the bar, which should be a good thing, because he pours with a heavy hand. He also knows I'm partial to Glenfiddich. He already has his hand on the bottle as I make my way to the counter.

One glance at the label, though, and I'm earwormed with Frank Sinatra, which is ridiculous, because this bar only plays loud rock music. My mouth fills with the taste of Scotch spun with cream, and Millionaire Malts are a stupid idea, and anyone who orders one should be shot on sight.

"I'm going with Grey Goose tonight," I tell Henry.

He raises his eyebrows but doesn't say a word, which automatically triples his tip. My double on the rocks is more like a four-in-hand, and that's the fucking knot Patrick uses on his neckties, and I'm closer to tears than I've been since Madden beat me black and blue.

"Here you go, beautiful," Henry says, pushing the drink over to me. I catch my breath, because that's the sort of thing Patrick would say. I wait for my body to betray me, for my pulse to pick up, for the traitor between my legs to soften with a lazy, spinning swoop.

But none of that happens—nothing at all. I tell myself I'm grateful, because what sort of woman can go through life falling apart at a single kind word? But really, I'm devastated. I'm aching. I'm terrified that I've lost that feeling forever, that Patrick's ruined my pussy, and I'll never come again.

I gulp my drink like it's water and gesture for Henry to work his magic again.

He gives me a wary look, but he pours. This time a double is exactly what it's supposed to be. Exactly what I deserve.

I sip, because I'm pretty sure he'll cut me off if I chug this one. Henry nods once, a sign of approval that ices all my insides. He heads over to the sink as a man steps up to the bar.

"It's busy in here for a Monday," he says.

I tell myself that's a perfectly reasonable opening for a conversation. I remind myself to smile. I take a look at his glass, and he's drinking something clear—gin and tonic, I'm guessing, from the lime.

Good. I can kiss him, and he won't taste like Jameson.

"I haven't seen you here before," he says. He takes just the right amount of time to eye my outfit. He appreciates the buckles. He's curious about what I'm wearing beneath my skirt. But he doesn't stare. And he doesn't reach out to answer his question without an invitation. "I'd remember," he says.

His smile is lopsided. He's got sand-colored hair that was probably blond when he was a kid. His eyes are light—blue or green, I can't tell in the bar's dim light. He's wearing a white cotton button-down, expensive, tailored to fit his trim waist.

"Law?" I ask. "Or finance?"

He smiles again. His right front tooth is chipped. "Banking law," he says.

"Want to fuck?"

That takes him by surprise. But he laughs a little, and then he says, "I'm used to a little foreplay before I jump right in."

I clutch my glass like it's the last parachute in a plane that's going down. For just a moment, I think I'm going to faint. I take a deep breath. Hold it for a count of four. Exhale on a count of four. Realize I'm breathing like Patrick and once again fight the urge to cry.

Or scream. I could scream instead.

But I choose a third option.

I reach out with my left hand, the one that isn't holding my drink. I cup Mr. Banking Law's crotch, just enough to feel the leap of his dick beneath my fingers. I squeeze once. "There. That's foreplay. Ready to fuck?"

This isn't right. This isn't what I want to do. It's not what I want to say, what I want to think, how I want to feel. I'm standing on the edge of a cliff, looking into a canyon, and if I take one more step, I'll fall for the rest of my life.

Mr. Banking Law shakes his head. "Sorry," he says. "I think you're looking for another guy."

He takes his gin and tonic and heads back to his table.

I barely make it to the ladies' room before I start to puke. The vodka burns a hell of a lot more coming up than it ever did going down. It takes a long time for my stomach to empty, which is ridiculous, because there's hardly anything in it.

I'm Fiona Fucking Ingram. I'm supposed to feel strong. I'm supposed to be powerful. Men drool like dogs when I spare them a single glance. Women stare in awe.

I flush the toilet. At the sink, I wash my hands, and then I rinse my mouth. I stare at myself in the mirror—at my smudged eyeliner, at my smeared lipstick, at my hair, which looks like I've run it through a blender.

I can't fix this. Too much is wrong. It's time for me to give up and go home.

But the worst part is, I won't look any better once I'm there.

No. That's not the worst part. The worst part is I'll spend the night alone in my big, empty bed. I'll toss and I'll turn and I'll dream about every mistake I've ever made.

And no Daddy will ever be there again, to make it even a tiny bit better.

38

PATRICK

The first week without meds, I feel like Superman.

I put together a new workout routine—crunches and pushups by the hundreds, squat thrusts, mountain climbers, all followed by miles-long runs.

I take the pen and notepad from the drawer in the hotel desk, and I start a list of every place I want to see in the world. There's plenty of Ireland I've never been to—my family's all from County Sligo—but there are other places too. The Eiffel Tower. The Taj Mahal. The Great Wall of China. I write everything down.

I start one of those language apps on my phone. I've got enough Spanish to work a drug deal with the Colombians, and that carries over to Italian when I'm dealing with old-school mafia eejits. But I've thought for a long time about picking up some Russian. The alphabet's a pain in the arse, but I force my way through, one word at a time.

Sure, I sleep like shite, but waking every hour gives me a

chance to check my perimeter. I can keep an eye on the hotel hallway. Make sure no one's getting into the Chevy.

Each morning, I think about reporting to Kelly. But in twenty-five years, I've never gone on holiday. I've never had three consecutive mornings I can do what I want. Three days stretches to four stretches to five, and then it starts to feel like I've been lying to my boss.

I haven't. He hasn't needed me. I still get Fishtown texts on my phone, so I can see Kelly's running the Boys out of his new house. He's watching the build-out on his new bar, the one where he'll keep a back office. The clan's going just fine without me.

Eight days after I get to Philly, I finally track down Rory O'Hare. I trained the man to be my second. I've watched over him for the last ten years, so I know I'll find him at Mimi's on a Monday night. He'll have a go at one of the girls. Treat her to a drink after. And at midnight, he'll be walking home, sticking to the shadows on Second Street.

I step out from the doorway of a boarded-up bank, taking a stand in the middle of the pavement. O'Hare drops into a fighter's crouch, his fingers near the Beretta he keeps in an ankle holster.

"Forget it, boyo," I say. "You'll never draw in time."

"Jaysus," he says, standing to his full height and offering me a handshake. "Moran! What are you doing here?"

"Checking up on your sorry arse. You're keeping Himself safe?"

O'Hare gives me a rundown on all he's done for the Boys. They've been warring with the mafia for months. Things have gone to hell since February, when a summit put things to rest for a short while.

That's the meeting Fiona ran when her da was too sick to manage.

Fiona... The squirrels treat me to a split-second slideshow—

her body moving under mine, her face flushing as I call her beautiful, her voice calling my name as she comes—

I snap my attention back to O'Hare. "Who do you have driving for Himself?"

He's deployed his men well. He's keeping track of all his boss's household—Kelly, and his wife, and the girl they're raising as their own. O'Hare's put some thought into his men's needs too. He's increasing responsibility for the best of the junior enforcers. He's doubling up where a yoke's not quite up to speed.

He's good at this job. The best.

"So when'll you be back from Boston for real?" he asks.

"I'm not sure."

"I've still got that Mini in the garage. The one you told me to nick."

That's Fiona's car, the one she left at Madden's. The Bell clangs, urging me to act, not think. "Sell it," I tell O'Hare. "Send the money to the Corman Museum up in Boston. Make a donation in Fiona Ingram's name."

"Then Ingram's girl is doing all right?"

"She's fine," I lie. Or maybe I'm telling the truth. I don't know. Fiona's not my business anymore.

She might be mine, if I'd held my fucking tongue. If I hadn't lashed out, aiming for her most vulnerable bits. If I'd given her half a chance to get past my killing Kevin Joyce.

Fuck Kevin Joyce. And while I'm at it, fuck Aran Dowd too. He's the one who sent out Joyce. He's the one who meant to drag Fiona back to the *dún*.

He meant to kill me, too.

The brain squirrels perk right up at that. They're grateful for a new tree to run, a new excuse to gather nuts, to start to bury them left, right, and center.

And standing here in the dark of a Philly street, talking to an enforcer who's working at the top of his game, I realize that

Aran Dowd just might be the reason I've tracked down O'Hare tonight.

Dowd's doing more than trying to take Fiona. More than trying to kill me. Dowd's met with a federal agent, with Mike Barbieri. He's betrayed the Crew. And now he needs to die.

But I still need more proof. I need help from the type of man who can dig deep into computer records. Who can scan phones. Who can screen video.

I ask O'Hare about one of the Fishtown Boys: "Is Fitzgerald still living on Cabot Street?"

"Declan?" O'Hare looks surprised by my change of focus. "He's there, yeah. Licking his wounds."

"Wounds?"

O'Hare shrugs. "Boss brought in someone else to set up the new house, a guy named Wolf. One of those billionaires from that tax place, down in Delaware."

Declan Fitzgerald's served the Fishtown Boys for a decade. I'd question Kelly's own loyalty before I'd throw darts at Fitzgerald. So if Kelly brought in this Wolf guy, he's good. Maybe good enough to work the miracle I need.

O'Hare's waiting for me to say something. To do something. He acts like I'm still his boss.

"Go on, then," I say. "Keep up the good work." I offer him my hand. But just before he takes it, I add, "No need to tell Himself I was checking up on you. You've earned that much."

O'Hare's hand is firm on mine. I chose well when I put him in charge of the Fishtown Boys enforcers. I stare at his back until he turns a corner, knowing I've worked myself out of a job.

39

FIONA

My life turns into *Groundhog Day*, everything the same, over and over and over.

Every morning, I groan awake after hours of nightmares. I'm determined to get my life under control. I stare at the fridge, but nothing looks good for breakfast. I go for a walk, but I lose interest before I've made it to the first corner.

Every afternoon, I vow I'll do something to make myself stronger when I'm captain of the Old Colony Crew. I study banking and accounting, but the numbers just bleed in my head, and I know I'll never be better than Q. I read about great organized crime empires—the mafia's early days in New York, the bratva's rise in Brighton Beach, the shaky foundations of South American cartels—but times have changed and they're no longer a good model for the Crew. I fill notebook after notebook with ideas for new schemes—ransomware and cryptocurrency and online gambling—but it's all too big, all too complex, and I can't begin to act on any of it until I'm Queen.

Every night, I realize I've squandered another twenty-four hours. I open a can of soup if there's one in the cupboard. I eat a carton of yogurt. I choke down an entire apple.

I take my birth control pill. Because I'm *going* to find another man. I'm *going* to take someone to bed. I'm *going* to get over Patrick Moran. I have to.

With Aunt S gone, there's only one person in the world I want to talk to. One person who's seen me at my worst and managed to still love me. One person who can tell me everything will be okay.

Oona.

There's no way in hell I can drop by the *dún* just to talk with her, not with Uncle Aran's living there. He'll have me dragged off to a priest at gunpoint, the instant I set foot inside the house. I'll be married before I can blink.

But there's another way I can get to Oona. One place we'll both be safe.

It's absurd to think I can pull this off. It'll take money—a lot of it. I need to pay a bribe, one large enough to stop even a hint of gossip from reaching Uncle Aran.

But thanks to Rónnad, I have fifty thousand dollars locked in a safe at the back of my closet. I count the money. And then I steel myself to place a phone call, putting my plan into motion.

40

PATRICK

Alix Key says, "Of course I remember you, Mr. Moran. I hope you and Ms. Ingram are both doing well."

"We are," I say, because it could take me a lifetime to explain the truth. I've already wasted a week, planning to call her, getting distracted, convincing myself I should make another plan instead of trusting a stranger.

There isn't a better way. I need to take the feckin' leap.

I say, "I hope you can help me get in touch with one of your clients."

Alix's voice cools noticeably. "And who would that be?"

"He's been working with my...colleague, Braiden Kelly." I barely stumble over *colleague*. I don't know what Kelly and I are anymore. "I understand this man's a computer expert. His name is Wolf?"

Alix says, "For privacy reasons, I can neither confirm nor deny that Mr. Wolf is a client of Diamond Freeport. I'm sure you understand."

"Yes," I say, like I'm reciting lines in a play. "Of course. Well, thank you very much for your time."

"My pleasure," Alix says.

I end the call, and the brain squirrels immediately start their burrowing. I spin my fidget ring, but that doesn't begin to take the edge off. I drop and pump out a quick twenty pushups. Twenty more. Twenty after that.

It's pissing down rain outside, and the thought of lacing up my runners and hitting the road makes my soul shrivel. But that's what I think it will take to buy myself a little peace.

I get one shoe on, and then I remember the search I ran on my phone before I called Alix. I'm spending a feckin' fortune on this hotel. I could rent a three-bedroom house in the Philly suburbs for what I'm spending on this one room.

Telling the feckin' squirrels to roast in hell, I try to concentrate on the listings. All I have to do is visit a few rentals. Sign a lease and settle down.

My foot is cold. I find my other runner and lace it up. Three miles might be enough to help me to focus. If not, four should do the job. Maybe five—

My phone rings.

It's a blocked number, which is exactly what I expect. Alix Key works quickly, even if the squirrels made it seem like hours.

"Moran," I answer.

"I understand you're looking for someone to handle some computer work."

"Mr. Wolf, I presume?"

"Diamond Freeport gave me your number. Alix Key vouched for you."

Alix Key doesn't know me, not really. But she knows Kelly. And that means I owe another debt to my old boss. They're piling up.

I stretch the truth a little. "And Braiden Kelly's vouched for you."

"What sort of job do you have in mind?" Wolf's voice thaws

as we complete our verbal handshake, but he's still pure business. I appreciate a man who doesn't waste my time.

"I need a full investigation on a man in Boston." There's no reason to mince words. If Wolf's going to get scared off, I need to know now. "Someone highly placed in the Old Colony Crew. In the Boston mob."

"I have some limited familiarity with the Crew. But you need to understand—I'm not a private investigator."

"I'm not looking for a PI. I want to get into this man's phones. Into his computers. I need proof that he's doing business with a certain party."

"Most men working for organizations like the Crew are sensitive to surveillance. Who's your *certain party?* It might be easier to get into their records."

"The FBI."

Fifteen seconds of silence is a lot longer in the real world than people imagine it will be. I don't know if Wolf is second-guessing targeting the mob, or if he wants to steer clear of the federal government, or maybe he's realizing Alix Key might not be his best source for new business.

But he finally says, "Let's work things from that angle, then. Who's the contact at the FBI? And what's your target's name?"

I feed him everything I have on Aran Dowd.

41

FIONA

"In the name of the Father, and of the Son, and of the Holy Spirit. My last confession was one week ago."

Oona's familiar voice chisels into the stone box around my heart. I want to fling open the door on my side of the confessional and drag her out of the wooden booth. I'm dying to throw my arms around her and bury my face in her soft neck and never need to face the world again.

But I paid Father Bertram a small fortune for these few minutes. I can't afford to waste a single second. "Oona," I say. "It's me."

"Fiona?" Her watery blue eyes are framed by the carved screen between us. "What in the name of the Blessed Virgin—"

"I needed to see you. I'm going crazy, and there's no one else who knows me, no one who understands…"

"What's wrong, *coinín beag?*"

Little rabbit. For just a moment, I'm sitting on her lap in the nursery on the third floor of the *dún*. I'm holding Bunbun, my fingers wrapped around his ears as she works a comb through my snarled hair.

Bunbun.

I hear Patrick's voice, rough with need the first night we fucked in the apartment. *That's your safeword. That's what you'll say when you need me to stop.*

And then I hear my voice, gasping the word I never thought I'd use, rushing it out, even though I thought he'd ignore me, even though I thought I was lost.

But he listened. He heard. He stopped.

"Fiona, love?" Oona's voice rises half an octave in concern.

"It's Patrick," I say.

"What's Paddy done now? You tell that boy I won't make the bannock he likes, if he doesn't treat you like the queen you are. Send him round. I'll give him a talking to."

"He's gone!" I hiccup when I say it.

"Gone?" Oona asks, like she doesn't know the word.

"We fought," I tell her. "Two, no, three weeks ago. I lost my temper and—"

"What have I told you about minding your tongue?"

I can't count the number of times Oona has told me I need to calm down, slow down, take the time to let my brain catch up with my mouth. I try to justify myself now, the same as I always have. "But he said things too!"

"I'm certain you remember that two wrongs never made a right."

"Tell *him* that!"

"I would, if he were the one who sent away Father Bertram and caught me all unawares like this."

She sounds so prim, my cheeks heat with embarrassment. We don't have much longer, and I have to make her understand why I've cornered her here. "I thought he was different, Oona. I thought he was special."

But then I remember the look of disgust on her face when I called him Daddy in her kitchen.

Wiping my palms on my thighs, I try again. "He took care of me when he didn't have to. He helped me when no one else would. He told me when he thought I was full of shit, but he stood by me anyway."

"Sweet Blessed Mary," she says, and I see her making the sign of the cross. I think she's going to lecture me about swearing in church, but instead she says, "You love him!"

"I don't—"

"I wasn't sure you'd ever trust a man like that, a man in the life. Not after what you've seen in the *dún*. Not after being raised by a wolf like your da."

"I don't love him, Oona. I can't."

"And why not?"

"*He left me!*" I barely remember not to shout the words. They come out as an agonized hiss, like a candle dropped in a bucket of tears.

"He'll come back." Oona says it with the simple confidence another woman would use to say two plus two equals four. Three teaspoons equals a tablespoon. Eight ounces make a cup. Patrick Moran will return to the *dún*.

No. More than that. Patrick Moran will return to *me*.

"How can you possibly know that?" I ask.

"I've seen the way he looks at you."

"Oh, please."

Oona says, "I've known Paddy since he was half your age. He has his own wolves. He met his own demons at the *dún*."

"So you're saying he's as fucked up as I am."

Oona tsks. "Keep using language like that, *coinín beag*, and I'll head straight for home."

"Oona…" I draw out her name, the way I used to do when I was a little girl, when I wanted her to read me one more story before she turned out the light.

"Talk to him," she finally says, like that's the simplest thing in the world.

"Yeah," I say. "Right."

282 | ALIX KEY

"Don't take that tone with me." She holds up her hand, close enough to the wooden screen that I can see her long life-line slicing across her palm. "No, no, I don't want to hear it. You have a thousand reasons why you can't do what's right. But there's one reason you should."

"Because…" I know what she means. But I can't make myself think the words, much less say them.

"Because you love him," she says. Straightforward. Matter of fact. Like when she told me I'd get my period. When she cleaned me up after what happened in the chapel. When she told me Aunt S had died. "Talk to Paddy now. Because your uncle…"

I hear something in her voice, just before she trails off, something I never thought I'd hear in a million years. Oona Maguire is scared. "What?" I ask her. "What's going on?"

She says, "The men in that house—they think I don't pay attention. They think I'm blind and I'm deaf and I won't repeat a syllable they say…"

"Oona. What is Uncle Aran planning to do?"

"At the vote next month, for the Grand Irish Union. Your uncle says he'll run the meeting."

"He can't do that. I'm the one who booked the rooms."

Oona makes a dismissive sound with her lips. "Anyone can book some rooms." She lowers her voice so much I have to lean forward to hear her. I catch my breath to make out her whispered words. "He says he'll sit for Boston. He'll cast the Old Colony vote for general. And the morning after oaths are sworn, he's bringing in a priest, to marry you in front of all the others. He'll drug you if he has to. Beat you if he must. And once his ring's jammed onto your finger, he'll have all those other captains name him King of Boston."

None of this is news. I've known Uncle Aran's plan since he shoved his tongue down my throat in his office at the *dún*.

But bringing a priest to the Union meeting? Drugging me in front of all the other captains?

He's crazier than I ever imagined. He won't give up the Crew without a fight.

I'm suddenly aware that Uncle Aran might have followed Oona today. He has the resources to pay for access to my phone and track me that way. He's purchased contacts on the police force; he can put out a missing-person claim and offer a reward to would-be Good Samaritans—tell them I'm sick, that I need help, that I'm off my non-existent medication.

Horror shivers through my belly like hairs rising on a tarantula's leg.

"Holy fuck," I breathe, which is probably the first time those two words have been said inside the confessional—at least on the priest's side of the box.

Oona tsks again. But then she says, "Talk to Paddy. Tell him the truth. Together, you'll stop him."

"*How?*" This time, I can't keep my voice low.

"Talk to Paddy," she says one more time. "You'll figure it out together."

"If I could fucking talk to—"

"That'll be three Our Fathers," Oona says serenely. "And three Hail Marys. Go in peace, *coinín beag.*"

She leaves before I do. I sit back on the hard wooden bench and try to figure out how to track down Patrick.

What I can possibly say to make him forgive me.

How I can get him to help me before it's too late.

42

PATRICK

I don't know what makes me finally wake up and smell the feckin' coffee.

Maybe it's pure exhaustion. Without Fiona's body to sedate the goddamn brain squirrels, I haven't slept more than two hours at a time in weeks.

Maybe it's handing over my credit card for yet another week of staying at the hotel. I hate these four walls. My clothes are tangled on the floor of the closet. The cheap snacks I've pretended are meals tumble on top of the dresser. I'm sick of drinking Jameson out of a white plastic cup that looks like it's made to hold piss samples at a doctor's office.

Maybe it's the report Cole Wolf has finally compiled, two weeks after I hired him. I drive down to DC to pick up the encrypted thumb drive he made because I won't chance it to any courier. As he walks me through what he's captured—thousands and thousands of phone records, computer files, and transcribed notes of in-person meetings—I wonder if Wolf ever sleeps.

Because he's delivered proof that Aran Dowd is pure sin.

Sure, the feds have the fecker on Crash distribution. With enhanced sentencing for endangering the lives of minors, they can send him to prison for the rest of his natural life.

But Dowd is singing like Maria Von Trapp in the Austrian hills. He's already handed over the Crew's entire banking system —everything Fiona and I learned from Q, all the offshore accounts, all the crypto. The feds have access to every new deposit, to each withdrawal Dowd's made "for the good of the clan."

He's given them the Old Colony's structure too—Clan Chief and Warlord and Quartermaster, the brigades of sworn soldiers, and runners who are still being tested. The feds keep pressing for specific names; they have long lists of candidates. Dowd's resistance is shredding like the roof of a thatched hut in the middle of a category five hurricane.

And the feds are leaning hard to get the same structure on every other clan in the country. Whenever Dowd gets cagy about his own crew, Michelangelo Barbieri switches to asking questions about the others.

I'm ready to boke when I finish going through all the garbage Wolf's raked up. I thank him and I authorize a bank transfer into his account with more zeroes than I've ever spent in one place. At least my personal banking hasn't been handed over to the feds. Yet.

When I get back to Philly, I place one call: To Doc Kelleher. He tells me to come by direct, and he gives me a month's worth of meds from the stash in his office. He says he'll email the drugstore up in Boston, get the scrip on record for the coming year.

I dry-swallow the pills on my way back to the hotel. It takes me five minutes to throw my things into bags. Fifteen to argue with the clerk at the front desk, asking for a refund for the rest of the week, the days I paid for yesterday. He can't give me any satisfaction, but we agree to let the manager decide things overnight.

I spend the night in a Boston hotel room that's a clone of the one I left in Philly. I can't say I sleep well—my body still misses Fiona's—but I wake feeling calmer than I have in weeks. More focused. Like I'm the one calling the shots instead of the feckin' squirrels.

Must be the meds.

Showered and dressed, I'm ready to drive to one of the big box stores on the edge of town. I need a computer to handle all the data Wolf's found because there's no way to plug the encrypted drive into my phone. Once I have a decent machine, I can start the hard work of reading every page of evidence. Of building a case that will take down Aran Cocksucking Dowd forever.

But there's one stop I need to make first. One part of my life that isn't the mob, that has nothing to do with the Old Colony Crew.

The tables are already set up outside Yankee Roast. Three people are in line at the counter, taking their time choosing their breakfast treats. Hannah Mulroney is at the register, her young face breaking into easy smiles as she rings up each customer.

Kimi's nowhere in sight.

When I get to the front of the line, I order a cup of drip coffee and a blueberry-corn muffin. I have my wallet ready, and I tip more than the total for my meal. Hannah's already looking past me to the next customer when I ask, "Is Kimi in the back?"

Hannah stiffens for just a moment, like the sole of her shoe rolled over a sharp stone. Recovering quickly, she says, "Kimberly's a little under the weather today."

Today. I don't believe her for a second. I think about my sister-in-law's jaundiced face, her drawn cheeks beneath her tight-wrapped headscarf. "I hope she feels better soon," I say, and I mean it.

When I pick up my computer, I'll get a pad of paper too. A box of envelopes. Stamps if they sell them. I'll write Kimi a note. I don't have a return address to put on the letter, nothing to scare her off from opening it. She might get a few lines into my apology before she decides to throw it away.

I'm halfway to the door when Hannah calls out, "Excuse me!"

When I look back, she nods toward the counter that stretches across the shop's front window. "If you have time to take a seat? I'll just finish up here and..."

I don't know what goes after *and*. But I take my coffee to one of the high stools while she finishes with the customers in line. I make the cup last, same as I do the muffin. I watch the traffic walking by outside the bakery.

It's a beautiful late-July morning. The sun catches on a patch of cobblestones exposed beneath the asphalt street. The afternoon will be hot. People are already wearing shorts and T-shirts.

I want to see more days like this. I want to watch the summer turn to autumn, turn to winter, turn to spring. I want to breathe the city's rhythms, from Red Sox to Patriots to Bruins, and back again to baseball. Somewhere, deep in my bones, my body knows I'm home.

"Freshen that up for you?" Hannah's holding a carafe of coffee.

I hold out my mug.

"You're my Uncle Pat, aren't you?"

For one panicked moment, I want to deny it, but that's absurd, because this is the entire reason I came here this morning. Fighting the urge to spread a hand over my tattooed sleeve, I say, "I am. I was married to your Aunt Jenn."

Hannah nods. "There's a picture of you on my mother's mantel, from your wedding day. You look so young there."

My lips twist in something that might be mistaken for a smile. "Time flies."

A faint blush spreads beneath the freckles on her cheeks. "I mean, you both looked so in love."

"We were."

She hooks a foot on the stool next to me, pulls it out, and sits down. "Mom's not just out today. She's back in the hospital. She had a bad reaction to her last round of chemo."

"I'm sorry to hear that."

"I'll be sure to tell her you asked after her."

I stare into my coffee cup. "Maybe that's not such a good idea. I don't want to make anything more difficult for her."

"Naw," she says. "She's tough. She can take it."

"I hope so. I really hope so." I take a napkin from the dispenser on the counter. I pat my pockets, but I don't have a pen—I never do.

Hannah fishes one out of her apron. "Will this help?"

I scrawl my phone number on the paper. "If you need anything... You or your mom."

She glances at the number as I hand it over with her pen. "Yeah," she says. "Um, thanks." For a moment, I worry that she thinks I'm making a pass. But her eyes have grown glassy, and she's trying hard not to blink. The set of her shoulders tells me she's changing the topic on purpose when she says, "Let me pack up a box of those tarts. Your wife seemed to like them."

My wife...

I must look as confused as I feel, because Hannah's voice takes on the sing-song tone of a kindergarten teacher, like she's reminding me of something I forgot two decades ago. "The cherry tarts. She ate them the last time you were here."

"How the f— *hell* do you know what my wife ate?" Hannah wasn't even born when Jenn died.

"I gave them to her. After Mom made you sit outside. At first I was embarrassed that Mom made such a scene, but then I saw how cute you two are together—"

"How cute..." I repeat, because I'm finally beginning to

understand the confusion. Hannah isn't talking about Jenn. She's talking about Fiona. She thinks Fiona and I are married.

"Oh, crap," Hannah says. "I've embarrassed you. What can I say? I'm a hopeless romantic. And when I see two people who pay that much attention to each other... You're so... I don't know. What's the word? Attuned?"

"Fiona and me?"

Hannah glances at my hand, the one that's gripping my coffee mug so tight the pottery might shatter. "Crap," she says again. "You aren't married yet."

"There's no *yet*. We're just friends. We *were* friends."

Her look is full of skepticism, like I've just told her I left my wallet at home and can't afford to pay for the breakfast I've finished. "Right," she finally says. "Whatever."

I debate how much of an explanation I owe this woman because—however unlikely—I *am* her Uncle Pat. Before I can settle on an answer, my phone buzzes in my pocket.

My stomach registers the letters on the screen before my brain does, and I regret my second cup of coffee. I look around the bakery like I expect to find a hidden camera. Or maybe there's a microphone taped beneath the counter.

Hannah glances at the screen and cracks up—a full belly laugh that crinkles her eyes and shows her teeth. "Go on and answer that," she says. "I've got dishes to wash."

I barely notice her walking back behind the counter. Instead, I'm busy clearing my throat. I'm fighting to draw a full breath. I'm telling myself to let the call go to voicemail.

But my hand doesn't listen to my feckin' brain. My finger lands heavily on the bright green icon. I raise the phone to my ear and try to sound normal as I say her name: "Fiona."

43

FIONA

I didn't think this far ahead.

It's been a week since Oona told me to call Patrick. A week that I've been telling myself she's wrong. She doesn't really know me. She still thinks I'm a child, that I'm her *coinín beag*. Not Fiona Fucking Ingram.

I *am* still her *coinín beag*. And I'm Fiona Fucking Ingram. And I'm...whatever the fuck that word is that Patrick calls me, the one I've never managed to find online or in print, even though I've bought three different Irish-English dictionaries.

And I'm going to be Aran Dowd's wife if I set foot outside this apartment. If any member of the Crew finds me anywhere in Boston.

So I finally call.

I'm convinced Patrick won't answer. I'll hang up. I won't even bother with voicemail. That's how civilized people use their phones, right? We look to see what calls we've missed, and we phone back if we want to.

"Fiona," he says again, and his voice sounds strange. "Are you okay? Give me a number between one and five if someone's keeping you from speaking freely."

"Patrick," I finally say. I'm laughing, because the first thing he thought was that he had to save me. And he's laughing, probably because I didn't give him a number. "Where are you?" I ask, and I pray he doesn't say Philadelphia, because I know him. He's loyal, and it would make perfect sense for him to go back to Braiden Kelly. Back to the one clan that's ever welcomed him with open arms.

"At the bakery."

"The bakery?"

"Yankee Roast. Where we met Rónnad."

Thank God. But I don't say that out loud. Instead, I say, "Then you can be here in half an hour."

"Here?" he asks. It's only one word. Four little letters. But it carries more than a month of all the bitter things we said on that golf course, all the hateful words we spewed inside that car.

"Beacon Street," I tell him. "The apartment." And then I add, "Please."

There's a pause, and I wish I could see his face. I wish I could reach out, that I could take his phone, that I could set it aside and pull his mouth to mine.

I can't think.

I can't breathe.

I can't speak.

But finally he says, "I'm on my way."

Relief soars over me like a jet rising off a runway. "Hurry," I say. And just in case he doesn't understand, in case he doesn't know what I'm thinking, how I really feel, I whisper: "Daddy."

44

PATRICK

My key still works in the lock.

I expect to find Fiona standing just inside the door, strapped into black leather, chin raised in a laughing challenge. She isn't.

I turn toward the couch, where I think she'll be waiting, wrapped in scarlet vinyl and a smile. She isn't.

I look toward the kitchen, wondering what she'll taste like covered in whipped cream and sin. She isn't there either.

I put my keys on the counter, along with Wolf's thumb drive and a white pasteboard box. The hallway is ten times longer than it ever was before. It stretches as I walk, the floorboards wavering and shifting. I run my fingers along the wall to keep from breaking into a sprint.

She's stripped the bed down to its fitted sheet. Her feet are splayed wide, two neckties lashing her feet to the footboard. Her black vinyl skirt is smaller than my handkerchief, and it's rucked up around her waist, showing off a scrap of lace that's meant to pass for knickers.

The barely-there triangle is pulled to the side. Her pussy's as bare as it was the night I found her in Philadelphia. This time, though, she's awake. She's inviting me in. This time, she's gloating at my stuttering breath, at the three steps I take to get close enough to catch the scent of her soft, wet folds.

My strangled groan makes her laugh. I can't see her belly beneath her boned black corset, but her tits are bare at the top. Chains fan across her nipples, framing those rock-hard cherries like engraved invitations. Her arms stretch over her head, her wrists locked in handcuffs that wrap around the central post of the headboard. The key gleams by her head, where she clearly dropped it.

"Welcome home, Daddy," she says.

The words are pure Fiona—taunting, promising. But the crease between her eyebrows belongs to another girl. Someone doubting. Someone afraid.

She called me, and I came. But she's still not sure we belong here. She's still not sure this is *right*.

I could show her. I could peel off my clothes and kneel in the V of her legs. I could rip off those knickers and pinch her clit before I fuck her with my tongue. I could get her off three times, four times, five, before I decide to open those cuffs with their silver key.

She'd be sated. She'd be exhausted. She'd be mine.

But I'm her Daddy. She's my little girl. That means I owe her more than orgasms. I need to protect her. I need to keep her safe.

The knots around her ankles are pulled tight. My first impulse is to go to the kitchen for a knife. But she needs a few minutes to shift out of her headspace. I pick at the knots with my fingernails, and I tell her what she needs to hear. "You were a brave girl, calling me."

She flushes, as if my words bare more than all her lace and leather.

When her right ankle's free, I kiss the arch of her foot.

"You thought this through," I say. "I don't know any Daddy in the world who could get a better gift."

Her smile is crooked. She doesn't understand why I'm ruining my present, why I'm denying us both the chance to play.

Her left foot's free. I run my hands up her calf, supporting her until I'm sure her muscles won't cramp now that they're freed.

I have to put one knee on the bed to reach the key to the cuffs. She turns her face toward me. Her lips are quivering now. Her chin trembles with shame or need or sorrow; I can't be sure.

"You're fine, little girl," I say. "You haven't done anything wrong."

I release her right hand and ease it to her side. The chain between the cuffs slides around the headboard's central post. I circle her wrist with my left hand as I use my right to spring the lock.

She rolls onto her side. Her knees curl into her chest. She buries her face in her hands.

"Don't be like that, little girl," I say as I toe off my shoes. I shift my weight until I'm sitting at the top of the bed, my back braced against the headboard. I rescue the handcuffs and move them to the top of the nightstand. "Come here, baby. Let me hold you, *Scáthach*."

It's the Irish word that breaks her. She lifts her head. Starts to turn over. I close my hands over her arms and pull her to sit between my legs. My knees come up on either side of her, and I ease her head back until it rests above my heart. My fingers lace across her belly, and it's all I can do not to trace the bottom hem of her wicked corset.

Instead, I rest my chin on the crown of her head. "That night on the golf course," I say.

I know she'll stiffen. I'm ready for it. I hold her closer.

"You would have made the shot. You could have taken out Joyce. I was trying to protect you. But you didn't need that. You didn't need *me*. And Christ, when I realized that, I wanted you to hurt as much as I did. So I said you'll never be captain. I hit as hard as I could. I'm sorry, *Scáthach*. I was wrong."

For a long time, I think she won't respond.

But then she speaks, her voice so soft I have to hold my breath to make out her words. "I was wrong, too. I know how hard you fight to stay on track, with the meds and the fidget ring, and your breathing. And you've never given me a reason not to trust you. Not once."

"Well," I say. "Maybe once. When I shot the man you said you were ready to kill."

She doesn't smile. "I shouldn't have called you...that."

"Say it," I urge her.

She shakes her head.

"It's just a word."

"One that hurt you."

"Sticks and stones..." I tease. But then I get serious again. "Go on. I want to hear you say it."

"Cujo," she finally whispers.

I kiss her hair. "See? Just a word."

She draws a ragged breath. I feel her start to say something. Stop. Start again. She sighs, and pulls her elbows in close to her sides, as if she's trying to disappear.

"What?" I ask. And then all I can do is wait.

When she finally speaks, she sounds like a lost orphan. "It's over then? You're not my Daddy anymore?"

My arms tighten around her. "Of course I'm your Daddy."

"But you... You said you were wrong."

"Daddies can be wrong."

She shakes her head. I might as well have told her Daddies can fly to Mars.

Sweet Jesus. Her da never admitted to being wrong, not

once, in Fiona's entire life. Her world doesn't have room for a man who makes mistakes. For a man who says he's sorry.

"I'm older than you are," I tell her. "Obviously. I've experienced a lot more. I have a hell of a lot more context than you do, for the Crew, for the world, in this bed. But you have to believe me. I'm not perfect. And that night, on the green, I was wrong, little girl."

Little girl.

I feel her start to soften at the pet name.

I let my fingers slip beneath the edge of her corset, purposely keeping my touch light enough to tickle. "Got that, little girl?"

She squirms.

"What, little girl? I can't hear you."

She giggles.

My fingers brush the soft skin beneath her tits. "What's so funny, little girl?"

She's laughing now. But she throws back her shoulders and challenges me. "You said you're more experienced than I am in bed."

The chains across her tits stretch tight. If my cock weren't trapped in my trousers, it would be pushing its way into the crease of her arse by now.

"Ha!" she says, as if I've proven her point. She reaches between us, going for my zipper.

I catch her wrist and bring her fingers to my lips. I mean to kiss her, to edge my lips across her knuckles, then finish our talk.

But when her hand is beneath my nose, I'm flooded with the smell of hot, excited girl. She started without me, when she tied herself up. She pulled her knickers to the side, and she exposed her pussy, and she couldn't resist slipping her fingers into her own dark heat.

When I pull her hand down to her waist, I feel her breath catch in her throat. She wants this. She needs this. This is how we get back together.

"Did you touch yourself, little girl?" I lower my voice to a dark growl.

She tilts her head to the side, a remarkable performance of turning shy. "Maybe?"

"Did I give you permission to finger-fuck your pussy?"

Her chin dips to her chest. "No."

"What happens to little girls who break the rules?"

She swallows hard. "I don't know," she whispers. "Tell me, Daddy."

I move fast, shifting my legs over the side of the bed. At the same time, I pull her onto my lap. She's on her belly, balanced across my knees. The angle's awkward, and her arse rises in the air.

I push that tiny vinyl skirt up roughly. I tug at her knickers, not caring if I rip them, yanking them to her knees. I lay the flat of my hand against her superheated skin, and I say very slowly, very clearly, so there's no chance for either of us to misunderstand: "They. Get. Spanked."

45

FIONA

His hand lands on my bare ass, harder than I expect. The jolt sends a lance of fire straight to my clit. I moan, and his cock presses into my belly. I arch my back, trying to feel more of his length.

I didn't realize my motion would force my ass higher into the air. "You're a naughty girl," he rumbles, and each word ripples through my core. He smacks my bare flesh again, fingers spread wide, gripping hard before he pulls back.

I'm panting now, breathing through my teeth. Part of me is trying to bleed off the pain, to cool the hand-shaped brand he's set on me. But part of me is trying to ease the muscles tightening inside me, trying to keep from coming. I clutch the fabric of his pants with both hands. "Please…" I beg.

"Please spank you again?"

Before I can lie, before I can deny that I'm asking for more punishment, he does it. This time, when he pulls his hand away, he dips one finger between my thighs. He glides through my wetness, and his cock twitches with his wicked laugh.

"You're a dirty girl, aren't you?"

I *am* a dirty girl. I dressed for him, because I knew it would drive him wild. I'm pressing against him, because I want to feel his cock. I want to suck him off until precum leaks onto my tongue and then I want to ride him, our mouths locked, my fingers tangled in his hair, until he explodes deep inside me.

"Little girl?" he says. "Answer Daddy when he asks you a question."

"Yes," I say. "Yes. I'm a dirty, dirty girl."

That earns me another spanking, the hardest one yet. I balance on the knife edge of pleasure and pain. I pound my fist against his thigh. I squeeze my eyes closed.

"You're so, so red," he says, brushing his hand against my stinging flesh, barely feathering me with his palm. "So beautiful…"

I unravel.

Every fiber in my body comes undone. I can't breathe, because I don't have lungs. I can't scream, because I don't have a mouth. I'm nothing but a hollow of pure sensation, an endless, timeless stretch of ecstasy.

When I come back into my body, I'm lying on my back. My arms are flung out to either side. My ass hangs off the edge of the bed.

My legs are splayed, and the backs of my thighs rest on Patrick's bare shoulders as he kneels on the floor. He's taken off his clothes, which makes a distant part of me sad, because I wanted to watch him do it. That sadness, though, disintegrates when he buries his face in my pussy.

"No," I moan as his tongue thrusts between my fluttering folds.

But Patrick and I have a language of our own. He's my Daddy. I'm his little girl. The first night we fucked here, he gave me my safeword. So *no* means yes. *No* means more. *No* means don't stop, don't stop, don't stop, don't...

I break around him, great heaving breaths ripping my throat as I come.

This time, I'm conscious when he shifts my body. He eases my legs onto the bed. He runs his hand over my corset. He pinches my nipples where they're framed by chains, but all my nerves have fired, and I don't stir.

He settles his lips by my ear. "Little girl," he whispers.

"Daddy." I shape the word with my mouth.

"Do I need to wear a johnny?"

He's telling me he knows how much we hurt each other. He's saying he trusts me to tell him the truth. He accepts me, whatever I've done in the time we were apart. He understands.

I shake my head. "No," I say. "You don't."

His fingers are nimble on the hook and eye closures that fasten the back of my corset. He sighs as he pulls away the leather. He traces the imprints of the chains like a blind man studying the *Venus de Milo*.

Finding the zipper on my skirt, he peels the vinyl from my body. The top edge dug into my hip bones; there's a bruised red line like an angry bikini. He traces it with his tongue.

He licks my navel. My sternum. My throat. He sucks on my left nipple, and then my right. His mouth finds mine, and our tongues lock. As he drinks me, as I drink him, his cock comes home.

I shift my hips to give him a better angle. I gasp when he glides inside me, because he's bigger than I remember. "I want *everything*," I whisper. "Don't hold back."

He fills me. And when we're as close as any two humans can be, when my thighs tremble against his, when my breasts quiver under the weight of his chest, he begins to move—long, slow strokes that slay me, leaving me helpless beneath him.

"Sweet Jesus," he groans as his fingers close around my wrists, pinning my hands above my head. And then he says,

"You're incredible, little girl." His voice is low and steady, like he's reciting some sort of truth he memorized a lifetime ago. "You were so brave, reaching out to me with that phone call. You showed so much trust, tying yourself up for me. You took your spanking like a warrior queen. You're my strong girl. You're my good girl. You're perfect."

I break before he does—*perfect* does it. He slides deep as I fold around him, as I bury my face in his shoulder and mew, mew, mew with an orgasm so hard I literally see stars.

And when he starts to come, the stars turn into snow-white leaves, raining down on both of us, burying us in light. I hold him, and he holds me, and my Daddy's right—we're perfect, together.

I don't know how much time passes before I feel him stir. He slides open the nightstand drawer, and he reaches for something far in the back. I hear the sound of plastic on plastic, but I don't have the energy to open my eyes.

The smell of rosemary and sage reaches my nose as his hand smooths the cream over my ass. His touch is firm enough to keep me from squirming, light enough to spare me pain.

"Arnica," I say, and my voice is rougher than I expect it to be. The scent of the cream carries me back to that first night, after he found me in Madden's apartment. "So, we're back to where we started."

"Not exactly, *Scáthach*."

"Now will you tell me what that means?"

"That depends. Are you ready to open the cigar box?"

I groan as I stretch beside him.

We lie there for a few minutes. But then I realize I want to ask him a different question. I *need* to. So I trace the outline of the lighthouse on his biceps and say, "That night on the golf course. Kevin Joyce said you'd end up dogshit. Like your father."

He stills, and the air in the room suddenly feels dangerous. But I want to understand him. I need to know everything about him. So I fan my fingers across the storm clouds on his arm and ask, "What happened to your father?"

"He betrayed the Crew."

"I know that. How?"

It takes Patrick a century before he decides to answer. "The feds got Da on a heroin rap. Distribution. A high-school kid ODed in the jacks so Da was looking at a mandatory twenty to life. He sold out his clan instead."

"What happened?"

Another century passes. But Patrick finally says, "Your father caught mine wearing a wire. Rivers worked Da over, in the basement at the *dún*. In the tile room?"

I nod to let him know I've seen it.

"After, your da sent me downstairs to find him. Told me to bring up a case of Guinness. To hurry."

Patrick stares at something I can't see in the distance. His muscles turn to steel beneath my palm. Finally he says, "Da was still alive when I got there. He was tied to a chair. Both his legs were broken, above and below the knee. His arms were shattered too. His face was chopped meat, and a dead rat was shoved between his lips."

I catch my breath. I've always known what happens in the basement at the *dún*. I've never seen it myself.

I think Patrick won't say anything more then, but I'm wrong. "I took the rat out of his mouth, and he said my name, as best he could without a tongue. He begged for help. Even after the worst Keenan Rivers could do, he wasn't ready to die."

Patrick closes his eyes. Now I'm sorry that I asked him. I want to take back my question, even though I know I can't. But more than that, I want Patrick to know I understand. I care. I trace the jagged heartbeat tattooed across his wrist.

And finally he says, "I took out my feckin' phone. I punched in 9, 1, 1. And I stood there without placing the call. I held the phone in front of him and then I watched him die."

I feel Patrick's pulse under my hand, steady and strong. "There was no way to save him," I say.

He shrugs, like he doesn't believe me. "I brought the Guinness upstairs," he says. "Your da told me to go back down and butcher that hunk of meat in the basement. To grind it into dogfood."

I can hear my father issuing orders. I can see the cruel glare in his eyes as he waited to be obeyed.

Patrick says, "I had to prove he could trust me. That I was different to my da. And nothing I did was going to hurt my father any worse. So I fed Tommy Moran to the fucking dogs."

I think that's the end. I think it can't get worse. I'm wrong.

Patrick's voice gets softer. More strained. "When I got home, my wife knew all about it. Aran Dowd had phoned. Told her she should be proud of me, and why. Jenn wrapped our car around a tree that night. She died, and our unborn son too. And two days later, Mam had had enough. She jumped off the Longfellow Bridge. Hit the water head-first, a witness said. They had to drag the Charles to bring her up."

It sounds like some dark fairytale from centuries past, the type of stories told to little kids when they won't eat their vegetables or refuse to go to bed. I half expect him to say, "And the moral of the story is…"

But there isn't any moral to the story. There's just my uncle's cruelty and my father's rules and decades of pain bleached gray by time.

I don't have any words to comfort him. But I want to give him something. Tell him something. Share, the way he just dared to share with me.

So I say, "There were two of them."

He gets very still.

I hurry on before I can chicken out. "In the chapel at my school. One held me down on the cold stone floor while the other tore away my panties. He shoved his way in like I was some plastic doll, and I kept thinking it hurt so much because it wasn't my wedding night, because he wasn't my husband, because I was committing a sin."

"Little girl…" Patrick says, but I shift my fingertips to his lips. I need him to know this about me. I need him to understand.

"After the first one finished, there was blood between my legs. I felt so fucking ashamed, like I'd started my period in public. My legs were shaking so hard I couldn't stand, but I tried to crawl away. And that's when the second one grabbed me. He choked me. Put both hands around my throat."

"Jesus," Patrick breathes, and I know we're both thinking about *Bunbun*, about how I used my safeword.

It's my turn to close my eyes, because that will help me get out the rest of the story. "The second one took longer to finish. He was still inside me when Father Colin came into the chapel. Father was carrying a… what do you call it? The thing with incense?"

"A thurible."

"A thurible. Newly polished. Father told the boys to go down to the gym. To clean up in the locker room, then go straight home. He reminded them about some paper they needed to turn in for New Testament Ethics."

"Fucking gobshite," Patrick says, and his fingers grip my hip so tightly I know they'll leave a mark.

"Father Colin took me to his office. He said I was the reason the boys did what they did. I was Eve's daughter. Sin incarnate. He gave me lines to write, one hundred times for each of the boys: *I will not use my body to tempt innocent boys into sins of the flesh.* I was still bleeding when I finished."

Patrick's hand trembles against my body. "You went to your da," he says. "And he said *a good King chooses his battles.*"

He remembers what I told him when I was feeling sorry for myself, downing my third boozy milkshake in an hour. I nod and say, "I'd been thrown out of so many schools by then. For skipping class. For fighting—girls and boys. For talking back to

Sister. So Da said he was done. He wouldn't help me. He washed his hands of all of it."

When I fall silent, Patrick finishes the story. "So you took care of things yourself. Both boys. And the fucking priest. Your first three kills."

I nod again.

"You were brilliant, *Scáthach*. Feckin' brilliant."

For the first time since he's called me that, I don't want to know what it means. I just want to lie here next to him, feeling the heat radiate off his body. He's heard the worst I've ever done, and he still thinks I'm a prize.

A long time goes by before he says, "What are you thinking, little girl?"

We can't take any more truths, neither of us right now, so I force myself to grin. "Honestly?"

"Always."

"I'm starving. And I'm trying to remember if there's anything left to eat in the kitchen."

"There is," he says.

I don't want him to leave. I hate when he's gone. But he's back in less than a minute, sitting up against the headboard. I curl against his side as he shifts a white cardboard box closer.

"What's that?" I ask.

He raises the lid. A dozen miniature tarts are lined up in three rows of four, cherry filling gleaming against rich, buttery crust. I shove one in my mouth by reflex.

"Mmmm," I moan, which makes him raise his eyebrows. "You waited around to buy these, after I called?"

"Hannah wouldn't let me leave without them."

"Who's Hannah?" I ask as I down a second tart.

"The girl at the bakery," he says. "Careful. You'll get crumbs in the bed."

Still chewing, I press a third tart against his lips. He takes it between his teeth, and something flips deep inside of me.

I'm debating another tart for me when I see the black plastic rectangle folded against his palm. "What's that?" I ask.

"Dynamite."

I sit up a little straighter and reach for the device. It's a thumb drive. I turn it over, but there's nothing written on the shell, nothing to hint at what it contains. "What are you going to blow up?"

"Not what. Who."

"Who," I repeat, and I look into his face.

The first time I saw Patrick Moran, I thought he was old. Wrinkles fanned beside his eyes. In some light, his hair was more gray than black. He was Braiden Kelly's Warlord. He was the Crew's failed soldier. He was a stranger, hardened and locked down, distant and aloof.

Now, he's *Patrick*.

"Who are you going to destroy?"

He eyes me steadily. "Aran Dowd. And you're going to help me do it."

He tells me what's on the drive, all the evidence from the feds. I've spent my entire life in the heart of the Irish mob. I drank down loyalty with every bottle Oona ever fed me. I've watched brave men make sacrifices and cowards die in shame, all in the name of the Old Colony Crew.

My uncle's betrayal feels like a physical wound. My stomach aches like I've eaten bad clams. A headache sparks behind my eyes, and I realize I'm grinding my teeth.

"How long has this been going on?" I ask Patrick.

"They turned him when he was in jail. When he was waiting for his trial."

Seven months ago, then. Maybe eight.

I thought Uncle Aran's stint in prison was a good thing for me. My father had to lean on me. He sent me to Philadelphia in his place. He trusted me to broker a peace between Braiden Kelly and his mafia counterpart.

But now I understand that Uncle Aran's time behind bars

might be the worst thing that's ever happened to me. If the FBI acts on everything they know, they can take the Crew away. They can devastate the clan.

I thought I'd felt anger before. When Father Colin called me a liar. When Da refused to punish the boys who hurt me. When my father declined to name me his heir.

But those disappointments are nothing compared to the wildfire that sweeps through me now. I want to shred something into tiny pieces. I want to blow something up.

"We have to devastate that motherfucker," I say.

"Exactly," Patrick says, and his smile is amused. "And if you agree, here's how we can do it, *Scáthach*."

46

PATRICK

I t takes a week and a half.
   Fiona insists on reading every incriminating word herself. She sorts the documents, putting them in folders. She sets up spreadsheets. She figures out a timeline and cross-references it with places and names. She's spent her entire life tapping away at computers and phones, and she's better at it, faster than I'll ever be.

Every new revelation sharpens something inside her. The entire time I drove back from Philly, I worried that the truth would break her, that she couldn't handle the scope of Dowd's betrayal.

But here, in our war room at the Beacon Street apartment, she proves she has a spine of steel. She's like one of those skyscrapers in a city plagued with earthquakes—shocks sway her for a moment, and then she's as solid as before.

And ten days later, when she's read it all, when she's thought about it, when it's become part of every cell in her body, she says, "I'll do it."

I'm standing by the counter in the kitchen, stretching to relieve an ache in the small of my back. "Do what?"

She looks at me like I've forgotten my ABCs. "I'll kill Uncle Aran."

The Bell goes off like a fire alarm. Fiona won't be the one taking down Aran Dowd. I will. For the Crew. For Jenn and Athawn. For myself.

But I remember Fiona standing on the golf course green, Joyce's gun in her hand and vengeance in her eyes. I need to keep her from executing her uncle without driving a stake into all we've built between us. So I tell the feckin' Bell to stop its clanging, and I force myself to say, "Tell me more."

"My da would do it if he were still alive—a captain taking out his traitor Clan Chief—and the Crew would have his back. I'll *be* captain, and I'll have the Crew behind me, but to get there, I have to go through Uncle Aran. It's too dangerous to wait. Who knows what he'll tell the feds today or tomorrow or the next day? He needs to be cut down now. Before he can do any more harm."

It's a pretty argument, but she's wrong. "Captains don't make their own kills. They have soldiers. A Warlord. They don't risk getting their own hands dirty."

"That's not true. Braiden took care of his brother."

It's the first time she's let on that she knows what happened to Madden Kelly. I wince, because I don't want her thinking about what that fucking gobshite did to her. I don't want to remember how my own hands were tied, how I couldn't get revenge.

But I say, "Kelly didn't make that kill as captain. He was taking care of family."

"*I'm* not killing Uncle Aran as captain. *I'm* taking care of family."

"The shitehawk's not your blood." She starts to respond, but

I don't let her get the words out. "And the things he's done—they didn't hurt family. They hurt the Crew."

Her sharp inhale is a little scream of frustration. "You're dragging me around in circles."

That's my intention. I want her seeing there's no way she's going after Dowd.

Before I can lie, she grits out, "He has to go because he's hurt the Crew. I'm the next Old Colony captain, but I'm not there yet. I can't name a Warlord. I have to do my own dirty work."

"That's not true." The Bell's ringing so loudly I can barely hear my own voice. This may be an impulse, it may be deadly, but it feels like the most brilliant thing I've ever said or done. "You don't have to do this on your own. Make me your Warlord. Now."

She opens her mouth. Shuts it. Tries again. Finally, she settles on, "You can't do that." She swallows hard. "You can't stay."

I hold her green gaze, knowing not to blink. "I can. I've been Warlord in Philly. I'll do it here for you."

"But Braiden—" she says.

"Was a good boss. Things change. I haven't been his man for more than three months now."

All the color has left her face. She tries to lick her lips but stops. Her tongue must be too dry. "Patrick…" she whispers.

"What do you want me to do? Take an oath on a Bible neither of us believes in?"

When she doesn't answer, I kneel in front of her. The kitchen tile is hard on my knees but I take her left hand, hold it between both of mine. "I'm yours, Fiona Ingram. I'm your Warlord, if you'll have me."

She puts her right hand on my bowed head. Her fingers tangle in my hair. "I'll have you, Patrick Moran. Sweet God, I'll have you."

I bite off a groan as I push to my feet. I want to kiss her, but this isn't about her being my little girl. This has nothing to do with my being her Daddy. So I say, "Good. That's settled. I'm getting Dowd."

But Fiona shakes her head. "You can't do it, either. Not before I'm Queen. Because to all those men in the *dún*, you're still one of the Fishtown Boys. Some of them still believe Braiden killed my da. If you take out Da's Clan Chief, they'll come after you, and I'm not sure I have the power to stop them. Yet."

"We'll tell them what we know. Show them all this shite." I wave vaguely toward the computer and all its records.

"And when someone puts a bullet through your skull before they've finished reading?"

I want her to be wrong. I want to say that I'm the one with bullets. I've got half a dozen weapons, and my own bare hands, and I'm taking down Aran Cocksucking Dowd.

But for now, she's right. And I'm not sure I truly believe it, but she thinks she'll be my Queen. So I might as well learn to give in when she issues a direct order.

"If you can't do it," I say. "And I can't do it, then who is going to kill that motherfucking dry shite?"

"Keenan Rivers," she says, like she's just remembered the words to a song.

My belly turns sour. "Rivers?"

"He's still the Old Colony Warlord, until a new captain is named. We'll send the information to him—just the heart of it, the meat. We'll show him what Uncle Aran's done, and we'll let him make the kill."

I hate the solution. But it keeps Fiona from getting her pretty arse shot. And it keeps me alive for long enough to figure out how to get her on the Old Colony throne.

And Rivers knows how to make men suffer. I close off the picture in my mind, of Da tied to that chair in the *dún's* basement.

"Rivers," I say.

In the end, we pull together five documents:

One: A letter from Dowd to Barbieri, written on a sheet of plain white paper, presented with an envelope showing the return address of his prison cell, asking for an in-person get-together to "come to a meeting of the minds."

Two: A transcript from that meeting, where Dowd calls Kieran Ingram a "bog-jumping dry shite without the bollocks to lead three men in the St. Patrick's Day parade", along with Dowd's promise to deliver the Old Colony Crew "on time and all complete so long as all state and federal charges are dropped."

Three: A phone log from a burner phone, showing a long list of calls to Barbieri, along with a pair of texts to Dowd's lieutenants—proof who owned the cell.

Four: A black-and-white photograph with a timestamp in the lower right corner, proving it was taken three weeks ago— Barbieri sitting across from Dowd in a restaurant booth, as the fat bearded fuck counts a wad of cash.

Five: A transcript from another in-person meeting between Dowd and Barbieri, the one where Dowd gives up the entire structure of the Crew. There's a quote half-way through, Dowd responding to an FBI question: "No, goddammit. Pay attention. *Rivers* is the Warlord. The chief enforcer. He's signed off on every Old Colony hit in the past ten years."

Fiona says, "Do we send it tonight? Or do we wait until after the Union meeting tomorrow?"

"No reason to wait," I say.

I hand her a clean burner. She attaches the files. She has Rivers' number; she checks it twice before she hits Send.

Both of us release a sigh once the documents are gone.

If I wasn't such a feral bastard, I might feel a flash of pity about the execution we've set in motion. Dowd doesn't stand a fucking chance.

⁓

I delay calling Braiden Kelly as long as I can. But he's a good captain. A fine leader of men. He deserves a straight conversation before he walks into that Four Seasons conference room for the Grand Irish Union meeting.

He answers on the first ring. "Kelly."

I bite back my instinctive reply—*Boss.* Instead, I say, "It's me."

He's no fool. He lets my reply sit between us for a full thirty seconds before he says, "Patrick."

"You'll be at the Union vote tomorrow," I say. I don't make it a question, because it isn't one.

"I'll be there," he says. "And Samantha too, as my second."

I've heard rumors, read threads on the group text for all my enforcers. For all *O'Hare's* enforcers, that is. They aren't mine anymore.

"Herself is a good choice for the job." Samantha Kelly is fierce as a dragon. She's smart, too. She's the match my former boss needs.

"I somehow doubt you're calling to comment on my employment choices." Kelly's voice is as dry as Death Valley.

"I wanted you to know I'll be at the meeting." I'm careful with my words. He needs to know I'm not asking. I'm telling him how things will be. "As Fiona's Warlord," I say.

There's another pause, this one longer than the first. Then, finally: "She's lucky to have you by her side."

"Thank you." We both know I'm not thanking him for the praise. He's setting me free without a fight.

"I was lucky to have you as *my* Warlord," he says gruffly.

I'm not prepared for that. I say, "Tell O'Hare—"

"O'Hare's doing fine."

"He can—"

"He can run things as he has done, since April."

There's a sting in that, but it's nothing more than I deserve. I clear my throat. "About that," I say, because it bothers me that I didn't tie off my own loose ends. I didn't get Fiona the revenge she deserves. "About Madden," I say.

"Fuck Madden," Kelly says, like the name of his own brother is soap in his mouth.

"Fuck Madden," I agree. I wait, in case there's anything else he wants to tell me. I'll never know how his bastard brother died. But I know Braiden Kelly understands how to make a man suffer.

"I'll see you tomorrow," he finally says.

That's as clean an end as I can ask for. "Tomorrow," I say.

When I end the call, I sign out of all the group texts for the Fishtown Boys. They know how to reach me if they need me.

They won't.

I take off my golden ring, the one cut deep with a Celtic knot, and I shove it in my pocket. I'll send it back to Kelly. He can give it to the next man to join the Boys.

Fiona's waiting for me in the bedroom down the hall.

47

FIONA

P atrick and I take the elevator to the Four Seasons conference room. I twitch at the hem of my leather bustier. The scarlet matches my lips; it's the exact shade of my fingernails. Folds of leather are sculpted into two elaborate roses that cover my breasts. I smirked when I told Patrick he could look, but he could not touch.

Not yet. Not until I've finished running this meeting.

I'm steady on my four-inch heels as we walk down the hall. I don't even flinch when I see Uncle Aran standing beside the door.

Part of me hoped Keenan Rivers would have taken him out by now.

Part of me is glad my uncle's still alive. I want him to see me run this meeting. I want him to know—in those final moments before Rivers kills him—exactly how I'll run the Crew. I want him to see me in charge.

Uncle Aran has brought one of the Old Colony lieutenants

to serve as his second in this meeting. Angus Miller doesn't have the decency to meet my gaze.

Patrick reaches the meeting room door first. That gives me the right to enter before all three men. I'm halfway to the head of the table when I glimpse the last man on earth I want to see in this room.

Keenan Rivers is leaning against the near wall, surveying everyone else who's arrived. His shoulders are back. The sole of his right foot rests beside his left knee. His arms are crossed over his chest, and his white-blond hair is clubbed at the nape of his neck.

I'm not the only one who has dressed in leather for this meeting. Rivers looks like he just left a motorcycle outside some seedy backstreet bar. His well-worn pants are dusty, and his leather jacket fits like armor.

He pushes off the wall and comes to the head of the table with three long strides. "Fiona," he says.

"Keenan," I answer evenly.

Patrick and I sent the documents from a burner. There's no way Rivers knows we're the source. But he holds my hand a fraction of a second too long when we shake. Or maybe that's just my own adrenaline, spiking my reactions.

A man flickers in Rivers' wake, one of the Clan's newer enforcers serving as a second. I've never spoken to him, which reflects badly on me. Once I'm Queen I'll know every member of my clan by name.

For now, I'm wondering if I can distract the pair of them. Create some sort of forced error. Get Rivers and his second thrown out, so my chosen assassin can work on what's really important—destroying Aran Dowd.

But if I'm caught squabbling with anyone from Boston, I'll look like an amateur. A pretender. Not like the captain I want all the other mob families to see.

Fuck.

I sit at the head of the table before Uncle Aran or Rivers

can stake a claim to the most prominent place in the room. As the other men scramble to drag over their own chairs, Patrick leans forward to whisper, "Head high. Eyes straight ahead."

That's what he said when he saved me at my father's wake. He's feeding, me power. He's giving me strength.

I look around the room and see that everyone else has arrived. San Francisco and New Orleans and Chicago. New York and Baltimore and Philadelphia.

Philadelphia. Braiden Kelly, with his wife, Samantha, sitting behind him as his Clan Chief. I catch a glimpse of a gold ring on her hand, a Celtic knot like Patrick wore until yesterday.

My eyes meet Braiden's across the table. I haven't seen him since Easter. I could fill volumes with what's happened to me since I left his mansion, since I gave up on annoying the living crap out of him. Someday, I'll tell him I'm sorry.

But not today. Not with Union business the most important thing at hand.

I clear my throat sharply, and every man in the room falls silent. Drawing on my da's most pompous delivery, I begin: "Grand Irish Union tradition—"

Rivers cuts me off, his voice like a guillotine made of ice. "Gentlemen—"

Uncle Aran follows suit, notably louder to make up for being a fraction late: "As you know—"

The three of us are still jockeying for control when the Chicago captain pounds the table with his fist. "All right," Mickey Reardon says. "We're all here for the same reason—to select our next general. So let's skip the greetings and the gossip and go straight to what matters. I'm stepping forward to serve."

Braiden takes exception to that. "It's good of you to volunteer, Mickey," he says. "But I'm thinking I should be our next general instead."

Uncle Aran and Rivers explode in predictable attacks. They shout that Braiden killed my da. They bring up old grievances. I let them go on because it makes them sound petty, like pasty-faced bookkeepers instead of like leaders of men.

Braiden parries their attacks smoothly, never letting his temper get the better of him. I risk a glance at his second, at Samantha.

I'll never admit it in public, but I might have overstepped a bit when I lived in Philadelphia. Before I knew Patrick. When I still believed Da meant me to be his heir.

It's unheard of, a woman serving as Clan Chief. Nearly as outrageous as a daughter filling her da's shoes as captain. So I give Samantha a small, tight smile. She returns the gesture, which is as close to making amends as we can come today.

Reardon's had enough of the bickering over my father's death, and he lumbers to his feet. Towering over the table, he says, "I hardly need to remind you, *dearthaireacha*, what I bring to the Union."

I know enough Irish to understand he's calling them all his brothers. Before I can point out there's a sister in this room, Reardon starts to present his arguments for why he should be general.

He has a few good points—he's the oldest man in the room, he manages a massive territory, and he handles a lot of money. But it takes him over an hour to make his pitch.

An hour, when all the men at the table become increasingly restless.

An hour, when I long to look at Rivers, to see if I can read murder in his eyes.

An hour, when Uncle Aran begins tapping his index finger against the table, a sure sign that he's thinking about cutting off the Chicago captain's speech.

My heart feels like it's being battered by hummingbird wings, but I can't let on that anything's amiss. I can't risk Uncle Aran figuring out that I know more than I did the last time we saw each other. I can't chance interrupting any vengeance that Rivers has set in place.

Forcing myself to look bored, I swallow a yawn before I ask, "Braiden?"

Even if my plot against my uncle goes awry, this is a good time to remind everyone that I'm running this meeting. I'm the best captain Boston could ever name.

Uncle Aran doesn't like my taking the lead. "Come now, Little Fee—" he starts.

Rivers cuts him off. "The man deserves to make his case."

My uncle's beard bobs as he takes offense. I order myself not to stare at Rivers, not to question if he's arguing because he wants to be seen as Boston's King or because he's been made aware of treason so abhorrent he can smell blood.

In any case, Braiden rolls over both of them. He says, "I've shared the Jameson with all of you over the years. You know I've run a tight ship since I took over from my da. I've always paid heed to the Union, playing by its rules even when that's cost me dosh. I'll take a stand for the GIU against anyone who means us harm—mafia or bratva, yakuza or the law. By now, you all know what happened to Antonio Russo. And I suspect you've heard what I did to my own brother when he turned traitor on us all. I respect the Union. I respect you. And I'll be your next general."

It takes me a moment to realize that's his entire speech. When I do, I hurry to fill the gap. "All right, then, captains of the Grand Irish Union."

Rivers, though, interrupts before I can call a vote. "Anyone else putting his hat in the ring?"

Turning my voice to steel, I repeat, "All right, then, captains of the Grand Irish Union. Following our tradition, Boston votes first. Then, we'll proceed in increasing order of seniority." I don't give Uncle Aran a chance to interrupt. Instead, I announce: "Boston votes for Kelly."

Uncle Aran's wailing must wake Da in his grave. He's calling me Little Fee. He's saying I have no right. He's saying he's Boston, and he'll make the call, and the rest of the room should ignore me because I'm a spoiled brat who's barely out of diapers.

I'm spitting my reply when Rivers closes his fingers over my shoulder.

Maybe he's trying to push me aside so he can forcibly shut Uncle Aran's mouth. He's probably just trying to get my attention. He doesn't mean to brush against the petals of my bustier's leather rose.

But Patrick snarls, leaping to his feet like he's ready to rip out Rivers' throat with his teeth. That puts Angus and Rivers' Unknown Soldier on their feet.

Patrick's left all three of his guns—the Glock, the Magnum, and the little Ruger we took from Kevin Joyce—back home, in deference to the Union captains. He looks angry enough, though, to kill with his bare hands.

I clear my throat to get his attention, but that doesn't do the trick. He's breathing through his teeth, short sharp pants. I didn't see him take his meds this morning. Maybe he did, and the extra tension of wondering if Rivers received our information is what's pushing him over the edge.

Whatever the cause, Patrick is dangerously close to snapping, the way he was on the golf course. I'm pretty sure I can break his murderous concentration if I say his name out loud. But I don't want to sound like I'm calling my dog to heel. I don't want to break him in front of all these men.

And that assumes I can still reach him, that he'd obey.

"Shut it!" The command comes from Braiden.

Braiden Kelly has the power to shut Patrick down. They have years of working together, decades of mutual respect. Braiden's command pierces the scuffle like an icepick.

"Today isn't about Boston," he says. He looks from Uncle Aran to Rivers to me. "We aren't here to decide which of you has the better claim. That's a question for your own clan to debate, for your own men to manage. But none of us leave this room until we've decided on a general. So each of you state your choice. Boston's vote is the majority, between the three of you."

What the fuck is he doing?

I already cast Boston's vote. I already gave him my support. *Why the hell is he undermining my position?*

But the answer comes to me before I can glare my fury. Braiden truly *doesn't* give a fuck about the Old Colony Crew today. He doesn't know that Patrick and I sent secret evidence to Rivers. He hasn't heard about Uncle Aran's betrayal. He doesn't even care if I become the Boston captain.

He just wants to be general. And he thinks he'll get one step closer to that by diluting my vote.

Reardon finally agrees to accept a three-way Boston ballot. Uncle Aran wastes no time proving he's not beholden to me. He cast his vote: "Reardon."

Rivers cold blue eyes narrow. I can't tell if he's weighing an attack on me, an evaluation of my traitorous uncle, or the matter actually in front of him—choosing the Union's general.

I can't breathe. I can't turn to Patrick. I can't do anything but wait, hoping, praying that I'll be able to parse whatever he says next. Rivers' vote is like a clump of tea leaves spread across a cup, and I'm the witch trying to read the future.

"I vote for Reardon too," he finally says.

So he's siding with Uncle Aran, against me. Is he ignoring all the evidence we sent? Refusing to believe it? Has he even read it at all?

But everyone else in the room is playing a different game—the Grand Irish Union game—so I force myself to shrug. I pretend I planned to side with Chicago all along. "Boston votes for Reardon, then," I say.

The voting proceeds around the table. San Francisco votes for Reardon, and of course Reardon votes for himself. New Orleans and Baltimore go for Braiden. He casts his own vote, so they're tied, three-three.

Connor Boyle, New York's captain, is a giant of a man. He

takes his time, looking first at Reardon, then at Braiden. And then he says, "I vote for Kelly."

Just like that, Braiden Kelly is the next general of the Grand Irish Union.

Following tradition, he pours a toast for each of us from a bottle of Jameson that was twenty-two years old when my da was sworn in. Samantha carries the glasses around.

I take one, as do Uncle Aran and Rivers. Patrick follows suit, and Angus and the Unknown Soldier. We wait until Samantha raises her own glass, until she calls out, "To Braiden Kelly, general of the Grand Irish Union!"

I make my answer, loud and clear: "To Kelly!" The whiskey is smooth, coating my throat with a complicated blend of oak and chocolate and just a hint of dried winter apples.

Uncle Aran pushes forward, making sure he's the first of us from Boston to shake our new general's hand. He acts like he's forgotten that he cast his vote for Reardon; he's bent on wiping clean the slate and starting new.

He makes a point of recognizing Samantha, too, touching his glass to hers. He's building bridges, forging allies against the storm for control of the Crew.

For now, I hold back. Braiden knows he had my support. Samantha saw my bid to set things straight after the differences we had in Philadelphia. There'll be time enough for me to speak after the visiting captains have had their say.

Patrick moves forward to shake his former boss's hand. There's a moment between them. A silence. A wait.

But then Braiden takes Patrick's offered grip. He does more than that, he pulls his former Warlord in for a quick one-armed embrace. They both step back, and they turn to me at the same time. Braiden raises his glass. Patrick meets my gaze.

I lift my own glass, high enough that my stays dig into my sides. I consider calling for limericks, but this isn't the time or the place.

The sworn captains will gather with their new general this

evening. They'll crack the seal on a new bottle of well-aged Jameson. There will be secret oaths, ones I've never heard before, but I understand they're made on blood and fire.

Down the road, *I'll* swear to my general. After Uncle Aran's dead. After the Old Colony Crew makes me its Queen.

Braiden's taken away by someone else offering congratulations. Patrick starts to make his way across the room, to me.

Uncle Aran's still lingering among the others. He doesn't understand his place in this crowd. He doesn't know he's about to be destroyed.

I look around the room for Rivers.

He's nowhere to be found.

48

PATRICK

Fiona and I have a hotel room for the night, close enough to the captains that we can manage any Union problems that arise. I wait until Fiona's closed the door before I tell her what I've been thinking from the moment she called the meeting to order. "You were brilliant."

Her blush matches the leather roses covering her tits. "I bet you say that to all the Mob princesses you know."

I close my hands on her hips, bringing her close enough to feel my hard-on. "Every single one."

Her mouth is hot under mine. Needy. I think about revising my plan, about throwing her on the bed, or maybe taking her into the shower. A couple of hours can't make that much difference…

But no. Even one hour could mean the difference between freedom and the rest of our lives behind bars. The knife scar across my belly begins to itch. I feel like we're already too late.

When I pull away, she groans, nearly undermining my

resolve. I shake my head, though. "No games today, *Scáthach*. If Rivers does what we're counting on him to do, you and I need air-tight alibis."

"The entire Grand Irish Union is meeting in the Royal Suite. They'll say whatever we need them to say."

"Exactly," I tell her. "Criminals like us don't make reliable witnesses in court."

Rivers is a Warlord, same as me. And if I had the assignment he has, I'd come to the Union meeting, just as he did. I'd watch my prey in public, let everyone see me, let everyone know I have an excellent reason to be in the vicinity. That'll solve any problems that come up in the future, unexpected security cameras or hotel staff with shockingly good recall of guests.

And once my victim left the safety of the meeting, I'd trail him. I wouldn't wait long to strike. Wouldn't take a chance that he shared more secrets with the feds. That he somehow found out I was sent to take care of him.

So while Fiona ran the meeting, I made a few discreet queries on my phone. I have some weapons up my sleeve— which will have to remain a metaphor for the next twenty-four hours. We'll be passing through metal detectors, where we're going. My bare hands will be the only weapons at our disposal.

I hope I don't need to kill.

Fiona's still waiting for more of an explanation about why we can't play. "In any case," I say. "The captains would throw us out within the hour." I glance down at her slim ankles. "How far can you walk in those shoes?"

She looks at me like I've asked a question in Swahili. "Several blocks? A mile? How far do you need?"

"That'll do. Let's go."

I gesture for her to go in front of me on our way to the elevator. I take her hand as we cross the lobby, lacing her fingers between mine.

This is the first time I've touched her this way. The first time we've broadcast to the world that we're a couple. I'm doing it for show—I want every security camera in the lobby to catch us. But I have to admit, it's a pleasure telling the world she belongs to me.

Outside, I call an Uber, because I want a record of our trip. It's early, still, getting to Fenway. The gates won't open until ninety minutes before today's baseball game, but there are plenty of bars around the stadium. I tell our driver to let us out a couple of blocks from the actual ballpark. The nearest bar is conveniently next door to a bank. If the ATM cameras don't pick us up, the security one over the door will do.

The crowd's already lively by the time we shoulder our way up to the polished wood bar. I hoist Fiona onto the single stool that's open in the middle of the row. Stepping close to steal a kiss, I capture our hands between us. My tongue brushes the line of her lips as I slip my fidget ring onto her finger. It's too big, of course. But I fold her thumb over the metal band, showing her how to hold it in place.

She's still looking down in surprise when I shout, "Barkeep!" I layer on my Irish brogue like icing on a cake. "My girl's agreed to be my bride! Drinks for everyone are on me!"

A woman dressed head-to-toe in Red Sox gear squeals like a dog's squeeze toy, grabbing at Fiona's hand like there's a prize for the first to congratulate her. Fiona's quick. "It's a family heirloom," she says, about the titanium band. "It means so much more to me than a diamond ever could."

The team behind the bar serves up glass after glass of pale American beer, along with some generous shots of rail drinks. For a thousand bucks or so, I've guaranteed no one in this place will forget us. We're good for a couple of hours.

"We met in this very bar on Opening Day last year," I tell the crowd. "I couldn't propose anywhere else." If anyone thinks we're dressed oddly for a ball game—my black suit, Fiona's killer leather outfit—they're too happy for us lovebirds to say anything about it.

The place starts to empty out an hour before first pitch. I

help Fiona down from her bar-stool throne, and we both accept a final round of congratulations, substantially more drunken ones than before. As we join the line of fans waiting to get into the stadium, Fiona says, "Engaged, huh?"

"Sorry I didn't have a diamond available." I hold out my hand. "I'll take it back now."

She folds her fingers into a sweet little fist. "I don't think so," she says. "What if we run into any of our new best friends?"

She's right, of course. It just makes sense for her to keep my ring. But I make her move it from her finger to her thumb, so it doesn't go missing.

Holding her hand again, I do my best to protect her from the jostling crowd, but Fiona doesn't seem the least bit concerned by rowdy baseball fans. She's in her element here. In her city. In her home.

Our tickets are on my phone, which is scanned at the gate. "When did you get those?" Fiona asks after we've passed through the turnstile.

"While Reardon was presenting his feckin' resumé. I had plenty of time to plan this entire evening."

She laughs. We follow the signs to our seats, moving deeper and deeper into the stadium until Fiona finally asks, "Where, exactly, are we going?"

At just that moment, we emerge from a darkened hallway into a stunning summer evening. The grass shines like a field of emeralds around the bases. The famous Green Monster forms the left-field wall.

Our seats are three rows up, directly behind home plate.

"Let me guess," Fiona says. "The first night we met in that bar, I told you my lifelong dream was to watch the Sox from seats like this?"

"Pretty much," I say. "The first two rows were taken. I could only get these because Kansas City isn't a major rival for the Sox. And I was willing to pay six times the ticket price."

She stares at me. "Six times?" She gestures toward the

stands behind us. "I'm not a big baseball fan. I would have been fine up there."

I shake my head. "No cameras up there."

"No…" Once again, she's fast to catch on. "We'll be on TV for every batter."

I spare an appreciative glance for those red leather flowers across her chest. "And I don't think anyone will miss us. At least not any straight man who can see."

She throws back her shoulders, and the bustier has to fight to do its job. For just a moment, I weigh the merits of taking her up on her sly little offer, but ballpark security would certainly throw us out.

We need to cement our alibi. Plus, if tonight goes the way I plan, we'll have days and days for Fiona to deliver on promises like that.

The game is a sloppy one—plenty of hits, defensive errors on both sides, and both starting pitchers are knocked out by the fourth inning. Any true baseball fan would be exasperated by the poor play spread out over almost four hours. I'm just happy they end the ninth tied at seven apiece. Extra innings give us another hour of rock-solid alibi before the Red Sox finally win.

That eighth run means the bars are full after the game. We head to the one closest to the park; I don't want to stay unseen for too long.

It's easy enough to get everyone's attention. Fiona's magic always works well on drunk and stupid men. She gets them working on limericks—baseball-themed ones at first, and then the usual filth.

My job is to stay close enough that no one gets too handsy. I make sure Fiona eats as well, something that passes for nachos, along with a broad array of deep-fried snacks, and that's on top of the ballpark food she polished off during the game.

We close the place down at two in the morning. Fiona leans into me, nestling her head under my chin. "We can go home now?"

332 | ALIX KEY

"Not yet."

She's gorgeous when she pouts. "I'm tired."

"That's a shame. Because we still have several hours to kill."

She slips her fingers into my belt loops. "I'll make it worth your time." When I shake my head, her lips curl, and she whispers, "Daddy."

I know she feels my cock's answer, but my brain overrules my body. Our Uber pulls up to the curb as I take her hands from my waist. I kiss her knuckles before I hand her into the car.

The all-night diner on South Street has been there since I was a kid. Da sat me at the counter once, in the middle of the night. While he begged his bookie for a break, I dipped French fries in a chocolate malt.

Fiona and I are too tired to sit on stools at the counter. I put us in a booth, close to the register. When the night-faded waitress comes to take our order, I pretend not to be able to decide. "What do you think?" I ask Fiona. "Waffles or pancakes?"

"Or French toast," she says. "I never get French toast."

"Maybe an omelet?"

"Spinach and feta," Fiona says. "No! Ham and cheddar!"

I turn to the waitress. "I guess we'll get it all."

She chomps on her gum. "All?"

"Waffles, pancakes, French toast, one spinach and feta omelet, and one ham and cheddar omelet."

Chomp. Chomp. "You got money? We only take cash."

I take out my wallet and show her a stash of twenties.

She finally nods. "You want bacon with that?"

Fiona wants bacon. And Fiona wants country ham. And Fiona wants sausage, both kinds, the patties and the links.

My plan was to order enough that both the cook and the waitress would remember us days later, maybe even weeks, if that's how long it takes for the cops to ask us to prove our whereabouts. Fiona accepts the challenge like she's going for a gold medal in eating.

We both drink enough coffee to fill a tanker truck.

By six, the morning crowd starts to arrive. Fiona makes her usual scene, leaning over the counter to call a farewell to the cook. I ask for a cash register receipt, which earns me even more of a stink-eye than I get for the tower of plates stacked on our table. But I end up with a piece of paper saying we left the diner at 7:12.

One more Uber. We pay surge pricing because it's morning rush hour, but I don't give a damn. Fiona falls asleep with her head in my lap, poor little bit. I rest a hand on her shoulder, replaying how she slayed, running the Union meeting.

Traffic is worse as we near the hotel. Gridlock jams the intersections. Drivers lean on their horns, and my phone gives me a message that I'm paying Uber even more because my ride has taken longer than expected.

The driver keeps saying he doesn't know why this is taking so long, that traffic is never this bad, especially not in August. We creep forward, one block, another, another.

I shake Fiona awake as the car finally turns onto Boylston, one block from the hotel. She sits up slowly, with the dazed look of someone who should have had at least six more hours of sleep. "What—?" she starts to ask.

But she stops. And she stares. We both do.

A dozen police cars surround the brick front of the hotel, blue and white lights flashing like strobes at a fashion show.

49

FIONA

P atrick and I stand on the sidewalk across the street from the hotel, gawking like all the people around us. Dozens of cops scurry between cars, some in uniform, others in suits. I quickly realize their attention isn't on the front door of the hotel or the lobby. Instead, the police are focused on the side of the building.

Crime scene tape stretches across the entrance to an alley. A group of reporters has already gathered; they're shouting questions from the sidewalk, but no one gives them any answers.

Patrick grabs my hand and leads the way across the street, taking advantage of the traffic jam to keep from getting killed. He shoulders a path to the front of the crowd, pulling me with him until we both peer down the alley.

Three overfilled dumpsters line a brick wall, huge and green and stinking in the August heat. A dozen cops cluster around the middle one.

Uncle Aran lies spread-eagle on top of a pile of black trash bags. The front of his shirt has been slashed, the white fabric now stiff with darkened blood. A pile of entrails spills over his belt, their scarlet mottled with black.

His hands stick out from the ends of his sleeves. They're already swelling in the morning heat, but even from here, I can see that his fingers jut at impossible angles. His arms bend the wrong way, too. So do his legs.

There's a bullet hole in the center of his forehead, and a line of blood that runs into his tattered beard. A rat the size of a shoebox hangs out of his mouth.

A crime scene investigator approaches with a camera, and one of the cops moves to get out of her way. The policeman bangs his hip against the corner of the dumpster, and a cloud of flies swarms up from the pile of ruined meat that used to be my uncle.

I gasp, but the sound is drowned out by the frantic shouts of reporters. Patrick turns to me, his face a blank canvas.

I need to tell him I'm all right. I can manage this. This is what we planned for. This is the only logical end for a man who betrayed his family, his clan.

Before I can speak, though, my phone buzzes. It's tucked inside my corset, where I've held it the entire night. I'm inclined to let the call go, but Patrick reaches inside his own pocket. He pulls out the burner he used to send the kill order.

He taps the screen on his phone as I reach for my own. It only takes a moment for me to see the messages, identical, from an unknown number.

> Job complete
>
> My fee: Control of the Crew

～

Thank you for reading *Her Irish Savage*! I hope you enjoyed reading Fiona and Patrick's love story as much as I've enjoyed sharing it with you.

Their story continues in *Her Irish Protector*.

Buy *Her Irish Protector* Now!
https://alixkey.com/PB8US

BONUS SCENE

~

Remember Chapter 27, where Patrick teaches Fiona a trick from the Old Man's Manual? Have you wondered what he did? Well, here's your chance to find out!

Get your bonus scene by typing:

https://alixkey.com/Bonus7

into your phone or computer browser.

MORE DIAMOND RING

∾

Or maybe you'd like to learn more about Braiden Kelly and Samantha Mott, and how Fiona tried to work her way into their super-spicy relationship? (And, um, you're curious about how Jane Eyre might play out in a very modern setting…)

https://alixkey.com/dring200

into your phone or computer browser.

∾

One last thing: If you want an absolutely free full-length, totally stand-alone Diamond Ring novel, featuring a gender-switch Jack and the Beanstalk retelling and starring Irish mobster Connor Boyle, I've got you covered! Just type:

https://alixkey.com/sins

into your phone or computer browser.

THANK YOU

I can't thank you enough for choosing *Her Irish Savage* from among all the dark Mafia romances out there! Without readers like you, I would never have my writing career.

You may not realize it, but *you* can be my hero. Study after study shows that the number one reason a person reads a book is because that book was recommended by a friend.

So will you tell one friend about *Her Irish Savage*?

Of course, if you're dead-set on reviewing my book on Amazon and Goodreads, I won't complain! Honest reviews are hugely helpful because many advertisers require me to have a certain number of reviews before I can buy ads.

Leave a review on Amazon
Leave a review on Goodreads

Whatever you do, don't be a stranger! I look forward to hearing from you soon!

www.alixkey.com
alix@alixkey.com

ABOUT THE AUTHOR

Alix Key was born in Potomac, Maryland, where she grew up making her twin brother and all her dolls act out her favorite fairytales. When an all-grown-up Alix discovered that very real dangers lurk in the woods, she figured out how to rescue herself. She now lives outside Dover, Delaware with her own Prince Charming. When not writing dark romance, Alix serves as the Chief Operations Officer of Diamond Freeport.

You can learn more about Alix at her website, www. alixkey.com.